MW01069118

MAKE ME
SIN

Also by J.T. Geissinger

Bad Habit Series

Sweet as Sin

The Night Prowler Series

Shadow's Edge
Edge of Oblivion
Rapture's Edge
Edge of Darkness
Darkness Bound
Into Darkness

Novella

The Last Vampire

A BAD HABIT NOVEL

J. T. GEISSINGER

This is a work of fiction. Names, characters, organizations, places, events, and incidents are either products of the author's imagination or are used fictitiously.

Published by Montlake Romance, Seattle

www.apub.com

ISBN-13: 9781503951525
ISBN-10: 1503951529

Cover design by Eileen Carey

Printed in the United States of America

For Jay, always.

The moment I first heard love, I gave up
my soul, my heart, and my eyes.

—Rumi

Prologue

The last time I saw Chloe Carmichael, she threw a glass of champagne in my face and called me an asshole.

I deserved it, of course. I *am* an asshole. To her more than anyone else.

Seventeen days later and here I am, standing outside the trendy flower shop she owns in West Hollywood—the sign above the green awning reads, "Fleuret, a bespoke floral boutique," whatever the fuck that means—and I wonder what name I'll make her call me today.

I wonder if it will gut me as much as it did last time.

"A.J.! Are you comin' in or are you just gonna stand there with your dick in your hand?"

Standing under the elegant green awning at Fleuret's glass entrance door, Nico looks impatiently back at me, where I'm lingering at the curb. Barney, Nico's driver/bodyguard, has just dropped us off, and his fiancée, Kat, has already gone inside to talk wedding flowers with her girlfriend. Why the fuck *I'm* here is anyone's guess.

Oh, yeah. I'm the best man.

Two words that no one, ever, in any other situation, would use to describe me.

I take a final drag on my smoke and flick the butt into the street, which makes a MILF in a passing BMW shout at me from her open window. I flip her the bird and slowly make my way across the sidewalk, toward the entrance to my own personal hell.

I'm starting to sweat.

"If I had my dick in my hand, Nico, traffic would be stopped in both directions so everyone could witness the miracle of my enormous junk."

Nico doesn't even bat an eye. "If your junk is even half as big as your ego, brother, that *is* a miracle. Now get your surly ass inside this shop. And remember what we talked about."

Right. I'd gotten "the talk" several times already. Pearls of wisdom along the lines of "You don't have to like Chloe, you just have to get along for the sake of the wedding."

Horseshit. I don't "get along" with anyone I don't want to get along with. Other people's opinions of me count for nothing on A.J. Edwards's Give-a-Shit scale. Which Nico, having known me for years now, knows perfectly well.

Another gem: "It really upsets Kat when you're mean to Chloe." Translation: "My woman has my balls in a death grip, she's giving me mountains of lip over how you treat her friend, and I've lost all control over this situation. Please help a brother out."

Tough shit, Nico. You're the one with his stones in a jar in his girlfriend's freezer, not me.

But the best piece of advice I'd gotten from Nico so far about the Chloe Carmichael situation? The timeless "If you can't say anything nice about her, don't say anything at all."

If I took that advice, I'd be mute for the rest of my life.

Because I can't say anything nice about her. I can't say anything nice *to* her. I can barely even look the woman in the eye.

When I do, it gets hard to breathe. It gets hot, even if it's freezing cold out. And suddenly, I feel like I'm ten years old again, on the last good day of my life, unwrapping the last Christmas present I'd ever get from my mother before she's dead from the final bang of heroin that killed her, and I'm left alone in a ghetto brothel in southeast Saint Petersburg with nothing but a new toy drum and the clothes on my back.

Hope. Fuck you, hope. And fuck you, too, happiness. You're both two-faced, lying bitches.

I stride past Nico, push open the door to Hades disguised as a flower shop, and go inside.

Sorry, Chloe, but I'm about to ruin your day again.

It's the only way I can be near you without wanting to make something bleed.

I see him through the windows of my shop, and anxiety pretzels my stomach.

Ambling toward the front door, A.J. Edwards, drummer for the infamous rock band Bad Habit, is all careless swagger and cocksure smirks, yet he somehow manages to radiate a dangerous intensity, as if he's about to burst inside, brandish an assault rifle, and rob the place.

I wouldn't put it past him.

When I grit my teeth and look down at the design portfolios spread over the table between us, my best friend, Kat, glances over her shoulder and sighs. When she turns back, her green eyes are sympathetic. She knows how much I've been dreading this.

"Just ignore him, Lo."

"Ignore him?" I mutter, brows raised. "The fire-breathing dragon who looks at me like he wants to rip off my head? Will do. No biggie. Isn't everyone used to having random rock stars hating their guts for no apparent reason?"

She reaches over and squeezes my hand. "C'mon, he doesn't hate you. You're way too sweet for anyone to hate."

"Bet you ten bucks he proves you wrong before we're done here today."

"It'll be fine, you'll see."

What I see is that Kat is living in a fantasy land where A.J. Edwards is a gentleman, and not Lord Voldemort disguised as an enormous, tattooed musician.

When I say enormous, it's not an exaggeration. He's built like a mountain. A mountain I'd very much like to rig with dynamite and blow a hole clean through.

The bell on the front door jingles as the door opens and closes. The Jerk is now inside. Last time he was here, when Nico first bought flowers for Kat seven months ago at the beginning of their relationship, it felt as if all the air had been sucked out the minute he walked in. A.J. has a way of negating all the space that surrounds him. He's a dark hole that devours all the light.

I already feel devoured, and he hasn't even been here for ten seconds.

But he can't know that. I'm determined that he'll never again get a rise out of me, no matter what he says or does. So I take Kat's advice, adopt a casual tone, and say, "I was thinking we'd use white peonies as the focal flower for the centerpieces, bridal party bouquets, and gazebo, and incorporate lavender roses for a touch of contrasting color. That will give the design more dimension than an all-white palette."

Distracted from the talk of A.J., Kat asks hopefully, "We can get peonies in August?"

"They'll be imported from Holland, and therefore ungodly expensive, but considering how much they mean to you and Nico . . . yes. I'll make sure we get them."

She beams. Then Nico walks up behind her, leans down and kisses her on the temple, and she beams so bright she's incandescent.

I now have two members of the most famous rock band on earth in my shop, and all I can think of is how fast I can get them *out*.

Not that I have anything against Nico. Quite the opposite. He makes Kat so happy she floats, which is because he treats her like a queen. Which she totally deserves. We've been best friends since high school, and she's the funniest, most honest, and most loyal girl I know. But Nico comes with A.J., and A.J. comes with thunder-clouds boiling over his head, and now he's standing by my flower cooler glaring at a bucket of happy yellow gerberas like he wants to murder them. I feel a migraine coming on.

Sixty seconds and the man is already wreaking havoc on my nervous system.

This was such a bad idea. Stupid wedding planner and her stupid insistence on the "cohesiveness of the wedding party" and "including the men in the process" and yada yada yada. I don't care that I'm the maid of honor and A.J. is the best man and that we're both adults and should act like it—I can't stand the guy! He's just . . . *mean*. It's unnerving how easily he gets under my skin with nothing but a look.

A withering, arctic look like the one he's just turned to give me.

I pretend like I don't see it, or him, and smile at Nico. "Hey, Nico. Good to see you. I was just telling your bride that the peo-nies are a go."

Nico grins. This is like watching the sun burst through fog. He wasn't named *People* magazine's Sexiest Man Alive three years in a row for nothing. Jet hair, blue eyes, and a set of dimples that can kill a woman on the spot . . . Occasionally, I have to remind myself not to stare. It's not that I'm *interested* in him—he and Kat are crazy in love, and I'm perfectly happy with my boyfriend, Eric—but not appreciating Nico's looks would be as criminal as standing in front of the statue of David at the Galleria dell'Accademia in Florence and spending the entire time texting on your phone.

Right now I'm too busy not looking at A.J. to appreciate the full effect of Nico's beauty.

"Good to hear, darlin'. Unless there's some other flower you can recommend that's a symbol of a happy marriage, peonies are definitely what we want." Nico sits down next to Kat, stretches out his long legs under the table, picks up her hand and kisses it. Slanting her an adoring look, he murmurs, "Make sure we get plenty of lavender roses, too."

Lavender roses are symbolic of love at first sight. Long story short, Nico grilled me once on all the different meanings of the colors of roses before he chose lavender for an outrageous birthday surprise for Kat. If only Nico's best man could channel an ounce of that sweetness, I wouldn't be sitting here acting indifferent toward the third ugly sneer he's sent my way.

Not that I'm counting.

Only I am, because the experience of being loathed by a complete stranger is new to me. If I'm being perfectly honest, it kind of freaks me out. Okay, it *really* freaks me out. Almost as much as when Grandpa Walt stuck his dentures in the mouth of the pig my father spit-roasted for the luau-themed birthday party my parents threw for me when I was fourteen.

I had nightmares of grinning pork chops for months. To this day, I still can't eat meat.

Continuing my charade of indifference, I say, "How about if we add some Stephanotis into Kat's bouquet? They smell amazing, and they symbolize marital happiness, too." I show Kat and Nico a picture of the tiny white star-shaped Stephanotis. They both nod in agreement.

As Kat, Nico, and I continue our conversation, A.J. begins to rove around the shop like a restless tiger in a cage, sniffing things out. I find that even more unnerving than his bad attitude. He's supposed to be participating in this meeting, or at least feigning interest to support the groom, but instead he's . . . what? Ogling the merchandise? Looking for something to break?

I watch from the corner of my eye as he rifles impatiently through the Lucite rack of designer greeting cards by the cash register, fingers flicking over them in contempt. He abruptly abandons the cards to strut past the tiered display of French buckets filled with fresh cut orchids because he's spotted the dishy brunette in the short shorts and stilettos browsing the scented candle shelves near the back.

Of course he'd spot the brunette. This is a man who drafts women like they're fantasy football picks. Most of whom are of the paid variety. From what I've read, seen, and heard, A.J. makes Charlie Sheen look like a choir boy.

"Chloe?"

Kat's voice snaps me back to attention. She and Nico are looking at me expectantly. I realize one of them has said something I haven't heard. "Sorry. What was that?"

One corner of Nico's mouth curves up. I suspect he knows exactly where my attention has strayed.

I will kill him with my bare hands if he mentions anything to A.J.

Kat says, "Nico talked to his publicist yesterday about the wedding. The press, and all that."

The two of them look like they're sharing a delicious secret. I have no idea why. "Um. Okay?"

"We've sold the photo rights to *People* magazine."

"Oh. Wow. That's amazing! I hope they're paying you a boatload of money—"

"No, honey, that's not what I'm trying to tell you." Kat leans forward over the table. She's smiling like the Cheshire Cat.

I look back and forth between her and Nico. "What then?"

Kat waits a beat before she speaks. When she does, I'm not sure I've heard her right. "Along with the coverage of the wedding, they're going to do a feature on Fleuret!"

Behind us, the brunette giggles at something A.J. has murmured. They're too far away for me to make out what he's said, but her laugh sounds distinctly sensual. I resist the urge to turn and find out if money is changing hands. "What do you mean a feature? Like, they'll mention my shop?"

Nico laughs. It's his signature husky chuckle, genetically designed to make a woman's ovaries sit up and beg. I'm immune to it now, having heard it so many times; however, judging by the look on Kat's face, she's anything but.

I love how completely in love they are. It's beautiful. Even if watching them together sometimes makes me feel like I'm missing out on the world's greatest inside joke. Which is silly, because, like I said before, I'm perfectly happy with my boyfriend.

But.

Like death, the concept of true love is one of those things that's really hard to grasp until you *see* it. Once you do, there's no going back.

Nico says warmly, "No, darlin'. They're not gonna mention your shop. They're gonna do a *spread* on your shop, and you. As in, an entire article about the florist we used to accompany the wedding story."

Words swirl around in my mouth, but none of them decide to land on my tongue. Heart racing, I stare at Nico and Kat in utter disbelief.

Delighted by my obvious astonishment, Kat laughs and claps her hands. "We made it a condition of the deal. If they wanted exclusive coverage of the 'wedding of the year,' they had to do a special article about our wedding florist. Fleuret's going to be famous, Lo! *You're* going to be famous!"

Actually, what I think I'm going to be, is sick. I whisper, *"Dude."*

Kat laughs louder. Nico says, "You deserve the recognition, Chloe. Your arrangements are fuckin' amazin'."

Nico's Matthew McConaughey southern drawl makes everything sound sexy, even when he's cursing. Which he frequently is. Right now, he could be reciting every curse word known to man and I wouldn't care.

"You guys." It's all I can say because my throat is getting tight. My eyes fill with water.

All I've wanted since I bought the shop from Mr. and Mrs. Feldman when they retired three years ago, was to turn it into the best floral design studio in LA. My parents thought I was insane to try to rescue a failing flower shop—considering the tuition they spent for me at USC while I was pursuing that English Lit degree I'll never use, I can hardly blame them—but I've always loved flowers, and I jumped at the chance to make Fleuret mine and turn it around. I'd started working at the shop part-time in high school, and it's been my first love ever since. I put every dime of my trust fund into it. I've put every dollar I've earned back into it. I've put countless hours of sweat equity into it.

And now my best friend and her superstar fiancé are telling me they've arranged for me to get press for the shop. Not just any press. *People* magazine. And not just a little mention. A *feature*.

This is quite possibly the best day of my life.

Holding back a sob, I jump from the chair and crush Kat into a hug. Then I crush Nico into a hug. Then I start laughing madly like the Sicilian from *The Princess Bride* just before he keels over dead from drinking the iocane-laced wine.

I think I might be losing it.

At precisely the height of my joy, a sarcastic voice speaks from over my shoulder. "Let me guess. Sale on grandma panties at Neiman Marcus?"

On a scale of one to ten, my dislike of A.J. shoots from about a nine to a solid, searing twenty. I stiffen, releasing Nico. Face flaming, I remember that the last time I saw A.J., he called me a "stuck-up, frigid rich girl." Who, additionally, "wouldn't know a dick if it hit her in the face."

Who apparently also wears grandma panties.

And this is how he sees me. *I don't care. I DO NOT CARE!*

Without missing a beat, Nico drawls, "You'll probably need to run over and stock up so your little ol' mangina doesn't get chilly under those jeans, A.J."

"Nah," says A.J., giving it right back, "I never wear underwear. Too restrictive. My mangina's huge, brother. It needs room to breathe."

A new piece of information about A.J. Edwards I could have gone my entire life without knowing: he goes commando. I'm not allowing myself to think about the other part. The "huge" part. Though judging by the size of his boots . . .

Without turning around, or otherwise acknowledging his existence, I say to Nico and Kat, "Seriously, *thank you*. And now I'm not doing the flowers for cost; I'm doing them for free."

Kat waves her hand dismissively. "Out of the question. And you're not doing them for cost, either. We already talked about that, dummy."

"But it's my wedding present to you guys—"

"Just having you do the flowers is enough of a present—"

"Kat, there's no way I'm making money off you—"

"Why the hell not? If we weren't using you, we'd have to pay some other florist! I'd rather give you the money."

"And I'd rather be Beyoncé, but that's not happening, either."

"Chloe—"

"Kat—"

"Shut up, girls," says Nico with affection, effectively ending the argument.

Except it doesn't, because I'll never send them a bill. Even if Kat wasn't my best friend, the kind of publicity she and Nico are giving me is priceless.

A.J. has moved to my right side and is looking down at the portfolios of my work with an expression I interpret as nausea. He glances up and finds me looking at him. His amber eyes—eyes that could actually be beautiful if they weren't so cold—narrow. He says flatly, "Yeah. Shut up."

"A.J.," Nico warns, but I hold up a hand.

Without looking away from A.J., I say to Nico and Kat, "Could you guys excuse us for a second?"

There's a long, uncomfortable silence. I refuse to break eye contact with A.J. From beneath the collar of his black T-shirt, a flush creeps up his neck.

Fine. Be angry. I've had enough.

"We'll be in your office." Kat takes Nico's hand, and then A.J. and I are alone.

He pulls himself up to his full height, folds his arms across his chest, and looks down his nose at me. Which means I have to look *up*—at five foot ten, this is an unusual experience for me. And today I'm in low heels, so my height is easily over six feet . . . and I'm still looking up. *Way* up.

I can never wear heels around Eric. I banish that thought as quickly as it arrives.

I demand, "What's your problem with me?"

I'll give him this: the guy has an amazing poker face. There's not a single telling change in his expression. He doesn't even blink.

He also doesn't answer.

I scowl at him. "Fine. I suppose it doesn't really matter. But Kat and Nico matter. And their wedding matters. And whatever the reason is that you hate me so much—not that I think I've done anything to deserve it, but whatever—I won't let you ruin what's supposed to be the happiest time in their lives by being so . . . so . . ."

"Mean?" he supplies with a smirk, seeming almost satisfied.

"Selfish," I correct with quiet vehemence.

Now he blinks. Then his brows lower. A crackle of something passes between us, bright as danger.

"Selfish," he repeats. His gaze, electrifying, flicks over me. He takes a step forward, staring into my eyes. This close I can see the flecks of brown and green in his gold irises. His lashes are impossibly long, golden brown and thick. He leans in and softly says, "Princess, you have no fucking idea what you're talking about."

My heart pounds wildly. He's big, and probably dangerous—did I read somewhere he'd spent time in prison for assault?—but I'm not afraid of him. What I'm feeling isn't as clear-cut as fear. I have to take a slow, steadying breath before I speak. "The wedding is only a few months away. After that, we never have to see each other again. Let's just try to ignore each other until then. For Kat and Nico's sake. Okay?"

There's another long, uncomfortable silence. A.J.'s gaze on me is burning. I catch a whiff of him, a warm, masculine scent of skin and musk and maybe cigarette smoke. I notice details about him I've never noticed before, like the way his hair is every shade of blond, from darkest copper to palest wheat. It needs to be cut. Stubble glints gold along his jaw. There's a small white scar above his left eyebrow. On his neck, there's a tattoo that disappears into his collar. I can just make out the shape of a cross.

His gaze drops to my mouth. When he looks into my eyes again, his voice is husky. "You were wrong, before."

Confused, I frown. "About what?"

His jaw works. For the first time, there's a flash of emotion in his eyes, something other than contempt. "About not doing anything to make me hate you. You've done plenty."

He turns on his heel and stalks away, out of my shop. I stand frozen, watching him go, watching as a white convertible Audi pulls up to the curb and a woman waves from it.

The brunette.

A.J. swings his bulk into the passenger seat, slams shut the door, shoots me a smirk, and they're gone. I release the breath I didn't know I'd been holding. So much for trying to strike a peace accord with the fire-breathing dragon.

I won't make the same mistake again.

And Kat owes me ten bucks.

Chapter 2

By the time I get home from work, it's dark, there's no parking available on the street, and the migraine that had been threatening me earlier has descended in full force. My head feels as if it will explode.

I wish it would. Then at least I wouldn't have to deal with the play-by-play, slow motion reruns my brain is torturing me with of the meeting with the Jerk today. At least Kat and Nico were happy with the way the meeting went. I fibbed and told them A.J. and I made a truce so they wouldn't worry my feelings had been hurt. They have more important things to think about. Then I told the truth and said he'd left to spend some time with his new special friend he'd met in the candle aisle. Kat snorted. Nico rolled his eyes, trying to hide a smile, and said, "Figures."

It "figures" that he runs off with a woman he just met to have sex. Probably amazing, animalistic sex. In her convertible.

In my next life, I want to come back as a rock star.

I circle the block four times, crawling through traffic, until finally someone pulls out from the curb just in front of me and I whip into his spot before it's stolen by all the other apartment dwellers circling behind.

When I moved in last year, the sales girl from the management company that maintains the building failed to tell me that finding a parking spot in this neighborhood after five o'clock is as likely as finding a winning lottery ticket on the sidewalk. She failed to mention several other important things, too, like how when she described the building as "full of character," she actually meant "decrepit." The faucets drip, the pipes rattle, the walls are so thin I've become uncomfortably familiar with the nighttime intimacies of my neighbors. But since I sank all my money into Fleuret, I can't afford to move. And there's no way I'm taking any money from my parents. I'm going to make this work one way or another, without their help.

I drag my sorry self from the car, sigh at the sight of the security gate cocked open because the lock is still broken, climb three flights of stairs—elevator's on the fritz again—and let myself into my apartment just in time to hear the phone ringing. When I pick up, it's my mother.

"Thank goodness! I was just about to call the police to report a missing person."

I lived at home until I was twenty-four. My mother is having a hard time letting go. She's also convinced that living in this part of town, I'll be raped and killed in my sleep. I've reminded her that if I *were* raped by an intruder in the middle of the night, I'd probably wake up before I was killed in my sleep. She didn't find my logic amusing.

Wearily, I drop my purse on the floor, sink onto the couch, and close my eyes. "You should try my cell, Mom. I'm hardly ever here."

"Well. I don't want to bother you at work."

There's a slight emphasis on "work." This is an old argument. I'm in no mood to rehash it again. "How are you? How's Dad?"

"I'm fine, dear, thank you. Your father is . . ." A faint, ladylike sigh comes over the line. "Well, he's taken another pro bono case."

She says it as if she can hardly bear the shame. To my mother, there's only one thing worse than working, and that's working for free. No matter that my father makes eight figures a year in his law practice, a single pro bono case will set her teeth on edge for months. I steer clear of that landmine, and head into safer waters.

"And Gigi?"

Her voice warms. "My baby is so sweet. We went to the groomer's today for a bath."

I smile at the thought of my mother and her pampered bichon frise puppy taking a bath together at the dog groomers. When she talks about the dog, it's always "we," like they're a single entity. She bought Gigi as part of her empty nest adjustment, and I swear she loves that dog more than anything else in her life. Probably because the dog is as much of a snob as she is.

"I'm calling because your brother's coming into town this weekend, dear. Will you and Eric come for dinner Sunday?"

My smile grows wider. "Jamie's coming out? Awesome! Business trip?"

"I think it's an immigration reform conference or some dreadful thing like that. You know your brother. Champion of the downtrodden."

My brother's an attorney who works for the largest immigration law firm in Manhattan. The way she discounts his job always grates on my nerves. "He's doing good work, Mom."

"Of course he is. But there must be plenty of people in this world better suited to help the poor." She launches into a rant I've heard a dozen times before. "James graduated summa cum laude from

Princeton. He's brilliant, handsome, and comes from a good family. His grandmother is a countess, for God's sake! He should be in politics, or marrying some heiress, but instead he's earning an associate's salary and rubbing elbows with the hoi polloi." She sighs. "Honestly, I don't know where I went wrong."

I have to bite my tongue in order to not recite a list. "Seven on Sunday?"

"As always."

"Okay, Mom. I'm beat, so I'm going to hang up now. I'll see you Sunday."

"With Eric," she reminds me firmly. He's the one thing in my life she approves of, even if he does have to work for a living. I can't blame her. Compared to most of my exes, Eric is practically a saint.

We say good-bye and hang up. Immediately there's a knock on my door. It's probably another solicitor selling magazine subscriptions. Darn that broken security gate!

Not moving from the couch, I shout, "Who is it?"

"It's me, babe!" comes the muffled reply. "Surprise!"

Eric. I'm not surprised. He enjoys showing up unannounced. I sometimes wonder if he's trying to catch me with another guy. That would never happen because I'm not that kind of girl, but his tendency to drop by without calling is a little irritating. I rub my temples, drag a deep breath into my lungs, and then haul myself from the sofa.

When I open the door, I'm immediately engulfed in an enthusiastic bear hug. The kiss Eric gives me is wet, and a little sloppy. He's still in his police uniform. He smells like beer.

"Hey. Did you just get off work?"

He nods, grinning. I still haven't taken off my heels, so I'm looking slightly down at him. This depresses me beyond reason. It must be the headache.

"I thought we could have dinner together. You up for it?"

I momentarily brighten at the thought of being treated to a dinner out, but Eric dispels that idea by saying, "I've been dreaming about your lasagna all day."

He gives me another sloppy kiss, and moves past me into the apartment, not noticing that I've closed my eyes and am counting to ten.

This is one thing my mother got right. She never cooked or cleaned, so no one ever expected it of her. And if ever she got a wild hair up her butt and cooked something for us—even something as simple as toast—the entire family acted as if it were a Christmas miracle.

She might be a pampered snob, but she's no dummy. If you don't spoil other people, they can never take you for granted.

I close the door and join Eric in the kitchen, where he's rummaging through my fridge. He emerges with a beer, pops the top, guzzles from the bottle, and shucks off his shoes, all without closing the refrigerator door. "How was your day, babe?"

I sigh. "Long."

He doesn't ask for details. "Mine, too. I'm beat. And starving," he adds with emphasis, finally closing the door. Unbuckling the black utility belt around his waist, he deposits his gun, baton, radio, and all the other various accessories attached to it directly onto my kitchen counter. It makes a strangely ominous-looking mess. He drops his hat and badge beside the mess, strips off his navy short-sleeved shirt and regulation trousers, throws them over the whole pile, and turns to me, wearing only a pair of black socks, his white undershirt and briefs, and a huge grin.

He spreads his legs, props his hands on his hips, and declares, "Officer Eric Cox reporting for duty, ma'am! What's this rookie's lesson for today?"

I stifle another sigh.

Once upon a time, Eric's talent for kissing was as bad as my Grandpa Walt's practical jokes. It shocked me when we first started dating, because he's a great-looking guy with loads of self-confidence, and, I assumed, plenty of experience with women. Apparently that experience did not include learning how to control a violently enthusiastic tongue while kissing. I swear the man would stick his tongue so far down my throat he could taste my lungs. When I complained about the problem to Kat, she suggested I take matters into my own hands and show him what I liked.

So I made up a game called "The Rookie Gets Shown the Ropes." Far from being insulted, Eric took to our little game like a duck to water.

And now I have a monster on my hands.

I calmly fold my arms across my chest and lean against the fridge. "Well, Officer Cox, today's lesson is a very important one. It's called 'How to Order Takeout When Your Girlfriend Has Worked a Twelve-Hour Day and Has a Migraine That Might Compel Her to Rearrange Certain Parts of Your Face with Her Fists.'"

He laughs uproariously. He thinks I'm joking.

"Babe, you're so cute when you try to act like Grace! I love it! Do more!"

Grace is my other best friend. She's a marriage and family counselor, whip smart, older than me and Kat by five years, and a bona fide badass. If Eric was her boyfriend and he'd demanded homemade lasagna within the first five seconds of walking in her door at the end of the day, he'd be missing a few important body parts right now.

"Sure. Our second lesson today will be, 'How to Survive a Spanking with a Spatula with Your Dignity Intact.'" Without taking my gaze from his smiling face, I remove a wooden spatula from the jar on the counter next to the stove. I slap it against my thigh.

"And our final lesson is simply called 'Paying Attention to the Warning Signs of a Psychotic Break in the Tired, Irritated Female.'"

I smile sweetly at him, tapping the spatula against my leg. His own smile fades.

"Oh. Oops. Sorry, babe."

He might be a little oblivious, but I'll give him points for the apology, which I can tell he means.

Relenting, I toss the spatula to the counter. I give him a hug. "It's not your fault. I just had a terrible day, and I've got a splitting headache. I'm sorry I snapped at you."

He hugs me back, chuckling. "You didn't even raise your voice, silly. And I meant it when I said you were cute. If that's you snapping, then I'll take it anytime. My last girlfriend used to break stuff when she was angry. She's Italian," he adds, as if her nationality explained her urge to destroy things.

I rest my head on his shoulder, which strains my neck. Without his work shoes, he's lost another inch. "Do you mind if we just order a pizza tonight? I really don't feel up to cooking."

His voice registers concern. "Sure. Why don't you go take some Advil and put something more comfortable on, and I'll take care of it. And after dinner I'll give you a massage. How's that?"

I groan in anticipation. "That sounds amazing. Thank you."

He nuzzles my neck. His voice drops. "After your massage, you'll get something that will relax you even more."

I know he's trying to be sexy, but the odd and unwelcome image of him slipping a roofie in my drink has me wondering what's wrong with me. Eric would never do something like that. He'd never *have* to; in spite of what A.J. Edwards might think, I have a healthy appetite for sex, thank you very much.

A.J. Why does he look at me the way he does? Why does he treat me like I'm a leper? What's that scar above his eyebrow? And those tattoos on his neck and the backs of his fingers, what are those all about? Does he have more tattoos? Where?

Why am I thinking about A.J. when my boyfriend is kissing my neck?

I pull away from Eric so abruptly he looks at me oddly. "You okay?" He touches my cheek. "Your face is all red."

I can feel he's right. My cheeks are suddenly so hot they burn. "I just need those Advil, that's all. And some food."

"Say no more. I'm on it." He turns to the drawer where I keep the takeout menus and rifles through them. I turn and head for the bedroom.

"Lenzini's?" he shouts from the kitchen. I strip off my shirt and toss it to the bed.

"Sounds good," I shout back. I remove the rest of my work clothes, change into a pair of black yoga pants and a sweatshirt, and get the Advil from the medicine cabinet in the bathroom. Washing two gel caps down with a gulp of water from the sink, I catch sight of my face in the mirror.

I look like hell.

My makeup wore off hours ago. My complexion is blotchy, and there are black smudges beneath my eyes where mascara has strayed from my lashes. My hair looks as if a family of rodents has built a nest in it. My eyes are red and glassy, and there's a look in them I rarely see:

Fury.

Anger boils my blood, making my hands shake, my heart throb as if I've sprinted up a flight of stairs. I know the cause of this rage, and I'm disappointed with myself for letting him, once again, get under my skin.

In the short time I've known him, A.J. Edwards has managed to make me lose my cool more than I've lost my cool over the course of my entire life. I'm known for my even temper, for being able to get along with most anyone, for manners and ladylike ways. I never even curse.

Well, hardly ever; I've called A.J. a few choice names.

It's partly the way I was raised, but it's also just my nature. I'm a naturally happy person. I'm easygoing. I was voted Most Popular my senior year of high school, for God's sake! I'm likeable! I'm nice!

You're a stuck-up, frigid rich girl who wouldn't know a dick if it hit her in the face.

I have to stand at the mirror and breathe deeply for several minutes before I finally begin to calm down. Once I do, I realize the fury isn't the worst of what I'm feeling.

The *hurt* is the worst. For reasons unknown, A.J. hates my guts. It hurts me more than I'd like to admit.

I meet my eyes in the mirror one last time, and shake my head. "Suck it up, Chloe," I say to my reflection. "Not everyone has to like you. Let it go."

For not the first time, I resolve to move on from the mystery of why this stranger seems to wish me dead. Even if I knew the reason, I know I couldn't change his mind. He's not the kind of man who listens to what he doesn't want to hear.

When I finally leave the bedroom, I find Eric sprawled on the couch in the living room with the television tuned to a football game. His cell phone is gripped in one hand, the remote control in the other.

He's snoring gently, sound asleep.

I don't wake him. By the time the pizza arrives, Eric's snoring has reached chainsaw levels. I cover him with a blanket, pay the delivery guy, sit down at my kitchen table alone, and eat a slice of lukewarm pizza—picking off the pepperoni, because Eric forgot again that I don't eat meat—all the while trying not to be driven insane by the little voice inside my head that's whispering one thing over and over.

A.J.

A.J.

A.J.

I abandon the half-eaten piece of pizza on the table, turn off all the lights, and go to bed, where I lay staring at the ceiling in the dark.

I should be thinking about the future, about what an incredible opportunity Kat and Nico have given me; how if their wedding flowers are admired, my life will change for the better in all the ways I've dreamed; or even about why Eric smelled like beer when he arrived, when he said he'd just gotten off work.

But I don't think about any of that. I think about cold amber eyes and messy gold hair and a stare that burns right through me, until finally, mercifully, sleep overtakes me and I pass out.

Even in my dreams, I can't escape him.

It's Sunday afternoon at four o'clock. I'm on the phone with a customer, taking an order for a funeral spray, when I'm grabbed from behind and pulled against a solid chest.

"*Hello*, beautiful," a cultured voice purrs in my ear. "Come here often?"

I spin around. When I see who it is, I scream in delight. "Jamie! You're here!" I throw my arms around my brother's shoulders.

He laughs, squeezing me. "I'm here, little bug. Your drab, colorless existence will commence being extremely fabulous right about *now*." He gives me another squeeze for emphasis, then pulls back to examine me at arms' length. He grows instantly sober. "Dear God. You're even prettier than the last time I saw you. Are you in love?"

One of the many reasons I adore my older brother: he gives compliments like no one's business.

"What are you doing here? Did you just get in? I thought we'd see you later at the 'rents for dinner!"

He winks at me. I see exactly why every gay man in a fifty-mile radius has just achieved an erection, even if they don't know why. My brother is gorgeous, if I do say so myself. He's wearing a dove-gray suit, no tie, white dress shirt open at the collar. His dark hair is perfect, as are his teeth, his skin, and every accessory, right down to the silk pocket square peeking out of his jacket. He's tall and slender like a model, and has the cheekbones of a model, too, but with none of a model's self-consciousness. He's completely at ease in his own skin, in spite of growing up with parents who refuse to acknowledge he's gay.

I still haven't forgiven them for that. Miraculously, it doesn't bother James a bit. He accepts people's shortcomings without judgment, even when they're viciously judging him themselves.

He smiles warmly at me, hazel eyes crinkling around the corners. "I had to see how the infamous 'bespoke boutique' was doing. Couldn't miss an opportunity to rub your success in Mommy Dearest's face, now, could I?"

I roll my eyes. "As if Mommy Dearest would care."

He purses his lips and shrugs. "Mmm. She might care. If you ever land the cover of *Vanity Fair*, that is. Until then, if she can't brag about it to her social set, it's simply not worth the effort. Don't take it personally, bug, she can't help herself. Her mother is British aristocracy. If that wouldn't ruin you, I don't know what would."

We share wry smiles, then a tinny squawking distracts me. I realize I've still got my customer on the line. I hold a finger in the air for Jamie and whip the phone to my ear. "Mr. Thornton! I'm so sorry, please excuse me." I continue with the order as I watch from the corner of my eye as James begins politely poking his nose into my business.

He strolls nonchalantly around the counter, lifting a notepad here, opening a file folder there, quickly and efficiently assessing everything within sight. I see him mentally catalogue the entire operation in a glance, nodding in satisfaction every so often. He frowns briefly at the state of disarray around the cash register, where the young son of my last customer tampered with a display of enclosure cards. Jamie quickly and silently straightens the display, leaving it looking better than it had before.

He's always been like this. Inquisitive. Precise. Unobtrusively infusing elegance into everything he touches. I can't believe some lucky guy hasn't put a ring on his finger yet.

Just as I finish the call with Mr. Thornton, Jamie falls still. His lips part. His eyes widen. He stares in fascination at something behind me, looking over my shoulder as if a unicorn has just pranced into the room.

I glance in the direction he's looking, expecting to see some hot young underwear model or something of the sort. Oh, how wrong I am.

A.J. Edwards stands in front of my counter, as broad and imposing as Thor. Today he's wearing faded jeans that are stuffed into combat boots with no laces, a battered brown leather bomber jacket, and a pair of aviators that obscure his eyes. His long hair is tied into a sloppy knot at the nape of his neck. He's unshaven, as usual. He gives my brother a friendly chin jerk in acknowledgment. "Hey."

Jamie makes a faint noise, not quite a hello. I can tell he wants to fan himself.

A.J. turns his attention to me. I can't see his eyes because of the aviators, but I imagine I feel their intensity penetrating through. With slightly less acidity than he normally addresses me with, he says, "I need to place an order."

My central nervous system decides it's a circus. Acrobats catapult through my intestines. Clowns on pogo sticks bounce around in my brain. A chimpanzee twirls a baton and rides a unicycle back and forth inside my heart, and a strongman tightens a pair of bulging biceps around my throat, squeezing off all my air. I am paralyzed by the clamor of activity, and stare stupidly at A.J. as if he has just arrived from outer space.

He removes the sunglasses. He stares at me. He doesn't smile.

Jamie nudges me with his elbow, and I snap out of my stupor. "You can order online," I blurt, without an ounce of warmth. Jamie shoots me a surprised glance. I'm never this grouchy to people, but he doesn't know the history between me and the grizzly bear standing on the other side of my counter.

A.J. says, "Don't have a computer."

I take that in, wondering if he doesn't know how to use a computer, or if he's just one of those antisocial people who hates technology. I decide on the latter. "You can also call to place an order. You didn't have to come in."

"Don't have a phone."

It takes me longer to process that. "What kind of person doesn't have a computer or a phone?"

A.J. moistens his lips. He runs a hand over his unruly hair. Beside me, Jamie watches with unabashed fascination. Though I hate to admit it, I can't say I blame him. The simple gestures somehow look incredibly erotic.

"You going to help me out with the flowers, or not?" A.J.'s voice is gruff now. His strange new patience with me has already grown thin.

My ears go hot with anger. My voice, though quiet, drips with contempt. "There are plenty of other flower shops in this town with owners you don't despise. Why don't you go try one of them?"

That brings a hint of a smile to his mouth, which promptly fades, as if his lips aren't used to curving in any direction but down. "Nico said your shop is the best. I need the best." He shrugs, the picture of nonchalance. "I can put up with some aggravation in order to get it."

My eyes bug out. Aggravation? I'm aggravating? Of all the *nerve*—

"Of *course* we can help you! Let me just get an order form, sir, and I'll take care of everything."

My lead designer, Trina, sidles up beside me, commandeering the discussion she can see has just gone off the rails. I was aware of her watching the back-and-forth from her position to my right, where she's been processing bunches of roses, but now she's decided I can't be trusted to deal with A.J. any longer. She's taken the matter out of my hands before I lose my temper completely.

If I had to guess how she knew I was about to lose it, I'd say my red face, stiff back, and clenched fists are all pretty solid indicators.

I turn and stomp away from the counter. I banish myself to the back room, which is conveniently out of sight of A.J. and his mocking eyes. Jamie is right on my heels.

"I can't decide which is more interesting," he drawls, taking a seat across from me at the round table where I usually eat my lunch. He leans back and crosses his legs. "Big Daddy with the hottest man bun since Jared Leto, or your *reaction* to him. What's that all about, bug?"

"You have no idea what a *jerk* that guy is." I try to keep my voice low so it doesn't carry to the front of the shop. "He always treats me like I'm a piece of garbage that's stuck to the bottom of his shoe." I make a noise of frustration. "I can't stand him!"

Jamie looks at me closely for what seems like a long time. "Hmm."

"Seriously, this is the nicest he's *ever* been to me. He was almost civil. I've met him, like, half a dozen times before, and he hated me on sight. He once barked at me for being a guest in someone else's house, like *I* did something wrong by being invited! And I won't even tell you the names he's called me."

Instantly, Jamie's in protective-big-brother mode. He sits forward, his normally smiling face growing dark. "He's called you *names*?"

"Yes!"

Jamie's expression is a little scary. He might not be the burliest guy around, but he's tall, and not afraid of anything. "Like what?"

"He calls me *Princess*. And not in a nice way. It's like he's really calling me a snob!"

He waits for more. I don't think I've impressed him so far.

"And he said I was a stuck-up, frigid rich girl!"

Again, he waits silently for me to provide more examples.

"Who wears grandma panties!"

His lips twitch. Is he trying not to smile? I begin to feel desperate.

"Who wouldn't know a dick if it hit her in the face!"

Unfortunately, I shout this last sentence. There's a sudden silence from the front, where Trina has been taking A.J.'s order. I prop my elbows on the table, and drop my face into my hands.

"I can see why you're so upset," says Jamie. "That *is* dire."

"Shut up."

"I mean, a princess who doesn't know a dick if it hits her in the face, well . . . that's just tragic. What would she think it is, do you suppose? A random flying sausage?"

I lift my head and glare at him. He dissolves into laughter.

When he's composed himself, he leans over and ruffles my hair like I'm twelve. "Bug, you can't take everything so personally. He's a drummer. They're fire starters. They like to hit hard."

"You know who he is?"

Jamie nods, smiling. "I've dated my share of musicians. And drummers are *always* the most trouble. That one in particular."

Suddenly, I'm all ears. "What do you mean?"

He lifts a shoulder. "I dated this drummer for a while who was at Juilliard. He was amazingly talented, but his idol was your friend in there." He inclines his head, indicating A.J. "He thought the man could walk on *water*. Had posters of him all over his bedroom."

"How old was this guy? Seventeen?"

Alarmingly, Jamie sighs. "I wish."

I make a face at him. "Ew."

"At any rate, Big Daddy apparently has some rare neurological condition called synesthesia that allows him to see musical notes and certain other sounds as colors. No—chromesthesia, that's it. It probably makes him a little crazy."

When I stare at him blankly, Jamie provides further explanation.

"So not only can he memorize a song in one pass because he's using more than one sense to experience the music, he also has perfect pitch."

I make a sound that indicates I'm not getting it.

"Okay, imagine a fireworks show. You've got yellows, greens, whites, reds, blues, all the colors of the rainbow exploding in the air above your head."

I nod, following him so far.

"That's what it's like for people with this particular type of synesthesia. Every song they hear is a symphony of three-dimensional color they can see, not just musical notes they hear. They *see* the song. It hangs in the air all around them, like a living rainbow."

Stunned, I sag back into my chair. I try to imagine it, and fail. What must that be like, to live with a kaleidoscope of color all around you, flitting like butterflies in the air?

A terrible thought strikes me: Does A.J. hate me because of the way I *sound*? Does he see the color of my voice as a putrid vomit yellow?

Jamie cocks his head. "What?"

I whisper in horror, "Is my voice ugly?"

Because he knows me so well, he grasps my meaning without further explanation. He rolls his eyes. "No, bug, your voice isn't ugly."

Unconvinced, I cover my mouth with my hands. It suddenly makes so much sense. The way A.J. sneers at me. The way he seems to cringe in my presence. His inexplicable dislike.

I am killing him with my hideous voice. When I speak, he sees diarrhea flying through the air.

"Oh, for God's sake, Chloe, stop being so dramatic." Jamie stands and pulls me to my feet. "Honestly, if you just understood men, your life would get a lot easier."

I'm offended. "I understand men!"

His raised brows refute my statement.

"And what is that supposed to mean, anyway? How does it apply to Prince Charming out there?"

The look my brother gives me is almost as penetrating as one of A.J.'s. "You call the man you claim to not be able to stand *Prince Charming*?"

I produce an extravagant sigh. "I'm being sarcastic, obviously."

"Obviously. In exactly the same way he calls you Princess. Which irritates you so much."

His logic is irritating, too. "It's not the same thing! And he started it!"

Jamie's expression grows stern. "I'm going to pretend you didn't just say that, because you're better than that, Chloe Anne. And you're far too old to be throwing temper tantrums. If you don't like him—or anyone else for that matter—just be polite and move on. Show some class."

Immediately, I'm ashamed of myself. If it were my mother delivering this lecture, I'd be able to shrug it off with no problem. Coming from Jamie, it makes me feel about two feet tall.

"All right, c'mon," says Jamie, pulling me into a hug. He releases me and smooths a hand over my hair. "Let's go out there and show Big Daddy you have some manners, shall we?"

I grimace. "Will you please stop calling him that? It's so . . ."

"Hot? Like him?" Jamie grins.

"Weird."

He wiggles his eyebrows suggestively. "Sexy? Like him?"

"Ugh."

"Deliciously dirty, like him?"

"Enough!" I cry, covering my ears. "I do *not* want to hear how hot you think he is!"

He moves me toward the door with an arm slung around my shoulders. "Does that mean we're not going to talk about the size of his boots? Because honestly, bug, I've seen elephants with smaller feet. Can you imagine what he's packing—"

"James Augustus Carmichael, I will kill you where you stand if you say another word."

His answering smile is knowing. "Please. It's not like you haven't thought the exact same thing."

He ushers me out the door into the front room, and I'm relieved I don't have to lie to deny it.

When I reach the register, Trina is just finishing up with A.J. She counts his change, and hands him a receipt.

He pays in cash, I note, wondering if he has the same bias against credit cards that he does against phones and computers.

Trina says, "You're probably looking at four or five days before they deliver. International orders take a bit longer."

A.J. nods. "Not a problem. I was expecting that. As long as it's there by the twenty-fifth." He catches sight of me coming out of the back with Jamie. His face betrays nothing, but I imagine he's holding his breath.

For the first time since I met him, I feel pity for this hostile, exasperating man. He watches me in tense silence, waiting for Quasimodo and Frankenstein's monster to crawl from my mouth and hurl feces at him.

I'm so depressed by this thought, I want to turn right around and hide in the back again.

"All done! Thank you for your order!" chirps Trina brightly, dismissing A.J.

He doesn't budge. His gaze on me is so burning I feel like I might combust. He shocks me with what next comes out of his mouth. "Can I have a word?" He jerks his head toward the side of the store with no customers milling around.

I freeze.

Jamie leans down to kiss my cheek. "See you at seven, bug." Softer, only for me, he adds, "I want *every single* detail." He straightens, nods at Trina, smiles at A.J., who gives a friendly chin jerk in return, and strides away, leaving me stranded with a fluttering heartbeat and a pair of clammy, shaking hands.

What on earth could he possibly have to say? How am I going to answer without speaking and making him want to puke on my shoes?

A.J. turns and walks away. I now have to decide whether to follow, or retreat like a coward into the back room. I take a fortifying breath, give myself a quick pep talk, and follow him. My pulse pounds in my temples with a sound like the crashing of waves.

We stop next to the walk-in display cooler, where he growled like an animal at me the first time we met. Now understanding the reason, I'm mortified. My face flames red.

We stand there in silence until I'm so uncomfortable I'm practically vibrating with misery. While A.J. studies me as if I'm an insect under a microscope, I stare glumly at a pink and white rose bouquet I made this morning. Finally he says, "You told Nico and Kat we agreed to a truce. Why?"

His tone isn't hostile or accusing, only inquisitive. It takes me by surprise. I blink up at him, unused to hearing anything but contempt.

"I . . . uh . . ." Is he wincing? Is my voice making him sick? I lower my voice to a whisper, and lower my gaze to my feet. "So they wouldn't worry."

He waits for more, so I'm obliged to provide it. "I told you. They have too many other things to worry about. The last thing they need is to be playing referees for us."

He absorbs that for a moment, while I continue to stare at my feet as if the meaning of life can be found in my Pradas.

He prompts, "Right. You said I was being selfish."

I mutter something unintelligible. The next thing I know, a big hand is lifting my chin so I can no longer stare at the floor. I forget how to breathe.

"Why are you mumbling?" he demands.

He doesn't remove his hand from beneath my chin. The heat in my cheeks spreads to my ears and down my neck. I swallow, desperate to flee, and close my eyes.

"Hey. Goldilocks. You still with me?"

Humiliated, I open my eyes and look at him. "You don't have to be nice to me. I get it. I know why you don't like me."

His reaction is so strange. His eyes widen, his nostrils flare, and his lips part, exactly as if I've surprised him. And now I'm even more miserable, knowing that I guessed right.

With as much dignity as I can muster, I remove my chin from his hand, and cover my mouth. "Let's just . . . I promise I won't talk to you anymore. I don't want to make it worse. It's really frickin' embarrassing, but I'm sorry. I can't help it."

As I watch, his expression morphs from surprised to confused. "You can't help what?"

I want to groan. Is he enjoying torturing me? This is *awful.* "I know about your . . ." I make a futile hand gesture. "Thing."

With that one word, a wall of ice slams down between us. He leans closer to me, big and male and threatening. He growls, "And what fucking thing would that be?"

Maybe I should be scared. Or maybe I should be insulted. What I actually feel is scalding anger mixed with sweet relief, because now we can go back to hating each other and I don't have to be so confused.

I pull myself to my full height, look him in the eye, and snap, "Your color hearing *thing*. I know about it. And I hope every single word I'm saying right now is making you want to barf up your breakfast, you bad-tempered, arrogant, antisocial bully!"

Silence swallows the shop. Even the noise of the compressor on the cooler seems to cringe in the wake of my outburst. I stare at A.J., breathing hard, trying to stab him with my eyes.

Understanding dawns over his face. Oddly, this makes his scathing hostility disappear in a poof as if it were never there in the first place. "You think my chromesthesia is the reason I don't like you."

It's a statement, not a question. Humor underscores it. My anger falters, then fizzles, leaving me feeling even more wretched than before.

Clearly, I was wrong about my voice being the source of his dislike. It seems almost naïve of me now, to expect such a simple, innocent explanation.

But no. A.J.'s hatred of me is far more personal than the mere sound of my voice. I'm back to square one.

And now he's grinning. *Grinning*.

"You're a real piece of work, aren't you, Princess?"

I refuse to answer him. I won't give him the satisfaction. I can't let him bait me. Like Jamie said, I have to show some class, and let it go. Unfortunately, I can't seem to get my feet to agree with my brain's command to turn around and walk away. We stare at each other in silence.

He moves closer to me, his gaze never leaving mine. His voice drops so low it's almost intimate. "You want to know what I see when you open your mouth?"

He smells like something I'd like to eat. Something warm and sugary, like a fresh-baked cookie. My mouth waters, but I'm far too stunned by what's happening to examine my physical reaction to him. My heartbeat skyrockets.

He leans closer. He inhales, as if he's scenting me, too. He puts his lips right next to my ear, so close I feel his warm breath feather down my neck. It makes me shiver.

"Ask me what I see, Chloe."

It's the first time he's ever spoken my name. Electricity runs through my body, setting every nerve on fire. My nipples harden. My breath falters. Even if I wanted to, I can't speak.

He slowly turns his face, skimming the tip of his nose across the skin of my jaw. When we're eye to eye and nose to nose, he whispers, "Ask me."

The shop disappears. We're suspended in empty space, alone in an endless sea of black. All I see are his eyes, gold and gorgeous and haunting.

"W-what do you see?"

In near silence, with barely a breath, A.J. murmurs, "Ghosts."

All the tiny hairs on the back of my neck stand on end. My arms pimple with gooseflesh.

He turns and leaves me standing there, gaping after him like a fool.

"We're ready for dessert, Nina."

My mother's voice jerks me back into the present. I'm sitting at her elegant dining room table with Eric sighing contentedly beside me, holding my hand under the tablecloth. My father sits to my right. Jamie is seated across from me, watching me in bemusement over the rim of his china coffee cup.

In the past four hours, I've done nothing but obsess over A.J. Edwards and his cryptic final words. I haven't been able to come up with a single hypothesis that makes sense of them, or of his even more strange behavior toward me. I can't wait to get Jamie alone and grill him on whatever else he knows about A.J. Especially any details about the woman in Russia who he sent flowers to today.

Unfortunately, because my parent's cook, Nina, is about four hundred years old, bless her, this dinner is moving at a snail's pace. We might still be sitting here at the turn of the next century.

"That was *awesome*, Mrs. Carmichael. I love your cooking."

My mother accepts Eric's compliment with a gracious smile, as if she actually had anything to do with preparing the dinner. "Thank you, Eric. It's so nice to see a man enjoy a meal."

This is a not-so-subtle dig at my father, who usually takes one sniff at Nina's bizarre Thai-Peruvian-Japanese concoctions and heads to the fridge to rummage for anything resembling real food. Eric, on the other hand, will eat anything that moves. If we were ever involved in a plane crash and became stranded on a desert island, he'd be the last one to survive, happily devouring every beetle, worm, and flying insect in sight, without a bit of squeamishness. I'm convinced he doesn't own taste buds.

On the positive side, most of what Nina makes doesn't include meat, which is a plus for me.

My mother turns her attention to Jamie. "James, any new special lady friends we should know about?"

My brother smiles serenely. "Not in particular. Though if you'd like to know about any new special male friends I've recently made, that's quite another topic altogether."

My mother pales. My father changes the subject so fast my head spins.

"Chloe, we've talked about your brother's new case, my new case, and your mother's new art acquisitions, and you haven't yet said one word about yourself."

I'm pleased my father is showing an interest in my work. This isn't typically the situation. "Now that you mention it, I do have some important news to share."

"Oh? And what's that?" I don't miss the look that passes between my parents. They lean forward eagerly. I'm touched by their attentiveness.

"Fleuret is going to be featured in *People* magazine!" Feeling proud of myself, waiting for their follow-up questions, I take a swig of the silky Bordeaux my mother's served with dinner.

My mother blinks. "*People* magazine," she repeats slowly, as if she's never heard of it. "Is that the one that does all the stories about Kim Kalashian?"

My brother comes to my rescue, his voice dry as bone. "Kar*dash*ian, mother. You know, one of the most famous women in the world? And yes, that's the magazine Chloe is referring to. It's an incredible opportunity for her." He turns to me with a smile. "You didn't tell me about this today, little bug. Congrats. Good on you. When's it happening?"

"I didn't hear anything about this either." Eric sounds miffed. "Does this mean you're going to be working even *longer* hours now?"

I take another slug of my wine.

My father waves this unwelcome interruption off. "No, Chloe, I meant what's happening in your personal life. When are you and this fine young man going to get married?"

Wine sprays from my mouth like a geyser, drenching my chin, my dinner plate, and the white linen tablecloth around it in a fine drizzle of red. I start coughing, and can't stop.

Jamie laughs. My mother gasps, appalled. She leaps to her feet, calling for Nina to bring a wet cloth. My father simply stares at me with his bushy eyebrows halfway up his forehead, awaiting an answer.

Eric provides him with one before I can regain my composure. Sheepishly, he says, "I'm honored to hear you say that, sir. In fact, I'm glad you brought it up. I know Chloe and I have only been dating a short while, but we have so much in common, and we get along so well, and our values are so similar . . ." He clears his throat, shifting his weight in his chair.

I turn to him slowly, my eyes wide open. I squeeze his hand so tightly I must be cutting off the blood flow to his fingers. He smiles at me, and pats my hand. I realize he's mistaken my blossoming horror for overwhelming emotion.

"Well, if things keep going in the direction they're going, sir, I think we'll have an announcement to make quite soon. With your blessing, of course," he hastens to add.

My mother instantly forgets about Nina and the cloth. She clutches her pearls. Her cry of joy, though I'm not certain I've ever heard it before, is genuine. My father relaxes back into his chair and folds his hands over his belly, beaming like a happy Buddha. My brother slowly sets his coffee on the table, his face impassive, watching me carefully.

As for me? I burn. I smoke. I writhe in impotent fury, gritting my teeth so hard they're in danger of shattering.

No one has asked my opinion on the subject of marriage to Eric, most importantly the man himself. Almost worse is the glaring reality that, except for my brother, everyone in this room is convinced I'm wasting my time on my silly little flower hobby, and I should hurry up and get down to the real work of landing myself a husband before I turn into an unmarryable spinster. And lucky me, lo and behold! A gallant suitor has just offered his hand—for my father's approval.

I'm living in a Jane Austen novel.

It goes from bad to worse.

"Oh, darling, we're so *pleased*!" My mother hastens to Eric and grips his shoulder, as if he might change his mind and she'll be forced to hold him against his chair. "You certainly had to kiss your share of frogs, Chloe, but now that you've found your—"

"Prince Charming?" Jamie interrupts my mother's gushings with a tone just as pointed as his look. Before I can banish it, the image of a Viking god flashes before my eyes, a god with piercing golden eyes and a lion's mane of hair, thundering bare chested over a battlefield on a stallion.

I've been watching way too much HBO.

"Yes, James. Prince Charming. As I was saying, now that you've found him, we can put all this flower shop nonsense behind us and get on with the more important business of wedding planning!" She pulls a hankie from her sleeve and dabs at her eyes, sniffing dramatically. "Oh, this calls for a toast!"

No, mother, this calls for a mutiny.

I stand. I wipe the remaining wine from my chin. I place my napkin on the table. "Eric and I are not getting married."

The room comes to a screeching halt. Nina, who has just arrived from the kitchen with a wet towel, turns around and dodders out.

"Babe," says Eric, hurt.

"Not anytime soon, anyway, Eric. There are a lot of things we need to talk about first. And a little news flash: this isn't the nineteenth century. My father's blessing is nice, but it isn't necessary. I'll marry whomever I want. Probably someone who respects me enough to consult with me and ask my feelings on the matter before he makes a dramatic announcement to my family."

"Now, Chloe," my father says in his deepest, most commanding courtroom voice, "let's not get hysterical."

If he thinks this is hysterical, he ain't seen nothin' yet.

"We're simply thinking of what's best for your future—"

"You haven't asked what *I* think is best for my future—"

"You haven't shown great intelligence in that regard—"

"That's so unfair! Just because my choices aren't what *you'd* make, that doesn't mean I'm a complete idiot, or a failure for that matter—"

"You're upsetting your mother—"

"We're even, then, because she's upsetting me!"

"Enough!" My father pounds his fist on the table so hard all the glassware jumps, falling back with a clatter.

Silence descends. The grandfather clock in the corner begins a doleful chime.

It's eight o'clock on a Sunday evening in January, and I am finally at my wit's end.

I look at my parents. My mother, swathed in silk and pearls, my father, lord of the manor, master of all he surveys. I know these flawed but genuinely good people love me. They have provided me with a lifetime of constant—if somewhat distant—affection, have gladly paid for my extravagant education, have done everything in their power to ensure I've had every advantage in life. Yet what they don't know about me could fill volumes.

The terrible truth is that they don't want to know. They want their dream of the perfect daughter, the obedient, sweet-natured girl who marries the perfect man and attends all the right parties and knows how to manage a household staff.

I am not that girl. Or, if I was, I'm not any longer.

Quietly, I say, "I'm twenty-five years old. I'm not your baby anymore. I'm sorry if the person I've become is a disappointment to you, but this is who I am. If you're not willing to accept me this way, then

I think it's best if we don't see each other for a while." I pause, look at Jamie's face, at the gleam of approval in his eye, and add, "And by the way, your son is gay. Stop being such assholes about it."

The following silence is so total, it's almost deafening. Into it, James begins slowly to clap.

I turn and leave the table, and let myself out the front door.

Santa Monica Boulevard is surprisingly busy for a cold Sunday night. Then again, I've never walked down the boulevard on a cold Sunday night, so I really have nothing to compare it to.

Eric drove us to my parents' in Beverly Hills for dinner. Walking back to my apartment in Hollywood would take weeks. Or at least a few hours, which in walking time is the same thing. I have my handbag and cell phone, so I could call Uber, or even hail one of the taxis regularly passing by, but I need to walk for at least a little while. I need to clear my head.

I need to calm down before I get home, where I know Eric will be waiting for me.

My mother's final cry of "What's gotten into her, Thomas?" as I marched out of the house is still echoing in my brain.

Not what, mother. Who.

I can't get him out of my head. This new rebelliousness, the anger, the cursing . . . it all started when my life collided with A.J. Edwards. He sent me into a tailspin I haven't recovered from.

I know it's not actually his fault. He's not standing next to me holding a gun to my head, making me act all crazy and out of character, but he might as well be. He's infiltrated my brain like a ninja, and no matter how I try, I can't evict him.

I'm stewing so deeply in my juices, I don't notice when it begins to rain. It's only when I step into a puddle and my foot is soaked with ice water that I jerk out of my reverie, and look around.

Crap. I don't even have a jacket on. I'm getting drenched.

I dart into the first doorway I see, taking shelter. As I'm shaking the water from my hair, four beautiful young men glide by me, open the door, and enter what I now realize is a gay bar.

The blazing neon sign in the window—"Flaming Saddles" it screams—should have been my first clue.

Confession time: I love gay bars. They're places of uninhibited fun. Also, in spite of what some people think, gay men love women. They just don't want to sleep with them. The majority of gay men I've met have good relationships with their mothers and sisters, have tons of girlfriends, and have a healthy respect for the gender in general. As long as you don't say anything stupid along the lines of "I bet if you spent the night with me, I'd change your mind," they have no problem if a vagina-owning human shares drinks with them in their bars.

When my brother first moved to Manhattan a few years ago, he took me around to all the best spots, introducing me to some of the sweetest, least judgmental people I've met anywhere.

Outside of New York City, West Hollywood has the best gay bars in the country. It's been a crappy night, and I need some distraction. I'm going in.

Inside is an Oz of flashing rainbow lights and bar-dancing cowboy bartenders. Bonnie Raitt croons on the jukebox. A giant iron steer threatens to charge from a raised platform. There's sawdust scattered over the wood plank floor. The Wild West Saloon theme abounds right down to the old black-and-white westerns playing on the overhead TVs.

I slip onto a stool in a corner near the steer, and text Kat and Grace to see if they can join me. Neither one can, which means I'll be drinking alone like the sad sack I am. In celebration of the first time I've ever told my parents off, I order champagne.

Which is when I notice him.

On the opposite side of the room, in a dark corner beneath the mounted head of a longhorn, sits a man in a black hoodie. He's hunched over the table in front of him, nursing a beer, wearing aviators and an expression that could turn molten lava to ice. His shoulders are so wide, they almost completely block the neon Budweiser sign behind him. I don't even have to see the mass of dark golden hair tucked under the hoodie to know who it is.

"You've *got* to be kidding me."

The cute waiter returns with my champagne. "What's that sweetie?"

I realize I've spoken aloud. I look down at the table, embarrassed. "Nothing. Sorry. Just thinking out loud."

"I do that all the time, too. My boyfriend keeps saying someone will think I'm a homeless guy who's off my meds, but what do I care what some judgey stranger thinks? You go right on with your conversation, sweetie, and just raise a hand in the air when you're ready for another, mmkay?"

Balancing a full tray of drinks, he walks away with better posture than I can ever hope to have. I'm left alone with my champagne and a sudden conviction that the universe is having a go at me. I'm the butt of some cosmic practical joke.

Because the giant on the other side of the room has risen from his table, and is heading my way.

Everything inside me starts to pound. I practice deep-breathing exercises, until he's too close and I have to look up at him.

Without a word, he sits across from me, lowering his bulk to the chair with surprising grace. He removes his sunglasses. He takes a long swallow of his beer, wipes his mouth with the back of his hand, and waits.

"I'm not following you, if that's what you're thinking."

A.J. nods. I can't tell whether he's acknowledging what I've said, is agreeing with me, or is waiting for me to add more. He's making me uncomfortable with his silence. All the anger I felt at dinner—which had begun so nicely to quiet down—surges back with a vengeance.

I lean closer to him and declare, "You made me call my parents assholes tonight!"

"Did I now."

I think he's amused. His facial expression hasn't changed, but his eyes shine. In the low light they gleam like he's running a fever. I wonder what my own reflect back at him.

"Yes, you did." I don't offer anything else, finding it more important to finish my champagne in one huge gulp. I lift my hand, motioning for the waiter. Across the room, he nods, catching my eye.

A.J. says, "Maybe they deserved it."

"They absolutely did."

"I did you a favor, then. Now you owe me one."

He's toying with me. I can sense it in the look in his eyes, in the way his lips seem to want to lift at the corners. I don't feel like playing along. I stare at him so long it's his turn to get uncomfortable. He drops his gaze and frowns.

"What are you doing here?" he growls.

"I could ask you the same question. This is a gay bar."

His eyes flash up to meet mine. "Yeah. It is." He offers no apology or explanation.

"Are you coming out to me right now, is that what you're saying? You're gay?"

He examines my expression. He takes his time with it, slowly letting his gaze rove all over my face, until he settles for staring at my mouth for so long I have to restrain myself from squirming in my seat. Finally, in a husky, almost carnal voice, he says, "You know better."

If I don't, my uterus certainly does. The pulse of heat that floods between my legs makes me clench my thighs together. Mercifully, the waiter arrives with another champagne.

"Here you go, sweetie."

"Thank you. I'm also going to need a whiskey when you get the chance. Two fingers, neat."

His gaze slides from me to A.J. and back again. He purses his lips, lifts his eyebrows twice in a hubba-hubba gesture, nods, and turns away silently.

"So you're not gay. Congratulations."

"You got something against gays?"

I'm insulted. "No!"

A.J. shrugs. "Me, neither. In fact, I think they've got more compassion than most, having to put up with so much shit their whole lives. Can't be easy, being one way when society tells you you're not okay unless you're another."

I'm floored by this little speech. A.J. Edwards is the last person alive I'd have called enlightened. I briefly wonder how else I've misjudged him, but then decide he could just be screwing with me. I don't know him well enough to judge.

I hate that I don't know him well enough to judge.

I mutter, "That explains your attitude toward prostitutes."

A.J. squints at me. "You're in a worse mood than usual, Princess. What's up?"

Now he's being nice? "You're talking about *my* moods? Can I just say that your mood swings should be treated with medication and extensive psychotherapy?"

My whiskey arrives, placed delicately on the table by the waiter who retreats as fast as he appeared. He obviously senses my pending mental break. I shoot the whiskey, coughing as it scorches a path down my throat.

A.J. says quietly, "Probably. But I think therapy is bullshit. The only person who can fix you is you; paying four hundred dollars an hour to pour your heart out to a stranger is just an emotional jerkoff. In the long run, you're still stuck with yourself, problems and all. And I don't put anything in my body that will alter my state of mind. Life's too short to miss out on anything, even if it's pain."

There's something in his voice that makes me pause with the glass halfway down to the table. I look at him. He looks back at me with naked longing darkening his eyes. I blink, and it's gone. I might have imagined it.

"You're drinking a beer. I think alcohol qualifies as mind-altering."

He wordlessly turns the bottle around so I can read the label: O'Doul's. It's nonalcoholic.

This man is shattering every preconceived notion I've held about him. And about rock stars in general. *Except for the prostitutes,* I remind myself grimly. He's got that one down pat.

"Let me get this straight. You're a man who likes gay bars, but you're not a gay man. You drink, but only if it's nonalcoholic. You don't believe in therapy or taking medication for emotional problems, but admit you probably need both."

"Don't forget the prostitutes," he chides softly, and takes another swig of the beer that lacks any reason whatsoever to drink it.

"Okay, since you mentioned it, what's with that? You're not into normal relationships?"

"*Normal* relationships? No. I'm not. I'm into honest relationships."

I stare at him, a little light-headed from drinking two glasses of champagne and a whiskey in such a short span of time. "Honest relationships. Like those that require money to exchange hands."

He nods, holding my gaze. "A prostitute will only lie to you if you ask her if you were good. Even then, you both know she's not telling the truth. It's part of what you're paying for. Otherwise, it's an honest relationship. Straightforward. No bullshit. I want something. She wants something. We both get what we want, and go our separate ways. Some of the best people I've ever known have been prostitutes. And yes, the most honest."

I gape at him. "But—but—you're taking advantage of them! Of their situation . . . their lack of money, their desperation. How can you be so casual about using a person that way? It's inhumane! Those poor women!"

Then a miracle occurs: A.J. throws back his head and laughs. It's a deep, masculine, beautiful sound. I'm astonished by how much I like hearing it.

When he's finished, he looks at me with a combination of amusement and pity. "You've seen *Hustle & Flow* one too many times. I'm not denying that kind of shit exists; it does. But the 'poor women' I hang out with aren't streetwalking teenagers with pimps who beat them if they don't cough up enough cash at the end of the night. My 'poor women' are freelancers, fully in control of their own destinies, who charge thousands of dollars per hour, Princess, to do something *you* give away for free. And probably don't even like."

"You're right. I don't like it; I *love* it."

The words are out before I can censor them. A.J.'s expression loses all its humor and smug self-importance. He tilts his head, examining me with such piercing intensity I wish the floor would open up and devour me. Flustered, I blunder on. "And it's not even the same thing. If I have sex with someone it's because I *want* to, not because I *have* to. I do it in a context of caring and love, of mutual respect—"

"Bullshit."

I wish there were cutlery on the table, because I'm seized with the overwhelming desire to drive a fork into A.J.'s eye.

"Bullshit?" I repeat carefully, challenging him.

"Yes. Everything you just said is bullshit." His eyes flash. "Except maybe the first part. I think you were telling the truth about that."

The anger inside me feels like a nuclear bomb detonating in my solar plexus. I'm so pissed I don't even know where to start.

Dead serious now, A.J. says, "If you want me to explain *why* I think it's bullshit, Princess, you're going to have to tell me more truths. You up for that?"

My hands shake with the violent desire to curl around his neck. He's so arrogant, so *infuriating*! I'd like to . . . well, I don't know what I'd like to do to him, but it would definitely involve drawing blood!

I feign boredom. After over two decades of living with my mother, a woman moved to great emotion only if it involves a sale at Saks Fifth Avenue, this kind of composure is second nature.

"I'm not afraid of you, A.J.," I say, tranquil as a sphinx. "Ask away."

His smile comes on slow and wicked. He's obviously not buying my act. "Good. Question one: Have you ever had sex when you weren't in the mood?"

I open my mouth to say no, but stop. The truth is, it happened just last week. Eric was horny, I was exhausted from a long day at work, and I didn't want to have an awkward scene or make him feel like I didn't want him, so I just . . . sort of . . .

"I see the answer is yes. And let me tell you this: when you fuck a man just to shut him up or spare his ego, that's not mutual respect. That's manipulation. In other words, it's bullshit."

My mouth closes with an audible snap. I motion to the bartender for another whiskey.

"Question two: Have you ever faked an orgasm?"

A telling flush creeps up my neck. *If that pretty waiter doesn't get his skinny behind over here* right now *with my whiskey, I'm going to slap that beauty mark right off his face.*

"Another yes." A.J.'s voice grows softer. "And this is an even worse yes, because not only is it a manipulation, it's a flat-out lie. A lie that maintains your control, so you don't have to risk being honest by telling a man what really makes you feel good. You get to keep your safe little distance, feeling superior, while the poor stupid fuck who's trying so hard to do everything right is pumping away in ignorance, thinking he's with a woman who cares enough about him to show him her heart."

My face is flaming. I can't look at him. For some unthinkable reason, I feel as if I might cry.

"Question three—"

"Enough. You've made your point." But he isn't done with me yet.

"Question three: Have you ever had sex with a man you weren't in love with?"

I turn my head slowly and meet his gaze. "Does that make me a slut?"

He shakes his head. "Not at all. In my opinion, a woman should be able to sleep with whoever she wants, whenever she wants, for any reason she wants, without having to explain or apologize. But your exact words were, 'I do it in a context of caring and love.' Which means, at the very least, every time you've had sex there was a real connection, real caring."

His gaze, once again, becomes penetrating. "Which means you've never had a one-night stand. Or revenge sex. Or sex out of boredom, or when you've had too much to drink, or with a guy who liked you way more than you liked him and you needed the ego stroke. Right?"

I can't answer. I don't have to; he sees it all written plainly on my face.

"And you're the one judging them," he murmurs, effectively rendering me speechless.

The waiter arrives. He sets down my drink. "Can I get you anything else?"

Looking at me, A.J. says, "A side order of crow?"

The waiter, who by now realizes there's something odd going on, giggles awkwardly, hesitating only a moment before saying brightly, "Well, let me know! I'll leave you two alone."

When he leaves, I'm left gagging on the dry, crusty rinds of my own hypocrisy.

I pretend the glass of whiskey is a crystal ball. I stare into it, hoping to divine a way to salvage my self-respect. Because A.J. is completely right; what I said was bullshit. Self-righteous bullshit, no less. I gather my courage and meet his gaze.

"You're right about everything you just said. I owe you an apology."

I can tell this staggers him, but he has the good grace to shrug it off with a simple nod.

"I still feel bad for prostitutes, though, no matter how much money they make. It can't be . . . that can't be an easy way to earn a living."

After a long time he says, "No. It isn't."

I'm arrested by the unexpected melancholy in his voice. I stare at him in dawning wonder. "Oh my God."

He looks up at me. "What?"

"You defend them! You not only defend them, you have empathy for them, too! And you think women who *aren't* being paid for it should be able to sleep with whoever they want, without being slut-shamed!"

"Your point being?"

"You're a *feminist*!"

He snorts. "And you're drunk."

He's right. I'm definitely feeling dizzy. Still, I'm convinced I've glimpsed into the soul of the sad, beautiful Viking sitting across from me, and I want more. Unfortunately, at that moment, my cell phone rings.

It's Eric. "Babe, where the hell are you?" he yells.

Wincing, I jerk my head away from the earpiece. "I'm fine, Eric. I stopped on the way home because I just needed . . . I just needed some space. I'll be home later."

"Stopped? Where?" I hear the panic in his voice.

"Just this bar—"

"You're alone at a bar?" he shouts. There's an alarming lack of trust resounding in his voice. "Jesus, Chloe, what are you thinking? Which bar? I'll come get you!"

"Eric, please, calm down. It's fine, I'm not alone. I'm with . . ." I raise my eyes to find A.J. gazing steadily at me. His jaw is rock hard. "I-I'm with a friend."

There. I said it. I'm with a friend. A prostitute-loving, bipolar friend, who just this afternoon told me he had plenty of reasons to hate me.

I've gone completely off my rocker.

"What friend?" Eric roars, so loudly I pull the phone even farther from my ear.

Which is when A.J. takes it from my hand.

"You have two seconds to calm your shit down, brother, before I make Chloe give me your address so I can come and calm it down for you."

His voice is low and dangerous. A thrill of pure fear zings through me. On the other end of the line, there's crackling silence, until Eric finds his tongue.

"Whoever you are, you just threatened an officer of the law. You'd better hope we don't meet face to face. *Brother*."

"I have a feeling we will," says A.J., looking at me. He hangs up.

He sets my phone into my shaking hand. "Your boyfriend's a cop?"

I nod.

His eyes are black. His mouth is set into a hard line, harder even than the muscles in his jaw. "He have a temper?"

"He's never hit me, if that's what you mean."

He growls, "Plenty of ways to mistreat a woman that don't involve putting your fists on her."

My head is pounding. I decide this day has gone on long enough; it's time to leave. I try to stand, but stagger as my foot catches on the leg of the stool I've been sitting on. A.J. is out of his seat, righting me with his hand under my elbow, faster than my eyes can track the movement.

"Easy, Princess." He chuckles. "We don't want you to fall and bang up that pretty face."

I stare up at him. Though his face is shadowed beneath the hood of the sweatshirt, I can tell he's wishing he could take that back. I'm not going to let him.

"You think I'm pretty?"

His lips thin. He looks away, motioning for the waiter to bring the check. He mutters, "Never said I didn't."

"Oh, right." Tipsy, I laugh. "You only said you hated me. And that I was stuck-up. And frigid. By the way, I'd like to take this opportunity to correct you about something: I *would* know a dick if it hit me in the face. I can't claim to ever have had that experience, but I can say with all confidence that if a dick suddenly flew out of nowhere and whacked me across the nose, I would *absolutely* know it was a dick." I hiccup. "One thousand percent sure. The hairy balls alone would be a dead giveaway."

Apparently deciding not to wait for the check, A.J. reaches into his pocket, produces his wallet, and throws a wad of cash on the table, all without releasing my arm. I'm impressed. I remind myself he must have perfected the art of handling women in various stages of inebriation. Picturing a chorus line of half-drunk prostitutes kicking their legs in the air as A.J. rushes to keep them all from falling, I giggle.

"How much did you have to drink before you got here?"

His voice is stern. He gazes down at me as if he's very disappointed in my behavior. I sheepishly admit I had two or three glasses of red wine with dinner.

"So. Two or three glasses of wine, two glasses of champagne, and two glasses of whiskey. You've had at least six, possibly seven drinks in the past few hours. Four of them in the last thirty minutes. Two of *those* double whiskeys. That about right?"

I close one eye because the room has, just slightly, begun to spin.

"I have many talents, Mr. Edwards, but I'm not all that great with math." Another hiccup. "I'll have to take your word on this one."

"Let's go, Princess." Without waiting for a reply, A.J. half drags, half carries me to the door.

"Where are we going?" I cry, alarmed. I'm even more alarmed by what he says next.

"Home. You need to go to bed."

A.J.'s car is nothing like what I expected. Because it's not a car. It's a motorcycle. He informs me he doesn't own a car.

Item number four thousand seven hundred eighty-two on the list of things normal people own that A.J. Edwards doesn't.

"I can't ride on that!" I stare at the ginormous black Harley parked in the back lot. It glitters with chrome and menace. Under the flickering fluorescent lamplight of the parking lot, it seems to leer at me.

One saving grace, at least: it's stopped raining.

"Of course you can." A.J. opens one of the leather side bags strapped to the back of the bike, produces a helmet that looks as if half of it is missing, and hands it to me. "Put this on."

He mounts the bike and starts it with a brisk kick of his leg. It roars to life, exhaling fumes. I cough and fan a hand back and forth in front of my face. "I'll die on that thing!" I shout over the racket. "Forget it! I'll call a cab!"

He shoves the hoodie off his head, pulls his hair out of the elastic that's been holding it in the messy man bun at the nape of his neck, and straps on a helmet, all while gazing calmly at me. "Chloe, get your ass on the back of my bike."

The way my body responds to this command is ridiculous. Hormones I never knew I had start screaming gleefully through my veins, tossing confetti and blowing party horns. I bite my lip, hard, and stare at him.

This is dangerous territory. *A.J.* is dangerous territory. I should know better. I have common sense. I have a *boyfriend.* I have a deeply ingrained sense of loyalty to said boyfriend, even if we are in a fight.

A.J. has a deeply ingrained fondness for ladies of the evening.

He says my name again, softer this time. His eyes caress mine. Under their warm golden glow, I melt. "Fine. But if you kill me on this thing, it's up to you to explain to my parents what happened. Good luck with that. My father will most likely disembowel you."

"She's not a *thing.*" Defending the honor of his motorbike, A.J. ignores the threat to his bodily unity. Perhaps he isn't as fond of his bowels as most people are.

With zero elegance, I clamber onto the back of the motorcycle, clutching his shoulders for balance. They feel like boulders beneath my hands.

"She's a custom V-Rod with a titanium chassis and a top speed of two hundred and fifty miles per hour."

It seems the alcohol has engaged my selective hearing because I glide right over that last piece of data as if it had never been spoken. No wonder they say ignorance is bliss. "How is a motorcycle a she?" I demand. "Wouldn't they all be *hes*, if they're supposed to be so macho and dangerous?"

"Helmet."

I don my helmet, fumbling with the chin strap. When I'm finished and he appears satisfied with my efforts, A.J. asks, "You ever watch Jacques Cousteau?"

Hello, left field, I see the fly ball approaching. "That might be the strangest segue I've ever heard."

"Answer the question."

I do this thing that's part belly-deep burp, part hiccup. I'm convinced it's the single most unattractive noise to ever exit my body. Horrified, I clap my hands over my mouth. A.J. looks amused. It's a relief, but it shouldn't be, considering I don't care about his opinion. I recover my composure quickly, and answer. "Yes. My mother loved him. She used to watch reruns of his show all the time when I was growing up."

He nods. "Mine, too."

Whoa. He has a *mother*. The thought has never occurred to me. My fuzzy brain launches into a stumbling frenzy of related questions about siblings, family life, his youth and hobbies and education, until it exhausts itself and falls flat on its face, and I just stare at him, waiting. The process takes all of five seconds.

"There's this thing that Jacques Cousteau used to say that always stuck with me. Put your arms around me."

"Jacques Cousteau used to say 'put your arms around me'?"

"No, Chloe. Put your arms around me. You have to hold on for the ride." He waits for me to follow this simple direction.

"Oh! Gotcha." With gargantuan effort, I marshal every ounce of faux disinterest at my disposal, and slide my arms around his shoulders. My hands don't touch on the other side. *He's bigger than my arm span.*

This leaves me in an awkward predicament. I can lower my arms to his waist, which will allow me to grasp my hands together, but I run the risk of an embarrassing encounter with his crotch.

Especially if, as he has said, and his shoe size and stature surely indicate, it's huge.

He senses my hesitation. "What's wrong?"

My voice comes out tiny. "I don't think I'm doing it right."

He takes my hands, and gently lowers them to his abdomen, locking my fingers together over a hard expanse of muscle that definitely isn't his crotch. "Better?"

I sigh in relief. *"Best."*

He revs the throttle. The bike rattles and hums beneath us, itching to leap into motion.

I prompt, "So—Jacques Cousteau?"

"Right. He used to say that the most beautiful creatures are always the most dangerous."

I recognize this saying. It's one of Mr. Cousteau's most famous. "No, what he actually said was, 'Zee most beeyooteefool creetoors are also zee most dangeroos.' "

Hearing my terrible French accent, A.J. laughs, a second miracle for the night. Loving the sound of it, I grin.

"That he did, Chloe, that he did. So I figured, following his logic, every dangerous creature therefore has to be female, because females are the only creatures who are really beautiful. Compared to them, us guys are just a bunch of slobbering idiots."

He looks at me over his shoulder. His smile is devastating. My heart skips a beat, then stalls out altogether.

Holy mother of all craps.

At the exact moment we pull out of the lot and zoom off into the night, I realize just how much trouble I'm in, and that, in more ways than one, it's too late to jump off this ride.

Because, reckless fool that I've become, I want too badly to see where it's going.

I'm being carried up stairs. My head rests on a heated, solid surface. I feel safe, relaxed, and completely at ease.

I have no idea where I am.

I snuggle closer to the sweet-smelling warmth that surrounds me, and sigh in profound contentment. I could stay here in this gently rocking, protective cocoon forever. My fingers find strands of silk. I begin to twist the silk through my fingers, smiling at how lovely it feels on my skin. I bring the silk to my nose and inhale.

Cinnamon. Sugar. A hint of smoke and musk. I love that smell. I'd happily drown in it.

A jarring, metallic clang makes me jerk. I whimper. A voice mutters, "Goddamn useless security gate."

More stairs. The sound of even breathing. The slow and steady thump of a heartbeat beneath my ear. The voice comes again, gentler this time. "Chloe. Wake up, Princess, I need the key."

"Mmm." I nuzzle my face into the warmth that is both unyielding and sinfully soft, like velvet laid over granite. I tighten my arms around it, because somehow I can. Wherever this place is, it's *heaven.*

I hear a low, strained groan, as if someone is in pain.

"Shhh." I press my lips against the silken heat. I hear myself make a noise deep in my throat, like a purr. The groan comes again, more anguished.

"Chloe. For the love of God. Give me the key."

Through my fog of contentment, I consider the word: key. I keep the key . . . "Spare," I mumble. "Top o' the frame."

A moment's pause, some rustling and gentle movement, then I hear a satisfied grunt. Now I'm somewhere darker than before, because the red light behind my lids has been extinguished.

Home. I'm home. The thought floats to me on a leisurely breeze. I recognize the orange-blossom scent of the candle I forgot to blow out before I left for dinner, which is still burning on the coffee table in the living room. It gutters as I glide by noiselessly, effortlessly, on my way somewhere else . . .

I'm laid down on a soft, soft surface. My limbs are gently arranged. My shoes are removed. It's not as warm as before, nor nearly as pleasant. I frown, trying to open my eyes, but my lids are like lead. I wrap my arms around myself, trying to regain the heat I've lost. A weight settles over me: a blanket. I burrow deep under it, sighing in contentment once again.

Something downy touches my forehead, the barest whisper of pressure. Sparks sizzle in its wake. The voice from before speaks softly into my ear. But now it speaks guttural, primitive words I can't understand.

"Idi spat, laskovaya moya. Spat."

"Don't go," I beg, fretting at the good-bye I sense in the gentle whisper. "Don't go yet. Please."

A moment of silence follows, then I hear an exhalation. "I won't," murmurs the voice in words I can grasp. "I'm here. I'm right here."

I'm awash in relief. He's here. He's not going. I can sleep, safe and sound.

And so I do.

I'm jolted awake by the sound of a garbage truck lumbering down the alley outside a nearby window. I bolt upright. My heart hammers. Confused, I look wildly around the dim room for a few moments before I realize I'm in my bed, at home.

I'm still fully dressed. My head pounds. My eyes are gritty. My mouth is a desert.

I pad to the bathroom, use the toilet, and pop two Advil with a gulp of water from the faucet. By chance, my gaze lands on the digital clock on the counter. I have a heart attack when I realize I was supposed to be at the downtown flower market three hours ago to pick up fresh flowers. It's Monday, Fleuret's busiest day of the week, when the majority of our corporate accounts have to be installed. Before lunch.

There are two dozen local business owners who are going to be furious with me today.

Not even bothering to brush my teeth, comb my hair, or otherwise make myself presentable, I run to the bedroom and shove my feet into a pair of sneakers, leaving the laces untied. I grab a jacket from the closet and drag it on while I dash to the living room, frantically searching for my handbag. It's on the coffee table. I fly out the door, and sprint down the stairs, out the building, and across the sidewalk. I fall panting on my car.

It's 5:50 a.m. In ten minutes, my shop staff will arrive, and there will be no fresh flowers for them to work with.

Desperate to find a solution, I begin a series of wild calculations. It will take me twenty minutes to get downtown, at least an hour or two to shop for the flowers—if I'm fast—another twenty to get back to Fleuret. Best-case scenario, I'm looking at an arrival time of approximately eight o'clock.

Right when the driver arrives to start loading the delivery van with all the arrangements that won't have been made.

I pound on the steering wheel. It makes me feel a little better, but doesn't help the situation. I dig my cell from my purse, hit Contacts, and select Trina's name. I need to send her a text to let her know she needs to be ready to start putting out fires today.

But I've already sent Trina a text, this morning at one thirty. It's there in black and white. I stare at the message, befuddled.

Can you do the market this morning? Feeling sick. So sorry. Will be in as soon as I can.

I have no recollection of sending it.

I sit in my car, staring at the text, until a tentative honk makes me look up. An older woman in a battered Volvo is motioning to me. She wants to know if I'm leaving. Even at this hour parking spots are at a premium.

I wave at her, start the car, and head to work.

When I arrive, I'm relieved to see Trina definitely got my text, because the shop is buzzing with activity.

"Morning, Carlos," I say to the young Latino guy who processes the flowers. There's a mess of leaves and stems around his feet from the stem chopper. He's starting to sweep up.

He smiles, nodding. "Morning, Miss C."

Farther inside the shop, hidden from the main sales floor behind a wall, are the long stainless steel design tables, where Trina and Renee, my junior designer, are standing chatting while they arrange. White plastic buckets of flowers surround them. Trina's working on an extravagant, modern piece for a Beverly Hills plastic surgeon's office—I can tell whose arrangement it is because they spend the most, and it's composed almost entirely of cut phalaenopsis orchids, one of the most expensive flowers available. Renee's dropping trios of white roses wrapped with wire into little blue bud vases for the desks of the attorneys at a law firm.

I'm impressed; they obviously started early. "You guys are awesome!"

Trina says, "You're here! I thought you were sick! How're you feeling?"

"I'm okay. Better now. Thanks for handling the market, Trin, you saved my behind."

She waves off my thanks. "No worries. When I got your text, I texted Renee to see if she could come in a little earlier since we'd be down a man. I'm happy you're here, though. Mrs. Goldman left a message that she's having a lunch at Spago and she needs flowers for it."

"Another lunch at Spago? Doesn't the woman eat anywhere else? Or cook?"

"Apparently not. Fifteen guests today. She needs it delivered by eleven."

"Of course she does." I drop my purse on the desk, make myself a coffee, and get to work.

Two hours later, Jeff, our driver, arrives, and starts loading up. I can finally take a break.

I've been distracted all morning. On the back burner of my mind simmers everything that happened yesterday. My parents, Eric, A.J.

Especially A.J.

I remember leaving the bar with him and getting on his death mobile. I remember parts of the ride home. There's also a hazy, patchy memory of being carried, though it has the quality of a dream, so I'm not sure if it's real or not. That's about it.

I distinctly do *not* remember giving him my home address.

I check my phone. There are six missed phone calls, all of them from Eric. He hasn't left any voicemail messages. I get a sick feeling in my stomach when I realize I'm going to have to tell him that I left a bar with a guy he's never met. Who then drove me home on his motorcycle.

Who then may or may not have tucked me into bed.

Idi spat, laskovaya moya.

Ghostly and indistinct, the strange words appear in my mind like a warm breath blown on a cold pane of glass. I don't know what they mean, but I do know that the tone they were spoken in was anything but angry.

The tone was tender. Almost . . . loving.

I'm tempted to think my mind is playing tricks on me. But there's something . . . I don't know. There's something that tells me it wasn't a drunk dream. Something tells me I really heard those words, in those sweet tones.

I'm staring off into the distance, lost in thought, when Trina comes up behind me and nearly scares me out of my skin.

"I forgot to tell you—jeez, jump a little, why don't you?"

"Sorry." I put a hand over my thundering heart. "I was just spacing out. You surprised me."

She peers at me. "You okay today? You've been spacey all morning."

I clear my throat. "Just . . . yeah. Still not feeling a hundred percent. I've got that . . . er, flu that's going around."

The wine flu, Kat calls it.

"What's up?"

She holds out an order form. "That order Big Daddy sent—"

"Oh no, not you, too," I interrupt, grimacing.

She grins. Behind her trendy glasses, her big brown eyes sparkle. "Yeah. I heard your brother call him that and thought it was totally apropos. That dude is just a big ol' huggy bear of a man. Grrrr!" She makes a growly bear noise and sticks her butt out like she's awaiting a slap on it. "Hey Big Daddy Bear, Little Baby Bear has been baaaaad! She needs a *spanking*!"

"Please never do that again, or I'll demote you to bucket scrubber."

Straightening, Trina laughs. "Don't worry, it's not me he wants to spank anyway." She gives me her signature *you know what I'm saying, girlfriend* face, which is a bizarre combination of pursed lips, wiggling eyebrows, head nodding, and hair tossing that always manages to make her appear as if a blood vessel in her brain has just burst.

I'm too busy rewinding what she's said to fully appreciate it. "What? Who? *Me?*"

Rolling her eyes, Trina sighs. "Did you, or did you not, attend elementary school?"

I did in fact attend elementary school. It was a private school that my parents paid thirty thousand dollars a year in tuition for, so I could finger-paint and bang on drums and "learn music, theater, dramatic play, athletics, and environmental awareness, all of which stimulate the senses and support different ways of learning."

Trina went to public school in Venice, where she was in a girl gang.

I simply answer, "Yes."

"Okay. So you remember that little asshole kid who would pick on you, and pull your ponytail in class, and try to trip you when you were walking past him at recess?"

I frown. "How did you know about Mikey Dolan?"

"Because every girl has a Mikey Dolan, dummy!"

I stare at Trina. "Did you smoke a bowl before you came to work? Because you're sounding a little stoney."

"Ugh. Never mind." She holds out the order form. "What I needed to tell you was that order from Big—excuse me," she amends when she sees the warning look on my face. "That order from *Mr. Edwards* is a no go."

"Why? What's wrong with it?"

She shrugs. "The address is wrong, or incomplete. They sent an email from the wire service to let us know. So they need a correct address, or a telephone number, so they can call the recipient. They're going to hold it until we get back to them."

I take the order from her hand and review it. It's for one hundred long stem white roses, which we charge seven hundred dollars for. He's not kidding around.

"There's no message for the enclosure card."

"He didn't want one."

Trina and I share a look. The only time men don't want to include a message with a bouquet of flowers they're sending is if the woman they're sending them to is married to someone else, or if he's a stalker.

"All right. I'll follow up on it, thanks."

Exactly how I'm going to follow up on it is a mystery, because there's this fun little device called a phone that's missing in the equation. I have no way of contacting A.J.

Directly, anyway.

Deciding it's too early to call Kat, I look up the address on Google Maps. The street and city names are a tangle of unpronounceable words. I type slowly, looking back and forth from the order to the screen, making sure I'm entering it right: *4, Prospekt Devyatogo Yanvarya / 66a, Prospekt Alexandrovskoy Fermy.*

Google produces the result. I'm looking at a link for the Preobrazhenskoe Cemetery in Saint Petersburg, Russia.

My hands fall still on the keyboard. A little shiver runs down my spine.

You want to know what I see when I look at you? Ghosts.

I look at the name of the intended recipient. Aleksandra Zimnyokov. I murmur several variations of the last name, trying to get the pronunciation right, but give up quickly. Whoever this woman is, I'm sure she won't appreciate me butchering her name.

I look back at the computer, thinking. Into the search box I type "A.J. Edwards Bad Habit."

There are, no joke, nine hundred eighty-three thousand results. I click on the Wikipedia link near the top and start reading.

Alex James Edwards (born 9 July, 1987), known professionally as A.J. Edwards, is an American musician and singer-songwriter, best known as the drummer for the rock band Bad Habit.

He's twenty-eight, three years older than I am. Funny, I thought he was older. Maybe that's because he always seems like he's got the weight of the world around his neck. I keep reading and learn he was born in Las Vegas, Nevada, to a pastor and his homemaker wife. Due to their religious beliefs, he was homeschooled for his entire education.

I have a hard time imagining A.J., tatted, surly, antiestablishment A.J., as coming from such a square background. Although being homeschooled by *my* mother would certainly have made me jump off the deep end, so I shrug, reading on.

For one of the members of such a famous band, there's surprisingly few personal details about him. He has no siblings. His parents died years back. Most of the information involves his musical career and the bands he played with before Bad Habit, which he joined five years ago. The drummer Bad Habit had before A.J. had a severe cocaine addiction and died of a heart attack after a three-day drug binge.

"That's awful," I murmur.

There's a considerable section on chromesthesia, the neurological anomaly he has.

I read aloud, "Chromesthesia or sound-to-color synesthesia is a type of synesthesia in which heard sounds automatically and involuntarily evoke an experience of color. As with other variations of synesthesia, individuals with sound-color synesthesia perceive the synesthetic experience spontaneously, without effort, and in a way that the individual learns to accept as normal. The exact mechanism by which synesthesia persists has yet to be identified. Given that synesthetes and non-synesthetes both match sounds to colors in a nonarbitrary way, and that the ingestion of hallucinogenic drugs can induce synesthesia in under an hour, some researchers claim it is reasonable to assume that synesthetic experience uses preexisting pathways that are present in the normal brain."

I wonder if I can find hallucinogenic drugs so I can try to re-create what A.J. sees when he hears music. I bet Trina could find me some.

When I continue with the article, I note that in almost every accompanying picture of him, A.J. wears sunglasses, and something covering his head. Usually it's a hoodie. Sometimes it's a hat, pulled low over his forehead. Even in the rare picture that captures him without sunglasses, he never looks directly into a camera. His face is always lowered, or hidden, or turned to the side. Even in promotional shots for the band—even on the pictures for the CDs and singles—he hovers in the background. Nico, Bad Habit's extroverted lead singer, is always front and center, flanked by the other members of the band, but A.J. is almost always in the shadows.

Just looking at the photos for a few minutes, I can tell it's deliberate.

I want to know why.

I tap my fingernails on the desk, calculating how long I have to wait before Kat's up, and I can call and get her to ask Nico for A.J.'s home address.

Chapter 8

When I get home that night, there's a team of men from the management company just leaving. The security gate at the front of the apartment building which has been broken since I moved in, is miraculously fixed.

On the narrow concrete steps in front of the gate sits Eric, staring dejectedly at the ground.

I tense. *Can I do this now? Do I need more time? What will I say?*

But it's too late. He's seen me, standing motionless in the street beside my car, and stands. I have to go in. He waits for me with his hands shoved into his pockets, shifting his weight from foot to foot.

We haven't talked since A.J. hung up on him last night. I'm full of anxiety about what might happen next.

When I'm within arms' reach, he reaches out and wordlessly engulfs me in a hug. He buries his face in my neck, breathing me in. He's shaking. His nose is cold against my throat. I wonder how long he's been sitting here, waiting for me to show up.

"I'm sorry, babe. I was an idiot. I never should have said anything to your parents. The way I handled that . . . and then you wouldn't answer my calls . . ." He pulls back, looking at me with worried eyes. "Are you all right?"

I nod.

Softer, he asks, "Are *we* all right?"

The tension ebbs from my shoulders. It isn't going to be World War III. I sigh, nodding again. "I meant what I said at dinner, though. We have some things we need to talk about."

"Of course, of course." He's relieved, too, reassuring me, squeezing my arms. I can tell that no matter what I say, he'll agree. He doesn't want to lose me.

What I'm not so sure of is whether or not I want to lose him.

Into the lockbox on the gate I punch the security code I've never used. It's the same number as my apartment, and therefore easy to recall. The gate swings open. We trudge upstairs. We're silent the whole way.

Once inside, I head straight to the fridge. There's no beer left, which I know Eric prefers to drink, but we'll need something to lubricate this jagged encounter, so I open a bottle of cabernet. I pour a glass for each of us. We sit on opposite sides of the coffee table in the living room, silent and tense, looking at everything but each other.

I wonder if this is what it feels like to be married.

Eric clears his throat. "I want to say something." He sets his wineglass on the coffee table, rests his elbows on his knees, and steeples his fingers beneath his chin. "I don't know who that guy was that you were with at the bar last night, but you said he was a friend."

Our eyes meet. He's waiting for confirmation, or a confession. I nod, meaning yes, he's only a friend. Eric inhales a deep breath, lets it out sharply. He's relieved.

"Okay. I believe you. So I won't bring it up again. You've never given me a reason not to trust you. I know I have a tendency to be suspicious, which probably comes from my line of work. I'm not using that as an excuse, it's just the reality. But I know you don't deserve that." He pauses. "I also won't ask how, or when, you finally got home. I didn't come here and wait for you last night, because I thought . . . it seemed like you didn't want to see me. You said you wanted space. I was trying to respect that. And I can't blame you for needing it, after how inconsiderate I was at dinner."

His voice drops. He looks at the floor. "That thing about getting married . . . it just came out. I didn't mean to be patronizing, or make it seem like your father's permission mattered more than your feelings about it. Honestly, I was just amazed that someone like him would think a cop is good enough for you. I just blurted out the first thing that came to mind."

My throat constricts. His confession is so unexpected, I don't know what to do. If the shoe were on the other foot, and some mystery girl pulled the phone away from Eric at a bar and threatened me after he and I had a fight and he walked out on me, I *know* I wouldn't be giving him this mea culpa right now.

Overwhelmed, I swallow some wine.

Eric slowly raises his head. Our eyes lock. I remember the first time I saw him, he had so much swagger, such adorable, cocksure charm, I was smitten on sight. He's a clean-cut, all-American quarterback type with a vulnerable side that's completely disarming, with a cleft chin a girl could get lost in.

Now there's no swagger. There are no cocksure smiles. There's just a man whose feelings for me are so big they're taking up most of the space in the room.

"I know I'm not good enough for you." His voice cracks. "But I love you. And I'd do anything to make you happy."

I cover my mouth with my hand. My eyes fill with tears. Though we've been dating for six months, Eric has never said he loves me before now.

I whisper his name. It's like fitting a key into a lock; it releases all the emotion he's been holding back.

He leaps over the coffee table and onto me, knocking the wineglass out of my hand as he crushes me against his body, sending us crashing down to the couch. I've never been kissed so desperately, or needed so desperately to be kissed. Every doubt and worry fly away, and I let myself be swept along in a tsunami of emotion. I feel more passionate, more elated, more *hungry*, than ever before.

In between ravenous kisses, he tears off his shirt, then mine. My shoes come off next, my socks, my pants, my underwear; I'm naked. He rips open the button fly of his jeans. He falls on top of me, kissing my breasts, positioning himself between my thighs. Incoherent words of adoration fall from his lips. I groan, arching into him, wanting wanting *wanting*, and he bites down just hard enough on my nipple that I cry out in pleasure and pain.

He freezes.

I'm reeling, not sure why he's stopped. "What?" I pant, blinking. "Eric, what's wrong?"

He withdraws from me as if I'm a giant pile of turds that he's just had the misfortune to fall face-first into. His expression is horror stricken.

It's also enraged.

He hisses, *"What did you call me?"*

It's my turn to freeze. I try to think, but my mind is blank. "I . . . nothing?"

He looks as if he might be sick. "You called me, 'A.J.' You called me another man's name!"

Ice water is instantly injected into my veins. I stare at him, all the cells in my body crystallizing into snowflakes. It can't be. I didn't say anything, I only made a small sound—

Eric leaps from the couch, snarling. I sit up and cover my breasts with my hands.

"Eric, I-I don't know what to say . . . I don't think I *did* say anything—"

He whirls around and shouts, "Oh, believe me, you did! Is that who you were with last night? A.J.? From the fucking band?"

Oh God. Of course he knows who A.J. is. My mouth hangs open, but no sound comes out.

He stands over me, livid with rage and betrayal, his face red, veins popping out in his neck. "Tell me the fucking truth, Chloe!"

And I can't lie. I want to. With every fiber of my being, I want to lie. But I don't.

White and shaking, I whisper, "Yes."

With a guttural groan, he turns away. He snatches his shirt from the floor and yanks it over his head. On his way to the door, he grabs a vase from the niche in the hallway and hurls it across the room. It hits the opposite wall and shatters with a sound like a bomb.

He yanks open the door, then slams it behind him so hard the entire building shakes.

I sit naked on my living room sofa, tears sliding silently down my cheeks, watching the shards of a million tiny glass fragments twinkle like diamonds on the floor.

When the phone rings a few hours later, I'm still naked in the living room. I've taken the time to wrap myself in a blanket and lock the front door, but I went right back to the sofa where I've been lying since Eric left, crucifying myself.

I pick up the handset from the table next to the sofa. "Hello."

"Why do you sound like your cat just died?"

It's Grace. "You know I don't own a cat."

"True. Give me a mulligan. Why do you sound like you've just returned from a funeral?"

"I'm a whore."

There's a pause. Finally, she says, "Really? What nasty deed did you do? And how much did you get paid for it? I want all the details, I'm thinking of writing a book."

"I didn't get paid anything."

Grace scoffs, "Then you're not a whore."

"Fine, I'm a slut."

She says warmly, "It's one of the things I most love about you, sweetheart."

Staring at the shadows crawling across the ceiling from passing headlights, I heave an epic sigh.

"All right, out with it. What's wrong?"

With Grace, it's best you get right to the point. As a therapist, she's always got one eye on the clock while you're telling your sad story. Also, she was involved in a car accident when she was in high school that killed her parents and left her with no memory of her life before the crash. Other, weaker-willed people might have coped by turning to drugs or freaking out, but Grace decided to handle it by living every moment as if it were her last. For her, there is no past or future, only the present. She has zero tolerance for anything that wastes time. So I launch right in.

"Eric and I were fooling around and I called him another guy's name."

Raucous laughter. I should have known she'd find that amusing. When the snorts and guffaws have finally died down, she says, "And I take it Mr. Law and Order took exception to your little faux pas?"

"It's more than a little faux pas, Grace! It's practically adultery!"

"It's not adultery if you're not married, Chloe."

I glare at the ceiling. She should *not* be excusing me with semantics right now. "Fine. It's practically cheating, then."

"Don't be silly," she says breezily. "Every woman thinks of someone other than her partner from time to time when she's having sex. It's completely normal. Your only mistake was opening your mouth."

"Yes, well now my foot is permanently inserted in that mouth. Eric stormed out of here like he was headed toward a murder spree."

Grace mutters, "Or to put a choke hold on some innocent person of color."

"Grace!"

"I'm sorry sweetie, but he's a white Republican police officer, who grew up in Alabama and still sees his fraternity brothers from college twice a year for hunting trips in the bayou. You *know* there's a pointy white hood somewhere in a locked trunk in his garage."

"I'm hanging up on you now."

"Okay, I give! He's a lovely person who rescues cats stuck in trees and helps old ladies cross the street when he's not too busy teaching the disadvantaged youth of the inner city how to read. Satisfied?"

"Sometimes I think you're a bigger snob than my mother, Grace."

"Thank you!"

"It wasn't a compliment."

She snorts. "That's what you think."

I grit my teeth. "If you were really my best friend, you'd be giving me a lecture on how rude and unforgiveable it is to call the man who cares so much for me another man's name while he's getting down to business."

"Wait—*getting* down to business? You mean he wasn't even inside you yet?"

"You know, the things you find important are really baffling to me. That's not the point!"

"Was his dick, or was his dick *not*, inside you at the time of the incident in question?"

I don't dignify that with an answer. She knows it already anyway.

"Well there you go!" she crows.

"There I go *what*?"

She exhales in exasperation. "You weren't even having sex, Chloe! It doesn't count!"

"Really? Try telling that to my boyfriend, who broke my favorite vase on his way out the door to go burn down A.J.'s house."

There's a long, cavernous silence. Then Grace tentatively asks, "You're telling me that you called Eric . . . A.J.?"

"That's what I'm telling you."

"The same A.J. that you absolutely detest?"

I close my eyes. This is so embarrassing. "The very same."

"The same A.J. that you wasted a perfectly good glass of champagne on when you threw it in his face, not two weeks ago, after calling him a certain smelly body part?"

"Grace."

"The same A.J. who dates sluts named Heavenly?"

"Actually she's a prostitute," I correct. "He pays her. And all the rest of his girlfriends, near as I can tell."

Grace begins to chuckle. It's a low, throaty laugh that would make a phone sex operator green with envy. When she's through enjoying the depth of my humiliation, she says cryptically, "Chloe Anne Carmichael, there's hope for you yet."

I throw an arm over my face. "I don't even want to know what that means."

"It means it's time for a meeting of the sisterhood of the traveling panties. Lula's, half an hour. I'll call Kat."

She hangs up. I know, from past experience, if I call her back she won't answer. And if I don't show at the appointed time, they'll come and get me.

I drag myself from the couch to go get dressed.

"Oh, sweetie, I'm so sorry. That must've been terrible for you." Kat looks at me with big, sympathetic eyes and squeezes my hand.

We're at Lula's, a local Mexican restaurant where the three of us always meet in Venice Beach, at a table loaded with margaritas, baskets of tortilla chips, and a vat of salsa. Kat and Grace sit across from me. While Kat has been carefully listening to my retelling of the story about what happened with Eric, Grace has been fidgeting, anxious for me to get to the good part.

Right on cue, she demands, "Chloe, enough already. Get to the good part."

Kat looks confused. "How can there possibly be a *good* part?"

I send Grace an evil glare I learned from watching A.J. practice it on me. Completely unfazed by it, she says, "That's interesting. Did you pick up that little voodoo stare from your new boyfriend?"

It sucks when your friends are smarter than you.

I put my nose in the air and act like she hasn't spoken. "What Grace means by 'good part,' Kat, is actually the *worst* part."

Kat's eyes narrow. She looks me up and down, as if checking for bruises.

I throw up my hands. "What is it with everyone assuming that because Eric's a cop he's going to beat me!" I glare at Grace. "Or burn a cross on someone's lawn! On behalf of our police force, I'm insulted! Besides, you guys have known him for months, he's a sweetheart."

Kat—apologetically, I have to admit—says, "We also knew Jeremy for months before we found out he was the one stealing all your underwear. And wearing it."

Grace points out with her usual dastardly logic, "And I wouldn't call a man who destroys your favorite vase in a snit just because you had a tiny tongue slipup a 'sweetheart.' I'd call him unbalanced, and then I'd call him a cab and send his sorry ass home."

"Calling a man another man's name in a moment of passion—no matter if there was penetration—is not a tiny tongue slipup, Grace. It's unforgiveable."

"Oh, honey, give me just a slight break, will you? I've called men by the wrong name when they were doing everything from eating my cookie to plowing my corn hole! That boy just needs to grow thicker skin."

With a groan, I drop my head to the tabletop and hide my face in my folded arms.

Someone says a tentative, "Excuse me."

I look up and see a wide-eyed girl of about seventeen standing tableside, clutching a rolled-up magazine and a pen. The style of her clothes and general lack of sophistication suggest she's a Midwestern farm girl. She stares adoringly at Kat.

"A-are you Kat Reid? The makeup artist? Nico Nyx's fiancée?"

Kat and I look at each other. Wow. This is weird. Nico and Kat aren't even married yet, and she's already a celebrity. This girl wants her autograph.

Grace takes charge. "Oh, she gets that all the time, don't you, Hortense? I hear the resemblance is uncanny."

Farm Girl looks unconvinced.

"Honestly," Grace insists, "would Nico Nyx's fiancée be out having dinner in a crappy Mexican restaurant with no bodyguard?" Her laugh is indulgent. "I don't think so."

I know for a fact that she does have a bodyguard, Barney, who discreetly watches us from his position near the kitchen door. Knowing Nico, there are also half a dozen ninjas posted around as well, lurking under manhole covers or hanging upside down from the rafters like bats. His protectiveness of her is legendary.

The girl squints at Kat, then makes up her mind. "You're right. I'm such a silly willy!" She wags the magazine in Kat's general direction. "You're *much* thinner than she is."

She trots off. Grace bursts into gales of laughter.

"Oh, be quiet, Grace. You know the camera adds ten pounds," says Kat, disgruntled.

She's got the figure of a fifties sex symbol, all boobs and butt and tiny waist, and is a little sensitive about it. Personally, I think she's beautiful. Guys are always going gaga over her curves. Standing next to her, I feel like an underfed giraffe.

"Ah, the perils of fame!" Grace says between hoots.

"Can we get back to the important topic here? Mainly, what was the worst part of your story, Chloe?"

I have to take several long swallows of my margarita before I work up the courage to speak. "The worst part . . . was the name I called Eric. Which . . . was . . ." I clear my throat. "A.J."

Kat frowns. "Well, obviously that's a mistake. You couldn't have possibly been thinking of A.J., you're not even attracted to him."

I pull my lips between my teeth and stare at her.

Her mouth drops open. *"No!"*

Grace squeals and claps like a ten-year-old who's just been given a pony at her birthday party. "Yes! Ha-ha! Isn't it fantastic!"

Kat looks at me as if I'm possessed by the devil himself. "No! You *hate* him! He hates *you*! I've seen this all up close and personal! You can't *stand* each other!"

"I know," I say miserably. "Only now I sort of . . . don't."

Grace sighs. It's a happy sigh. It sounds as if she's just won a hundred million dollars. It irritates me so much I down the rest of my drink.

"You're *supposed* to be my friend. You're *supposed* to feel bad for me. You're *supposed* to tell me what to do to make up with Eric! Instead you're acting like this is the best thing that's happened since you had that affair with the Italian cultural attaché!"

Grace pushes her long red hair off her neck in an elegant sweep of her wrist that is supremely her. "It's not *that* good. But seriously, Chloe, as far as I can tell—and please forgive me, because I say this in total love—you have never been properly fucked."

"Gee, don't hold back, Grace. Tell us how you really feel." I toss a chip into my mouth, crunching on it violently, wishing it were Grace's head.

"All I'm saying is once you get a taste of a real man, nothing else in the world ever tastes the same. If you're going to have a fling, A.J. Edwards is the. Perfect. Man for it."

Kat pulls a face. "He's also the perfect man if you're interested in contracting a life-threatening venereal disease. I went on tour with those guys. You should *see* some of the hos he hangs out with."

"Literally," I mutter.

Grace isn't buying it. "He's too smart to get VD, Kat. He probably owns stock in a company that produces titanium condoms or something. There's no way a player like that doesn't take *every* precaution. Plus, high-end prostitutes are certified clean. I mean, really, they have papers to prove it. The clients expect it. You can't charge five thousand dollars a pop and have the clap. Or worse."

A chip falls out of my mouth. It lands on the table. Five thousand dollars? When A.J. told me he paid "thousands" for his high-rent hos, I thought it was an exaggeration.

"Dear God," says Kat. "What kind of skills do you need to have to charge that kind of money for sex?"

I can tell Grace is about to provide a laundry list by the look on her face. I hold up a hand to stop her. "No! I don't want to know!"

She gazes steadily at me. Her steely-grey eyes look even more steely than usual, which means I'm about to get a lecture. "Chloe, if you're going to sleep with a man whose preferences run toward women who know how to expertly massage the prostate with anal balls while giving a blow job, you might want to brush up on your bedroom skills."

"Gross!"

Vindicated, she sits back, shaking her head. "It's like shooting puppies in a barrel."

I turn to Kat. "Help me out here."

"Hey, you're the one who has the hots for him."

"I never said I had the *hots* for him! I just don't hate him so much anymore . . . is all."

Grace drawls, "Riiiight. You just don't hate him so much. Which is why you're calling out his name during sex."

I need to get new friends. These two are the worst.

Something terrible occurs to me. I bolt upright in my seat and grab Kat's hand just as she's lifting a loaded chip to her mouth. Salsa flies all over the place.

"Hey! I was going to eat that!"

"You *cannot* say a *word* to Nico about this. Promise me you won't."

"Chloe, even if I did, he would laugh me right out of the room. He's seen you two together. He'd never believe it in a million years. When I told him you needed A.J.'s address, the first thing out of Nico's mouth was, 'Why, is she going to plant a bomb under his porch?' "

That makes me feel a little better. I release her wrist, and sit back in my chair.

"Needed his address?" Grace repeats, a little cattily I think.

"It's not like that. He placed a flower order for some chick in Russia, and the address was wrong. Trina probably wrote it down incorrectly. It ended up being some cemetery. Anyway, the dude doesn't own a phone, or a computer, which means he has no email, so I have no other way to contact him." I add a teeny, tiny lie. "I'm going to send Jeff over to get it."

Kat and Grace stare at me.

"What?"

Kat says, "Russia?"

Grace says, *"Cemetery?"*

I shrug, plowing into the salsa with two chips. I'm trying to make a chip-and-salsa sandwich. "Yeah. I know. What's even weirder is that he told me when he looks at me, he sees ghosts."

Grace starts laughing again. "He sees dead people? Like the kid in that Bruce Willis movie? This shit is solid gold!"

Kat isn't laughing. She's just staring at me with this really weird look, like she can't decide if she wants to say something or not. So of course I have to know.

"Tell me right now or I'll throw my chip sandwich in your face, girlfriend."

She dusts off her hands, takes a swig of her drink, and wipes her mouth with her napkin. It looks like she's stalling. Finally, she asks, "Have you guys ever noticed A.J.'s accent?"

Grace and I repeat in unison, "Accent?"

"Yeah. His accent. His oh-so-subtle-but-definitely-there European accent."

Grace says, "You're on crack."

Kat shrugs. "That was almost exactly Nico's response when I asked him about it, too."

But I don't dismiss it so lightly. Kat is really intuitive about certain things. Like, *scary* intuitive. She's the one who told me I should check my ex-boyfriend Jeremy's closet for my missing underwear.

"He grew up in Las Vegas. How could he have a European accent?"

Instantly, Grace has me pegged. "You Googled him, didn't you?"

Crap. I motion to the waiter to get me another margarita.

"His tattoos *are* a little Russian prisony looking, though," she adds thoughtfully.

"Prison? What?" I'm totally confused, but Kat picks up Grace's train of thought right away.

"That's what *I* thought! Those tattoos on the backs of his hands are totally Viggo Mortensen in *Eastern Promises*!"

Grace licks her lips. "God, he was so hot in that."

"And when we were on tour, one time I saw him without a shirt. It was a total accident. I walked into the wrong dressing room. You've never seen a guy go sideways so fast, though. He was so pissed I thought he was going to explode. He acted like I'd caught him fucking a chicken or something."

A chicken? I look to Grace, the expert. "That's not a real thing, is it? Please tell me people don't have sex with poultry."

She smiles at me like I'm the village idiot and pats my hand.

Kat says, "If you think fucking chickens is weird, you should've seen some of the stuff we saw in the red light district in Amsterdam when we were on tour." She shudders. "I'll never look at bananas the same way again."

"You guys are really starting to freak me out."

"Moving on: Is his chest as lickable as it looks underneath all those stupid hoodies he's usually wearing?"

Grace is more interested in hearing about A.J.'s naked torso than I'm comfortable with.

"I was too busy being goggle-eyed by all the tattoos to really notice. You'd never know it, but he's got full sleeves, wrist to shoulder, in addition to stuff just everywhere, all over, front and back. Nico has lots of tats, but I'm talking hard-core. I'm talking *full-on* hard-core."

I remember his face when he told me to get my ass on the back of his bike. I remember the look in his eyes. Now I imagine he's naked, covered in tattoos, and, with that same look in his eyes, ordering me to strip and get my ass in his bed.

I drop my face into my hands. What's happening to me? I'm a *good girl*!

"Look." Kat digs her cell from her handbag, types something, waits, then hands it to me. It's a website depicting various types of tattoos, in particular the types criminals in the Russian penal system are known to have.

"Okay, so the tattoos on A.J.'s hands might look similar to some Russian prison tattoos. That's not evidence of anything! Maybe he just likes the culture!"

"Maybe." Kat puts the phone back in her bag. Then she gives me a look that says *or maybe not.*

"It's not like she'll ever find out, anyway." Grace toys nonchalantly with a lock of her hair. "Since she's so full of guilt over her 'unforgiveable' name-mix-up episode with Eric that she's going to beg him to take her back and forget all about the crazy-sexy secret Russian spy she's dying to do the dirty deed with."

I roll my eyes. "He's not a secret Russian spy!"

She pounces. "Aha! So you don't deny you're dying to do the dirty deed with him?"

"You're fixated on sex, you know that?"

"Why do you think I became a marriage therapist? Not only do I get to enjoy my own sex life, I get to hear all about everyone else's!"

"Then why didn't you just become a sex therapist?"

She wrinkles her nose. "Too tacky. Might as well own a massage parlor that gives happy endings."

I blink. "That's not a real thing, either, right? Happy endings at massage parlors are just urban legends." I look at Kat. "Right?"

Kat and Grace look at each other, pick up their glasses, and clink them together in a toast.

"Oh, screw you guys," I mutter.

Kat slurps the salt off the rim of her margarita glass. Casually, she says, "Well, if you do ever find out anything . . . strange . . . about A.J., my advice is to keep it to yourself. In my experience, it's best to let sleeping dogs lie."

Equally casually, Grace asks, "That sounds interesting, Katherine. Care to share more?"

Kat's face grows serious. She sets down her drink. She meets my gaze. Suddenly, in place of my normally lighthearted friend, there's a stranger looking back at me. A stranger who's older, and wiser, and has endless dark shadows in her eyes.

"You know what I went through," she says, her voice quiet. "And I learned that people keep secrets for all kinds of reasons. Sometimes they're sad reasons. Sometimes they're selfish reasons. And sometimes . . . they're dangerous reasons. If—and I'm only saying *if*—A.J. has secrets, they belong to him. And they're best left alone."

Kat's talking about Nico's crazy brother, Michael, who's in prison for trying to kill her, among other things, and Nico's crazy sister, Avery, who overdosed due to the complete insanity of her life . . . not least of which was the incestuous affair she was carrying on with Michael since she was a kid. The whole thing was a complete mess. Kat came out the other side okay, but there's the occasional moment, like this, when it seems like her world was knocked off-kilter, and she hasn't quite found her way back to center yet.

In the silence that follows, I think of how A.J. never looks into a camera lens. How he sits alone in a dark corner of a gay bar on a Sunday night, when the rest of the world is at home with their families. How when he looks at me, all he sees are ghosts.

I heave a sigh, and fill another tortilla chip with salsa. Around my chewing, I say, "I think this might be a good time to tell you guys about what happened *last* night. Then tell me if you think I should let this particular sleeping dog lie, or pat it on the head and wake it up."

Four days later, at half past three on a sunny Friday afternoon, I stand outside my car at the end of a long dirt road in the Hollywood Hills, shading my eyes with my hand as I stare at a rusted chain-link fence bisecting the road.

It's locked with a padlock. A sign warns, "Private Property. Intruders Will Be Shot."

I'm very confused.

On Monday at Lula's, I eventually admitted to the girls that I was having some pretty conflicted thoughts about A.J. After hearing the rest of the story about my night with him at the gay bar, Grace's opinion was that it ultimately didn't matter what secrets A.J. might be hiding, because I really only needed him for what was between his legs. (She's sentimental that way.) She said go for it, have a crazy fling, learn a few new tricks in the sack, then go marry Eric or some other normal person, have my two point three babies, and live the life I was brought up to live.

That made me vaguely depressed.

Kat's opinion was more ambivalent. She doesn't want me to get hurt. She also knows you can never, ever judge a book by its cover, so even though A.J.'s particular cover is mad and bad, what's on the inside might be anything but.

"First," she cautioned, "you need to sort things out with Eric."

I have repeatedly tried to do so, but he isn't cooperating. I can't get him to return my calls. When I mentioned that to Grace, she said, "So there you have it," as if I were now free and clear to shop my vagina all over town.

I left Eric another apology message, asking him to call. I waited another full day to hear back. When the crickets got too loud, I decided I wasn't going to wait any longer. Now here I stand, befuddled.

According to my GPS, this road is supposed to lead to the address Kat gave me where A.J. lives, but I can't get around the darn locked gate. Which, by the looks of it, no one else has gotten around in a long time, either. Except . . .

Off to the left side of the road, where the dirt gives way to wild grasses and trees, there's a man-height, oval break in the fence. It's almost hidden behind a wall of shrubbery, but I see it, and go over for a look. The grass beneath it is flattened, and bald in some patches. There are slim tire tracks in the dust.

It's a way in. A way in that someone on a two-wheeled vehicle is regularly using.

Oh, goodie. I found the entrance to the bat cave. I wonder if Bruce Wayne is at home.

I maneuver the car so it's parked off the main part of the road, lock it, and continue on foot. It's a pretty good incline, and soon I'm sweating. I don't normally mind a good sweat—I love to run, and take regular hikes up Runyon Canyon—but I really don't want to see A.J. when I'm looking like I just hopped off a treadmill.

After another ten minutes of walking, I realize I've left my phone, along with A.J.'s flower order form with the incorrect address, in the car.

I stop in the middle of the road, and look around. I see only gently rolling hills covered in trees and low shrubs on either side of me. Where perhaps, my mind inconveniently suggests, murderers and rapists are hiding. I chew my lip, undecided. Do I go back? Do I keep going?

Then a dog barks off in the distance, and I think I might be getting close after all.

I continue on. After another half mile or so, I crest the top of the low rise, and stop dead in my tracks.

"Oookay," I say aloud, staring. "*That's* not creepy."

The road dead-ends in a broad, circular driveway perhaps three hundred yards ahead. In the center of the circle is a dry, cracked marble fountain choked with weeds. Beyond it is a sprawling, dilapidated, abandoned hotel. It looks right out of that horror movie where Jack Nicholson plays the writer who goes crazy and tries to murder his family.

Parked in front of the hotel, gleaming in the afternoon sun, is A.J.'s death mobile.

I stand gaping until the dog I heard earlier trots into sight around the rusted hulk of a dumpster on the side of the building. He's a pale caramel color, thin and small. He has only three legs.

He spots me and freezes. His ears flatten. He seems to shrink closer to the ground.

"Hey, buddy. It's okay, I'm not going to hurt you." I kneel down, holding out my hand.

He starts trembling. He skips backward a step. Poor thing, he's terrified of me. Then, somewhere inside the hotel, music begins to play. The dog turns its head, perks its ears, and tears off in the direction it came, faster than you'd think a dog missing a leg would be able to.

I stand, listening for a moment, trying to identify the music. There's a lone, piercing flute or clarinet, accompanied by a soprano, who is singing in . . . Italian, I decide.

Inside the abandoned hotel, with a three-legged dog as company, someone is blasting an Italian opera. This is getting weirder and weirder.

I move toward the massive double doors at the front of the building. It's obvious this place was once beautiful. Now it's a ruin. The tall beveled-glass windows are streaked with dirt. The carved lintel about the door is sagging and warped from both moisture and age. The roof was probably last repaired in 1930. Paint peels off the façade in long, curling flakes. But an echo of its majesty remains. Up close, it's a little less creepy.

A little.

I walk up three rotted wood steps, cross the porch that runs the length of the first floor, and try the knob on the front door. Just like I've seen happen in the movies, it breaks off in my hand. The door swings slowly open, revealing a tantalizing glimpse of the interior. I toss the knob and go inside, feeling like Nancy Drew.

If I hear a disembodied voice hiss, *"Get ooouuuttt!"* I am so out of here.

The room opens into a grand foyer flanked by twin staircases that sweep upward to a second level. There's no furniture, or anything on the walls except faded floral wallpaper, dotted with slightly brighter squares where paintings once hung. An enormous crystal chandelier, dull with dust, dangles precariously from a frayed cord on the ceiling two stories above.

The soprano sings on.

I know more than I should about opera, as I grew up with a mother who believed children should be introduced to such things. Culture and whatnot. So I recognize this particular song. It's "Il

Dolce Suono," or "The Sweet Sound," from the opera *Lucia di Lammermoor* by Donizetti. It's about a woman, Lucia, who's in love with a man, Edgardo. But, for various reasons that only make sense in operas, she marries another man, Arturo. There's lots of angst and threatening of duels, and Lucia finally goes crazy and stabs her new husband to death on their wedding night. Edgardo, desolate at the rejection by Lucia, then kills himself.

In short, it's a tragedy about star-crossed lovers. It's basically the Italian opera version of Romeo and Juliet.

Trying not to take it as a sign, I straighten my shoulders, reminding myself what I came here for. Which—allegedly—is to get a correct address for A.J.'s flower order.

Because I couldn't have just asked Kat to pass along the message to Nico, right?

Following the music, I ascend the sweeping staircase. The second floor branches off in two main wings. I turn east. The song plays on. Now I hear another noise, a repetitive, low, *thump, thump, thump*. I have no idea what it could be, but it doesn't stop.

Finally, at the end of the wing, I stop outside room number twenty-seven. The music comes from inside. A painted glass window set high in the wall coaxes in the afternoon light in brilliant beams of saffron, emerald, and gold, illuminating the threadbare carpet beneath my feet. Heart pounding, I knock on the door.

Nothing. No response. The music continues. The strange thudding continues at erratic intervals.

I look at the door handle. Do I dare?

I knock again, louder, longer, a little desperately. When it produces no result, I tentatively turn the handle, crack open the door, and peek inside.

The room is cavernous, with vaulted ceilings and dormer windows that showcase views to the surrounding hills. The only furniture is a mattress on the floor in a corner, a cracked leather sofa, and a dresser. Half-melted pillar candles are strewn in clusters around the floor, and also line the windowsills. One wall is covered, floor to ceiling, in bookshelves, which are packed tight with CDs. A boxer's heavy punching bag dangles from a metal chain from the rafters.

Sweating, shirtless, and barefoot, A.J. dances around the bag, punishing it brutally with his bare fists.

I'm transfixed. I'm fused to the floor. I'm hot, and cold, and thrilled, and scared. I think he's the most glorious and also the most frightening thing I've ever seen.

Kat was right about his tattoos. They are legion, covering the flesh of his arms, chest, abdomen, and back, in colorful, intricate designs. I see a dragon. I see a woman's face. I see an angel, kneeling on the ground, his wings broken and black. I see crosses and skulls and roses and what looks to be lines from scripture, all of it rendered in vivid detail.

None of which compare to what lies *beneath* his skin.

His body is a masterwork of muscle. Thick, bulging ropes of hardened muscle flex with every movement. His shoulders, arms, and back are slick with a sheen of perspiration, which only serves to further highlight his incredible physique. His hair is tied back, but a few strands of dark gold have escaped and are plastered to his forehead and neck. He wears nothing but a pair of black nylon shorts and a look of intense concentration. He hits the bag over and over, grunting, fists flashing, dancing and turning, until finally he spots me standing agog in the doorway.

He jerks, and staggers back as if he's been electrocuted. Chest heaving, eyes wide, he stares at me. His hands shake. His knuckles drip blood onto the floor.

"I . . . I'm so sorry. I didn't mean to intrude."

I don't know if he's heard me over the music. His expression is part shock, part confusion, and part pleasure, if I'm not mistaken.

It gives me a little courage. I walk a few steps further into the room. As soon as I do, all the emotion on his face is wiped away. It becomes a mask of stone.

"What are you doing here?"

I freeze. "I-I'm . . ."

He steps forward, still breathing heavily. His eyes flash fire. A vein throbs in his neck. "What the fuck are you doing here, Chloe?"

I swallow. Clearly this was a terrible idea. "Your order . . . the flowers . . ."

He strides over to the wall of CDs. There's a stereo, slim and modern, hidden between two shelves. He pushes a button and the music stops. The sudden silence is jarring. Without looking at me, he says, "You should go."

"No."

He's just as surprised by that as I am. He turns his head, looking at me from the corner of his eye. He waits, unmoving.

I moisten my lips. "I came because of the flower order you placed. The address is wrong. I tried to reach your manager but he wouldn't call me back, so I asked Kat to get your address from Nico so I could . . . because you don't have a phone."

He stares at me.

Blood suffuses my cheeks. "I-I'm sorry to interrupt you like this. Had I known . . . I thought . . . I don't know what I thought." I glance nervously around the room. "But I wanted to make sure the flowers were delivered—"

"The address is correct." His words are low and clipped. He still hasn't turned toward me. He's visible mainly in profile. I wonder if that's deliberate, if he doesn't want me to get a closer look at what's on his chest and back.

"No, it can't be. It's a cemetery."

He nods, once.

A shiver runs through me. Something cold unfurls in my stomach. "Oh. Well . . . they'll still need a plot number, to put it on the right gravestone."

He turns his head away. His hands curl to fists. "The cemetery management knows which gravestone. They'll know it's from me. I've been sending the same thing every year since . . . forever. Just send it. And leave."

I hear anguish in the husky timbre of his voice. Anguish, and a loneliness so vast and deep it makes my heart ache. Whoever this dead Aleksandra is, she clearly meant a lot to him.

I say his name. He leans his arms against the bookcase, closes his eyes, and hangs his head. He whispers, "You shouldn't be here."

I fight the violent urge to go to him, put my arms around him, and murmur words of comfort in his ear. I'm almost moved to tears by this spartan room, by the way he lives here, in a crumbling old ruin high in the hills, alone. Kat told me he's lived here as long as Nico has known him. He goes to a pay phone at a liquor store off Sunset Boulevard once a day to check in with the band's manager, who receives all his mail and phone messages. Anyone who needs to contact A.J. knows to go through the manager, and anyone who doesn't know him would have one hell of a hard time finding him, if they ever could.

It's as if he's exiled himself from the world. As if he's removed himself from the human race, from any chance of a random encounter.

As if he's doing penance.

If A.J. has secrets, they belong to him. And they're best left alone. I wonder if Kat knows more than she's telling.

A.J. breaks the tense silence by saying, forcefully and with surprising bitterness, "Just go. Call your boyfriend to come and get you, and go."

"We broke up."

He lifts his head. He turns toward me, intense and intimidating, eyes blazing. "Was it because of the other night, what I said to him on the phone?" His burning gaze rakes over me. He snaps, "What happened? Did he hurt you?"

Here we go again. "*No*, he didn't hurt me."

Clearly not believing me, A.J. prowls closer. His energy is dangerous, yet I know it's not directed at me. His gaze darts all over my face, my body. He's looking for any sign of injury. That alone gives me the courage to say what I say next.

"And it wasn't because of the night you and I were together."

He waits, watching me in molten silence. A muscle in his jaw flexes over and over.

I whisper, "It was because I called him by your name."

My face burns. So does his. We stand there staring at each other wordlessly, until I hear a soft whine from behind me.

Trembling, the three-legged dog cowers in the corner of the hallway, his thin tail between his legs. He gazes up at me in terror. His big brown eyes, which take up half his face, dart to A.J. He lifts his snout and yips.

He wants to come in.

A.J. kneels and holds out his bloodied hands. The dog, keeping a wary eye on me, hops slowly forward into the room until he's past me, then breaks into an awkward run. He leaps into A.J.'s arms. A.J. stands, cradling his frail body and stroking his ears, murmuring softly to him. The dog snuggles closer to A.J., licking A.J.'s chin, wagging his scrawny little tail.

And I melt into a puddle like a stick of butter left out in the sun.

"What's his name?"

Still stroking the dog's head, A.J. says, "Bella."

So he's really a she. "She's yours?"

"As much as anything can be."

I don't know what to make of that. But the dog has softened something in A.J., and I want to keep him talking. I move a little closer, noting the tattoo on the left side of his neck. It's two black crosses, with a third, larger, in between. "Was she a rescue?"

His jaw tightens. I think I've asked the wrong question. When he answers, I realize it's not annoyance with me, it's a bad memory that's making him frown.

"I found her in the back parking lot of Flaming Saddles one night last year. Some drunk asshole ran her over, left her there to die. Took her to the emergency vet, but they couldn't save her leg."

So Flaming Saddles is his regular hangout. Obviously he hasn't made any friends there, either.

A.J. murmurs tenderly to the dog, "Doesn't seem to bother you too much, though, does it, baby?"

The dog wriggles in glee in A.J.'s arms, responding to his gentle coo with a frenzy of licks to his face, and I think I might faint from shock.

A.J. loves this dog.

A.J. loves something.

So it's possible. My heart, which clearly has no intelligence or sense of self-preservation whatsoever, trips all over itself in fluttering ecstasy.

"Can I . . . can I pet her?"

He glances at me. There's an awful moment when I think he's going to tell me to go jump off a bridge, but then he relents with a curt nod. Judging by the look on her face, Bella isn't completely convinced I'm not going to murder her. But, with a reassuring word from A.J., she lets me approach.

I pet her between her ears. She's smooth and soft, like velvet. She nuzzles her wet nose into my hand, sniffing me. When she wags her tail, I know I've passed muster. "Good girl. You're a sweetie, aren't you?"

A.J.'s knuckles are swollen and split, clotted with blood. He doesn't notice, or doesn't care. He's too intent on watching my fingers stroke Bella's head. Heat radiates from his body. Sweat runs in meandering rivulets down his chest. I'm possessed by the need to lick it off.

To distract myself from the vivid image of my tongue lapping at A.J.'s tattooed, sweaty skin, I casually say, "That's quite the CD collection you've got."

He doesn't respond. In the awkward silence that follows my even more awkward attempt at conversation, I make a mental list of A.J.'s hobbies: *Boxing. Opera. Dog rescue. Drinking alone at gay bars. Making me uncomfortable.* Other than what I read on the internet—oh, and his fondness for hookers, of course—that's really all I know about him. I wonder if maybe I open up and share something, he will, too. I take a deep breath.

"I like opera, too."

He grunts. "I would've pegged you more for a Britney Spears fan."

"Pop and Top 40 aren't really my favorite music genres. Mostly I listen to eighties rock."

His brows rise. Slowly blinking, he slides me a look. I think if I had lashes that long and thick I'd spend all day staring at myself in the mirror, practicing batting them to disarm unsuspecting strangers. Now I'm even more flustered. I start to babble.

"The seventies were good, too. I mean, you have to love the classics: AC/DC, Queen, Zeppelin, Aerosmith, the Rolling Stones, Black Sabbath—"

"*You* like Black Sabbath?"

I forget my intimidation and discomfort for a moment, and just answer like I would if I were speaking to anyone else. "Dude, they're only the best metal band of all time!"

He considers me in silence for what feels like four thousand years. My face grows redder and redder. So much for forgetting the discomfort.

I finish with a lame "But eighties rock is really my thing. Love and Rockets, you know them? That's my favorite band."

Bella smiles up at us, tongue lolling in delight. She has decided she likes this new game where she gets petted by both her master and the incredibly stupid, crimson-faced girl.

A.J., releasing me from the prison of his stare, looks down at Bella. He rubs her belly thoughtfully. After a moment, he says, "It's the quality of the voices."

I wait, then mutter a hesitant "Um . . ."

"In opera. The voices are exquisite. In rock, pop, rap, R&B, pretty much every other genre of music, the quality of the singer's voice isn't as important as his sound. Which is to say his vocal style, not the purity or range of his voice. That can be dressed up in a million ways, especially today with all the auto-tune bullshit. But when an opera singer opens her mouth, you're listening to an artist who's honed her natural talent for hours a day, every day, for years. Like Inva Mula singing 'Il Dolce Suono.' She's a lyric soprano. Her voice is laser pure, laser focused. And the *colors* . . ."

He closes his eyes.

I watch him in open fascination, because I can. I'm intoxicated by the way he looks right now, relishing the memory of the color of a woman's voice. I find it impossibly, almost painfully, beautiful.

"Can you describe it to me?"

He inhales. His exhale is slow, deep, relaxed. Without opening his eyes, he says, "Only in comparison. A bass voice is like . . . a stormy midnight sky. Sapphire blue and deep purple, rich and opaque. Baritones are slightly lighter, still night, but a clear night, shimmering with stars. Tenors are the like hours just before dawn, when it's not daytime yet, but it's no longer full night. There are bolder blues, cobalt, emeralds, even hits of lavender at the higher ranges.

"Then there's the lowest female voice, the contralto. That's dawn. Orange, fuchsia, and red. Glimmering. The next higher range is alto, then mezzo-soprano, both lighter, more vibrant, sparkling pinks and aquamarines, a clear midmorning, headed toward high noon."

He pauses. I'm completely enthralled. He inhales again, and his voice lowers an octave.

"Finally there's the soprano. For me a lyric soprano voice is the brightest, most brilliant of all sounds. It's like . . . looking up at a midday sun, squinting, your eyes watering because it's so searingly bright. It's gold and yellow and crystalline white, glinting and weightless. It's like standing on a mountaintop on a perfect winter's day, feeling snowfall on your upturned face. It's like being showered in diamonds."

I'm so moved by his words, I forget to stop staring when he opens his eyes and looks at me. His amber eyes are the softest I've ever seen them. My heart squeezes inside my chest.

He says quietly, "There's one voice even more beautiful than the lyric soprano's, though."

I can hardly find the words, but somehow, beyond the sudden sense that the world has stopped turning, I do. "Which is?"

His gaze drops to my mouth. A ghost of a smile lifts his lips. "The coloratura. It's a very rare, agile soprano."

I'm breathless. I'm weightless. I feel my pulse in every vein in my body. "What's it like?"

He lifts his eyes to mine, and gazes at me for a long, excruciating moment. "I don't think I can describe it in color. It's bigger than that. Deeper. It's more like . . ."

For a moment, he struggles for words. He turns to look out the windows, lost in thought.

"It's like a feeling. Like that feeling you get when you've been away from home for far too long, and you're tired and hungry, and just fucking *spent*, and your car is low on gas and it's getting dark, and you're sick of cheap hotels and cheap diners and every song on the radio and every thought in your head, and all you want to do is crawl into your own bed and fall into a dead sleep . . . and then you turn the last corner, and there it is. Home. All your troubles melt away with one big sigh, and you hit the gas hard, because you just can't stay away one second longer."

He turns his head, and looks so deeply into my eyes I feel naked.

"It's like coming home to your own brightly lit house after wandering alone for years in the unwelcome dark."

Again, he's moved me almost to tears. I've never heard a man speak so eloquently, with so much emotion, such raw honesty. It's like he's just let me glimpse at his soul.

I wonder if he can hear my heart beating. I wonder what he would do if I took his face in my hands and kissed him, just went ahead and did it because I know he never will.

I whisper, "A.J."

Emotion wells in his eyes. His brows furrow. He swallows, hard.

Sensing the sudden shift in mood, Bella lets out a soft, worried bark. Just as quickly as it happened, our peaceful little interlude evaporates with an almost audible *poof*.

A.J. withdraws. He sets the dog gently down on the mattress, where she curls into a little ball by his pillow and promptly falls asleep. There's a white T-shirt near the pillow, which A.J. snatches up and yanks over his head, pulling it down to cover his abdomen.

Coldly, he says, "It's time for you to leave."

"A.J.—"

"Leave!" he booms, whirling around to glare at me. "How many times do I have to ask you?"

I leap backward with a cry. He advances, forcing me to retreat. I stumble over my feet in my haste, and nearly lose my balance. Gasping, I fling my arms wide, but, once again, A.J. is there to steady me before I fall.

He grips me by my upper arms, staring down at me, his face red. He backs me against the wall next to the door. He demands harshly, "Why did you really come? What is it you really want, Chloe? You looking for a cheap thrill, something you can brag about to your girlfriends? Oh, wait, that's right—you only fuck if it's in the context of *'love.'* Is that what you came looking for, Princess?" he sneers. "Love? Well you're looking in the *wrong fucking place.*"

Only a few days ago, this crass, angry speech would have made me livid. But now it's too late; I've peeked behind the golden curtain. I know the kind of man that's lurking inside, how sad he is behind his mask. How layered and complex behind the façade of swaggering, skirt-chasing sneers.

How lonely.

Looking into his eyes, I say softly, "You don't fool me."

His entire body stiffens. His lips part. Into his eyes comes a look of pure torture. He whispers a halting, "W-what?"

"I see you, A.J. I *see* you. All the way past your big scary exterior. You don't have to let me in; I can't make you, and it's obvious you don't want to. But *I* want you to." My voice breaks. "Think about that while you're up here all alone with your tragic Italian operas and your only friend, Bella."

I yank my arms from his grip and turn to leave. In one swift move, he slams the door shut, blocking my way, and pushes me back against it.

He stares at my face, my mouth, my eyes, my hair. He breathes raggedly, his gaze devouring. He trembles with the effort to hold himself back. It's so clear; what he wants is to crush his mouth against mine, just as badly as I want it.

He fights. He fights himself so hard, it makes my heart bleed.

In a flash of comprehension, I understand. All his strange behavior, all his anger, all the flip-flopping of emotions he seems to go through whenever I'm near.

I reach up and touch his face. "I hurt you, somehow, don't I? Being near me hurts you."

His lashes flutter. In a low, choked voice that sounds like it rises from the deepest pit of hell, A.J. answers, "Being near you makes me want to die."

Pain pierces my heart. Tears well in my eyes. No one has ever said anything even remotely like that to me before, and it hurts so much I'm breathless. I'm being hollowed out by knives.

"Why?"

He laughs. Somehow it's even worse than what he's just told me. The sound is vicious, heartless, totally without mercy. "Because you have a smile like a sunrise and eyes that could end all wars, and you have no idea, you have no fucking *clue*, that when you look at me, you're looking at a dead man."

His face twists with misery. His eyes are wet. When he speaks, his voice cracks. "But mostly because you give me hope. You fucking *haunt* me with hope. And I can't forgive you for that. Now get the hell out and don't ever come back!"

He shoves me through the door, out into the hallway. He slams the door in my face. He turns the deadbolt with a decisive, dismissive *clack*.

I stare openmouthed at the door. Seconds pass to a minute.

From behind the closed door, A.J. roars, "GO!"

I'm jolted into motion by the fury in his shout. I turn and flee, running at top speed. My footsteps pound down the empty corridor.

My vision wavers from all the water pooling in my eyes. I take the staircase three stairs at a time, stumbling and cursing, hanging on to the gritty handrail and holding back sobs, until I burst through the front door. I stop to catch my breath on the porch, leaning over with my hands on my knees.

Music blasts at top volume from upstairs.

I lift my head, listening. It's not opera this time, but a rock song. As soon as the bass joins in, I recognize it, and the knife twists a little deeper into my guts.

It's Love and Rockets, my favorite band. The song?

"Haunted."

The tears I've been holding back finally succeed in breaking out and spill down my cheeks. I straighten and run all the way back to my car.

I don't look back once.

I stand in front of the bathroom sink, staring at my reflection in the mirror. My face is twisted in misery. My lip quivers. My eyes are red and wild.

The hand holding the blade to my throat shakes so hard I cut myself. A single drop of crimson wells from my skin, slides down five inches of sharpened steel, and drops off the end. It lands in the sink with a soft purple *splash*.

I can do it. I need to do it. I need to do it *now*, while I still have any control left.

She's been gone ten minutes, but her colors still blind me. Her colors are everywhere, saturating everything, the air itself. She shows up at my door like an apparition, like a demon, promising everything with those goddamn swimming-pool blue eyes, those beautiful, innocent eyes, and she makes me want to kill myself.

Worse, she makes me want to fall on my knees and beg for a forgiveness I know will never come, because it isn't deserved.

Ready now, I inhale. I press the blade harder against the pulse in my throat. Just one flick of my wrist. A single, effortless slice—

Bella pads into the bathroom. She sits at my feet. She looks up at me, wags her tail, and whines.

She's hungry.

Trembling, I slowly lower the blade from my skin. My laugh is shaky, and sounds just this side of insane.

I drop the bloodied blade into the sink, and go to make dinner for my dog.

There's always tomorrow.

I spend the weekend cleaning my apartment and licking my wounds.

The encounter with A.J. has left me so raw I don't trust myself to talk to anyone. So I hide, ignoring phone calls, scrubbing the kitchen floor, reorganizing my closet, and dusting things that haven't been dusted since I moved in. It's therapeutic. By Sunday night I've regained some semblance of my former sense of balance. I sit down with a glass of chardonnay at the kitchen table to think.

I've had my fair share of boyfriends—not as many as Grace, lord knows, but I suspect that number is in the triple digits—and, prior to A.J., I thought I had men pretty much figured out. I thought most guys were basically just the bigger, louder, smellier version of girls. But this one has really thrown me for a loop. I just can't get my head around his whole mess. I have so many unanswered questions about A.J., so many puzzle pieces that don't fit, I'm at a loss as to how to proceed.

Two things: First, I'm not that girl who chases guys. Especially guys who have clearly said they're not interested. Or, more gallantly, "you make me want to die." I don't think that could possibly be interpreted as anything remotely romantic. Although I'm sure there are girls out there who would take that statement as a challenge, I'm not one of them. I don't want to be the nail in anyone's coffin, thank you very much.

Second, I don't think it's fair or realistic to ask other people to change for you. If you want to change for them, knock yourself out. But if you're thinking your relationship would be perfect if only he would do (or not do) this or that, you're doomed to misery. Let him go, and find someone who fits you better. Nobody likes a nag.

Which leads me to the only logical conclusion.

A.J. is a no-go.

Forget the thermonuclear chemistry between us. Forget that he's maybe the most soulful, beautiful, and—when he wants to be—sweet man I've ever met; he obviously comes with so much baggage, any relationship we could attempt would sink like a mafia rat thrown off the docks with his feet encased in cement.

Also, there's the matter of the prostitutes.

I can just see it now. "Mom, Dad, I'd like to introduce you to my new boyfriend, A.J.! He's super angry and unstable, is an expert at sending mixed messages, and just *loves* hookers! Don't you, honey!"

I sigh, and drink my wine.

The phone rings; it's my brother. This is one call I won't avoid. Smiling, I pick up. "Hey, big brother, how are you?"

"Bug," he says, his voice warm, "I'm glad I caught you. I'm great, back in the Big Apple where I belong. But the real question is: How are *you*? That little performance of yours the other night at the 'rents was straight out of an episode of *Downton Abbey*."

I can tell he's impressed. Jamie and I have always had a great relationship. He's older than me by seven years, but it doesn't feel like it. We've always been close, so I tell him the truth.

"I'm confused, a little depressed, and, according to Grace, in need of a good rogering."

His response is dry. "Aren't we all."

"I'm being serious."

"About which part? Because I might be able to help you out with the first two problems, but that last one is a little TMI, even for me."

I puff out my lower lip and blow my hair off my forehead. "It's just, you know. Men."

His chuckle is knowing. "Men, plural? Or are we talking about one man in particular? Because I can see how that might be a problem, considering the size of those shoes."

I glide right past the subject that he's obsessed with, and move on. "How'd you know I wasn't talking about Eric?"

There's a short silence. "Because I've seen you with Eric. And you've never looked at Eric the way you looked at that scruffy blond sex god who walked into your store."

I'm that obvious. Wonderful. I rest my forehead on my hand.

"Don't worry, I don't think anyone else can tell. Except for maybe the man himself. Honestly, bug, it was a little weird standing there while the two of you eye-fucked each other over the counter."

Embarrassed, I bristle. "We were arguing, not eye-fucking!"

He snorts. "Don't get testy, sis, I'm just calling it like I see it. And what I saw was two people trying to pretend they dislike each other enormously when what they really want is to get into each other's pants."

I deflate just as quickly as I snapped. "Anyway, it's not going to happen. There's only so many soul-killing statements a girl can take before she gets the hint."

"Soul killing? That's a little dramatic. Did he call you a princess again? Maybe something worse, a duchess, perhaps?"

"Are you ready for this?" I pause for dramatic effect. "He said, and I quote, 'Being near you makes me want to die.'" I slap the table for added emphasis and sit back in my chair.

Jamie sounds disturbed. "I have to admit, that's a little different than calling you Princess. Was he laughing when he said it?"

My voice grows quiet. "Actually, he looked like he was about to cry."

"So what did you say?"

In order to give it the proper perspective, I rewind and tell him the story, beginning from when I bumped into A.J. at Flaming Saddles last Sunday night, and ending with Friday, when I pulled the genius move of showing up unannounced at his haunted hideout. When I'm finished, Jamie is silent for so long I have to ask if he's still there.

"What you're describing is a man in a great deal of pain. You realize that, right, Chloe?"

He's dead serious. He even sounds worried, like he's warning me. "Why do you say that?"

"Because when it's in pain, an animal hides. And, if cornered and feeling threatened, it lashes out. Your friend is doing both."

My lungs constrict, making it harder to breathe. "I know."

"So here's my piece of big-brotherly advice. Do with it what you will."

I listen hard, my heart beating a little faster.

"Wait."

I frown at the phone. "What do you mean, wait? He's not going to change—"

"Not for him to change."

"What then?"

"For him to decide what he wants more: his pain, or you."

I drink my wine, swiping angrily at the moisture in the corner of my eye.

"And in the meantime, live your life. I'm not saying sit by the phone and pine away. I'm just saying that it might take him a minute or two to come around. You can't push it. But the way you two looked at each other . . . I don't think you should throw the idea out the window just yet. So just wait. Leave him alone. Let's see what he does if he doesn't feel cornered."

Because this little pep talk is giving me too much hope, I blurt, "He's into prostitutes. Like, *really* into them. They're all he dates."

Jamie calmly asks, "Male or female?"

"Female! Geez!"

"I'm just trying to get my facts straight, don't get all excited."

"Excuse me, but why don't you seem more disturbed? *He pays for sex.*"

"Because no man in the history of the world has ever done that."

Exasperated, I say, "Jamie, come on!"

"Would it shock you to know I've done the same?"

My brows shoot so far up my forehead they almost fly off. "Yes, as a matter of fact it would. When? More importantly, *why*?"

There's a shrug in his voice. "Because I was horny, and lonely, and I could."

I decide not to ask for details. "I'm sorry, I just don't get it. The whole thing seems so seedy and pathetic to me."

"Well, you're not a man."

I groan. "That's such a sexist statement."

"When did you become so judgmental, anyway?"

"Hello, it's illegal? And dangerous? And totally gross?"

"How would you know it's gross? Maybe it's the hottest sex you'll ever have, but you're so busy looking down your nose at it, you'll never know."

My eyes bug out. "You're advocating your little sister hire a gigolo to get some firsthand experience in the area, is that it?"

He goes all practical on me. "Well, if you do, I know this guy in LA—"

"Please stop talking now."

"Look, I admit it's . . . not mainstream."

Suddenly, I'm angry. "No, Jamie, that's not it at all. This has nothing to do with me being narrow-minded or judgmental. *It's wrong.* I'm sorry if it makes me sound like a church lady, but screwing someone for money is wrong."

"Why aren't you mad at the prostitutes, then? They're the ones taking his money. If there were no prostitutes, men couldn't visit them."

I almost curse at him. "You're *such* a lawyer."

He shoots right back, "And you're too quick to point fingers. Nothing in this world is black or white. *Nothing.* I don't know much about this A.J. of yours, but if he *only* can be with a woman who he pays, there's something to that. And besides, if that's really the case, this entire conversation is moot." He adds, "Unless you're willing to send him an invoice, that is."

I mutter, "I'm sure they get paid up front. You don't want that much money in receivables."

"Really?" He sounds interested. "How much are we talkin'? Two, three grand?"

"Try five."

He whistles. "*Damn.* And I thought Dad charged a lot per hour. He'd freak out if he knew a hooker had thirty-five hundred bucks on his going hourly rate."

It's my turn to be shocked. "Dad charges his clients fifteen hundred dollars per hour?"

Jamie laughs. "Only for old clients. For new ones he charges twenty-five hundred."

Holy guacamole. I honestly had no idea. "That doesn't even seem like it should be legal!"

His voice turns wry. "You weren't complaining when it was paying to put you through USC. Or padding your trust fund. Or financing that graduation trip you took to Paris with all your girlfriends—"

"Point made. No need to rub it in."

"All right. I know I'm being a little hard on you, but I just want you to keep an open mind. At the very least . . . try to have compassion. You never know what it's like to be someone else until you've lived what he's lived."

"Walk a mile in his shoes, that whole bit?"

"Exactly. And don't sound so snarky, it's true."

Annoyed with Jamie, with the conversation, with life in general, I stand and go to the living room window. Outside it's growing dark. Cars flash by with their headlights on, in traffic even at this hour, on the weekend. The streetlights are winking on.

"When will you be in LA again?"

"I don't know. I'm giving Mom and Dad a little room to breathe after your dramatic announcement at dinner. I think they might finally be realizing their son is never going to marry Bunny Anderson's very homely, very rich daughter."

"Are you angry with me for that?"

"Never. I've never hidden who or what I am, they've just chosen not to see me. But you always have, and you've always accepted me just as I am. I love you for that, bug."

I'm touched. We don't often say these things to each other. Stiff upper lip and all that. "I love you, too, Jamie."

"Gotta go. Call me if you need any more man advice."

I say wryly, "Or if I need the number of that gigolo."

His laugh is loud. "Right. And bug?"

"Yeah?"

There's a pause. "It doesn't always have to look good on paper."

"What do you mean?"

He sighs. "Only that you can't find love on a checklist of must-haves. You know: A good education; A stable, upwardly progressive career; A nice car; Good hair. It's never that easy. Sometimes what looks like perfection is nothing more than a chocolate-dipped turd. And sometimes what you find in the gutter covered in mud that *looks* like a turd is really a diamond. A big old, chunky diamond that some other fool threw out because she couldn't see that all it needed was a little TLC to make it shine."

With a soft click, the line goes dead.

I lower the phone to my side. My breath catches; across the street, under the glow of a streetlamp, a man stands staring up at my window.

As he turns and walks away with a lowered head, he tightens the drawstring on his hoodie.

Chapter 13

For two weeks, I hear nothing from either A.J. or Eric. I work, I hang out with the girls, I do my thing, trying not to obsess. I fail spectacularly at not obsessing. Those two weeks contain the longest nights I've ever spent. I could draw every crack and miniscule bump in my bedroom ceiling from memory.

Then one crisp morning I walk out to my car on my way to work, and someone has left something on my windshield, resting against the wiper.

It's an origami bird, crafted from fine, pale blue linen paper.

I hold it in my hand, inspecting it. I remember making origami forms when I was a kid. I had a teacher, originally from Japan, who taught a class on the ancient art of paper sculpture. I could only ever make a crane, the simplest of beginner folds aside from a paper airplane.

This bird is no simple crane. What I'm holding in my hand is a work of art.

It's three-dimensional, with an elegant body, layers of delicate feathers, even tiny feet. Whoever made it took painstaking care. I see no mistaken folds, no telltale creases where one was begun only to be abandoned for another, no blemishes on the paper at all.

It's perfect.

I look up and around, hoping to find a clue as to who might have left it, but there's no one looking back at me, just cars whizzing by and an old man walking his chubby beagle across the street.

I unlock the car and carefully set the beautiful paper bird on the passenger seat. On the drive to work, I glance at it frequently, half expecting it to open its wings and take flight.

The next week, there's another bird on my windshield.

This one is even more elaborate than the first. It's made of foil-backed paper, a rich violet on one side and reflective hot pink on the other, so the folds reveal layer over layer of lush color. Enraptured, I stare at it. I know for certain now the first wasn't some kind of fluke.

These beautiful birds are meant for *me*.

I try to picture the hands that made such intricate, delicate things. I can only envision a woman's hands, fine boned and elegant, deft and precise. Yet I know of no one, male or female, capable of such eccentric, whimsical artistry.

After the third week, and the third bird—this one an incredible canary yellow with black-and-white striped wings—I clear a shelf on the bookcase in my bedroom, and start a collection.

I also start trying to catch whoever is leaving them for me.

Every day for the next two weeks, I get up early, before dawn. I wait, watching from the window. I know the birds can't have been left out all night, or the paper would be damp with the night air. If not sodden, at least a bit limp, feathers and beaks wilting. It's still spring in LA, and the nights are chilly. But the crispness of the paper belies the truth of the timing of their appearance: after sunrise, at least.

My surveillance fails utterly. The fourth bird appears on the windshield of my car when I take a two-minute bathroom break. The fifth, when I go to the kitchen to make myself a cup of tea.

Which can only mean one thing.

I'm being watched.

Yet I see no one. I see nothing out of the ordinary. I see normal life happening on the street below: cars, joggers, mothers with baby carriages, people on bikes.

I know who I want it to be. But whoever it is doesn't wish to be seen, so he isn't.

I don't tell anyone about the birds, not even Kat or Grace. They're my little secret, a locked treasure chest hidden away in my brain that only I can open and play with. Kat had said she learned that people keep secrets for all sorts of reasons: sad, selfish, dangerous. I don't know about sad or selfish, but this little secret of mine definitely feels dangerous, as if by the mere act of not sharing with my best friends, I've taken the first step down a dark, uncharted road.

I don't care. I'm no longer afraid of the dark.

I've discovered an extraordinary creature who lives there.

"What'll it be today?"

"I need a triple espresso, a Venti chai latte, a Tall Americano, and . . ." I eyeball the refrigerated display in front of the counter. "Ooh! One of those lemon bar thingies. The big one on the end."

The barista smiles at me. "You and your lemon bars. You should try our new double chocolate chunk brownie, they're really popular."

I shrug, handing over a twenty. "I'm more of a sour girl than a sweet."

"No way, Chloe, you're *totally* sweet." He smiles wider, flirting.

I shake my head and walk to the end of the counter to await my order.

I've been coming to this Starbucks nearly every day since I opened Fleuret, and all the baristas know me by name. Pathetic, I know, but people in the flower business are total caffeine addicts. You would be too if you had to go to work in the dark every morning, then stand on your feet for twelve hours, wielding a wickedly sharp design knife that you'd cut yourself with every so often. As in, five times a day. Some of the junior designers use clippers, but a knife is a much faster tool to arrange with, so that's what I use.

Hence the sorry state of my hands. Today, for example, I have a Band-Aid wrapped around the tip of my left thumb, a slice on the middle finger of my right hand that isn't healing as well as it should be because of the dirt lodged in it, nicks on both my pinkies, and the usual calluses galore on my palms. If there's one thing I'm certain of, it's that I'll never be a hand model.

I pick up the *Times* and browse the front page while I wait, until I become aware that someone stands silently brooding a few feet away to my left. Brooding, and staring right at me.

When I lift my head, I'm looking at Eric.

He's in uniform. His eyes are bloodshot, his shirt is wrinkled, and he's unshaven. He looks like he's just woken up from a three-week bender.

My heart thumping, I set the paper back on its rack. "Eric . . . hi."

Unsmiling, he nods slowly. "Chloe."

"How are you?"

He doesn't answer right away. Finally he says, "I've been better."

I can see that. At the same time I realize I don't like it, that I don't want him to suffer for any reason, especially if it's on my account, he says quietly, "Not that it's your concern."

That stings. In fact, it hurts. He must see it on my face, because he steps closer, lifting a hand as if to touch me. He thinks better of it and lets it fall to his waist.

"I'm not trying to be a jerk."

I look away. "Okay." What does he want me to say?

After a moment, he wordlessly takes my arm. He gently steers me through the morning crowd into the back hallway near the bathrooms. I let him, wondering if I've thrown away a perfectly good man for a long shot bet on a dark horse that probably won't pay off anyway.

We stop beside the payphone. He keeps his hand on my arm.

"Look at me."

I do. He's solemn, but not angry. I have to stop myself from brushing the hair off his forehead that's about to fall into his eyes.

"I mean it, I'm not trying to be a jerk. I just . . . you can't know what that felt like for me."

But I can imagine. It's not a pretty picture. My voice small, I say, "I'm sorry. I don't know what else I can say. It was a terrible mistake, one I wish I could undo. I never intended to do that. I never meant to hurt you. I really, *really* apologize."

I flounder for anything else to say. He lets me writhe in agonizing silence for a while, watching me squirm. He removes his hand from my arm, and lowers it to casually rest on the butt of his sidearm. I find the simple move incredibly menacing.

Then he asks abruptly, "Did you sleep with him while we were together?"

My head rears back. "No!"

I can tell he believes me. His eyes glow with intensity. He moves closer. "You just fooled around with him then?"

My face flushes with heat. I have to work to keep my voice down. "No, Eric. I didn't fool around with him. I never cheated on you. I've never even kissed him."

Surprise registers on his face. "You're not with him now?"

I shake my head.

He stares at me intently. "Let me make sure I'm getting this right. You're not together with him, you never fooled around with him while you were with me, and you never even kissed him."

"That's right."

His jaw works. "So you just *wanted* to screw him."

The acid in his voice makes me feel as if I've been slapped. "Eric!"

"You were just *thinking* of screwing him, while my hands and mouth were all over you."

Believing I deserve to endure this—at least for a while longer—I stand glaring at him silently, my cheeks as red as the scarlet letter I imagine sewn on to my shirt.

"I think I deserve an honest answer, Chloe."

Oh, really? Because I think you deserve a kick in the shin. "The answer is no. I wasn't thinking of him that night. I don't know what happened." He looks relieved, for all of two seconds, until I speak again. "But if you want total honesty, which is what I've always given you, then yes. I'm attracted to him."

He pales, then reddens. His lips thin to a line.

"But I never would've acted on it. I made a stupid mistake that night, and believe me, I regret it. I've been kicking myself over it for a month. But you didn't give me the chance to explain, or make it up to you, which I think at the very least I deserved, seeing as how we were together for *six months* before that happened. You just completely froze me out. And if the situation were reversed, maybe I would have done the same thing as you and walked away, but at least I would've let you say your piece before I did."

I fold my arms protectively across my chest, and stare in misery at my feet. I should walk away. Part of me wants to. Another part of me is glad I finally got to apologize, because what I did to Eric is one of the lowest things I've ever done.

No matter what Grace says.

"Hey."

The softness in Eric's voice makes me glance up. He seems taller than I remember. Maybe it's because I'm slumped over so far in shame.

He looks away, then back at me, and I can tell he's having a hard time deciding what to say. I don't let him off the hook. I just stare at him, waiting, trying to ignore the old Vietnamese lady sitting at a table near the end of the hall, openly eavesdropping.

He blows out a short breath. "I, uh . . . you're right. I kind of freaked out."

When I give him the stink eye, he relents. "Okay, I *really* freaked out. I've never felt that way before. I lost my mind. I just wanted to break something."

I refrain from reminding him he did break something: my favorite vase. He also put a sizeable dent in my self-respect, not to mention the living room wall. I know it was a crap situation, but in retrospect I think he might have handled it with a little more maturity. Or at least a little less Raging Bull.

His voice grows even softer. "Especially after what I'd told you, not even two minutes before."

I love you. It's amazing how three such small words, when spoken together, can either take you to heaven or shoot you in the hooha with a high-caliber rifle.

"I know," I whisper. "If I could take it back, I would."

Watching his reaction to my words, the way his face softens, the vulnerability in his eyes, I'm having a ton of crazy mixed emotions. I still have feelings for him, most of which, if you made a list, would fall in the pros column. He's (usually) thoughtful, kind, and polite. He's (usually) sweet, responsible, and funny. He's always charming. Until now, he's always been upbeat. He's the kind of guy parents love, because he's easygoing, well-educated, and successful. He loves kids. He has a great relationship with his own parents, and has a core group of nice, stable friends.

In short, he's good marriage material.

In the cons column, underlined in red, would be his jealousy. If I were more like Grace, I'd get it, but I'm not. Prior to the A.J. incident, I'd never given him any reason to distrust me, yet he often acted as if I had the male escort line on speed dial.

Just below the red-lined jealousy would be a big question mark after the word "beer."

Because I'm pretty sure I smell beer on him right now, at eight o'clock in the morning, and I don't know what to do with that disturbing fact.

"Chloe!"

The barista calls my name; my order's ready. I'm so relieved I want to burst out in hysterical laughter. I don't think I can take this tension one second longer.

I light a match under the unwelcome thought that if I were standing eyeball to eyeball with A.J. with this kind of tension, I'd never want it to end.

"That's me."

Eric nods, glancing at the barista like he'd like to remove the poor guy's spleen. His voice drops. "Listen . . . can I call you? Maybe we could just talk a little more?"

When he looks up at me, his eyes are dark.

Though I'm wearing a sweater, I rub my arms for warmth against a sudden chill. "Sure," I say, nodding. "Okay."

He tucks a strand of hair behind my ear like he used to do, one of those intimate gestures lovers make when they're in public. As his thumb brushes my cheek, I notice the man standing across the street beside the bus stand, staring in through the windows of the coffee shop.

Sunglasses obscure his eyes. His hands are shoved into his pockets. He's tall and broad, motionless as a statue, until one hand reaches up to pull the hoodie he wears farther down over his forehead.

By the time Eric turns to follow my stare, A.J. is gone.

Sweating and gasping, I wake at one a.m. the following morning from an intensely erotic dream wherein I was being ravished by a man in a hoodie who'd broken into my bedroom in the middle of the night.

If my mother knew I was having fantasies about the very thing she warned me about, I'd be cut out of the will.

In the boy shorts and ratty, sleeveless ZZ Top T-shirt I wore to bed, I pad barefoot to the kitchen, not turning on any lights, and stand in front of the open refrigerator door, chugging orange juice from the big plastic jug. I know I'll never be able to get back to sleep.

That damn dream was the sexiest thing that's happened to me since . . . well, since *ever*.

I groan softly, trying to forget the way the stranger pinned my arms to the pillow above my head. How he tied my wrists to the headboard with a pair of my own pantyhose. How his mouth felt on my skin. How his rough voice murmured all kinds of filthy things in my ear as his big hands groped me, fondling my breasts, pinching my nipples, sliding against the wetness between my legs—

Gah! I really need to get laid.

Frustrated, I toss the juice back into the fridge and slam the door. Yawning, I scrub my hands over my face. I check the clock; I've got three hours to kill before the alarm goes off.

I could get dressed and go to the flower market now. It opens at eleven p.m., so getting in would be no problem. Plus all the best stuff goes early. Instead, I find myself wandering restlessly around the apartment in the dark, my thoughts drifting.

Until I stop dead in front of the living room window. My skin prickles.

"This is getting to be a thing," I murmur in disbelief, staring down at the man pacing back and forth under the streetlight across the street. I always thought having a stalker would be an incredibly creepy experience, but then again, I never thought I'd know exactly who my stalker would be. That shaves an edge off the creep factor, leaving me more fascinated than frightened by this new development in my life.

Even at a distance, A.J.'s agitation is clear.

He paces in long, even strides. He flexes his hands open, then closes them to fists. It appears that he's muttering to himself. Every few feet he turns abruptly and goes back in the opposite direction, starting the whole process all over again.

Without thinking about what I'm doing, I turn on the lamp beside the window, flooding the room in light.

A.J. stops pacing. He looks up at my window. I stare down at him, waiting, hands shaking, heart racing, wondering if I've just made a terrible mistake, while simultaneously not caring if I have.

After a lifetime of holding my breath, I watch as he slowly steps off the curb and crosses the street.

When he's out of view around the front corner of my building, I run to the front door. I press my ear against it, straining to hear any sound. The elevator was fixed a few weeks ago, so now I can't hear steps on the stairs, but I do hear the cheerful *ding* as the elevator stops on my floor and the doors slide open.

It's a few excruciating moments before heavy footsteps begin to move toward my door.

They pause just outside. My heart feels like a trampoline with a dozen fat ladies jumping up and down on it. After a moment, A.J. says my name. His voice is barely audible. He knows I'm standing here.

I take a deep breath and open the door.

He dwarfs the doorway. He's in faded jeans, boots, the signature black hoodie that shadows his face. His hands, trembling, hang at his sides. His eyes burn a hole right through me.

In a gravelly voice, he says, "Tell me to leave. Tell me to go away and shut the door in my face."

Before I can change my mind, I reach out, grab the front of his sweatshirt and gently pull him into my apartment.

He stares down at me with those burning eyes, his face hard. "One last chance. Tell me to leave."

"I don't want you to leave."

Without looking away from me, he swings the door shut behind him with a flick of his hand. We stand for a moment, tension thick between us, until he says, "Bedroom."

That single, husky word wreaks havoc throughout my body. I swallow, licking my lips, hesitating, but A.J. shakes his head.

"Too late, Princess." He bends and sweeps me off my feet, into his arms.

This is a move that I, who reached my full height of five foot ten in junior high school, never would have thought possible. It takes a man as large and strong as A.J. to make lifting me look as easy as lifting a piece of paper from the floor. Along with being surprised and thrilled, I'm deeply impressed.

Also impressive are his shoulders, which I'm now clinging on to for dear life, because he's walking across the living room.

He doesn't need to ask again where the bedroom is; it's pretty obvious. I'm hyperaware of every movement of his body, of the sound of his breath, of my own shrieking nerves. He pauses just outside my open bedroom door, and sets me gently on my feet.

"Invite me into your bedroom, Chloe."

Trying not to faint becomes my top priority. "I . . . um . . ."

He takes my chin in his hand, forcing me to meet his eyes. "Invite me in."

God, he's hot. Smoking, crackling hot, and also incredibly intimidating. I can't tell what expression he's wearing. It fluctuates somewhere between murder spree and kid on Christmas morning. When I lick my lips again, he watches the motion of my mouth and tongue with an almost predatory look, his eyes flashing in the shadows.

I whisper, "Come in."

His lids briefly close, then his eyes go right back to roasting me alive. Satisfied, he nods, brushes past me, and goes directly to my bed, where he stands looking down at the rumpled sheets. In one swift motion, he pulls the hoodie off over his head, and drops it to the floor.

He's not wearing a shirt underneath.

Now I'm gaping at his ripped, tattooed, naked upper body. Someone turned on the heat, because it flashes over me like I just stepped out of an air-conditioned room into a tropical rainforest. He looks over at me.

"Get in bed."

Normally I'm not one to take commands from men. Or from anyone else, for that matter. But A.J.'s voice weaves a wicked spell over me, one I feel helpless to resist. Oddly, irrationally, I trust him. So that takes care of my brain. As for my ovaries, they're partying like it's 1999. Parts of me I didn't even know I had are clenching, aching, nervously twitching in anticipation.

Never before has a man had such an effect on my body. If he told me to jump out the window at this point, I'd seriously consider it.

I climb into bed, sit against the headboard with my knees drawn up, and pull the sheets up to my chin. Wide-eyed and breathless, I stare at him. My mind goes a million miles per hour. Starlight and lightning bolts fly through my veins.

Shucking off his boots, he holds my gaze. Without removing his jeans, he slowly peels back the sheets. He slides in bed next to me, and, with one arm wrapped around my waist, pulls me from my sitting position until I'm lying flat on my back next to him. He whispers, "Roll on your right side."

I do. He slides an arm beneath my head, tightens the other one around my body, pulls his knees up behind mine, puts his face into my hair, and inhales. A delicate shudder runs through his chest.

We're spooning. Holy Jesus, A.J. is *spooning me.*

I can't breathe. I'm having some kind of cardiac event.

"Take a breath," he murmurs against the back of my neck. My lungs obey him. After a minute or two I can feel my toes again.

I'm too wired to say anything. My thoughts are too scattered. All I can do is lie in my bed with his arms around me, and feel.

And lord, do I.

I'm aware of everything, from the way the material of his jeans feels against the backs of my bare legs, to the way his warm breath stirs the hair on the nape of my neck. I feel my pulse in my throat.

I feel his breathing, his chest rising and falling against my shoulder blades, the heat and solidity of his body, flush against mine.

I feel his erection, straining against his zipper, digging hard into my bottom.

But he makes no move to do anything other than lie with me, and breathe me in. After a while, I get past the sheer shock of the situation, and begin to relax.

His lips moving against my skin, A.J. says, "Good."

I want to ask questions. I want to grill him about why he's here, what he wants from me, and what the hell happened between us at his home, but I don't. I understand instinctively that we're on his timetable. This is his game, and, if I want it to go further, I have to play by his rules.

The Spanish Inquisition isn't in those rules.

The arm he's thrown over my body is heavy, but the weight is pleasant. Though the bedroom light isn't on, there's a bit of illumination from the living room, and I can see the tattoos on his forearm and knuckles. Hesitantly, I touch his hand. When he doesn't react, I slowly trace the outline of a small tattoo with the tip of my finger.

It's a flower. On one of the petals is the letter A.

"What's your mother's name?"

My finger freezes. *He's asking about my mother?* "Elizabeth."

He doesn't wait a nanosecond to ask his next question. "Your father?"

"Thomas."

"You have a middle name?"

"Anne. With an e."

"And your brother is Jamie."

"Yes. James." I know A.J. saw him at my shop, but he was never introduced as my brother. Or introduced at all, for that matter.

"Any other siblings?"

"No."

"Grandparents living?"

"Two. My mom's mom. She's a British countess. Countess Chloe Harris of Wakefield, West Yorkshire. I was named after her."

He pauses. "That explains a lot, Princess. The other one?"

"My dad's dad, Walter." I tell him the luau pig story about why I don't eat meat. There's an even longer pause.

"I'm a vegetarian, too."

There are no words to convey my astonishment. While I'm busy putting my eyes back into my head, he adds thoughtfully, "I read *Diet for a New America* by the Baskin-Robbins ice cream heir when I was seventeen. I'll never forget the stories about how slaughterhouses treat the animals. How they die. I never touched meat again. I couldn't bear to think of being part of all that suffering."

My heart dissolves around the edges. But A.J. isn't done with giving me the third degree.

"How long have you owned the flower shop?"

I clear my throat, still recovering from what he's just told me. "Three years."

"You want to be a florist since you were little?"

"I always wanted to do something creative. And I knew I wanted to work for myself. I started working at Fleuret during high school and fell in love with it. When I graduated college, I bought the store. It's hella hard work but I wouldn't give it up for the world. It's just . . . mine. It's all mine. And no one can take it away from me. If it fails, it's because I didn't work hard enough, or smart enough. I can never be fired. That's important to me: to stand on my own two feet. To make my own way. To never be at someone else's mercy."

My unplanned confession seems to satisfy him in some profound way, because he nods, and makes a masculine sound deep in his throat. After a moment of silence, the questions resume.

"How long have you lived here?"

"Just under a year."

It goes on like this. He asks about where I went to school, how long I've been friends with Kat and Grace, what my favorite food is, my favorite color, my favorite place to vacation. He asks what TV shows I watch, and if I'm a reader, and what kind of music I like other than eighties rock, bang, bang, bang. It's like he's trying to pack a year of getting to know me into one night, like he can't exist for another moment on the earth without finding out everything he can about the woman he's wrapped around.

And I *love* it.

The one line of questioning conspicuously missing is about Eric. I know he saw us together at Starbucks, but he never brings it up.

When, after what seems like an hour of the third degree on every other subject, I try to turn the tables and ask A.J. why he moved into that abandoned hotel, he cuts me off with a curt "No."

I turn my head. "No?"

His exhalation is low. He sounds exhausted. "I'm not here to talk about me."

I swallow. *Be brave, Chloe. Just ask him. Do it.* I whisper, "Why are you here?"

This is when I feel—I actually, physically feel—his erection twitch. The damn thing is chomping at the bit! My heartbeat skyrockets.

He says, "Because I haven't slept in six weeks."

A few things happen in quick succession following that statement. First, I'm doused in cold disappointment. He's here to sleep? As in, sleepy-sleep, nighty-night, sweet dreams, and see you in the morning kind of sleep? Huh. Not what I would have guessed. Especially because of that rocket ready to blast a hole out of his pants.

Which, my inner slut points out with a wink, hasn't deflated an inch since he got here.

Second, my brain latches on to the fact that it was six weeks ago that I went to his house. Am I the reason he hasn't slept in all that time?

Eerily reading my thoughts, he says, "Yes. Since that day."

I'm at a loss for words. I'm thrilled, confused, turned on, worried, and a little weirded out. This is so far beyond my normal experience with men, I simply have no idea what's the best course of action.

But my heart knows. Instinctively, my heart guesses what he needs from me. I understand why he came, and it's not just because he needs to sleep.

He needs to escape. And the only way he can escape what gnaws at him is to surrender to it.

I take a deep breath, let it out. I don't understand what drives him, what reasons he's both so repelled by and attracted to me. Perhaps I never will. He doesn't seem inclined to share.

What I do know is that I like having him here. I like his heat. I like his smell. I like the sound of his voice and the way he moves, the way he looks at me like he's starving. I like the sheer size of him, cradling me in his strong arms so I feel completely safe and secure. I like his tattoos. I like his husky laugh. I like the way he looks at the world, in acceptance and forgiveness, without judgment or fear.

I like the way he protects and cares for Bella. The way he cares about a bunch of faceless animals he'll never even meet, enough to change his eating habits for a lifetime.

He's fascinating to me. He's also a total enigma.

I ask, "Can I have one question?"

His arm tightens around my waist. Against my skin, his lips curve. He's smiling.

"One."

Chewing my lower lip, I think. There are too many to pick just one. *Why do I make you want to die? Who is the dead woman in Russia? Why do you never look into a camera lens? Are you going to keep stalking me? Is it you who's leaving the origami birds? What's up with the damn hoodies?*

Instead I blurt, "Are you a spy?"

There's a moment of silence, until he starts to laugh. The sound is something I'll never get used to. I wish I could listen to it forever.

"I could tell you, but then I'd have to kill you."

I smile into the dark. "Very funny. Answer the question."

He shifts his weight, adjusting his arm so that his left hand lies flat against my belly. He pulls me closer to his body, sealing any gaps between us, until we're fused from top to toe. His bare feet tangle with mine. He lowers his mouth to my neck, to the place where it meets my shoulder, opens his lips over my skin, and bites me, just hard enough to sting.

His voice husky with want, he says, "The answer is no. Now stop talking because it's taking every ounce of strength I have not to tear off your panties and your stupid ZZ Top T-shirt and fuck you, Chloe Anne with an e, until we both come so hard we pass out."

I bite back a moan. A shiver of desire runs through my body, followed by blossoming heat. My nipples are so hard they could cut glass.

Apparently my brain also decides it's time for a nap, because I breathlessly ask, without a hint of hesitation or shyness, "You want to fuck me?"

His answer is a low, dangerous growl. His hand on my belly spreads wide. His fingers dig into my flesh.

I can't help it; I arch against that hand.

His reaction is instantaneous. His entire body stiffens. His arm becomes an iron band around my waist. His right hand fists into my hair. He hisses, "More than I want my next breath. But I won't. I never will, you understand? *Never.*"

That hurts so unexpectedly, I suck in a breath. I feel like I've just been punched in the stomach. "Why not, because I won't charge you for it?"

My bitter dig only seems to make him sad. The tension drains from him. He releases his grip on my hair, and gently combs his fingers through it, fanning it over the pillow. "No, Princess," he whispers. "Because I'm not that goddamn selfish."

I lie there in silent misery for a few seconds, blinking back tears. I don't know what he means, and I'm too mad to care. Right now, I just want him to leave so I can rub one out, cry into my pillow, and call it a night.

Behind me, there's a deep sigh. His hand on my stomach slides over my waist, and he begins to caress my back. "It's just over two hours before your alarm goes off. Get some sleep."

I tuck my head into the space between the crook of his elbow and the pillow beneath. I'm hiding. "You know what time my alarm goes off?"

His hand doesn't falter. He just rubs me, slowly, his strong fingers kneading the tense muscles of my neck and shoulders, his palm following the line of my back down to my waist, then up again. It's a nonsexual touch, but I'm aroused by it. Even though I'm mad and exhausted, I'm still aroused.

He murmurs, "Don't ask questions you already know the answer to, songbird. Just go to sleep."

Songbird. I think of the origami birds, the beautiful, painstakingly crafted birds. In the dark, my heart sings.

"I have something to say. It's not a question," I hurry to add, as his hand freezes.

He waits, listening.

I blow out my breath, hard, and bury my head deeper into the pillow. "I'm mad at you right now. And I'm so freaking confused my eyes are crossed."

I feel his head move closer to mine. His forehead touches my shoulder. He whispers, "I know."

"But . . ." My voice drops. "I'm glad you're here."

For this, I'm rewarded with my first-ever kiss from A.J. It's feather soft and achingly sweet.

It's on my shoulder.

Who are you? I drift as his hand continues to caress my back. Its warmth and softness soothe all the ragged edges that he's torn just by showing up, by being his incomprehensible self.

Unexpectedly, I fall asleep.

When the alarm jolts me awake at four, the space beside me in bed is empty. On the pillow next to my head sits an origami bird, white with its head tucked under its wing.

A dove. Sleeping. It's made of the same plain white paper I use in the printer on my desk.

I touch the sheets where A.J. had lain.

They're still warm.

Chapter 15

I'm in a fog of sleep deprivation and hormonal overload all the next day at work. I can't concentrate on anything. When the phone rings at three o'clock, I answer robotically, without my usual chipper, please-be-calling-to-spend-thousands voice.

"Good afternoon thank you for calling Fleuret this is Chloe speaking how may I help you."

The snort on the other end of the line is all too familiar. "Well good afternoon to you, too, sweetheart! Did someone wake up on the wrong side of the bed this morning?"

My lips curve upward. If Grace only knew what had happened in my bed this morning, her head would explode.

"I slept blissfully, thank you very much."

There's a pause. "Why do you sound like you're smiling when you say that?"

Damn, that girl is sharp. I wipe the smile from my face and sit up straighter in the chair. "No reason. I'm not. Anyway, how are you? What's up?"

There's another pause. I worry she's going to grill me, in which case I'm toast because Grace can sniff out a lie like a shark can sniff out a single drop of blood in ten thousand gallons of water. But she lets me off the hook.

"What's up is the time. We're waiting for you over here!"

Frowning, I look at the clock. "Here? Where?"

Grace groans. "You're in so much trouble."

"What are you talking about?"

"The first fitting is today, genius! You forgot!"

"Oh, crap." She's right; I did forget. At this very moment, I'm supposed to be at the Monique Lhuillier atelier in Beverly Hills, getting fitted for my outrageously expensive, incredibly gorgeous, floor-length, sage-green silk chiffon bridesmaid's dress. "I'll be there in twenty. Make sure there's champagne ready."

Grace chuckles. "You're *so* going to tell me what's up with you the *minute* you walk in the door. Did you by any chance see our friend the surly drummer slash Russian spy?"

I try to sound nonchalant. "You wish. I'll see you soon." I hang up before I can do any more damage.

When I arrive at the bridal salon, having left the shop in the capable hands of Trina and Renee, I've worked myself up into a bit of a lather about what, if anything, I'm going to tell Kat and Grace about A.J. It's not that I want to keep anything from them, it's just that what's happening with A.J. feels so . . . delicate. Intimate. Strange. I don't know how I'd describe it, or if I even could.

All I know is that I'm hoping with every fiber of my being that when I look out my window tonight, he'll be there, waiting.

Or stalking. Whatever.

I haven't the slightest clue what I'm going to do about Eric. I don't even know if he's really going to call me, like he said he would. For now, I've decided to cross that bridge when I come to it. There are only so many fires you can try to put out at once.

And damn, am I on fire. I'm burning so hot, I'm surprised everyone can't see the flames.

I'm a little breathless when I walk-run into the elegant, white-on-white salon.

Kat and Grace stand on a raised dais in front of a wall of mirrors. Kat's all rocker-chick chic in skinny jeans, pointy-toe high heeled boots, and a leather jacket, her long dark hair pulled back in a ponytail. Looking like an Amazon warrior goddess gussied up for a ball, Grace is in the sage-green dress. It's one shouldered, fitted and shirred through the bodice and waist, with a side slit that exposes her toned leg all the way to her hip. A seamstress kneels at her feet, pinning the hem. The blade-thin salesgirl who helped Kat find her wedding dress when we shopped here with her a few months ago is fluttering this way and that like an emaciated butterfly, pouring champagne into crystal flutes. Kenji, Bad Habit's stylist and Kat's third bridesmaid—er, brides*man*—is admiring himself in a full-length mirror near the dressing room.

He's wearing the same gown Grace is.

"Hi! Sorry I'm late!"

Everyone turns to look at me. Kat smiles. Grace narrows her eyes. Kenji puts his hand on his hip, looks me up and down, and whistles. "Well, hellllooo, white chocolate! Who's been nibblin' on your little ol' Wonder Bread crusts?"

"I would answer that, but I don't even know what language you're speaking." I toss my handbag onto a white leather chair. The salesgirl scowls at me. I want to tell her to eat a hamburger. Then I remember that's exactly what A.J. *did* say to her when we were here last, and a flush creeps up my neck at the thought of him.

"Allow me to translate," says Grace, eyeing me with one elegant brow arched. "What Kenji said was, 'Hello, normally uptight white girl who suddenly has a mad, hip-shakin' strut, you look like you've recently gobbled down a giant cock sandwich, and we'd all like to know whose it was.' "

I stare at Grace. "Honestly, dude. Sometimes I wonder about you."

She smiles serenely. "Don't change the subject."

"Leave her alone, Grace." Kat winks at me. "And go get your dress on, Lo, we have to be out of here by four. They have another group coming in."

I'm so relieved I want to sigh out loud, but I pretend nonchalance instead. "Just point me in the right direction."

The salesgirl ushers me into the dressing room and helps me into the gown. When I turn and look at myself in the mirror, I'm pleasantly surprised. The color and style are very flattering on me.

"You won't need any adjustment to the length," the salesgirl purrs, fussing over me. She's pleased by my height. She's also obviously pleased by the fit around my waist and chest, because she says, "It's not often we have girls who can fit into the sample sizes. Usually if they're as tall and slender as you are, they have those hideous bolt-ons to go with."

Grimacing, she spreads her hands in front of her chest like she's holding a pair of watermelons. This is one area where the salesgirl and I agree. I think fake boobs are false advertising. Or maybe I'm just jealous. Unless you're a runway model, B-cups aren't exactly all the rage.

They did come in handy for volleyball, though. I played on a team all through high school and college, and never once did I have a nip slip.

"Let's go show your girlfriends, dear."

The salesgirl—whose nametag reads "AINE," a word I have no

idea how to pronounce, so I don't even try—leads me into the main dressing area by the wrist. She announces, "Here we are!" and golf claps like I've just won Best in Show.

I curtsy, because it seems like the thing to do.

Kat squeals in delight. "Oh my God, it's perfect! You look fucking *amazing*!"

Grace, sounding impressed and also a little disgruntled, says, "If anyone has the genes to wear couture, it's definitely you, sweetheart."

Kenji says, "Bitch." He struts to the middle of the room. The dress drags behind him like the train of a wedding gown. At four foot nine, he's going to need a lot of help from the seamstress if he's really going to wear that thing, as he's repeatedly insisted he will. Even his signature zebra-print platform boots aren't much help.

He announces, "In light of current events, Kenji must reevaluate his wardrobe selection." He lifts the dress over his head, and flings it dramatically to the floor.

Aside from the platform boots, he's wearing nothing but a pair of Spider-Man briefs. His body is nut brown, slender as a young boy's, and entirely hairless. I wonder if he shaves it, like he does his head.

Hands on hips, he executes a perfect catwalk turn, then sashays off to the dressing room, where he slams the door.

Kat yells after him, "You left an eyelash out here!"

She's right. One of his big fake eyelashes is stuck to the neckline of the dress. Kat, Grace, and I look at each other, and laugh.

The salesgirl is in the corner, chugging champagne.

"You girls sound like you're havin' fun. We interruptin'?"

The amused voice comes from the doorway. We turn to find Nico leaning against a mirrored armoire near the entry, arms crossed over his chest, grinning.

"Baby!" Kat leaps from the dais and flies into his open arms. I should have known he'd be here; he can't let her out of his sight for more than thirty minutes at a time.

Then I freeze. *We. He said "we."*

My heart turns somersaults. I slowly turn to look into the main room of the salon behind them, and my mouth goes dry.

Unmoving beside a display of white wedding gowns in the other room, A.J. stands watching me. He's in a battered leather bomber jacket instead of a hoodie, and no sunglasses cover his eyes. His hair is loose around his shoulders, a golden lion's mane, and he's freshly shaven. He looks rested.

His eyes are the color of warmed whiskey. His stare is fierce.

He's so beautiful, I can't look away.

Silently, he lifts his hand and makes a "turn" motion with one finger. So I lift the delicate material slightly away from my legs, rise onto my toes and pirouette, a ballerina en pointe, an ice skater in a spin. I feel weightless. I feel breathless. The dress whispers around my bare legs, billowing, airy. When I come to a stop, my hair cascades over my right shoulder, the dress sighs and falls still.

And everyone is staring at me.

"Very pretty," says Grace. "And will you be playing the jazz flute for the talent portion of the pageant, Miss California?"

I flush and look away.

Then A.J.'s in the room, standing next to Kat and Nico. "Sorry for barging in like this. You know how twitchy my boy here gets if he's away from his woman too long." Smiling, he claps his hand on Nico's shoulder.

I wonder who this cheerful stranger could possibly be.

Flustered, I hurry across the room, take a glass of champagne from AINE, and pretend to examine the dress in the mirror. My face is the color of a beet. Grace steps down from the dais, stops beside me and murmurs, "Not the jazz flute then. The skin flute, perhaps?"

I don't respond. I can't; I'm too busy being mortified. Or hornified, not that that's even a word. But dear lord, what's happening to my body? I feel like I might spontaneously combust, like all the drummers in the movie *Spinal Tap.*

Grace can tell. She kisses me on the cheek. "I love you so much right now it hurts."

"You'll be hurting a lot more when I kill you," I hiss under my breath. "Behave!"

She beams at me, pretending to get misty eyed. "My little girl is finally growing up."

I growl, "You're an evil, twisted harpy!"

"And you give the best compliments. Now stop pretending your panties aren't melting, and go over and talk to him. I promise I'll be quiet."

"Not quiet," I warn. *"Mute."*

She makes a zipper motion across her mouth, then floats away into the dressing room. I hear her call out to Kenji, "I have an idea for you, sweetheart. Let's abandon the dress altogether and start with something fresh. I'm thinking peacock feathers."

There's a beat of silence, then Kenji answers, "Ooooooo."

I chance a look in the mirror in A.J.'s general direction. He's looking at me. His gaze hungrily roves up and down my body. He's undressing me with his eyes.

You want to fuck me?

More than I want my next breath. But I won't. I never will, you understand? Never.

Kat says, "This is a nice surprise, A.J. How are you?"

He nods, a hint of a smile hovering at the corners of his mouth. "Good."

He's still staring at me.

Nico says, "We finished up the session earlier than scheduled, so we thought we'd stop by and see how it was goin'."

"It's going great! I mean, Kenji isn't happy, but we'll figure something out. How did the session go?"

"Actually . . ." Nico slides A.J. a look. "My man here came up with a pretty fuckin' ambitious new track. Very 'Stairway to Heaven'–esque. Not sure if my pipes can handle all the upper extensions, but it's a hell of a song."

"Yeah? What's it called A.J.?"

"Shipwrecked Soul."

His voice is quiet when he speaks, quiet yet intense, and his eyes are intense, too.

My throat constricts. I'll never understand him, or this thing between us. It's obvious he wants me, just as obvious that he doesn't *want* to want me. His ambivalence is a big, fat slap in the face, and suddenly *I* feel shipwrecked.

What am I doing? This is foolish. I'm a fool.

I don't want to be a fool.

"Is there anything else I need to do?" I ask AINE, my eyes lowered. I can't look at anyone right now. I'm feeling a little too raw.

She says, "Nothing. It's a perfect fit. You can have this sample for a discount if you'd like, or I can order a new one that hasn't been worn."

"This one is fine," I whisper. As I'm practically broke, I'm grateful for a discount. I'll have to put it on my credit card and pay it off over the next several months. Hopefully by the wedding date. I hustle into the dressing room and change.

After a few minutes, there's a hesitant knock on my door. "Lo? You okay?"

I'm finished changing, so I open the door, avoiding Kat's eyes. "I'm fine. I just need to get back to work."

I try to brush past her, but she blocks my way, standing in front of me with crossed arms. "Yeah. I call bullshit. It's A.J., isn't it? Spill."

I close my eyes, drag my hands through my hair, and sigh. "It's A.J."

"I didn't know he was coming, I promise. And I haven't said anything to Nico, either, so you don't have to worry about that. He thinks you two still hate each other." She pauses. "Although if you keep staring at each other the way you do, he's bound to figure it out."

"That's just it. There's nothing *to* figure out. He might as well hate me for all the good it's doing me."

"Meaning?"

"Look . . . it doesn't matter. There's nothing going on between us, and he's made it clear there never will be—"

"Why? What did he say?"

I fiddle with the buttons on my shirt. "Let's just say he made no bones about the fact that he'd rather lose a limb than sleep with me."

She snorts. "And you believed him?"

"No, I didn't! Which is even worse! He's either the biggest liar in the world or he's totally screwed up in his head! What am I supposed to do with that?"

She says softly, "I don't know. What do you want to do with that?"

I put my face into my hands, and groan. "I don't do complicated. You know this about me, Kat. I hate complicated."

"So make it simple, then."

I lift my head and stare at her. "You mind telling me how?"

"Just lay it on the line, straight out. 'I dig you. Do you dig me, yes or no? If yes, get naked right now. If no, go fuck yourself.' End of story."

"Tch. If only life were so easy."

She grins. "I know I'm oversimplifying."

"Gee, you think?"

"But the basic premise still stands. If you want to put yourself out of your misery, just talk to him. Tell him what you want." She cocks her head. "But first you have to *know* what you want. Do you?"

The vivid image of a naked, sweating A.J. pounding into me as I grip his ass and cry out in ecstasy floods my brain.

Kat's grin returns, even wider. "Oh, yeah. You do."

I sigh. "We've all been spending too much time with Grace."

"Well, she might be an incurable horndog, but at least she's clear on her priorities."

From a few dressing rooms down, Grace says, "You geniuses know I can hear you, right?"

Together, Kat and I say, "Shut up!"

Then Kenji appears in the doorway behind Kat. He's still wearing nothing but his boots and Spidey underwear. And the one false eyelash. Pointing at me with a look of incredulity, he says, "A.J. and . . . *you*?"

"Oh, no!" I moan. He heard everything!

"You *cannot* repeat a *word*," Kat snaps, wagging her finger at him.

Kenji throws up his hands. "Of course I can't, because I can't believe a word of what I'm hearing! It's a figment of my imagination! I'm obviously on drugs! We're talking about a man who eats virgins for lunch and a woman who makes nuns look slutty! There is no universe in existence where these two paths cross!"

"Why does everyone think I'm such a prude?" I shout.

Grace calls out, "Have you ever taken it up the ass?"

"Dude! Gross! No!"

Kenji asks, "Have you ever had sex with another girl?"

"I'm not gay!"

Kat says, "You don't have to be gay, you could have just experimented when you were younger or something, like the rest of us."

I gasp. "*You've* had *sex* with another *girl*?"

Chuckling, Grace says, "Case closed."

I clench my hands in my hair. I hate everyone!

AINE appears in the dressing room with us, looking all sorts of nervous. "Excuse me, but there's a gentleman here to see you?"

I frown. "A gentleman? Who?"

"A policeman. He says his name is Officer Cox?"

All the blood drains from my face. Kat and I share a horrified look.

Kenji says, "I watched a movie with an Officer Cox in it just last night." He smirks. "That boy had a huge *talent*."

From the far dressing room comes Grace's delighted laugh.

Trying to appear calm, I walk through the mirrored dressing area into the main salon. I don't look at Nico, who's talking to someone on his cell. I also don't look at A.J., but I feel his eyes burn into me like two hot pokers as I pass.

In the front room, Eric stands rigidly with his hands on his hips, staring out the windows to the street.

"Hey."

He turns. His face is red. He obviously knows who's in the back.

I cross my arms over my chest, hoping this isn't going to be a scene.

Eric shoots a glance in the direction I just came from. "I wanted to surprise you, so I stopped by your shop instead of calling. Trina said you were here." He pauses, a muscle in his jaw jumping. "Surprise."

I feel an explanation is in order. "I didn't know they were coming. They just showed up about five minutes ago when I was getting ready to leave. You know how Nico is."

Eric's dealt with Nico's overprotectiveness of Kat before. There was an ugly scene during which Eric and his partner were called to deal with some paparazzi who showed up at her house when she and Nico were first dating. And the night Nico's brother abducted Kat, Eric was part of the squad who found her.

"Yeah, I know how Nico is. What I don't know is why A.J.'s here." He gazes long and hard at my face. His voice drops. "Or maybe I do."

My face flushes. "He's the best man, Eric."

"Since when does the best man go dress shopping with the bridesmaids?"

There's an awful pleading tone in my voice that I hate, but I'm desperate to keep this civil. There's nothing more embarrassing than couples arguing in public, and I'm still trying to spare Eric's feelings. "Kat and Nico hired some froufrou wedding planner who insisted on having the guys involved in the whole process. I know it's crazy, but it's not my fault—"

Eric steps closer. "You want me to believe this was the *wedding planner's* idea? Like that Neanderthal would take orders from a woman? Do you even know anything about him, Chloe?" His voice rises, and I know it's on purpose. He wants what he's saying to carry into the other room. "Did you know he's been arrested *eight times*?"

He nods at the look of shock on my face. "That's right! For everything from misdemeanor battery to felony assault with a firearm! He's *dangerous*, Chloe. He's—"

"You pulled his record?"

"Yeah, so?"

His defiant, defensive tone makes heat blaze up my neck. My desire to keep things civil goes up in smoke.

"*So* my father is one of this town's best criminal defense attorneys. And he's talked a lot about his cases over the years, so I happen to know that police officers don't have access to a citizen's criminal record at the touch of a button. You have to formally request it through the Criminal Offender Record Information unit of the Department of Justice, and it's on a need-to-know basis." I pause, trying to get my breathing under control. "What exactly was your legal need to know, Officer Cox?"

He looks at me with steam coming out of his ears. "You're defending that loser?" he hisses.

"Actually what I'm doing is trying to find out if I've completely misjudged a person I thought was trustworthy."

This is the wrong thing to say. Eric goes from merely indignant to thermonuclear in two seconds flat. He grabs my arm and shouts, "You're talking about *me* being trustworthy? *Me?* This from the girl who called her boyfriend by some whoring, violent criminal's name while he was trying to make love to her?"

To my left comes A.J.'s voice, deadly soft. "Take your hand off her, or I'll break it."

Eric turns his head. I follow his gaze. There stands A.J., all six foot six of him, legs spread, shoulders back, bristling. What I see in his eyes could make Freddy Krueger run screaming in terror.

Eric drops his hand from my arm, and turns to face A.J. He rests his right hand on his gun. "That's the second time you've threatened me."

"It's the second time you've deserved it."

"Why don't you mind your own goddamn business?"

"She is my business."

It hangs there between them, a lit stick of dynamite with a very short fuse.

Nico walks up, eyeing A.J. and Eric. His glance flicks to me. "What's goin' on, kids?"

No one answers. The tension is so thick I could cut it with a knife.

Nico casually says, "Officer Cox, good to see you. Actually this is great timin', because I've been meanin' to call you about this charity concert I wanna put together. I was hopin' I could get the support of the LAPD . . . you got a minute?"

I've never seen Eric so angry. Cords stand out on his neck. A pulse throbs in his temple. His left hand is curled to a fist, and it's shaking. Nico eases between him and A.J., and puts a hand on his shoulder.

"C'mon, Eric. Let's take a walk."

I know Eric likes Nico, and respects him, too. But I can see the struggle Eric goes through as he decides whether or not to allow Nico to steer him away from the cliff he's about to sail over.

Finally, he relents. He curses, turns away, and lets Nico lead him out the front door. When they're gone, I exhale and press my hands over my pounding heart.

"I'm sorry," I say to A.J. without looking at him.

"Not your fault. Love makes people do crazy things."

I meet his gaze. "I've never seen him this way. I don't know what's wrong with him."

A.J. says softly, "He loves you, Chloe. He's actually showing remarkable restraint. If you were mine, I would've burned down the entire city by now to get you back."

That takes my breath away. I look away, swallowing. "How do you know he loves me?"

"Princess. How could he not?"

His voice is so tender it makes tears well in my eyes. I can't look at him. Instead I watch Nico and Eric through the windows, standing outside on the sidewalk together, talking. Nico looks over Eric's shoulder, and catches my eye.

I see understanding on his face. Eric's telling him everything. His gaze moves to A.J., and I have to close my eyes to block out the new emotion that crosses Nico's face: fear.

Nico knows A.J. better than anyone does. And if he's afraid for me, then I should be afraid for myself.

I feel my heart break, just a little.

"So if you were me, what would you do, A.J.?"

Silence.

"Because I'm having a really hard time deciphering this new puzzle that's my life. It doesn't make any sense to me. I'm pretty much at a loss."

"Is he a good man?"

I open my eyes, and look at A.J. "I thought so. Before all this—"

"No. You know. Is he a good man? Overall. No one's perfect, but you know him. Deep down, do you think he's good?"

I whisper, "Yes."

He slowly nods. "Then my answer is, you should marry him, and live your life."

A knife twists in my heart. I hate it that my voice breaks when I speak. "Really? You think it's okay to marry someone when you have feelings for someone else?"

A.J.'s eyes flash. His nostrils flare. He shakes his head, silently, and I don't know if he's saying yes or no, or just telling me not to be such an idiot.

Because I am. I so am. I'm standing here with a man who's told me I make him want to die, and that I should go and marry Eric, and all I can think of is how badly I want him to put his arms around me, pull me against his chest, and kiss me.

A lone tear crests my lower lid and snakes down my cheek. With anguished eyes, A.J. watches it fall.

I whisper, "I'm not waiting up for you tonight. I won't be watching from the window."

A.J. nods, resigned.

"But the door will be unlocked."

His brows pull together. He says hoarsely, "Chloe—"

"If you don't come, that's the end of it. I can't do this anymore. If you don't come I'm moving on with my life, and we'll never speak of any of this again."

Before he can reply, I turn and run to the other room, grab my purse, say good-bye to Kenji and the girls, and flee.

It's midnight. I'm lying in bed, wide awake, staring at the same crack in the ceiling I've been staring at for the past three hours.

I'm a writhing ball of pent-up, white-hot, whirlwind emotions. Every nerve is stretched taut. Every time a car passes by on the street outside, I tense, holding my breath. Every little sound is amplified, until a fly buzzing against the windowpane sounds like a jackhammer. I don't know how much longer I can lie here like this before I suffer a serious mental break, start screaming, and never stop.

Then I hear the front door open, and freeze.

The door softly closes. After a moment's pause, heavy footsteps start down the hall. My frozen blood thaws, and begins to boil. I'm roasting from the inside out.

When A.J. reaches my open bedroom door, he stands just outside, peering in. There are no lights on in the apartment, but my eyes have adjusted to the dark, so I see how his eyes glitter. I see how brightly they burn.

Heart thundering, I sit up. The sheets puddle around my waist. I'm wearing no makeup and my usual bedtime outfit, boy shorts and a T-shirt, because the thought of waiting all dolled up in a nightie and being stood up was too much to bear.

But now he's here. I have no idea what lies on the other side of this moment.

And I. Don't. Care.

Without saying a word, I pull back the sheets on the other side of the bed. A.J. doesn't hesitate a fraction of a second. He crosses the threshold, pulls the hoodie off over his head, drops it to the floor, shucks off his boots, and crawls into bed next to me.

As his arms come around me and his knees draw up behind mine, I release a breath so relieved it's almost painful.

We lie together for a while in total silence. His breath is warm on the back of my neck. Against my shoulder blades, his heart beats fast and hard.

Into the soft darkness, I say, "Thank you."

"Don't thank me."

"I am. Because I know this isn't easy for you."

He presses his feverish forehead to my neck. "How do you see me so clearly, when no one else can?"

I think about it. "I don't know. Maybe I'm just looking closer than they are."

I hear him swallow. His thumb moves back and forth over my wrist. With a fingertip, I trace the flower tattoo on his knuckle. There are several more on his other knuckles, but this is the one I find most fascinating. "What does this tattoo mean? The flower one with the initials inside the petals."

The question is a risk, because I know how he hates questions. I'm not sure he'll answer. But finally he does, his voice thick. "It's a reminder."

"Of?"

"Everyone I've lost."

My finger stills. I count the petals.

Twelve.

I sit with it, resisting the urge to ask a rapid-fire succession of follow-up questions. He's lost twelve people. I assume by "lost" he means died, although without asking I have no way to prove that. I know the mysterious Aleksandra, resident of the Preobrazhenskoe Cemetery in Saint Petersburg, is one of the lost. His parents are, too. I remember from Wikipedia that they died years past. But who are the other nine? He didn't have siblings. Could they be other relatives? Friends?

In the end I decide it doesn't matter. A.J. has a dozen dead people in his past. I've never known anyone who's died. Not one. Even my two dead grandparents died before I was born.

I try to imagine my parents being dead, and can't. We don't always get along, but I love them. And I know they love me. Their absence would leave such a void I can't imagine it ever being filled. And if Kat or Grace died, I'd be devastated.

An unexpected feeling of tenderness wells up inside me. It's a warm, achy softness in the center of my chest, and it's all for the man in whose arms I lie.

I lower my head and gently press my lips against the flower tattoo.

Behind me, A.J.'s chest heaves as he gulps several deep breaths. His arms tighten around my body. He lifts the arm that's under my head and wraps it around my chest, so I'm cocooned in a pair of big, strong arms. I press the soles of my bare feet against the tops of his, and close my eyes.

Like an onion, layer by layer, my heart peels slowly open.

"When I was growing up, I was always the tallest one in class. Taller than all the boys. Tall and skinny, so I used to get teased. They'd call me giraffe or beanpole or Skeletor. My brother always stuck up for me, even though sometimes he'd get his ass kicked because he was pretty skinny, too. My mother would call the kids' parents and scream. And my father would call the principal and threaten to sue the entire school district. It wasn't really that big of a deal to me. I mean, it hurt, but I knew I'd eventually grow into my legs. That's what Granny Harris would always tell me when she saw me."

I mimic a posh British accent. "'When you grow into those legs, luv, you'll be the most gorgeous creature that ever walked the earth. You're just going through the same awkward stage everyone goes through. But I know a thoroughbred when I see one!' She was always saying nice things to me like that. My entire family always had my back. My whole life, I've always felt protected."

A.J. is quiet, listening. I feel the energy thrumming through him, the electricity sparking from his skin.

I gather my courage and whisper, "But I've never felt safer than I do right now."

He turns his face to my shoulder. His cheek burns against my skin. His voice comes low and hoarse. "I can't be what you need. I'm not the man for you. We both know that."

That's not what I want to hear. It's so far from what I want to hear, I childishly put my hands over my ears and shake my head.

He pries my hands off my ears. "Yes, Chloe."

"Then what are we doing, A.J.? What is this? Why are you here?"

His answer bursts out of him. "Because I'm fucking weak! I can't stay away from you! No matter what I do, you're there, in my head, smiling that heartbreaker smile! I can't stay away." His voice cracks, and it sounds as if he might cry. "And I'm so tired of trying."

He's trembling. His entire body is wracked with tremors, little earthquakes that shake me in his arms. He makes a desperate noise, like he's tearing apart, and I act on pure instinct.

I turn over and wrap my arms around his neck. He buries his face into my shoulder, shuddering, holding on to me as if for dear life.

I whisper, "It's okay."

"It's not okay. It won't end well. I'll hurt you."

"Only if you want to."

His laugh is ugly, choked. "That's the thing, Princess. I *don't* want to. But I will."

I smooth the hair off his face, force him to meet my eyes. His are filled with water.

"Okay."

He stops breathing. His eyes get wide. "What?"

"I said okay. So be it. If all I get is this, right now, tonight, and tomorrow you change your mind and never want to see me again, then okay. I'll take it. I'll take the one night."

He just stares at me. I've never seen an expression like his. It's one of horror and elation and disbelief, all at once.

"Um . . . that was your cue to ravish me, A.J. Let the ravishment begin."

He rears up on his elbows and pushes me to my back. He gives me his weight, pressing the full length of his hard—and very aroused—body against mine. He hovers above me, his hair falling down on either side of our heads so we're in a private little world, just our two curtained faces, our breath and beating hearts.

"You don't mean it."

"I do."

"You don't know what you're saying."

"Yes, I do."

"You'll change your mind in the morning. You'll regret it."

"I won't regret anything."

"What happened to 'I only have sex in a context of caring and love'?"

Very softly, I answer, "Nothing."

He understands without me having to provide more. His eyes devour my face. He whispers, "*Goddamn* you."

"Just kiss me, A.J. You can hate me all you want tomorrow."

"No."

"Why not?"

"I already told you why not."

My face is getting hotter by the second. "That eight-inch steel pipe in your pants would like you to kiss me."

His lips twitch. "Eleven-inch."

I bite my lower lip, hard, because my ovaries have just fainted. Then something terrible occurs to me, and I draw a breath. "Do you . . . is there . . ."

"What?"

I swallow, hugely embarrassed by what I'm about to ask. In a small voice I say, "Is there a, um . . . problem with it?"

He tilts his head, staring down at me. "What kind of a problem?"

"Um. Maybe the kind of problem that you'd only want a . . . prostitute . . . to see?"

He's frowning at me in total confusion. Then his face clears as he begins to understand. "Are you asking if my dick is deformed?"

I squeak, "Or do you have some terrible disease you don't want me to catch?"

Slowly, he lowers his mouth to my ear. His nose skims the outer rim, and I break out in goose bumps. He breathes, "I'm clean as a whistle, Princess. You?"

I nod, trying not to rock my pelvis against his.

Lightly, he takes my earlobe between his teeth. Then I get his lips, gently sucking. He murmurs, "And my cock is in perfect working order."

"Prove it."

He goes still. He's thinking so hard I hear the gears turning inside his brain. But I'm in no mood for delay, as my ovaries have recovered and have started flinging themselves lustfully all over my lower body.

I reach down between us, and curl my fingers around his erection.

He hisses out a breath, but doesn't move. We're eye to eye, staring at each other, and I'm challenging him with a look to stop me.

He doesn't stop me. My ovaries cheer.

Slowly, I stroke my hand down the length of him. I can tell he's not wearing anything beneath his jeans, because I feel every ridge, every throbbing vein, from crown to base. And he's *huge*. Thick, long, solid. I stroke my hand back up, to the tip, and rub my thumb back and forth over the rigid head. A little bead of wetness dampens his jeans.

My entire body explodes with want. The kind of want I've never felt. It's like some wild animal has just woken up inside me, ravenous, greedy, insatiable with lust.

Looking into his eyes, I say, "I want to see it. I want to suck on it. I want it inside me."

My throaty voice sounds like it belongs to another woman. I *feel* like another woman, someone wanton and confident. Someone far more uninhibited than me.

I squeeze his cock, and he groans. The sound thrills me, gives me even more confidence. I lean close to his ear. "I want to ride this big, beautiful cock until I come, screaming your name."

He pants, "Jesus, fuck, Princess, who *are* you right now?"

He's losing control. I feel it. I see it. His face is strained with the effort to hold back. His arms shake, his breath is ragged. He wants this just as badly as I do, but, for whatever reason, he won't let himself go.

So I do the only thing I can think of that might push him over the edge. I roll out from beneath him, rise to my knees, pull my T-shirt over my head, and toss it aside. My hair falls all around my shoulders, brushing my bare breasts.

He's frozen in shock. His eyes are big, drinking me in. He whispers my name.

I hook my thumbs into the waistband of my boy shorts, and begin to slide them down over my hips.

A.J. sits up abruptly and grabs my wrists, hard. He snaps, "Stop!"

So this is what rejection feels like. Man does it suck. I go limp and sink to my knees, hiding my face behind my hair. He doesn't release my wrists.

"Look at me."

I shake my head. I've never felt such crushing shame.

He pulls me up by my wrists, winds my arms around his neck. He hugs me, burying his face in my hair. My breasts are flattened against his chest. Beneath my cheek, his heart pounds wildly.

"I told you I'd never fuck you."

I don't say anything. What is there to say? He did tell me that, and, like a class A moron, I tried to change his mind.

He breathes me in, inhaling deeply into my hair, nuzzling his face into my neck. His fingers grip hard into my sides, and they're twitching.

I don't speak. Something is happening with him, and, selfish slut I've suddenly become, I don't want to interfere if it's going to wind up with me on my back, pinned beneath his hard, gorgeous body. Hoping against hope, I clamp my mouth shut, determined not to say a word.

I feel his mouth on my neck. His lips open over the pulse in my throat, he sucks, and I can't stop the low, breathy moan that escapes me. My head falls back, into his open hand. His other hand slides up my waist and stops just beneath my breast, gently squeezing. I arch against him, mewing like a cat.

"God, Chloe. The sounds you make . . ."

His voice throbs with desire. Heat sizzles through my limbs. My fingers sink into his hair, and I pull, lost in sensation.

When his thumb brushes over the hard, peaked nub of my nipple, I gasp and jerk. I'm about to unravel, all with the slightest touch of his fingers and lips.

"You need to come, don't you, baby?" His voice is low and harsh at my ear.

It's the first time he's called me baby. For some unthinkable reason, it makes me so wet and desperate, I moan again, grinding my pelvis against his.

It's that moan that finally breaks through his resistance. With a snarled oath, he pushes me onto my back, rips my boy shorts off my body, and buries his face between my legs.

I cry out, delirious, writhing as he grips my ass in his hands and sucks hard where I most need it. Every time I make a sound of pleasure, he makes a low noise in his throat that sends a pulse of vibration through my core. It makes me moan louder, which makes him suck harder. He slides two fingers inside me and I buck, crying out. I quickly build to a peak so hot and bright my entire body bows. My back lifts off the bed. My hands, clenched in his hair, shake.

In what feels like a nuclear detonation, I come. His name rips from my lips in a long, wavering scream.

Upstairs, my neighbor pounds on the wall, shouting for me to shut up.

Panting, I collapse against the mattress. The entire process from nipple flick to orgasm has taken approximately thirty seconds.

He crawls up my body, takes my face in his hands, and kisses me, deep and hard. I taste myself on him and nearly come again.

"Off!" I claw at the waistband of his jeans. I want him inside me so badly I can't wait *one second longer.*

Unfortunately, I'll be waiting a hell of a lot longer than one second, because A.J. says, "No."

I freeze, hoping I've misheard him. "Excuse me?"

"I said no."

My heart stalls, then reboots with a painful thud. "You've got to be kidding me."

"Chloe—"

"You have GOT to be KIDDING!" I try pushing at the mountains of his shoulders, but he doesn't budge. He rises up on his elbows, and pins my wrists to the pillow above my head.

"Listen to me."

I can already hear the excuses in his voice, all the *I'm so sorry*s and the *It's for the best*s. I groan, turn my face away, and squeeze shut my eyes.

"I already told you I wouldn't—"

"You *jerk*! What is this to you, some kind of game? Do you think this is funny, making me beg you for it? Watching me lose control and be completely pathetic—is that what gets you off?"

"Yes, watching you lose control gets me off! So does *listening* to you lose control, and hearing that perfect mouth tell me all the filthy things you want, and tasting your beautiful sweet pussy, and hearing you beg for my cock! It *all* gets me off and it's taking every fucking crumb of self-control I have not to bury myself balls-deep inside you *right now*!"

He roars the last part into my face. I lie there panting and livid under him, my eyes filling with tears.

"Then tell me why not. You've said you won't, but you haven't said why not. At least give me that."

He closes his eyes and drops his forehead to my shoulder. "Because you can't be mine. You can never be mine. And if I fuck you, baby, you'll be mine forever."

There's pain in his voice, pain, longing, and sorrow. I turn my head, press my lips to his temple. "What if I want to be yours?"

He shakes his head. "I told you. I'm not that selfish."

I whisper, "Please, A.J. Please help me understand. I don't understand."

Instead of answering, he rolls to his back and flips me on top of him, so my naked body is flush against his. He tucks my head into the crook of his neck, cradling it with one big hand, and smooths the other hand over my hair. He begins to rub my back, gently, his palm warm and rough against my skin.

I exhale, shuddering. He's not going to tell me anything more. He's given all he's going to give.

"I should tell you to leave."

His deep inhalation makes his chest rise beneath my cheek. "You don't want me to leave. And I wouldn't, anyway."

My nose is pressed against the tattoos of the crosses on his neck. I close my eyes to block the sight of them, because I know I'll never find out what they mean. I've come up against the brick wall of A.J.'s will, reached the sheer cliff of his sharing. There will be nothing beyond what I already have.

As he pets and strokes my naked back, his hands so tender and cherishing, somehow I begin to relax. The steady beat of his heart against mine soothes me, as does his breathing, the slow, rhythmic rise and fall of his strong chest. I'm more confused than ever, but, lying in his arms, I still feel safe.

I sigh, wind my arms around his shoulders, and snuggle closer to his body, as close as I can get.

He presses his lips against my hair. So, so quietly, he says, "You make me think there might be a God after all."

My face crumples. My heart feels like someone is stabbing it over and over with scissors. "I thought I made you want to die."

His hand drops to my bottom, and he squeezes. "Well, this ass *could* kill a man."

I raise my head and look at him. His face is solemn, but his eyes are sparkling. He's making a joke.

"Oh, it's time for funny A.J. to come out and play? Thanks for the heads-up. Let me just look around for my neck brace because I've got a nasty case of whiplash from all your prior mood swings."

He grins. "I love it when you give me shit."

"Really? Because I hate it when you give *me* shit."

His amused look turns smoldering. "Don't lie to me. You love it just as much as I do."

That heated stare of his sets off fireworks in my body. It's as if my hormones are just waiting around for him to do something sexy, and the minute he does, they all leap to their feet and run around like kindergartners on a sugar high.

He firmly cups my jaw in his hand and growls, "Look at that fucking look you're giving me. How am I supposed to maintain my sanity when the most beautiful woman I've ever met is staring at me with big eyes that beg, 'Please fuck me'?"

The most beautiful woman he's ever met.

My hormones graduate from kindergarten and go straight to college, where they throw a toga party of epic proportions and burn down the dorm.

I moisten my lips. A.J. watches the motion of my tongue, and I feel his heartbeat kick up a notch. I also notice that his erection hasn't flagged at all since he arrived. His mind might not be on board with whatever's happening between us, but his body definitely is.

And oh, do I have plans for that body.

"Thank you for the compliment. I'll assume that's a rhetorical question. But I do have an idea."

He watches me warily, his hand still firm around my jaw.

"How exactly would you define fucking?"

"Excuse me?"

"You said you'd never fuck me. But you just went down on me, and I'm lying here butt naked on top of you, so I'm trying to get a better grasp of the exact parameters of our little . . . situation."

One side of his mouth curves upward. His lids lower so his eyes are practically slits. "You trying to negotiate with me, Princess?"

I wrinkle my nose. The word "negotiate" makes me feel a little gross, especially in light of how his dates usually begin.

"No. I'm trying to determine if this, for instance, is allowed." I press my lips against his, softly, no tongue.

He watches me from beneath his lowered lids. "That's allowed." His voice is husky. His hand drifts down from my jaw to my neck. For some reason, I find his light grip around my throat unbearably sexy.

"Okay. And this?" I kiss him again, but this time suck his lower lip into my mouth. He doesn't resist, so I kiss him deeper, exploring his mouth with my tongue. His fingers tighten around my neck.

"That's allowed, too," he breathes when I pull away and look at him.

I nod. Without breaking eye contact with him, I lower my head and press a kiss to his chest. It's feather light, right above his heart. I wait for his answer, my heart beginning to pound.

"Allowed." He swallows. His voice is getting lower and lower.

Trying not to make any sudden moves, I ease myself down his body a foot or so, careful to balance my weight on my hands on the mattress on either side of his waist. As I move, my breasts skim against his chest. He inhales sharply, and I freeze.

He doesn't do anything, so I press my lips to his abdomen. It's as hard as rock, without an ounce of fat, tattooed and so sexy I just want to bite it. In fact, I want to sink my teeth into his biceps, his shoulders, his thighs, *everywhere*. I'm starving for him. I want to gobble him up. I want to taste every part of his body, every inch of his skin.

I lick a languid circle around his belly button, dip my tongue into the little depression, and suck.

Beneath my mouth, his muscles contract, quivering. His hands settle on either side of my head. They're trembling. I fall still, waiting.

After a moment, he whispers, "Allowed."

The feeling of power that surges through me is heady. When I glance up, he's staring at me, eyes hooded. All the humor is gone. Now there's only need.

Holding his gaze, I move my lips to a spot about half an inch above the waistband of his jeans. I press my mouth to his skin. His lips part, but he doesn't make a sound. So, still looking into his eyes, I kiss a soft, slow path right down to the denim, then slide my tongue just under the waistband.

He's frozen. I'm not even sure if he's breathing.

I lay my hand over the bulge in his jeans. Slowly, I stroke my hand up and down its twitching, hard length. I move my mouth to the pulsing crown at its tip, and suck, right through the denim.

A.J.'s groan is ragged.

"Allowed?" I ask, watching him. I give his erection a squeeze, and the muscles in his stomach contract.

"Chloe, fuck, Princess—"

"Say yes, A.J.," I softly demand, rubbing my hand up and down, squeezing and stroking.

He lies there, tense, panting, the occasional moan working from his throat as I continue my torture. But I won't go any further without his permission. I won't push him more than this.

He has to ask me for it.

He drops his head against the pillow, closes his eyes, and utters a soft, surrendering cry. "Yes *please* God *please* Chloe give me your mouth baby I need you so fucking bad—"

I rip open the fly of his jeans, and he's free.

His cock springs out into my hands. I gasp, astonished at the size, at how beautiful it is.

It's a masterpiece. It deserves a painting, or at least a commemorative statue carved in marble, set out in a public square. If I wasn't so stricken by lust, I'd want to grab a pencil and paper and sketch it, that's how fantastic I think it is.

I wrap a hand around the thick base. I wrap the other hand above the first. Even with two fists around it, there's still plenty of bare acreage on this baby. With a moan, I pounce on it. I take the crown into my mouth and suck.

The sound A.J. makes is so erotic I suck harder.

He shudders. His hips start to move. He says my name, his hands reaching for my head. His fingers settle lightly against my face, and he pushes my hair aside so he can watch me.

I take him as far into my throat as I can without gagging. Both my hands stroke him as he flexes his hips up and down, slowly fucking my mouth. His hips start to move faster. His eyes are glazed with lust and pleasure. He's making soft, helpless moans, watching my mouth and hands, my face.

He whispers, "You're so beautiful. My beautiful little songbird. My angel."

Thrilled by his words, I hum, and it makes him groan.

His eyes slide shut. His chest heaves as he pants, and he starts to buck against my hands and mouth. He's close already.

I keep one hand wrapped around him, but take the other and gently cup his balls. They're heavy in my palm, velvet soft. I fondle them as I continue to suck his head and shaft, my hand slipping up and down his throbbing length, squeezing and stroking.

His hands tighten on either side of my head. He hisses, "Fuck baby yes baby feels so goddamn *good*."

I open my throat and slide his cock as far down it as it can go, which is about half of his length. His entire body stiffens. He jerks and comes into my mouth, groaning and swearing, roaring like an animal.

The neighbors upstairs pound on the wall again.

He's still coming hard, grunting and twitching, his breath hissing in and out between his clenched teeth, all the muscles of his abdomen and arms flexed, his head tipped back into the pillow. I watch him, euphoric, feeling powerful and ridiculously self-satisfied and accomplished, as if I've just invented cold fusion or facilitated world peace.

Most of all, I feel incredibly *feminine*. I've just watched the sexiest man alive fall apart in my hands, and I want to purr in satisfaction.

A.J. collapses against the mattress as if he's been flung there by some giant invisible hand. I swallow—something I've admittedly not been too keen on in the past but at the moment I *adore*—and swallow again, then gently lick him clean, lapping up his salty goodness.

"You taste like hazelnuts."

His laugh is ragged. "You like hazelnuts, Princess?"

"I *love* them. They're my new favorite food."

His grin fades. He quickly grows serious, watching me lovingly clean every drop of what he's given me off his shaft, his crown, my hands. Somehow there are even a few splatters on his abdomen, and I lick those off like a kitten with a bowl of cream.

I feel like Cleopatra. I feel like Helen of Troy. I feel like the most beautiful, sexy woman who ever walked the earth. The irony isn't lost on me that I'm on my knees, in the position I'm in, but right now this feels like the most powerful position in the world.

Then I suffer a little twinge of paranoia. My tongue falters. My hands fall still.

A.J. is used to having professionals do what I just did. Professionals with vastly more experience than I have in the area.

He doesn't miss my sudden hesitation. "What's wrong?"

"Was that . . . did I . . . um . . ."

It takes him a nanosecond to catch my drift. He grabs my arms, hauls me up his body, positions me on top of him, and starts to chuckle softly into my ear. "Are you asking if it was good for me, too?"

I hide my face in his neck. "Maybe. But don't answer unless the answer is yes."

He gives me a squeeze, laughing now. "Princess, it was fucking *epic*. That blow job was a gold medal winner. I'll dream about it every night for the rest of my life."

Grinning, I look up at him. His eyes shine, amber and gilt in the shadows, bright beneath the dark chocolate curve of his lashes. His hair is mussed and his smile is soft, and he's so handsome it hurts. My breath hitches, and my heart does this odd thing where it expands and contracts at the same time. I reach up and press my hand against his cheek.

"I'd like to give you one of those every night for the rest of *my* life."

His laugh dies in his throat. His lips part, his brows draw together, the expression in his eyes turns haunted.

"No," I whisper, recognizing that look. "Stay with me. Don't go back into the dark."

He closes his eyes. A low, soft sound of despair escapes his lips. Gathering me closer, he presses his lips to my forehead, and leaves them there.

Slowly, with as much gentle loving as I can put into a touch, I run my fingers over his chest, his biceps, his tense, corded forearm. I don't know what to say, or if there's even anything that could be said to help him, to take away whatever pain he's so obviously in, so I try to convey with my touch that he's safe with me. That I know he's hurting, and, though I don't know why, I'm here for him.

With all my heart, I want to be what makes him feel better. I want him to feel as safe with me as I do with him.

Looking up at the ceiling, A.J. blows out a hard breath. I keep silently stroking his skin, listening to his jagged heartbeat, trying to soothe him. I try not to think of anything else, of what might happen next, of what tomorrow will bring. I told him I'd take only one night, if that's all he was willing to give, and I meant it.

At the time I meant it. Now, only a short while later, getting only one night with him seems like an impossibly cruel joke.

But I won't think about it. I'm here, he's here, right now we're both safe in the circle of each other's arms.

The sigh he heaves sounds resigned. When I look up at him, he's staring down at me with all the light extinguished in his eyes.

"You can't go now," I beg, terrified he's leaving.

"No, angel, I can't. That's the problem."

Without another word, he rolls me to my side and curls up behind me. Within minutes, he's sleeping deeply, as if he's been set free. I lie awake in the dark, listening to him breathe.

When the alarm goes off in the morning, A.J. is gone. On the pillow next to mine lies an origami sculpture. Not a bird this time.

A heart.

When I pick it up and cup it in my palms, it fans open like it's alive. It's blood red, the white copy paper saturated with ink from the fat red Sharpie sitting out on my desk. I lift it to my nose, inhaling the pungent, chemical smell.

I wonder how long it took him to make. I wonder if he watched me sleeping while he made it. I wonder what he thought about while he worked, folding, creating, his fingers deft and precise.

Outside my bedroom window a nightingale begins to sing, and my eyes fill with tears.

I can't remember ever feeling this happy.

Chapter 19

A.J. comes to me again the next night. And the next. And the next.

It's always the same. I leave the door unlocked, and lie in bed with the lights off, waiting. He comes very late, usually around midnight. He enters without a word, takes off his shirt and shoes, crawls into bed beside me. We talk for a long time, nestled back to front, limbs entangled. Each night his questions are more serious, more intimate, increasingly more difficult to answer.

Of what in my life am I most proud?

Of what am I most ashamed?

What's my most treasured memory?

For what am I most grateful?

If I only had twenty-four hours left to live, what would I do?

Sometimes I have to think long and hard before I answer. No one has ever asked me such things, and I'm not prone to introspection. But I never tell him anything but the entire, unvarnished truth. I don't hide. I don't lie. If I think an answer might not paint me in the best light, I tell him anyway. I want him to know me, warts and all.

I want him to see me, inside and out.

By the time he's exhausted his questions, my body is so high from his proximity, so strung out with the need to feel his hands and mouth, I'm nearly squirming in his arms. He always knows when I can't bear it a second longer. He laughs his husky laugh into my ear, then takes off all my clothes, and sates me.

There is no penetration. After the first night, he doesn't let me use my mouth on him again. It's like he got himself under control, decided on a format of Q&A followed by giving me a mind-blowing orgasm or three, and stuck to his plan.

Afterward, he sleeps like a coma patient, and I wake up alone.

It's wreaking havoc with my emotions.

Not to mention my face.

"Sweetheart, you look like shit. Are you coming down with something?"

Grace can always be counted on to pull no punches. We're at Lula's with Kat on a weekday night at eight o'clock, and I'm trying desperately not to fall asleep at the table and slump facedown into my steaming bowl of albondigas soup.

"Just tired," I mumble. I pick up my margarita and yawn into it before taking a swallow.

"Work going rough this week?" Concerned, Kat watches me as she munches on a tortilla chip. The ginormous diamond ring on her left hand nearly blinds me as it catches the light.

"Mmm. Sort of."

Both Kat and Grace narrow their eyes. Grace flatly says, "Chloe."

As I'm the worst secret keeper in the world, they've already got my number. I sigh, rubbing a fist into my left eye. "I can't talk about it. Not yet. I don't want to jinx it."

In slow motion, Kat lowers her half-eaten chip to the table. "Oh my God."

Grace asks, "What?"

I already know what Kat's going to say, but I'm too exhausted to get worked up about anything at this point. "She just figured out why I'm tired."

Grace raises her brows, looking back and forth between us.

Kat says, "You're sleeping with him."

Grace whoops in glee, pounding the table with her fist. "Yes! Finally! Is this why you haven't returned my calls for four days? You've been on a sex spree? Tell, tell, tell!"

Because the cat is clearly out of the bag, I don't bother to deny it. But it does need a little correcting. "Technically, yes, I'm sleeping with him. *Sleeping* being the operative word. Well, at least he is."

Grace eyes me. "That doesn't sound good."

I take a long pull of my drink, buying time. I look at my best friends, the two people who know me better than anyone else, who've spent countless hours in my company, with whom I've shared years of laughter and tears, been with during bitter breakups and many life milestones, and trust completely. In fact, I trust these women with my life.

And, if I'm guessing right, they don't know me as well as A.J. does after four nights.

That idea is seriously screwing with my head.

"Here's a little quiz for you, ladies: What would you guess, if asked, that I'm most proud of in my life?"

Kat blinks, frowning. "How does this relate to the topic at hand?"

"I have a point, trust me."

Always up for a challenge, Grace jumps right in. "Your business."

I shake my head. She immediately guesses again. "Your hair."

"Be serious."

"I am serious. Your hair is glorious. You could earn millions doing shampoo commercials. It's the only thing I'm jealous of you about. Well, I'm also pretty green over that Patek Phillipe your father bought you for your twenty-first birthday. It might be even better than your hair."

I sigh. "I knew I could count on you for some deep insights. Kat?"

Kat hesitates for a moment, sucking thoughtfully on the little red straw in her margarita. "Maybe your degree. I know how hard you worked to get it. I know how proud you were when you graduated. It was a huge accomplishment."

Slowly, I shake my head. "No. What I'm most proud of is my relationship with you two nitwits. You're both strong, intelligent, amazing women, who I admire tremendously, and you're the best, most solid thing in my life. I'd rather not know my own parents than not know you."

Stunned silence.

"Here's another one: Of what am I most ashamed?"

Grace quickly recovers. "That's easy. Cory McLean."

Cory McLean, who I'd conveniently suppressed the memory of until this moment, was a boyfriend I had in my freshman year of college. There was a drunken incident involving the hood of a convertible Porsche, an awkward striptease, and a cell phone camera. My father had to threaten legal action to have the video taken down from the web. It wasn't until my senior year guys stopped calling me "Coochie Carmichael."

"No. The thing I'm most ashamed of is the time I saw Jeff Douglas from my high school's football team kicking a homeless guy in the stomach behind the El Pollo Loco on Washington Boulevard, and I didn't stop him. Or tell anyone about it. The poor man was just lying there on the ground, getting beaten, and I didn't do anything. Because it was Jeff Douglas, Homecoming King, Jock of the Century, I just walked away. And I'll never forgive myself for that."

I look down at my soup. The tiny floating vegan meatballs seem as appetizing as clods of dirt.

"Sweetheart," says Grace, moved. "You never told us about that."

I look at her, then Kat. "I haven't thought about it in years. That's the way I've always lived my life: one thing after the next, set goals, achieve them, move on, don't think about anything sad or unpleasant. Shrug it off. Live in the here and now. But for the past four nights, A.J. has asked me questions I've never even asked myself, and I feel like . . . I'm getting to know myself better. Because of him."

Kat sits back in her chair, staring at me with understanding dawning over her face. Grace takes one look at her expression and her head snaps around like that girl from *The Exorcist* just before she spews green puke all over the room.

She gasps. "No. Abso-lutely-fucking-*no*!"

Kat nods. "Yep."

Grace covers her mouth with her hands. Her gray eyes look ready to pop from her head. From beneath her palms comes a muffled, horrified "You have feelings for him."

I can't deny it, so I take another swig of my drink.

"Jesus H. Christ on a crutch!" Grace shouts, jerking upright in her chair. The mother with her three young kids in the opposite booth shoots us a death glare, which everyone at our table ignores. "Chloe, for God's sake, I said have a fling, not fall in love! A.J. Edwards is NOT the guy you fall in love with! What the hell are you *thinking*?"

I look at her. My gaze is steady, as is my voice when I answer. "I'm thinking I underestimated him, and so has everyone else. I'm thinking he's pretty damn incredible. I'm thinking of putting my heart in his hands, and giving him a lot of rope to run with it, even though it scares me to death, because I'm thinking he'll be worth it. What I'm *not* thinking about is what's going to happen next." My voice drops. "Because what I've gotten from him the last few nights is enough to last me for the next fifty years."

Grace's mouth hangs open in horror like the guy in that Edvard Munch painting.

Kat knocks back the rest of her drink. "What about Eric?"

"I care about Eric. But I never felt this way when I was with him. I've realized he's not the one."

Grace says, "Please don't tell me you think A.J. is the one."

I seriously consider that before I answer. "I don't know yet what A.J. is. What I do know is that when I'm with him, I feel understood. And safe. And that's enough."

Kat says, "Last week you said he'd told you he'd never sleep with you. What changed?"

I stir my soup, take a bite. It's salty and delicious, and makes me think of A.J.'s taste. My lips turn up. "I told you, we're not having sex. Well, at least he's not. I'm having the most incredible orgasms of my life. He's doing a lot of sleeping. So basically, we're both getting exactly what we need."

Grace groans.

"Well, that's one mystery solved anyway."

Kat's sigh sounds resigned to the whole affair. I knew I could count on her. "What do you mean?"

"Nico said A.J.'s been acting strange lately."

I pause with another spoonful of soup halfway to my mouth. "Strange?"

She pins me with a look. "Yeah. Happy."

My heart swells. It gets a little harder to breathe.

"Not only that, he stopped smoking. Just quit cold turkey one day weeks ago. After that, he started writing all these songs, which according to Nico, are incredible. And . . ." She pauses, gazing at me meaningfully. "His hoochie mamas haven't been seen hanging around. In months."

I whisper, "Months?"

She shakes her head. "Apparently not since the day we came into your shop to talk about the wedding flowers."

"The day he left with the dishy brunette from the candle aisle, as I recall you saying," Grace points out.

"Which he made sure you saw, didn't he Lo? Almost as if he was making a point."

I think about Kat's question. In retrospect, it does seem possible. "So what do you think it all means?" My heart is in my throat as I wait for her to answer.

"I think," she says softly, "that you're not the only one in over your head."

Grace waves the waiter over. When he arrives, she rests a hand on his arm and looks at him in desperation. "Vodka. Straight. Make it a double. Get it here in less than two minutes and I'll tip you twenty bucks."

He sprints away, on the job. While she waits for his return, Grace props her elbows on the table and drops her head to her hands, moaning.

Inside my handbag, my cell phone rings. It's an unknown number.

"Hello?"

"You ran out on me the other day. And you're not answering my calls. We need to talk."

It's Eric. He sounds tense and unhappy. I close my eyes, already feeling defeated. I'm not looking forward to the conversation we need to have. "Yes, we do."

"I'm off in an hour. I'll come to your place."

He hangs up before I can say no, or suggest somewhere else. Feeling panicked, I look at the clock on my phone. Eight thirty. If Eric gets to my place by ten, I'll still have a few hours before A.J. shows up.

Unless he decides to come earlier.

Or Eric won't leave.

Kat asks, "Who was that?"

I slip the phone back in my purse. "Eric. He wants to talk. He's coming over to my apartment in an hour."

"Tonight? You're exhausted!"

"He didn't give me a chance to say no."

"Have you talked to him since the fitting?"

I shake my head.

"Well, I don't think you should be talking to him at your place, alone. Nico said he got a really weird vibe from Eric the other day when they talked outside before you left."

Remembering the look in Eric's eyes, how angry he was, a chill runs down my spine. "What kind of weird vibe?"

"Like a stabby vibe. Like he was ready to kill someone."

Into her hands, Grace mutters, "I told you."

I wave it off. "He's just upset. I'd feel the same way if the situation were reversed. We went from being happy one day to me calling him the wrong name and broken up the next without ever really talking about what happened."

The waiter arrives with Grace's drink. She sends him a smile that leaves him starry-eyed, and guzzles it. When she sets it back down on the table she looks straight at me and says, "You were never happy with him, Chloe. You were content. It's not the same thing."

I drop my gaze to the soup. Softly, I say, "I know. And it's only in the past few days I've really understood the difference."

Grace groans. "You are seriously *killing* me."

"Grace," says Kat sternly, "you warned me away from Nico at the beginning of our relationship, remember? And we turned out fine."

"Yes, but Nico doesn't have a mafia don's rap sheet and a harem of paid escorts that, if lined up, would circle the globe five times over."

Kat gives her a look. "Close enough."

"*And* he was crazy about you from day one. A.J. and Chloe hated each other on sight."

"I never hated him. I was just hurt by how much of a jerk he always was to me. And now I'm pretty sure he was doing that to keep me at arms' length." I finally raise my gaze and look at them. "To protect me."

Grace blinks. "Wait. You think all his assholeyness was because he was trying to protect you?"

I nod.

"From what?"

"From him."

There's a long silence as my friends process that. Finally, Grace says, "There's a hell of a lot you're not telling us."

"There's a lot I don't know."

Kat reaches across the table and takes my hand. "I know this might sound hypocritical coming from me after all I went through to be with Nico, but I'm saying it again: please be careful. I don't want to see you get hurt."

"That's the thing." I clear my throat, give her hand a squeeze, sit back in my chair. "I'm pretty sure I will. Especially since he flat out told me he'd hurt me. But I don't care. I still want him."

Grace's stare slices a hole through my head. "This is crazy. You're volunteering to get hurt? Do you hear yourself right now? You're too smart to sign up for that, Chloe!"

She's really pissed. Her face has flushed, her eyes glitter. I know it's because she loves me. And I know she'll be there for me at the tail end of whatever sad story I'm about to create for myself by falling for a man who's told me in no uncertain terms he's bad news.

"I love you guys," I say softly. "And I know you love me. So what I'm going to need from you is a soft place to fall if and when this thing with A.J. goes sideways. Because I can already tell it's going to hurt like hell."

Kat and Grace look at each other in silence while I finish the rest of my soup.

Chapter 20

When the knock comes on my front door just before ten, I'm ready. I've got the whole speech rehearsed.

What I'm not prepared for is the state Eric's in when he arrives.

He reeks of beer. His face is grim and unshaven. His eyes are bloodshot, and the look in them is anything but friendly. My nerves instantly slam into high alert.

Without a word, he pushes past me into the apartment. Alarmed, I watch as he paces circles around the living room. I close the door and go and stand with my arms crossed over my chest in the kitchen, watching him.

"Eric. What are you doing?"

"I know you're going to tell me it's over. I could tell by the tone of your voice on the phone." He laughs without humor. "I already knew anyway. I knew it was over the first time that piece of shit's name left your lips."

Hearing him call A.J. that makes me so angry I want to grab a plate from the cabinet and hurl it at his head. But that would be foolish, along with nonproductive. All I really want right now is for him to leave without making a scene. "I can see this isn't going to be a mature discussion. Why don't we just try not to say anything nasty, say our good-byes, and call it a night."

He stops pacing and looks at me with such burning anger, I take a step back, hand at my throat.

"You want a mature discussion, Chloe? Okay, how about this: break it off with him and get back together with me, or I'll make it my personal mission to ruin his life."

My blood turns to ice water. Stunned, I stare at him. "You don't mean that."

He says slowly, "Look at my face, Chloe."

I am, and it's scaring the hell out of me. Who is this man? I've never seen this side of Eric, and I have no idea how to handle him. I edge away from the counter, trying to put distance between us. "I told you before, I'm not together with him."

Eric moves closer, his gaze level, and so very dark. "You know what I used to love most about you, Chloe? You never lied. You weren't that kind of person. But you've changed, and I know what made you change. I know *who*."

"I think you need to leave now."

"Oh, is that what you think? Because *I* think you should get down on your knees and do something to convince me not to make his life a living hell." His hand drops to the fly of his trousers. A bitter little smile disfigures his mouth.

I'm so afraid I begin to shake. Though his tone is calm, the malice and madness glittering in his eyes make him look totally unhinged. My heart pounding, I walk slowly backward, heading toward the front door. "You're drunk. This isn't you, Eric. I know you—"

"This is what you've made me," he hisses, following as I retreat. "I *love* you, Chloe. We're good together. We fit. Until you decided to take a detour down whore alley, everything was perfect. I'm willing to forgive and forget, but you have to earn my trust back. And you're going to start by *getting down on your fucking knees* and begging me to forgive you."

He unzips his pants and pulls out his erection.

I don't know where it comes from, but the outrage that blasts through my veins is like electricity, sizzling hot and blazing, lighting me up from inside. I stand up straight, walk to the front door, yank it open, turn back to Eric and shout, "Get the hell out of my house!"

At that moment, my upstairs neighbor walks down the stairs. She's an older woman, single, recently divorced, the one who pounds on the wall if I'm too noisy. I've always thought she disliked me, and she takes the opportunity to prove it.

She takes one look at me standing in the doorway, and says, "You know, if you're going to keep having screaming orgasms every night at two a.m., you might want to buy the rest of the building some earplugs." She sends me an evil smile, then turns and continues on her way.

There's a split second before Eric reacts when I think it couldn't possibly get any worse. Then he lunges toward me, snarling, and proves me wrong.

He slams shut the door and wraps both hands around my neck. He pushes me against the wall and starts screaming. "You lying whore! You fucking bitch! You filthy little cunt, I'll kill you!"

Over and over, he bangs my head against the wall. He's breathing alcohol fumes into my face. His lips are peeled back over his teeth, his eyes are wild, and I'm convinced I'm going to die. The room gets fuzzy. I claw at his hands, desperate for air. I can't breathe.

Then I jerk my leg upward, hard, and knee Eric in the balls.

He cries out in agony and doubles over, staggering back. I fall to my knees, gasping and coughing, one hand on my burning throat, the other splayed on the floor, supporting my weight as I struggle to stay upright. Eyes watering, I crawl forward, reaching for the door handle, but Eric has recovered. He lunges at me again. He drags me to the floor, falls on top of me, and starts tearing at my clothes. When I fight him, he backhands me across the face. Pain explodes across my cheekbone.

His class ring. That'll leave a nasty mark. My brain is somehow removed from what's happening to my body.

Eric savagely rips open the front of my cardigan. Buttons pop off and clatter over the wood floor. He leans over me, panting, snarling obscenities, grabbing my breasts and squeezing them hard. My hands flail at his face, but he easily knocks them away.

And suddenly I'm floating above myself, looking down. The strangest sensation of calm sweeps over me, like I've flown into the eye of a hurricane, where everything is silent and still. My mind is clear, detached, and I can think.

I remember a newspaper article about my father that ran in the *Los Angeles Times* last summer, after he'd been hired to defend a famous basketball player from charges of domestic abuse. All charges were eventually dropped when my father unearthed the plot between the player's wife and her lover to try to cash in on the thirty-million-dollar contract the player had just signed. Subsequently, my father filed extortion, blackmail, and conspiracy charges against the wife.

The headline read, "Carmichael Goes for the Jugular."

I look at Eric's throat, pale and vulnerable above the open collar of his shirt.

Then I punch him in his Adam's apple.

He makes an awful gagging noise and clasps his hands around his neck. I get enough wiggle room to move, and shove him off me.

As he coughs and retches, I stagger to my feet, run to the kitchen, rip open the junk drawer, grab the bottle of pepper spray my mother gave me when I moved in, and run back over to Eric. I spray the crap out of him, all over his face and upper body.

He screams. Clawing at his eyes, howling and sputtering, he falls from his knees to his ass and starts rolling on the floor.

Panting, I stagger to the door. I have to get out of here. I can't think of anything else but *get out get out get out.* I run out of the apartment, leaving the door wide open. Eric's bellowing follows me out into the hall. I fall against the wall next to the elevator, banging my fist on the call button. Blood drips from my face onto my arm. There are splatters of my own blood all over my chest, my bra, the sleeves of my sweater. My throat is on fire; it's almost impossible to breathe. Badly shaking, I pull the sides of my torn sweater together over my chest, and start to cry.

When the elevator doors slide open, A.J. is standing inside.

He takes one look at me and makes a sound I've never heard a human make before, a guttural rumble of pure rage. Sobbing, I fall forward, collapsing into his open arms.

"Eric, it's Eric, he's in my apartment he went crazy I left him inside!"

"I've got you, baby."

I've got you. That makes me cry even harder.

One of the neighbors pops his head outside his apartment door. "What's all the screaming?" He sees me and gasps. "Oh my God. What's going on?"

A.J. lifts me into his arms. I cling to him, crying into his neck. He growls to the neighbor, "We need your couch."

There is no refusing, not if the neighbor wants to keep his head attached to his body, which he clearly understands. A.J. barges into my neighbor's apartment, sets me gently on the hideous, plaid, cat-hair-covered sofa, kisses me on the forehead, turns to the neighbor and snaps, "Call 911. Report an assault." He pauses for a moment. The look that comes into his eyes is murderous. "No. Report *two* assaults." He turns and strides out.

Moments later, there is more screaming from down the hall.

On the ambulance ride to the hospital, A.J. and I don't speak. So he can ride with me, I've told the paramedics he's my husband. He sits next to me, gripping my hand as I lie on the lumpy stretcher with tears silently rolling down my cheeks.

His knuckles are bloody. I find a perverse satisfaction in that.

In the ER, I'm taken straight in to see a bleary-eyed female doctor, although the waiting room is full. Apparently being covered in blood puts you to the head of the line. I haven't yet seen my face, and I don't want to; my cheek throbs so badly I feel it in my toes. I have a CT scan, which shows a hairline fracture of the zygomatic bone, then I get fourteen stitches to close the wound torn in my skin from Eric's ring. The doctor is concerned about the bruising around my neck; apparently swelling is a common side effect of trauma to the esophagus, and there's a risk my air passage will swell shut.

I'm admitted to the hospital, and kept overnight for observation. A.J. is by my side the entire time, bossing people around, grilling the doctor and intake staff, scaring the crap out of the poor nurses with his barked demands. He has a bizarre familiarity with medical terms, frequently sounding like a doctor himself. One more question to add to the queue, if he ever lets me ask.

I refuse the pain reliever the nurse tries to give me. I want to be totally lucid when I speak to the police, who've arrived and are waiting outside.

Then I tell A.J. to call my father.

"Holy mother of God."

Staring at me in white-faced shock, my father stands rigidly in the doorway of my room. Even at five o'clock in the morning, called to the hospital where his injured daughter is being treated after being brutally attacked, he's showered and clean-shaven, perfectly put together in a navy bespoke Brioni suit with coordinating tie and pocket square, looking every inch the wealthy, successful businessman he is.

Until I see him, I've gotten myself pretty well under control. The moment he steps in the room, however, I revert to a frightened five-year-old who needs her father to check on the strange noise she's heard underneath her bed.

My face screws up, and I start to cry. I whisper, "Daddy."

Moving faster than I've seen him move in years, he runs to my bedside and takes me in his arms. He silently rocks me, letting me cry all over his beautiful custom lapel.

When I'm a little better, I withdraw, leaning back against the pillow. He hands me his handkerchief. I blow my nose into it, conscious that I've just ruined a two-hundred-dollar square of Hermès silk, yet taking comfort in the knowledge that my father won't care one bit.

The third degree begins.

"How do you feel? How are they treating you? Is the doctor competent? I've called Dr. Mendelsohn; he'll be here in twenty minutes."

Dr. Mendelsohn is my family's personal doctor, kept on retainer like an attorney for everything from annual checkups to emergency treatment. My mother is a career hypochondriac and my father can't tolerate waiting for anything so mundane as an office appointment;

hence the ridiculous luxury of a twenty-first-century house-call physician, who will travel to any location in the world to tend to his employers at the drop of a hat.

Sometimes my parents are mortifying. Right now, I'm so grateful for them I could die.

"They're taking good care of me. I feel okay. My throat hurts. I think my face looks worse than it is."

My father's mouth tightens. Clearly he thinks my face looks pretty bad. "Have they fed you?"

"I got the regulation gruel half an hour ago. I'm expecting sepsis to set in any minute."

My lame attempt at humor takes the edge off the killer ferocity in his eyes. Now he looks merely furious.

"How long have you been here?"

"Since about eleven last night."

"And what tests have they done?"

I tell him about all the tests, and the results. He nods, grimly satisfied. "When do they expect to release you?"

"They haven't said yet. There was some concern about my throat closing because of swelling, but so far that hasn't happened . . ."

Murder has renewed in my father's eyes. I squeeze his hand.

"I'm okay, Dad. It could've been a lot worse; I got away." I try to be lighthearted. "Plus, I kneed Eric in the balls and got to use Mom's pepper spray on his sorry ass, so it wasn't a total loss."

We fall quiet. Because I know my father so well, I see he's struggling with guilt over our last meeting, the awful dinner when he asked when Eric and I were going to get married. "This fine young man," he called him. I wonder now if he'll ever forgive himself for that miscalculation. Usually he's even better than Grace at pegging people.

This time it's Grace who's won that call.

"What did you tell Mom?" I only ask because I know he didn't tell her the truth. At least not the whole truth. He makes his living defending criminals, after all; the truth can be a very inconvenient roadblock to keeping people out of prison.

"I told her I was needed at work." The ghost of a smile lifts his lips. "And don't give me that look. I *was* needed. By my baby girl." He strokes a hand over my hair.

Looking at each other, we share a moment of profound silence. I can see he's carefully weighing what he'll say next.

Finally, his voice quiet, he asks, "Who was the man who called me?"

"His name is A.J. He's here; he just went to go get some food. He's been with me all night. He's a friend of mine." My face reddens. I drop my gaze to my hands, and pick at the heartbeat monitor attached to my forefinger. "He's actually more than a friend. We're . . . close."

"I see."

Oh God, the weight of that. The assumptions, which I know are right. My father has just figured out the whole sordid picture, without having to hear more than a few words. My embarrassment is excruciating.

But my wonderful father bypasses any awkward conversation about the identity of the man who usurped his hoped-for son-in-law's position in his daughter's bed, and switches into professional-lawyer mode. "All right. Chloe, I need you to tell me everything that happened. Start at the beginning."

I do. I also tell him about my last few encounters with Eric, and his increasingly erratic behavior. When I'm finished, my father squeezes my hand so tightly I think he might be cutting off the circulation to my fingers. His eyes are bright and diamond hard.

"I'd like to kill that son of a bitch. I'd like to rip his heart from his chest with my bare goddamn hands. I'd like to burn him alive.

Then I'd like to slice both his Achilles tendons, dump him in the lion cage at the zoo, and throw knives at his head while they tear out his barbequed guts."

I'm shocked. I've never heard my father curse, or utter a speech so choked with hatred. I didn't know he was capable of such violent emotion.

He sees the expression on my face, leans forward and takes my face in his cupped hands.

"I wasn't always Thomas Carmichael, upstanding businessman, respectable, tax-paying citizen. Before I met your mother and turned my life around, I was Tommy Two-Time, repeat offender, biggest, baddest thug in Southie. All the other gang leaders in Boston would shit golden bricks when they heard my name. And if anyone was stupid enough to lay a finger on my family or friends, they'd lose that finger . . . and the rest of their arm."

My lower jaw comes unhinged, and hangs uselessly on my chest. After a moment I compose myself enough to say, "Gang leader? You're joking! Mom never would have married a thug!"

He kisses my cheek. "Of course not. I had to clean up my act before she'd even consider dating me."

I sputter, "B-but you met at a country club! Playing golf!"

My father smiles. It's a half smile, crooked and cunning. In it I see a flash of the old Tommy Two-Time, the thug from Southie who wouldn't know Brioni from a bagel.

"*She* was playing golf. I was inches away from getting fired from my job as snack bar attendant for stealing beer and candy bars. When I first laid eyes on her, I thought I'd been struck by lightning. I'd never seen a woman so beautiful, so elegant. I jumped over the counter, walked right up to her, and asked her out. She put her nose in the air, looked me up and down, and said, 'Get a haircut and a law degree, and I'll consider it.' So what do you think I did?"

Awed, I murmur, "You got a haircut and a law degree."

He nods, releases my face and sits back, adjusting his cufflinks. "Nothing gets in the way of what I want. You're like me that way. We're both fighters. Single-minded when we set a goal. Though thank God you got your mother's looks."

I have to laugh. It hurts my throat, and I cough. My father pours me a glass of water from the plastic pitcher on the table beside my bed, and I drink it, my brain spinning with this new information.

"How come I never heard that story before?"

"Because one condition your grandmother had for allowing me to marry her daughter was that my sordid past be buried under a nice, thick layer of respectability. So it was." He shrugs. "This was before the internet. People could still reinvent themselves back then."

I can't wait to grill my mother about this. All these years of judging my boyfriends and she married a gangster. Unbelievable.

My father turns brisk. "All right. Are you ready to give your statement to the police?"

Though I'm dreading rehashing it once again, it has to be done. I nod, paling a little.

"I'll be right here with you. Just tell them what happened, exactly how you told me." He pauses. A dark note creeps into his voice. "And don't let their attitude affect you."

"What do you mean?"

"They're LAPD, Chloe. They're his coworkers."

"So? Why should that make a difference?"

"There's a code of loyalty among police. It's a brotherhood, not unlike a gang, if truth be told. They have each other's backs. In cases of domestic violence, many times the responding officers won't report the attack if the perpetrator is another officer. They know he can be suspended, have his firearm taken away so he's forced to be reassigned to a desk job, even lose his job altogether. It's considered a relationship problem, a social worker problem, not real police work. I've heard policemen try to convince wives and girlfriends who've been beaten bloody that their man is just under a lot of stress at work."

I feel sick. "That's awful!"

He nods. "There are also cases, especially in custody battles, where women will falsely accuse their husbands of battery or child abuse in order to get the children taken away from them. Every officer has heard his share of those stories. So what I'm saying is don't expect to be believed. On the plus side, I'm here, and they all know who I am, so while they might not believe your story, they also won't be stupid enough to say it out loud. And I'll make sure the report is filed with the chief, and followed up on."

He rises from the bed, straightening his tie, squaring his shoulders. His voice gets low and rough. "And we're getting a restraining order. That son of a bitch is going to stay far away from you, or go to jail."

As I hide my shaking hands beneath the blanket, my father calls the officers into the room.

Chapter 21

It's not anywhere near as bad as my father has warned. For one thing, one of the two officers is a woman, an attractive young Latina who listens to me seriously, nodding, taking copious notes. For another, the male officer looks like he's been on the job all of two weeks.

I suppose he hasn't had enough time to be properly indoctrinated into the "brotherhood."

The entire interview takes about thirty minutes. At the end of it, the female officer, Garcia, her badge reads, casually mentions they weren't able to get a statement from Eric yet, who, to my horror, is somewhere in the same hospital.

"Why not?" asks my father.

Officer Lawrence, the young male, says, "Because he just got out of surgery."

My father raises his brows. "Surgery?"

"Yep. A dislocated kneecap and shattered tibia, a broken arm, a ruptured spleen . . ." He consults his notepad. "Three broken ribs, some pretty serious internal bleeding that took a long time to get under control, and a fractured jaw." He looks up. "Had to have it wired shut. He'll be sucking all his meals through a straw for at least a month."

A grim smile spreads over my father's face.

Officer Garcia says, "We'd like to talk to your friend, Ms. Carmichael. The man who accompanied you to the hospital? We need to get his statement also."

Fear slices through me like an arctic wind. If A.J. has done that much damage to Eric, will he be facing prosecution? Eric told me about A.J.'s prior record, I know all about the three-strikes law, and I'm pretty sure what he's done will be considered aggravated assault. To a *police officer*, no less . . .

Desperate, I look at my father.

Without missing a beat, he says, "He's my client. I'll need to be present when his statement is taken."

The two officers share a glance. Officer Lawrence says, "Of course. Is he here?"

From the doorway, a voice says, "He's right here."

Everyone turns. The officers share another look, but I'm staring at my father, holding my breath.

To anyone who hasn't been in A.J.'s presence before, he can be overwhelming. His sheer size, combined with his crackling intensity, tends to frighten people. The way he glares at you from under his lowered brows doesn't help.

And there's the matter of the tattoos.

But my father merely gazes at him with a look of intense scrutiny. There's no judgment, just a narrow-eyed, fierce assessment, a collecting of all the visual facts. He and A.J. stare at each other for what feels like a very long time.

Then my father relaxes slightly and does this thing with his head, a jerky upward tilt of his chin I've never seen him make before.

It looks suspiciously like a gangster greeting and a wordless acceptance, all in one.

Or maybe I'm making it up. I probably have a head injury in addition to everything else.

Officer Garcia asks, "Mister . . . ?"

"Edwards." A.J. steps into the room. When the male officer takes an involuntary step back, I try not to smile.

"Mr. Edwards. We'd like to speak to you about the incident last night. Your attorney has requested he be present."

A.J. looks at my father, then at me, then at the officers. He nods.

"Why don't we go to the commissary and let Ms. Carmichael rest—"

"That won't be necessary." My father interrupts Officer Lawrence with a pointed look. I'm not sure what's going on, until he adds, "I'm sure Mr. Edwards is comfortable giving his statement right here."

Then I get it. The police are trying to separate us, to see if our statements match. Or at least my father thinks that's what's happening. If it's true, the officers make no indication one way or another. They motion for A.J. to take a seat in one of the uncomfortable-looking plastic chairs by the window, but he opts to stand, announcing this fact by staying put and crossing his massive arms over his chest.

It's clear from his stance and his glower that he's not a big fan of the police.

After ten minutes of questioning, during which I sink farther and farther into the bed, soreness and a bone-deep fatigue setting in to every crevice of my body, Officer Lawrence asks A.J., "And after you left Ms. Carmichael with the neighbor and instructed him to notify 911, what happened?"

My eyelids, which had been drifting shut, snap wide open. My heart begins to pound.

This is the part where they arrest A.J. for aggravated assault on a police officer.

Without taking his unflinching gaze from Officer Lawrence, A.J. says, "Then I readjusted his expectations of living a long, pain-free life."

Officer Lawrence, clearly not the brightest bulb, asks, "The neighbor?"

"No. The piece of scum who beat my girl."

Officer Garcia sends me a sympathetic, over-the-shoulder glance. I breathe a tiny bit easier, seeing that look, but then rewind to the part where A.J. called me his girl, and suffer a minor heart attack.

Meanwhile, my father watches A.J. like a hawk tracking a meal. He looks more than a little scary.

"So just to be clear, you're saying you beat him up. You're the person who inflicted the physical damage to Officer Cox that necessitated his emergency surgery."

Before A.J. can answer the question my father interjects, "No one said anything of the sort. Additionally, not only was Officer Cox off duty at the time of the incident, and in plain clothes, there's no evidence my client knew he was a police officer."

Officer Garcia consults her notes. "According to Ms. Carmichael, Officer Cox was incapacitated when she left the apartment, due to her copious application of pepper spray to his face." She looks at A.J. "Is that correct?"

"Incapacitated? No. He was still able to form a sentence. He told me to go fuck myself. After *that*, he was incapacitated."

My father sighs. "All right. We're done here. Officers, thank you very much. If you have any further questions, here's my card." He produces two business cards from his breast pocket, hands them over, and opens his palm toward the door, a clear indication of the direction they should head.

Officer Lawrence turns and walks out like an obedient child. Officer Garcia, however, lingers behind. Her sharp brown eyes assess the three of us, not unkindly, but not in a friendly way, either. I get the sense she's trying to decide whether or not to say something she might regret.

"When he wakes, Officer Cox may very well want to press charges."

My father calmly says, "That stupid fuck is going to be facing so many charges of his own, he won't have time to think about anything else."

Garcia slowly nods, not rankled in the least by hearing my father's unflattering description of her coworker. She looks at A.J. "Mr. Edwards, I'd like a word with your attorney."

A.J. shoots a glance to my father, whose face reflects nothing, not a hint of surprise or worry.

The former Tommy Two-Time says with perfect composure and civilized sincerity, "Of course, Officer Garcia. Anything to assist our fine police department."

A muscle in A.J.'s jaw flexes. For a terrifying moment, I think he's going to snap, but then I see the fleeting depression in his cheek, a stray smile immediately suppressed, and I realize my father is being sarcastic, A.J. knows it, and Officer Garcia doesn't.

Two peas in a pod, I think, too exhausted and emotionally overwrought to decide how that makes me feel.

With a final, piercing glance at me, A.J. leaves the room.

As soon as he clears the threshold, Officer Garcia says quietly to my father, "When you present the charges to the chief, make sure to ask about any recent disciplinary action Officer Cox has been subject to."

"Meaning?"

My father is very, very interested in what she's saying, but he's playing it cool.

"Meaning the chief might find it extremely embarrassing if it were to be made public that he didn't act sooner on an officer who's had multiple Code of Ethics violations, along with failing a recent alcohol test." Her mouth pinches. "That last one alone should have gotten him fired on the spot."

Almost indifferently, my father asks, "Why didn't it?"

Officer Garcia's pinched mouth twists with a wry, knowing smile. "Because the chief is third-generation U of A, Officer Cox was one of the best running backs the university ever had, and, unlike any of the female officers on the force, they both share a small, brainless organ responsible for most of their decision-making. At least, that's my humble, *unofficial* opinion."

My father looks at her in a whole new light. Respect creeps into his eyes. "Not that you ever shared it, of course."

Her look is blistering. "Of course. And if anyone suggests otherwise, he might get a traffic ticket every week for the rest of his life."

My father holds up his hands. "Believe me, Officer Garcia, I long ago abandoned thinking with my small, brainless organ."

Her smile returns. "I've heard that about you." She glances at me, and her face softens. "Good luck. And try a little Arnica ointment for the bruising on your face and neck. In my experience, it helps."

In my experience. Those words tell me all I need to know about why Officer Garcia felt compelled to share the information about Eric. God only knows what caused that small, irregular scar on her chin.

I say, "Thank you."

She nods, then she's gone.

My father stares after her in unabashed admiration. "Jesus. If we had ten more of her on the force, crime would be eradicated in weeks."

A.J. comes back the moment she's left. He walks straight to my bedside and takes my hand, gently threading his fingers through mine. We look at each other for a moment, then he turns to my father, who's watching us from the other side of the room. In a low voice, A.J. says, "The only reason I didn't kill him is because I knew Chloe wouldn't want me to."

My father seems to take great satisfaction in that statement, because his grim, throw-the-bastard-to-the-lions smile returns. "We haven't had the pleasure of being formally introduced." He crosses the room slowly, holding out his hand. "I'm Chloe's father, Thomas. Call me Tom."

They shake hands. A.J. says solemnly, "Nice to meet you, Tom. Normally I can't stand lawyers because they're such money-grubbing fucks, but your daughter loves and admires you, so you must be all right."

I close my eyes. If anyone had tried to tell me this would be the first conversation between A.J. and my father—and under these particular circumstances—I would have laughed until I fell over.

Or maybe I would have cried.

Either way, it's completely out of the realm of what my brain can presently handle, so I simply lie there like a bruised zucchini, waiting for whatever comes next.

It turns out to be an amused snort from my father. "I *am* a money-grubbing fuck, but only because I want the best for my family." He pauses. When he speaks again, his tone is as lethal and cold as the sharpened edge of a knife. "There's nothing more important to me than them."

I open my eyes to see A.J. slowly nodding. As if something has been agreed upon, my father nods back. An unspoken understanding has just occurred between these two men, and I faintly grasp that my father may have just accepted A.J. as a new fixture in our family, while simultaneously threatening his life.

I feel like I'm in some kind of Tarantino remake of *The Godfather*.

My father releases A.J.'s hand and turns his attention to me. "You shouldn't go back to your apartment."

"Agreed."

My father continues as if A.J. hasn't just spoken. "You'll come home with me—"

"No." My voice is firm enough to give my father pause.

"All right. I'll book you a suite at the Four Seasons—"

"No."

My father chews on the inside of his cheek like he does when he's frustrated, but trying not to show it. "Fine, the L'Ermitage, then. It's small and very private—"

"I'm not staying at a hotel, Dad."

He bristles. "You're not going back to your apartment!"

"I can stay with Grace for a few days—"

"It might take more than a few days to get the restraining order, Chloe Anne, and I'm not taking any chances with your safety! You'll stay with your mother and me, or at a hotel. Those are your choices."

"There's another alternative."

Startled by the interruption, my father and I look at A.J. He's talking to both of us, but he's only looking at me. And his eyes . . . lord, his eyes are so deep and dark there's no end to them.

"Which is?" my father prompts.

"Chloe can stay with me."

The room fades to black. My father disappears. There's only me and A.J., our locked eyes, my heart drumming a crazy, improv beat. I whisper, "Yes, please."

My father's looking back and forth between us, but I can't tear my gaze from A.J.'s. Even if I wanted to, I can't.

Because everything I never knew I needed is right there, staring back at me.

My father says, "Eric or one of his buddies on the force can easily find out where you live."

"No they can't. Property title and all the utilities are in a trust, which doesn't have my name on it. The place is well off the beaten path. And only three people other than me know the address." As he gazes down at me, a smile lifts A.J.'s lips. "Four people."

When my father hesitates, my heart soars. This is a possibility. This could happen. I could be leaving this sour-smelling, antiseptic hospital bed for another one, a dangerous and thrilling one, hidden away in a candlelit room in an abandoned hotel high in the hills. The heartbeat monitor next to my bed goes crazy.

Without looking away from me, A.J. reaches over and hits an unmarked button on the side of the little green box, shutting off the sound. He says, "I'm totally off the grid, Tom. The safest place she can be is with me." He finally breaks our locked gazes to look at my father. "And if somehow the impossible happened and that bastard did find out where I live and showed up there . . . he'd never be seen again."

The total conviction in A.J.'s voice, the bald, unapologetic willingness to kill to protect me, is what finally seals the deal. Satisfied, Tommy Two-Time nods. When he looks back at me, the gangster has vanished and my loving father has returned, the cagey glint already erased from his eyes.

"You're to call me every day, Chloe Anne. No exceptions."

Pound, pound, *thud*, goes my heart. "I will."

"And if anything out of the ordinary happens—you see a strange car lingering around, the electric guy shows up for an unscheduled line repair, you hear some weird clicks on your phone—you tell me right away. Eric might be out of commission for a few weeks, but his buddies aren't. There are bound to be at least a few of them who'll want revenge on his behalf. Cops don't take it well when one of their own gets his ass handed to him on a platter."

I swallow, unable to answer because fear has flash-frozen my tongue. This is a possibility I've never considered. Will I be living with a dark cloud of paranoia over my head from now on, looking over my shoulder, suspicious of every stranger on the street?

"Don't worry." There's an edge to A.J.'s voice. "I've got a few tricks of my own up my sleeves. Anyone who gets some dumb ideas about payback will get the surprise of his fucking life."

I can tell my father is liking A.J. more and more with every word that comes out of his mouth. This entire incident is so bizarre I think there's a strong possibility I'm hallucinating it all, doped up and dreaming.

Into the room bustles Dr. Mendelsohn, clipboard in hand. He's sixtyish, bespectacled, bald as a cue ball, and scowling. "Thomas, good to see you. Chloe, my God, your face! Did they get Dr. Frankenstein to sew you up? Christ, these corporate surgeons are *butchers*."

Not too alarmed because Dr. Mendelsohn is as neurotic as my mother when it comes to matters of health, I merely shake my head. Then he notices A.J. standing there and does a double take that is cartoonish in its exaggeration. Brows raised, he looks back at my father.

Who snaps, "Just get to work, Mendelsohn! I don't pay you five hundred K a year to stand around gawking."

An hour later, reexamined and judged stable enough to leave, I'm released from the hospital into A.J.'s care.

In the rental car A.J. picked up while Dr. Mendelsohn examined me, I sit huddled in the passenger seat, blinking into the brilliant morning light. I'm swimming in A.J.'s hoodie, wrapped in his scent. My cardigan was destroyed in my fight with Eric, and since I didn't have any other clothes at the hospital, A.J. handed over his hoodie without a word when it was time for me to get dressed.

Luckily he'd been wearing a leather jacket over it, so he has something to leave the hospital in, too.

I'm trying not to think about the fact that his chest is bare beneath the leather. Honestly, I'm trying not to think about much at all, because if I do, my head will probably explode.

I've seen my face—glimpsed in the bathroom mirror as I dressed—and it's not pretty. My eye is swollen, livid purple-and-black bruises have blossomed across my cheek, jaw, and temple, and Dr. Mendelsohn was onto something when he asked if Frankenstein did the stitches in my cheek. They're black, irregular in size, snaking a few inches down the crest of my cheekbone. My father promised he'd schedule a consultation with a plastic surgeon, but I can't think about anything past this moment.

I don't dare.

We stop at the rusted chain-link fence bisecting the dirt road that leads to A.J.'s place. He gets out, unlocks it, and pushes one side open. He returns and drives past the gate, then gets out again and locks it behind us.

I notice the hole on the left side of the fence has been repaired. The glittering coil of barbed wire that tops it is new, too. I wonder if he had the fence fixed the day after I showed up unannounced here, but decide not to ask. There's only so much reality I can take right now.

A.J. parks the rental car behind the hotel, and for a moment I forget everything.

Drifts of brown leaves decorate the cracked bottom of a cavernous, empty swimming pool. Weeds have broken through the faded tiles of two enormous mosaic fountains that flank it. An incredible, thick arbor of waving purple wisteria decorates the crumbling remains of the marble colonnade that runs the length of the back of the property, curving around in a huge semicircle from the east and west ends of the building to enclose the pool and formal gardens, which are now nothing but a tangle of native shrubs and wild roses.

At the far side of the pool are clustered elaborate, old-fashioned ironwork tables and chairs partially consumed by creeping vines. Toppled statues, green with moss, are being reclaimed by the land. A family of deer munches on tender shoots of grass in a patch of dappled sunlight, oblivious to our presence.

In spite of the hotel's gentle ruin and its obvious abandonment, I don't find it as creepy as I did when I first came. Now I can see that into everything is imbued a sense of forlorn, forgotten magic, as if lonely wood fairies inhabit the wild gardens and empty rooms, just waiting for someone to invite them out to play.

This place, I think. *This place is enchanted.*

A.J. catches me staring. He looks around, following my gaze. "I bought it because it looks how I feel."

I try to decipher his expression, the hollow tone in his voice. "Alone?"

He shakes his head. "Corroded. Decayed."

My heart twinges. I reach out and take his hand. At my touch, he turns to me, startled. "It's not corroded. It's beautiful. It's bewitched."

He looks at me a long, silent moment. "Yes. Bewitched," he agrees in a murmur, and I don't think he's talking about his hotel. I flush and look down at our entwined fingers.

He clears his throat. "I'll stop by your place and get some clothes for you later. And anything else you need. Just make me a list. Right now you need to rest."

"I need to call the girls. Let Grace and Kat know—"

"Already done. I told them you're staying with me, and that you'll call them every day. And I called your shop, too. They're not expecting you back for a week."

His voice is rough. When I look up at him, he's gazing at me with hooded eyes. "A week?" I repeat.

He nods.

A week. Alone with A.J. for a week. I think about it, considering what needs to get done at work, swiftly calculating if I can take that much time off. I've *never* taken that much time off.

But the temptation to be with him is too great. Finally I just nod, because the fatigue is really starting to hit me and I can barely think anymore. I've been up all night, I'm sore as hell, and I look like I lost a twelve-round heavyweight fight.

But I didn't; I won. I got away. It could have been so much worse, and I know I'm lucky. As adrenaline from the memory of what happened floods my veins, my hands start to shake. I still can't believe it. How could Eric have done that to me? How could I have judged him so poorly? How can I ever trust myself to make a good decision again?

"Hey."

I look up to find A.J. staring at me with fire in his amber eyes. He takes my chin in his hand. "Don't go there. It's not your fault. You didn't do anything wrong."

"Grace tried to warn me. I didn't listen."

His fingers tighten on my chin. "You did not. Do anything. Wrong."

His tone makes it clear he's not going to let it go until I agree with him. I nod, until I remember that Grace has also warned me against A.J., and I'm miserable all over again. I put my face into my hands.

A.J. is out of the car and opening my door so fast my head spins. He lifts me into his arms, and kicks the door shut behind him. He kisses the top of my head. "All right, Princess. You're getting punchy on me. Time for you to go to sleep."

I wind my arms around his neck as he strides toward the back doors of the hotel. He leans down so I can turn the knob to open the door, then straightens and shoulders his way past it, careful not to jostle me or knock my head against the doorjamb. I think we're going to take an elevator, but A.J. carries me in his arms all the way up a back staircase to the second floor. He doesn't even break a sweat.

I rest my head against his shoulder as he ambles down the long corridor toward his room. "This is very impressive. You must work out with really heavy weights."

"Baby, you're the lightest weight I've ever carried."

This man speaks in riddles. He *is* a riddle. He says one thing, and means another. He wants one thing, and allows himself another. There's so much light in him, yet he is so very dark.

And I'm falling for him. I know it. I feel it. I want it, yet because I know there will be no happily-ever-after to this fairytale, I don't. If I allow myself to fall in love with him, I no longer think it will merely hurt, as I told Grace and Kat. I think it will be much worse than that. I think the fall might break me.

I think A.J. might have been right about this all along.

Still, I don't ask him to stop. I don't ask him to turn back around and drive me to my parents' house, or to a hotel. I allow him to cradle me in his arms, take me into his room, and lay me gently down on the mattress on the floor that he calls a bed. I stare up at him with wide eyes, unsure of what to do next.

Without another word, he takes off my shoes. He tucks a blanket around me, fluffs the pillow under my head. He straightens, goes into the little kitchenette adjacent to the main room, makes me a cup of herbal tea with honey, then watches me intently as I drink, propped up on my elbow. When I'm finished, he whistles. From down the hall I hear the sound of little toenails tearing against carpet.

Bella noses her way past the door, wriggling and barking happily when she sees A.J.

"C'mon, baby. Come help Chloe get better." He kneels, hands outstretched. Bella runs to him with her adorable, awkward, three-legged gait. He hugs and kisses her, then sets her beside me, gently encouraging her with pets and murmurs to snuggle up against me. Reluctantly, she does.

Her eyes are the most amazing liquid brown. She's a little afraid of me, but because A.J. has told her it's okay, she lets me stroke her head, pet her soft, warm body. As a feeling of peacefulness begins to replace the anxiety, I yawn, my eyes drooping. Bella licks my chin.

"I don't have enough food here. I need to make a run to the store—"

"Not yet!" My lids fly open. I'm panicked at the thought of him leaving. "Please don't leave me yet. I don't think I can be alone right now."

A.J. kneels next to the mattress. He strokes a hand over my hair. He murmurs, "You'll never be alone again, Chloe, not if you don't want to be. Okay?" Then he looks at me, really looks at me, letting me see the emotion in his eyes.

I hear what he's saying, what he's asking, and my vision gets blurry. All of my energy goes into trying not to ugly cry. "Okay."

A.J. leans over and kisses me. It's tender and beautiful, the softest, sweetest kiss I've ever had. When he pulls away, I have to hide my face in the pillow so he doesn't see my tears.

He stands and goes into the kitchenette again. I think he's giving me my space. Or maybe he needs space of his own. Because what's happening between us is huge, and it's happening fast.

I blow out a breath, snuggle closer to Bella, and shove all the worry away. I know I can worry as much as I want to when I wake up. Right now, I'm exhausted. I need an escape from the Category 5 hurricane howling inside my mind.

Within minutes, I'm asleep.

When I open my eyes again, it's early evening. The sun has set behind the hills, and the room is full of soft shadows. An opera plays low on the stereo. Warm pools of flickering light dance around the clusters of lit pillar candles gathered on the windowsills, grouped around the floor. Bella is gone.

I'm not wearing a watch and there's no clock in the room, so I can't tell the exact time, but judging by the light, I'd guess it's maybe six o'clock. I've slept the entire day. My throat is raw and scratchy. My head is pounding. I need to use the toilet.

"A.J.?"

No answer. I stand, groaning at the stiffness in my muscles, and stretch. My cheek feels hot and tight around the stitches; I should ice it. I move slowly from the bed to the kitchenette, hoping to find A.J. hiding in some corner.

He isn't there.

I try not to freak out, figuring he's probably taking Bella for a pee or something. I find ice in the freezer, wrap it in a paper towel, and press it to my face. Then I hear a low sound from the bathroom. I cock my head, frowning.

The faint sound comes again.

The skin on the back of my neck tingling, I lower the ice and move toward the closed bathroom door. I stand there a moment, listening.

"A.J.? Are you all right?"

Again, no answer. But my intuition is screaming that something is wrong, so I knock lightly, calling his name again.

"I'm fine."

In his voice I hear an unrecognizable emotion that makes my skin crawl. With my heart in my throat, I say, "I'm coming in." I don't give him much time before I open the door.

And there he stands at the bathroom sink, in nothing but faded jeans. He's staring at himself in the mirror.

"Are you okay? What's wrong?"

He just keeps staring at himself, as if he can't tear his eyes away from his reflection. "I don't recognize him."

He's referring to the man looking back at him in the glass. I get a sick feeling in my stomach. "I don't understand what you mean."

"Look at him. Look at his eyes, Chloe."

Now I'm really scared. What the hell is happening? Just when I'm about to ask, A.J. says wonderingly, "They're happy." He turns slowly from the mirror and looks at me. "My eyes are *happy*."

And they are. They're shining so bright, it's like he's lit up from inside.

He moves slowly away from the sink as if in a dream. He takes my face in his hands, gazing down at me in stunned disbelief. "I know it's wrong . . . that I should feel . . . when you've been hurt, you're so hurt, but just having you here with me, having you sleeping in the other room . . . I was in the kitchen and this feeling came over me, and it scared me so much because I didn't know what it was, and when I went into the bathroom and saw myself I realized . . . it's happiness. I think it is, I mean. I don't really remember what it feels like."

I drop the ice and wrap my arms around his waist, rising up on my toes. I kiss him softly on the mouth. "Welcome back to the human race, Prince Charming. We've missed you here."

A smile spreads over his face. It's heartbreakingly beautiful. "Angel," he whispers. And then his lips find mine.

The kiss starts out soft, but within seconds it turns violently passionate. We're desperately hungry for each other, clinging and voracious. His teeth draw blood as they press into my lower lip. When I make a small sound in my throat, he pulls back and sees the smear of red on my mouth. He tenses, his expression pained.

"Fuck! I'm so sorry—"

"Don't be. That's the best pain I've ever felt."

He's appalled, but also turned on, and can't decide whether to smile or frown. So I decide for him. I reach between his legs and grasp the throbbing bulge in his jeans.

He groans. "No. You're hurt."

"Shut up." I stroke him, ignoring his protests. When he doesn't stop me, I reach for his zipper.

In the same way he gutted me with humiliation the night in my bedroom, he grasps my wrists and commands, "Stop."

His face is flushed. His eyes are hot. I know he doesn't want me to stop.

"We've already been through this, A.J."

His eyes briefly close. "I mean, not like this. Not when you're hurt. Not now."

In spite of what seems like inevitable forward momentum leading to us finally consummating our relationship to become true lovers in every sense of the word, I suffer a moment of hideous insecurity. "But you do want to?"

He releases my wrists to once again cup my face. He strokes his thumbs over my heated cheeks, carefully skirting the area with the stitches. He breathes, "Sweet angel, I've wanted you since the first time I heard you sing."

That stops me dead. "Um . . . what?"

He wraps his arms around me, and rests his forehead on my shoulder. His heart thumps a steady beat against my breasts.

"I heard you singing to yourself one day. Nine months ago, to be exact. The day Nico and I first came into your shop to get flowers for Kat. I'll never forget it, no matter how long I live."

He turns his face to my neck. I hold my breath, sensing that what he's about to tell me might explain everything. Or at least shed some light on the mystery that is Alex James Edwards.

"I came inside the shop first. Nico was still talking to Barney in the car, but I'd been working in the studio all day and couldn't stand another second of being cooped up. And as soon as I opened the door and stepped inside, I heard your voice. I didn't know it was you, but I heard this woman singing to herself somewhere just out of sight. I thought I would die right there, next to the rack of Hallmark cards, from sheer bliss."

When he looks at me his eyes are endless, full of what I can only describe as love. "Your voice, Chloe. The colors of your voice are like . . . fucking . . . *heaven.*" He starts to sing the lyrics of a Journey song, one I instantly recognize.

"'Don't Stop Believin',"' I say, stunned. "It's one of my favorite songs."

He laughs, but it's choked with emotion. "You and your goddamn eighties rock. That's what you were singing. You were hitting all the high notes, too, all the hard ones, without missing a beat. And it was like the Fourth of July and a Vegas laser show and the northern lights, all rolled into one. I was blinded. Frozen. I couldn't move. I'd never heard or seen anything so beautiful. No occlusions or breaks, no cracks or wobbles, just pure, totally effortless perfection, surrounding me on every side, raining over me like a shower of precious jewels."

All of a sudden, I'm crying. Tears stream unchecked down my cheeks, stinging my stitches. "Then why did you act like you hated me so much? If you thought I was so beautiful, why did you always snarl at me and push me away? Why did you tell me I make you want to die?"

A.J.'s eyes are so soft it breaks my heart. "You remember the famous saying from Jacques Cousteau?"

I nod, sniffling.

"That's why. Because for a man like me, the most beautiful, dangerous creature of all is love. I fell in love with you sight unseen, just from the sound of your voice, and I knew if I didn't make you hate me, I'd do the most selfish thing in the world and try to make you mine."

I'm kissing him again; I can't help myself. Like breathing, it's an automatic reflex. I need to taste him, to feel him, to communicate without words what he does to me. How much I care.

"Angel. Angel." He murmurs it over and over as I kiss his face, his eyelids, his lips. I'm not particularly religious, but I feel like this is a form of communion. This moment is sacred, and I don't want it to ever end.

It does, though. A.J. takes hold of my shoulders, gently pushing me away. "You need to get back in bed."

I nod enthusiastically. "Yes, I do. *We* do."

His chuckle is soft and indulgent. He swipes the moisture from my cheeks with his fingers. "Easy, killer. One thing at a time. Sleep, eat, sleep more, then we'll talk. And then . . . we'll see."

"I just woke up from twelve hours of sleeping!"

He presses his thumb against the frown lines between my brows, smoothing them out. "Which was instruction number one. Instruction number two was eat."

As if on cue, my stomach growls.

A.J. grins triumphantly. "You like pancakes?"

"Pancakes? It's dinnertime!"

He shakes his head, the corners of his eyes crinkling. "Yeah, but that's all I know how to cook, so that's what you're getting."

I roll my eyes. "Okay. Pancakes. Then sleep again, then the other thing. Deal?"

"The *other* thing?" He smirks at me.

I say innocently, "Yeah, talking. That was instruction number four, right?"

He gathers me into his massive arms. I gaze up at him, falling, falling, falling.

His voice husky, A.J. asks, "Are you going to follow all my instructions from now on, Princess?"

"I would say yes, but we both know I'd be lying."

He nuzzles my neck. "How about just for one week?"

There's something in his voice, some kind of dark need that makes me go still. "You want me to do whatever you say for a week?"

He lifts his head and stares at me. The desire in his eyes tells me the answer is yes.

"Why?"

He struggles to find the words. "Because I need to be in control of this."

"Me, you mean?"

"No, baby. This. What's happening here. I have to be in control of it, so that when the week is up and you're gone . . ."

He doesn't finish his thought, but I think I understand. This has to be on his terms. So that when we both go back to real life, he can go on without me.

My heart takes a flying leap out of my chest. I stare into his eyes, finally comprehending why he's revealing all this, why he brought me here in the first place. "This is all I'm going to get, isn't it? This one week with you. That's all there will ever be."

He swallows, hard.

"Answer me, A.J. Is that what you mean? Is that what you want?"

"What I *want* is to wake up next to you every day for the rest of my life, angel. But I already told you this wouldn't end well. I already told you I'd hurt you. And you said you'd be willing to only take one night, so I'm thinking six more days is a good compromise."

Oh, God, the pain. It's like fire. It's like I'm being burned alive, from the inside out.

I shove him away. Red faced, I shout, "You just told me you were in love with me! You just told me you were happy! You said I'd never have to be alone again! What the hell is wrong with you?"

"Everything, baby. Everything is wrong with me."

The look he gives me freezes all my rage. There's something so dead about his eyes right now, something so unbearably bleak. Whatever he isn't telling me about himself—which is pretty much everything—it's bad.

"What does that mean?"

Silence.

"What are you hiding? What's your big secret, A.J.? Why won't you let me all the way in? Don't you trust me?"

"I trust you. It's myself I don't trust."

A nonanswer if there ever was one. Now I'm angry again. "Are you a serial killer?"

"No."

"An undercover FBI agent?"

"No."

"A drug dealer? A cartel leader? The head of an international prostitution ring?"

He winces. "No."

"What, then? Why do you hide from cameras, A.J.? Why do you live up here alone like this? Why would you bring me here and make me hope that you're going to give me everything I want you to give, and then pull the rug out from under me?"

In a voice that sounds like gravel, he says, "I hide because I'm ashamed. I'm alone because I have to be. And I brought you here because I was going crazy without you, and I might not be selfish enough to try to make you mine permanently, but I'm not strong enough to stay away from you, either. So we can have a week, or we can have nothing. The decision is yours."

That's all he gives me. He stares at me, his face closed off. I can't read anything in his eyes. Instinctively, I know we could go on like this for hours. Back and forth, questions that lead nowhere, uselessly spinning my wheels. I need to decide right now if I'm leaving or going, if I'm willing to accept all this on his terms.

I draw a deep breath, close my eyes, count to ten to try to get control of my ragged breathing. "And what do I get out of all this, A.J.? What's in it for me except heartbreak?"

The mask of hardness melts away from his face, and his eyes blaze with emotion. He pulls me against his chest. He cradles my face in his hands. He kisses me, deeply, with everything he's got. When he pulls away I'm breathless, clinging to his arms so I don't collapse at his feet.

Looking into my eyes, he says softly, "Let me love you, Chloe. Let me love you like you need to be loved. It won't be for forever, but it *will* be the best thing either one of us has ever had. I know it. It'll be enough to last us the rest of our lives."

I swallow a sob. I'd told Kat and Grace almost the same thing, that what he'd given me so far would be enough to last me the next fifty years. And I meant it. And I'd told him earlier I'd be happy with just one night, and meant that, too.

But I want so much more. I want all of him. Without limits, without secrets, without lies. If I can't have that, will seven days with zero answers satisfy me?

No. It won't satisfy me. But as I stare at him, as I see all the emotion and need and longing reflected in his eyes, I realize it will be enough.

He's enough for me. For one night or one week or any other measure of time, he's enough. I feel it to the marrow of my bones. And though it's crazy, I feel lucky. In entire lifetimes, some people never even get this. Some people will never know the joy of this small, enormous, effortlessly simple, ridiculously complicated thing:

Love.

I rest my head on his chest. I heave a deep, resigned sigh. I make a conscious decision to let go of everything, all the expectations, all the frustrations, all the questions I've been so desperate to ask. I let everything slide through my fingers and vanish.

In the steadiest voice I can manage, I say, "If I'm going to be eating pancakes for the next week, boyfriend, they better be awesome or I'm seriously going to kick your ass."

All the tension drains from A.J.'s body. He hugs me so hard I have trouble catching my breath. He says, "Honestly, baby, they're shit."

He laughs. It's like a sound a mourner makes at a funeral.

God, this is gonna hurt.

Chapter 23

I've seen hundreds of women sleep. Alone or in twos or threes or dozens, pillowed in satin or custom linens, shivering in freezing rooms under torn, filthy rags.

No one has ever looked like Chloe. Nothing on this earth is more beautiful than her.

She sleeps on her stomach like a child, arms flung out to the sides, legs splayed, face buried in the pillow. Lit by a moonbeam from the window, her hair is a shimmering spill of platinum and gold, messy around her shoulders, and I'm going insane with want and self-hatred.

What the fuck am I doing? This was so not the plan. But I had to have her with me. I had to keep her safe. Even when all this ends, I'll make sure she's safe forever.

I shut my eyes and press the heels of my hands into my eye sockets. Crying, something I haven't done since I was ten years old, is as easy as breathing now. All these stored up tears, now so eager to fall.

I have to fight to keep them from coming. Every time she looks at me with those eyes of hers, I have to fight not to break down and tell her everything.

If I did, she'd run away as fast as she could. So I keep my mouth shut. And I keep her.

I told her I wasn't selfish, but I lied. I'm the most selfish bastard who ever lived. She'll find out soon enough. And then she'll hate me, like I deserve.

My angel murmurs incoherently in her sleep. I stroke her back and she settles, sighing, burrowing farther into the pillow. When I press a kiss to her temple, she murmurs my name. It's like a thousand spear points piercing my heart.

Who knew love would be such utter, fucking misery?

Chapter 24

We spend the first evening together in almost total silence.

After I decided to stay, A.J. made me those pancakes. They weren't "shit," as he so eloquently described them; they were amazing. Even more amazing was his insistence on feeding them to me, forkful by fluffy forkful. It seemed really odd at first, but, in the spirit of "thou shalt follow my commandments" that we'd agreed on, I let him. Then I let him run me a hot bath in the giant claw-foot bathtub, put me in it, and wash my hair, along with every other part of my body. He was serious as he did it, a little detached, his hands gentle, missing nothing, yet I could tell his touch wasn't meant to be arousing.

Of course it *was* arousing, but I didn't let on. Well, there was that one little groan that slipped out when he ran the bar of soap between my legs, but we both pretended I hadn't made it. We also pretended not to notice the enormous bulge straining the fly in his jeans.

He dried me. He dressed me in one of his T-shirts and a pair of his sweats, rolled up at the ankles. He combed out my hair and put

Neosporin on my cheek, then he kissed me softly and put me back into bed. When he went to the kitchen to make me tea, I took off the clothes he'd just put on and acted innocent when he came back and stopped short, frowning.

My ploy didn't work. He ignored my nudity, ordered me to drink the tea, and got in bed beside me without taking off his jeans.

Apparently if and when we finally had sex was his decision as well. We fell asleep in our usual spooned embrace.

In the morning, there were more pancakes. After an inspection of the stitches, there was more Neosporin for my cheek. Then, because I was feeling a little more secure and thought I could be alone, A.J. went to my place to get my clothes and a few other things I'd asked for, and went shopping for food, while I busied myself snooping around his room, trying to find anything that would give me a clue about him.

Here's what I found: zilch.

His closet holds only identical pairs of jeans, boots, jackets, and hoodies, most of the items are black except for the jeans and a brown leather bomber. His dresser contains socks, underwear, and T-shirts, folded neatly in stacks. The medicine cabinet in the bathroom is like anyone else's. There is no junk drawer in the kitchenette, no photo albums in a bookcase, no mementos from trips taken, no receipts, no mail, no phone book, and of course no telephone or computer for me to try to hack into.

He could be anyone, or no one. It's as if he's a ghost.

The only thing of any interest is his CD collection. He has every genre of music, from opera to reggae, country to jazz, classic rock to punk and heavy metal, organized in sections and alphabetized by artist. Opera is by far the biggest section, followed by jazz. Bands and musicians I've never heard of make up a good chunk. I think about introducing him to an iPod so he can take his music on the go, but then wonder if he even has a credit card to buy music with. I doubt he'd be interested in anything that tracks his spending and purchase history.

I'm totally off the grid, he told my father. Looking around his place really drives that point home.

My detective work abruptly ends when he returns, arms full with my suitcase, a bag of groceries, and a bouquet of store-bought red roses wrapped in cellophane. He leaves my suitcase next to the bed, drops the grocery bag on the kitchenette counter, and, after kissing me lightly on the lips, presents me with the bouquet of roses.

I'm shocked, and pleased. I can't remember the last time a man brought me flowers. Eric once told me that buying a florist flowers would be like buying a jeweler a diamond ring, or a winemaker a bottle of someone else's wine. He thought it was bad manners.

"No one ever buys me flowers!"

"That's what I figured. Which is exactly why I did." A.J. smiles at me, and my heart melts. He seems happy, almost carefree, which makes me happy, too.

"Do you have a vase?" I look around the kitchenette, but see nothing that would be a likely candidate.

"Oh. No." He's momentarily crestfallen, but then brightens. "Maybe in the downstairs kitchens, though. There are all sorts of containers there. Or in the concierge closet, or one of the storage rooms. This place is full of stuff the prior owners left behind."

Whistling to himself, he starts to unpack the bag of groceries. It's a little thrilling, and a lot scary, how this domestic side of him turns me on. Though it's weird, it's also comforting, and comfortable. We could be just any other couple in their apartment on a Saturday morning, looking forward to spending the rest of their lives together.

And not just their final week.

I push that nasty thought aside, and busy myself with filling the small sink with water. I submerge the stems of the roses so they can drink until we can find a more appropriate container. I want desperately to ask questions, but know I can't, so instead I mount what I hope is a subtle fishing expedition.

"Speaking of this place, did you ever see *The Grand Budapest Hotel*? It totally reminds me of that."

"Hmm."

Okay, not exactly the explanation of how he'd come to live here that I hoped for. I try again. "Was it empty a long time before you bought it?"

"Years. It was originally built as a resort hotel but never made it. Too far from the beach I guess. Then it was bought by some religious sect. They had it for a few decades before the leader committed suicide and it went on the market again. Then a corporation bought it, tried to make it into an exclusive rehab center for rich drug addicts. Don't know what happened there, but it wasn't successful, so a private investor bought it, tried to fix it up and flip it, but the economy took a shit and he lost everything. The IRS repossessed it to cover his unpaid taxes. Then some old eccentric guy bought it at auction and lived here with his nurse until he died. It's been empty ever since."

That this poor, abandoned hotel that A.J. bought, because it looks like he feels, has had such a string of failures in its past makes me unreasonably depressed. I try not to think it might be jinxed, but of course I start to obsess over exactly that.

"Weird that it has such a checkered past," I mutter, staring out the window to the view of the hills.

From behind, A.J. snakes his arms around my waist. He kisses the back of my neck, nosing aside my hair to gain access. "That's one of the reasons it makes me feel at home."

His confession is so unexpected I blurt, "Because you have a checkered past, too?"

He doesn't growl or freeze me out, as I expect him to. He simply rests his chin on my shoulder and stares out the window. "Exactly, Princess. Birds of a feather."

He kills me when he's like this. His self-loathing is so deep. I wish I could take it away.

Without turning, I softly say, "If I found a magic lamp and a genie came out and said he'd grant me three wishes, they'd all be for you to be able to forget whatever bad things happened to you, and for you to be happy forever."

I can tell he's moved by my words, because a little tremor goes through him. He turns his face to my neck. "Not everything bad in my past happened *to* me, angel. Some of them were bad things I did to other people."

My heart beats faster. "Whatever you did, I know it was because you had to. I know it was because you didn't have a choice. You're a good man, A.J. I know that."

His arms tighten around me. "You believe that because *you're* good. You see the best in people. But we always have choices, angel. Even if they're hard, or shitty, every decision we make involves a choice." His voice drops even lower. "And you're wrong about me being a good man. I made every bad choice with my eyes wide open . . . even the ones that hurt other people. I always knew exactly what I was doing. There's no excuse for the things I've done."

Without hesitating, and with a vehemence I wasn't intending, I say, "I don't care what you've done. I don't care if you're Jesus or Hitler or something in between. None of that matters to me."

With his hands on my shoulders, A.J. turns me around. He stares down at me, his eyes devouring. "It should."

I shake my head. "It doesn't. And it never will, no matter what happens. No matter what you say to try to convince me, no matter what I find out."

"You can't mean that. Not if you don't know the facts."

I don't know how we got here so quickly, when all I was trying for was a few random tidbits to fill in my knowledge about how he came to own the hotel, but here we are. I'm not missing the opportunity. "Tell me then. Try me out."

"No."

"Why not?"

His lips part. His eyes burn. "Because I'm not ready to lose you just yet."

"I promise you won't lose me."

His smile is the saddest thing I've ever seen. "No."

"A.J.—"

"No," he repeats, more firmly.

Question-and-answer time is over. To underscore that, he withdraws from me, and finishes unpacking the bag of groceries. I watch him in miserable silence. The final thing he takes from the brown paper bag is a disposable cell phone. Without meeting my eyes, he hands it to me.

"I brought your purse but left your cell phone at your apartment." He adds, "This one can't be tracked."

Eric. Here he comes again, intruding with his jealousy and all the awful memories he's gifted me. "You think Eric might try to track me with my phone?"

"I think he's capable of anything, and I'm not taking chances, so you're using a burner from now on."

"What, forever?"

In his gaze is something dark and dangerous. "Until I know you're safe."

I'm about to ask more questions, but am seized by the irresistible urge to sneeze. I do—violently—jerking with the unexpected force of it. Thankfully I had time to cover my mouth and nose, or A.J. might have gotten doused with snot. "Ugh. Sorry," I say sheepishly.

Then I sneeze again. And again.

"Was it something I said?"

A.J.'s being funny, but all at once a wave of heat flashes over me, and I break out in a cold sweat. "Whoa."

"What's wrong?" Worried, A.J. steps closer.

"I'm not feeling so good all of a sudden." Warmth creeps up my neck, spreading over my face. My cheeks flush.

With a hand under my elbow, he marches me over to the leather couch, and directs, "Sit."

Feeling strangely weak, I do.

He goes into the bathroom and returns with a thermometer. "Open," is his next command, which I follow, allowing him to insert the slender glass tube under my tongue. In thirty seconds he removes it, looks at it, and frowns.

"Hundred and two."

Within minutes, my head is pounding. A.J. feeds me two aspirin. After an hour lying on the couch, sneezing, feverish, wracked with chills, I can no longer deny the obvious.

I've come down with the flu.

Is this the universe's way of trying to tell me something?

For five days, I'm completely out of it. I haven't been this sick since I had strep throat when I was twelve and had to miss ten days of school. Other than calling my father and the girls daily to check in, I sleep most of the time, restlessly tossing, dreaming unsettling dreams of waking to find A.J. gone, or of Eric chasing me down a dark alley, his fingers grasping for my neck. When I'm not sleeping I'm groggy, my head pounds, my body is clammy and clumsy. The only time I get out of bed on my own is to shuffle to the bathroom like a zombie to use the toilet.

What does A.J. do with himself while I'm so ill?

The broody, moody, badass drummer turns into Florence Nightingale.

He gently wipes my sweaty forehead with cold cloths. He buys me every available type of cold and flu medication. He frets over me, fluffing pillows and smoothing blankets and worrying about every sneeze and sniffle. When I'm too weak to sit up to feed myself, he props me against his chest and spoon-feeds me vegetable soup or organic ice cream he bought from the health store.

He even reads to me. There's a moldering library on the first floor, and in it he finds a copy of *The Princess Bride*. He spends hours sitting next to me on the bed, reading out loud, doing all the different parts in different voices.

I've never been this well looked after, not even by my mother when I was twelve. I feel cocooned. Though I'm terribly sick, I feel spoiled. Bella's even learned to love snuggling with me, on the pillow by my head during the day, at our feet at night while A.J. and I sleep.

And every morning when I awake, there's a new origami bird on the pillow beside my head. Today, my sixth at A.J.'s place, it's the most elaborate creation so far: a black-and-teal peacock, complete with a plume of real feathers for a tail.

I pick it up and stare at it in total disbelief. It's so perfect, so detailed, it looks manufactured by a machine.

I hear A.J. moving around in the bathroom, and call out, "How did you learn origami?"

He sticks his head out of the door. "Good morning! You're up!"

I can tell he's happy to see me talking. I think the most I've said to him over the past six days has been a series of grunts in answer to his questions or commands. To be honest, it's all a little blurry. I'm still weak, but at least my head is no longer pounding, and the chills are finally gone.

"If you can call this up."

I touch my hair. It's a nest of knots. A.J. has bathed me in the tub when I have the energy to sit up, but my hair has only been washed once, and it feels like dirty straw. I wonder if I have dreadlocks.

He strolls out of the bathroom, looking ridiculously hot in his little black nylon boxing shorts and nothing else. I can't resist ogling him as he moves toward me. I love looking at his tattoos when he moves; it's almost as if they're alive, dancing atop his muscles.

I decide I'm going to ask him what every one means. If I've only got one day left, I'm going to grill him about everything since I've missed so many opportunities to talk to him.

My heart sinks. I've only got one day of my week left. Or is today the last day? I've lost count.

A.J. drops to his knees on the mattress beside me. I hold out the bird.

"So? How did you learn to do this?"

He sits back on his heels, a smile quirking his mouth. "You like it?"

"Like it? No, I don't like it. I *love* it. It's *amazing*. Where did you get the tiny little feathers for the tail?"

"A shop called Mother Plucker. They have every kind of feather you can buy. Kenji introduced me to it."

He runs a hand through his long hair. The move is so blatantly sexual it looks like something out of a porn movie. With his naked chest and biceps on display, his muscular thighs open, I'm having a little trouble concentrating on what he's saying.

Because I know he's not wearing anything under those shorts.

Apparently my libido has recovered much more quickly than the rest of me.

"So was Kenji the one who taught you origami, too?" It seems entirely possible, though I'm probably just racially profiling because Kenji is Japanese.

A.J. says quietly, "No. I learned it from a Japanese whore."

And suddenly I hate this peacock in my hand with a passion that borders on violence. I want to crush it. I want to tear it to pieces with my teeth.

A.J. leans over and takes my chin in his hand. I wish I didn't like it so much when he does this, because I'm seriously ticked off right now.

"It wasn't like that. She was a friend."

I don't say anything. I just keep my gaze trained on the peacock. I imagine it's smirking at me.

"I was fifteen, angel. She was almost thirty years older than me. She was just a friend."

Scowling, aggravated, I look up at him. My mind is sharper than it's been in nearly a week, and what he's said makes absolutely no sense to me. "What's a fifteen-year-old kid doing hanging out with a middle-aged Japanese whore?"

The first thing out of his mouth is a hard "I was never a kid." Then, as if regretting his tone he adds more gently, "And for a long time, whores were the only friends I had."

I'm astonished. What's the correct reply to those two gems?

He sighs, releases my chin, and runs his hand through his hair again. "Yeah. I know it sounds weird."

"No, not at all! That sounds totally reasonable, A.J.! Doesn't every teenage boy surround himself with whores? I mean, I can't imagine they make the best choices for the soccer or football teams because of the stilettos, but I'm sure they're really great at wrestling!"

Head cocked, he looks at me intently, undisturbed by my sarcastic outburst. "Are you . . . jealous?"

My face flushes. I look down at the bird in my hand. Maybe it's because I don't have the strength for evasion at the moment, but I tell him the truth. "All those girls or women you call friends probably know a lot more about you than I ever will. So yes, I'm jealous. I'm so jealous if you cut me open I'd bleed green."

There's a moment of tense silence. A.J. finally breaks it by saying flatly, "Don't be. Every single one of them is dead."

The bird falls from my hand.

I think of the white roses he sent to the cemetery in Saint Petersburg. I think of the flower tattoo on his knuckle, the petals with the twelve initials of everyone he's "lost." I think about how he told my father he had a few tricks up his sleeve, and if Eric ever found out where I was and showed up here, he'd never be seen again. I think of how A.J. said he'd done terrible, unforgiveable things.

I think of how I told him I didn't care.

I'm shaking. I feel like I might throw up. When I look at him, he's watching me with narrowed eyes.

"What's going on in your head right now, Chloe?"

What's going on is chaos. The bells of intuition clang loud and insistent against the lazy, comforting reluctance of denial, and all I hear is ringing and buzzing, a relentless, rising noise, like a swarm of angry bees.

I swallow. My mouth is as dry as bone. "You're not from Las Vegas, are you."

It's not a question. He holds my gaze for what feels like forever. I'm not sure he'll answer, but then, slowly, he shakes his head.

Starting at my spine and working its way outward, coldness runs through my body. I can't move. I can barely breathe. "And your parents, the homemaker and the pastor? Were they a lie, too?"

I expect a denial or silence, but he answers immediately. "No." Then he closes his eyes. "And yes, sort of. They weren't my birth parents, but they raised me, gave me a new name, a new life. They adopted me." He opens his eyes. In them I see nothing but darkness.

"When you were a baby?"

Once again, he answers without hesitation. "When I came to this country when I was sixteen."

The noise in my head grows louder. The stitches in my cheek throb. I want to scratch at them. I want to rip them out. "From where?"

He's still as stone. He whispers, "You already know."

He's right; I do. Maybe I've known it all along. "Russia."

When he nods, relief overwhelms me. *At last.* I close my eyes. The terrible noise subsides, until there's only silence, clear and cold. "And your birth mother's name is Aleksandra Zimnyokov."

When I look at him again, A.J.'s face is a study in misery. His eyes glitter with tears. "She died when I was ten." His voice cracks. "She was a prostitute."

Oh God. Everything I've been missing begins to knit together with a swift, effortless clarity, like fingers interlocking. All the questions I have, all the mysteries about the man kneeling in front of me, hover around us, whispering, weighting the air.

With surprising strength in my voice I demand, "Tell me your real name."

A.J.'s face crumples. It's like watching a building burn to the ground.

"Alexei. My name is Alexei Janic Zimnyokov." A sob breaks from his chest. "I haven't said that out loud in twelve years."

My heart is going to burst. I can feel it, expanding inside my chest, stretching so wide it will explode and kill me.

Then he shoots to his feet and bolts from the room.

I follow him. Slowly, because I'm still weak, I make my way from room number twenty-seven down the long corridor, Bella trotting by my side. I take the stairs to the main floor. A.J. is nowhere to be seen.

At my feet, Bella huffs. I look down at her, and she's staring in the direction of the corridor that leads to the rear of the hotel. "Show me, Bella. Where's Daddy?"

She yips and trots away. I follow behind, my heart pounding, my knees like Jell-O.

The light is murky today; there's a storm coming soon. In A.J.'s room I saw the sky through the windows, slate gray, threatening rain, and downstairs there's little illumination as I walk barefoot through the silent halls. When Bella reaches the door that leads to the pool patio, she looks back at me, waiting. We go outside.

I see him right away, standing at the edge of the empty pool. He's motionless, looking down at the piles of dead leaves. Even from where I'm standing I can see how his hands shake. The clouds overhead cast everything in a shadowed half light, so though it's morning, it seems like we're headed toward night. When A.J. raises his head and looks at me, the first of the rain begins to fall.

His face is already wet.

The pull between us is so strong, I feel as if an invisible hand has reached into my chest and grabbed my heart. I don't even try to resist it. My feet move before I can stop them, and then I'm running.

When I'm a few feet away, he opens his arms. I slam into his chest at full speed, but it doesn't knock him off-balance. He wraps his arms around me and buries his face in my neck.

"You're still here."

His voice is hoarse. The fist around my heart tightens. "I still have one more day."

We're getting wet. The drizzle is turning into a downpour, which we both ignore. Under the patio awning, Bella barks, wanting us to come in.

"You don't hate me for lying?" he whispers, trembling.

And my heart, dear God my poor battered heart, just cracks wide open. I start to cry. "No, I don't hate you, A.J. I love you! I love you no matter who you are! I can't *not* love you, no matter what name you call yourself or what you've done! I don't care about any of that!"

My words make him groan. He takes my face in his hands. He kisses me deeply, passionately, his heart thumping hard against my chest. Rain catches in my lashes and slides down my cheeks, mingling with my tears.

He lifts me into his arms. I rest my face against his neck and close my eyes, shivering, my arms wrapped around his strong shoulders. He walks us out of the rain, into the hotel, and up the stairs. My heart beats like a hummingbird's the entire time. I can't stop shaking, or catch my breath.

He kicks open the door to his room. He strides over to the mattress, kneels on it, and lies down with me in his arms. He kisses me again, desperately, his body wet and hard against mine. When I respond with equal desperation, he rips off my wet T-shirt, sweats, and panties, throwing it all aside so he can stare down at my naked body.

His gaze is adoring. He kneels between my legs, running his hands down my thighs, over my hips and belly, and up across my breasts, slowly, as if he's memorizing every inch of my flesh. Everywhere he touches I arch into his hands, feeling like I'm ablaze.

"So beautiful," he murmurs, caressing my breasts. "You're so goddamn beautiful, angel."

I hold out my arms. He lowers himself atop me. I love his weight, the feel of his wet chest against mine, the smell of his skin, his hair. I want to drown in him.

His cock is hard against my thigh. The thin nylon shorts are no match for it; he might as well be naked.

When he kisses me, I rock my pelvis against his. He moans into my mouth. I slide my hands down his back and under the elastic of the shorts and grab his ass, sinking my nails into his skin. He hisses and draws back, looking like he's in pain, but I know it's not from my fingernails.

It's because he's still holding back.

I stare into his eyes. "I know you said you'd never fuck me. But you never said you wouldn't make love to me."

His cock twitches against my leg. Agonized, fighting himself, he stares down at my face.

Remembering what he told me before, that the reason he'd never sleep with me was because then I'd belong to him forever, I whisper, "I'm already yours, A.J. It's too late. All of me already belongs to you."

I see the exact moment it happens, the instant he decides. He teeters for one final breath, then, with a flutter of his lashes and a soft exhalation, he gives in.

He digs his fingers deep into my hair, fits his mouth against mine, and kisses me like I've never been kissed in my entire life. He puts his all into it, his body and his heart and even his soul, so that I feel like we're not even two people anymore; we're fused. It's incredible.

It's a claim.

By the end of the kiss I'm writhing against him, delirious with want. I jerk the thin nylon shorts down his hips, tearing at the fabric. He lifts his hips, allowing his cock to spring free between us, then lowers himself again so it's pressed, hot and throbbing, against my core.

He reaches his hand between our bodies and takes his erection in his fist. He slides the tip of his cock back and forth over my entrance, watching my face, listening to my whimpers and low moans. He whispers, "You on the pill, baby?"

I shake my head.

Without a word, he shifts his weight, reaches over to the side of the mattress and retrieves a little foil packet from beneath. He tears it open with his teeth, ripping the gold lettering "Magnum XL" in two. I watch in breathless anticipation as he quickly rolls the condom down the length of his stiff cock, then positions it again between my thighs.

When he eases it inside me, I gasp at the feeling of fullness. He's big, but I'm so wet and ready he doesn't have to go as slow as he's going.

A low rumble of thunder rattles the windows. Rain drums hard against the roof.

"More," I plead, rocking my hips, trying to get him deeper, but he's in control. He won't let me set the pace. He kisses me, then lowers his head and sucks my nipple into his mouth, hard, using his teeth. I arch, crying out in both pleasure and pain. Instantly he gentles, lapping my nipple with his tongue, suckling lightly, moving to the other nipple to lavish it with the same attention.

I squirm beneath him. It will only be seconds before I start to beg incoherently. He's still got only the tip inside me, and I need every beautiful inch of it. *Now.*

"Chloe. Keep still." His voice is firm, just this side of hard.

"I can't." It's true; my thighs tremble as I say the words. My fingers squeeze his ass.

"Do I need to tie you up?"

Now I freeze. My body falls completely still. Only my chest moves, rapidly rising and falling with my breath.

He lifts his head and breathes something in Russian into my ear. The tone is soft but the language is guttural, harsh, and incredibly sexual. I have no idea what he's just said to me, but I'm *on fire.*

He moves his hand and presses his thumb against my swollen, aching clit. Stiffening, I suck in a breath, trying not to move. I'm rewarded with low, satisfied praise.

"Good girl."

Still not sinking deeper inside me, A.J. lowers his mouth to my nipple again. He begins to suck it at the same time he rubs slow, gentle circles around my clit with his thumb.

My moan of pleasure is broken. My eyes slide shut. It takes every ounce of my concentration not to move, to resist the incredibly strong urge to flex my hips and arch my back, to buck against his hand.

"Perfect," he whispers, and slides farther inside me.

I feel myself stretch around him. I feel the heat of him, the hardness, the pulsing vein that runs the length of the crown to the base. I'm so close to orgasm I have to bite the inside of my mouth to keep myself still.

"Open your eyes baby."

I do. His nose is inches from mine. His face is strained, and his eyes are both soft and thrillingly hard. It's obvious that going this slow is as difficult for him as it is for me. I wonder why he's doing it.

"Tell me again."

"What?"

"You know what."

It can only be one of a few things. I moisten my lips. "I'm yours."

He slides in another inch.

I gasp, struggling to remain still. My fingers dig into the muscles of his ass.

"What else?"

"All of me belongs to you."

He presses in farther, another few inches, huge and hot, and I can't stop the groan that slips from my lips. My thighs shake with the effort not to wrap around his waist.

"And what else?"

"And . . . and . . ."

He waits, breathing shallowly, watching me with hooded eyes. He's balanced on one elbow, still massaging the bundle of nerves between my legs. I can tell he can't last much longer, either. I know now what he wants me to say, and what he'll do when I say it.

A sliver of lightning briefly illuminates the room in a jagged pulse of white. It's raining so hard it sounds like gunfire.

On an exhalation, looking into his eyes, I whisper, "I love you."

With a growl like an animal's, he shoves all the way inside me.

I cry out. My body bows against his. My eyes fall shut. My head tips back against the pillow. A.J. starts to thrust into me, deep and hard, over and over, one big hand beneath my head, pulling my hair, the other gripping my thigh, holding me open as he plunges inside.

So this is what I've been missing.

That's the last coherent thought I have before I come, screaming his name.

There are moments that brand you.

There are moments that alter you, that you recognize, even as they're happening, will leave you different afterward than you were before. It's these life-changing moments that make you who you are, more so than the family you were born into or all the experiences you had leading up to them.

For better or for worse, once you've lived through such a moment, you can never go back.

As I lie sweaty and sated in A.J.'s arms, my head resting on his chest, our legs entangled and our frantic heartbeats finally beginning to slow, I know that this is one of those moments. I'm different from the girl I was just this morning. I'm darker. More dangerous. In fact, I'm capable of anything.

Because now there's something I'm willing to lie, cheat, steal, or die for to protect. Something I don't want to live without.

Or some*one.*

And it's time for him to share. There can be no more walls between us, not after this.

"Tell me everything, A.J. Start from the beginning. Don't leave anything out."

His chest slowly rises with his deep inhalation, lifting my head. His right hand is on my scalp, fingers entwined in my hair, the left trails slowly up and down the arm I have flung across his chest.

"I was always bigger than the other boys. Even when I was little, I was always the giant of the bunch." His voice is slow, almost sleepy, neither sad nor happy, just matter-of-fact. "My earliest memory is of fighting. I don't know what it was about, but I was fighting a boy a few years older than me, and winning." He pauses. "Mostly I remember the screaming."

"The other boy's?"

"The crowd. People were standing around us, watching. Cheering me on."

"How old were you?"

He thinks silently for a moment. "Maybe four or five."

I picture a child, barely more than a toddler, fighting bare-knuckled in the street, surrounded by a rabid crowd of onlookers. It doesn't seem possible.

"Where was your mother?"

There's a shrug in his voice. "Fucking some john."

We're quiet for a moment, listening to the rain. Bella is nestled at our feet, dreaming. Her paws twitch in a dream run.

"I never knew my father. Don't even know his name. I doubt my mother knew who he was, either. It was common for the prostitutes to get pregnant in the slums; johns paid more when the girls didn't insist on protection. There was the threat of HIV and everything else, of course, but they always paid more if they didn't have to wear a rubber. I don't know why." He pauses again, and his voice turns dark. "Some of them paid more for a pregnant whore, too."

Pressing a kiss to his chest, I close my eyes.

"The brothel I grew up in was run by a woman named Darya, but everyone called her *Matushka*. Mother." His snort is derisive. "A wolf had more maternal instinct than that old bitch. Her girls had to work when they were sick, pregnant, on the rag, beaten up, starving, everything. There were even girls who were dying of AIDS who were still turning tricks. As long as you were breathing and could spread your legs, you were worth something to *Matushka*."

There's a longer, darker pause. "And if you weren't breathing, there were certain men who would pay special for that, too."

I lie perfectly still. I want to hear this—I need to—but I know it will gut me. I know it will be the worst thing I've ever heard.

A.J. exhales through his nose, a hard burst that stirs my hair. "*Matushka*'s girls were allowed to keep their bastards on two conditions. One: they kept earning during their pregnancy. And two: as soon as they could, the children would go to work. Not like that," he adds when he sees my horrified look. "At least, not until they were older. Girls had to be ten before they could start turning tricks. *Matushka* said it ruined their insides to start earlier."

I swallow. "And boys?"

"Six."

He says it without a trace of regret or sadness. It's just a fact of life. I think of my brother at six years old. I can only remember from pictures; I wasn't even born then.

"And so . . . you had to . . ."

A.J. produces a low, chilling laugh. "No. Not me. I was worth much more than what the chicken hawks would pay. I wasn't just a fresh little hole to fuck. I could *fight*. And for the house, taking hundreds of bets on a single fight is much more lucrative than a four-trick-a-day whore, no matter how many of them you have in your stable."

The bitterness in his voice breaks my heart. I'm suddenly ashamed by my privileged, first-world upbringing, of all the times I complained about clothes or cars or boys. Until now, real life was as real to me as Santa Claus or the tooth fairy. Real life was somewhere *out there*, beyond the safe confines of my pretty little bubble in Beverly Hills.

"So you started fighting for your keep."

He nods. "Earlier than most, because I was big, and always angry anyway. I didn't understand why I was so different, why I saw colors in sounds and no one else did. I felt like a freak. And because the more often I won, the easier *Matushka* was on my mother."

Bella growls in her sleep, and turns over. She settles again, burrowing into the covers, still making a warning grumble deep in her throat.

"My mother was an addict. Heroin, crack, booze, whatever she could get her hands on. When I was ten, she overdosed. On Christmas morning. I didn't tell *Matushka* for three days, until after my mother's body had already begun to decompose." He adds thoughtfully, "Only fresh corpses were commodities."

I whisper, "Oh my God."

"So I told everyone she was so sick she couldn't get out of bed. Luckily that week, *Matushka* had brought in a pair of fourteen-year-old twins from the country. Farm girls. Their father couldn't afford to feed them anymore, and *Matushka* paid well for rarities like twins. She could charge three times as much for twins as she could for a single whore. And all my mother's regulars wanted a turn with the twins, as did everyone else; word had spread. Most of the other whores idled for the first few weeks after the twins arrived. So by the time my lie was discovered, it was too late. *Matushka* couldn't make any money on my mother's remains."

He turns his face to my hair. His heart beats beneath my palm, banging against his breastbone like it's trying to break free.

"I paid for that lie with a beating so severe I couldn't get out of bed for ten days. But I had nowhere to go, so I took it without complaint. The other whores looked after me, nursed me, brought me food and water. Though I don't think *Matushka* expected it, I survived. And when I was able to fight again, *Matushka* put me up against a boy three years older than me. His name was Pavel."

A.J.'s voice cracks when he says the other boy's name. I glance up at his face, and his eyes are closed. His brows are pulled together. He seems in terrible pain.

Haltingly, he whispers, "He was the first . . . the first one . . . I killed."

My heart stops. I rear up on my elbow and stare down at him. When he opens his eyes, they glitter like he has a fever.

"I was so angry. About my mother, about my life. I just went wild on him. I was like an animal. And the sound of the crowd, urging me on, screaming louder and louder the bloodier it became, the colors of their voices, everything so black . . ."

He closes his eyes again, as if he can't bear to look at me. "When he fell on the ground I stomped on his throat and broke his neck."

He touches one of the crosses tattooed on his throat, a small one, the closest to his ear. Though he can't see it, his fingers trace the outline perfectly, as if they've done it a thousand times before.

My horror is so crushing I can only breathe in shallow, panted breaths.

There are three crosses on his neck.

"*Matushka* took better care of me after that. She made a lot of money from that fight. So she moved me into a nicer room and gave me better food, and told me I had a purpose in life. I had value. I could fight, and win, and so I had value. It didn't matter that I didn't want to. Survival was the only thing that mattered. By the time I was thirteen I was six feet tall, and famous in certain circles. *Medved*, they called me. The bear."

I think of Trina calling him a big ol' huggy bear, and I feel sick.

"I fought almost every week. I rarely lost. When I was fourteen I was matched with a boy my own age. He was too small. I don't know why they gave him to me, but I knew from the moment I saw him that he'd be number two. He'd be the next Pavel. By then I didn't care about hurting the boys I fought. I only cared about hearing the crowd scream and getting my money.

"His name was Maksim. He had a face like a doll's. Before the fight, I mean."

A.J. traces the other small cross on his neck, the one closest to his Adam's apple.

I'm shaking. Outwardly A.J. is calm, telling me this horror story in a tranquil, almost detached voice, but his eyes are filled with self-hatred and revulsion, and his face is very pale.

"After that fight, I was notorious. *Matushka* couldn't find a local fighter to go up against me, so they started coming in from the city. I just kept growing and gaining weight, getting harder with every fight, and it was easy for me. I was good at it. I was a fourteen-year-old, six-foot-three, two-hundred-and-ten-pound soulless motherfucker who stole and fought and lived with whores, and I thought that would be my life."

The rain is relentless, drumming against the roof, sliding down the windowpanes like silvery tears. Bella twitches in her sleep. I can't get warm, even though I'm pressed against the hot bulk of A.J.'s body.

"And then came Sayori."

He pauses for a long time, struggling, it seems, for words. Or maybe he's trying not to cry. I can't tell; his throat works like he's holding back great, unspoken emotion, but his eyes have gone blank, staring at the ceiling. I think he's lost inside himself, inside whatever terrible memory he's about to reveal.

"She was old for a whore. Usually the girls would overdose, die of disease or botched abortions, or be killed by a john by the time they got to be her age, but there were a few who survived into middle age. She was originally from Tokyo, the daughter of a rich businessman and a former geisha, raised to be a dancer. She was spoiled. Stubborn." His voice falls. "And beautiful. Right up until she took her last breath, she was beautiful."

Thunder booms in the sky. Startled, I jump. I realize I'm holding my breath.

"She came to Russia when she was still young, followed a man she'd fallen in love with. Turned out he was married. Turned out he didn't want anything to do with her when he found out she was pregnant. Her father cut her off when she left Japan to find her lover, so she had no one to turn to. And desperation makes whores of us all, one way or another. She took up with some lowlife who eventually convinced her to have an abortion and start selling herself to support them both. That was the beginning of the end. The lowlife abandoned her to another, worse piece of scum, who sold her to a collector who had a fetish for Asian girls. When she got too old for his taste—she was thirty by then—he sold her to someone else, who eventually sold her to someone else, until she wound up on *Matushka*'s doorstep. When we met, she was forty-four."

When he stays silent too long, I prompt, "And you were fifteen."

"She was kind," he whispers. "After my mother died, I didn't know any kindness. Sayori was the one who taught me how to read, how to appreciate music, how to make origami." His voice turns reverent. "Like you, she had the voice of an angel."

Ghosts, he'd said. *When I look at you all I see are ghosts.* I try to gather my courage, because I already know how this story will end.

"Why did she take such a special interest in you, do you think?"

"I was the only man she ever knew who never fucked her or fucked her over. That's what she said. She was like a second mother to me, for a while." His voice quivers. "So when she got sick . . . I couldn't say no . . ."

My body breaks out in gooseflesh. My heart pounding, I stare at his face.

Abruptly he rolls onto his side, turning me so I roll with him. He winds his arms around me, pulls his knees up behind mine, and bows his head, so his forehead rests on the back of my neck. His body trembles. His breathing is shallow and erratic.

"When the time was near, she was too weak to help herself. She was wasted away. I think it was cancer, though she never told me. She knew what happened to whores who died in *Matushka*'s house, and she didn't want that to happen to her. I told her I'd take care of her, that I'd get her out of there or make it so *Matushka* didn't find out until it was too late, but she said no. She said she'd only stayed so long because of me, and she didn't want me to get into trouble. So the problem, as she saw it, wasn't so much how to die, but how to leave a corpse too damaged for even the twisted tastes of one of *Matushka*'s special clients."

I want to put my hands over my ears now. I want to get out of this bed and run far, far away and hide. I thought I knew where he was going with this story only moments before, but now I'm gripped by a terrifying certainty that what I'm about to hear will be stuck in my head on repeat forever.

A.J.'s trembles turn to jerking shakes. His teeth chatter as if he's caught a death chill. All the little hairs on my body stand on end.

"I used a pillow," he says, his voice breaking over every few words. "I waited until early in the morning, so everyone was asleep. She kissed me good-bye first, told me I was the best friend she'd ever had. Then I . . . then I . . ."

He can't go on. He's shaking so badly he shakes me with him. The two of us make the sheets twitch, the mattress shudder. At our feet, Bella lifts her head and barks.

Then the words spew from A.J. in a broken, breathless rush, like he's vomiting poison out of his soul.

"When it was over I woke all the other girls and got them out of the house except *Matushka* she always slept so soundly so she didn't hear us leaving she didn't hear me sloshing petrol all over the floor she didn't hear the match I struck or the sound the petrol made when it caught fire the whoosh and the sizzle and the pop she only woke up when she smelled the smoke and by then it was too late by then the whole house was on fire and when she came out of the house in her nightgown into the street she was on fire too and her face was melting and all her hair had burned off and the smell oh god the *smell*—"

He bursts into full, body-wracking sobs.

After a moment, Bella begins to howl.

It sounds exactly like the noise inside my head.

Chloe's still here.

How can she still be here?

How can she be so calm?

She'll go soon. This calm can't last. She's just in shock.

Right?

It's been at least an hour since I told her. In that time she's held me, kissed me, wiped my eyes, made me tea, put on music, lit all the candles, fed the dog, and crawled back into bed with me. Right now she's fitted against my side with her head on my shoulder and her leg thrown over mine. She hasn't asked me any more questions. In fact, she's not speaking at all.

It's probably better this way. I don't know if I can stand to hear what she thinks of me.

I do know I won't be able to stand it when she tells me she's leaving for good. I know I'll beg. Fuck, I can already see it, me on my knees at the door, pathetic and broken—

"Are you hungry?"

Her soft question is so unexpected I don't answer for a second. She trails her fingertips up and down my forearm, waiting for me to respond.

"I . . . I could eat."

"I saw you got some spaghetti from the store. How about if I make that?"

She's just hungry. She's going to make some food, then pack her bags and leave. Don't get your fucking hopes up, idiot.

"That would be fine." My voice is thick. I turn my face to her hair and inhale. She always smells so good. Fresh. Warm. Clean. I guess that's because she's all of those things.

How the fuck is she still here?

She makes a move to get up, but I pull her back against me so quickly I think I scare her a little bit. Her big blue eyes get even bigger, and don't blink. I loosen my grip on her arms; the last thing I want is for her to be scared of me.

"I'd never hurt you." Now my voice sounds like a growl, low and harsh in my throat.

"I know."

She looks sincere, and a little confused. Maybe I didn't scare her. Now that I think about it, she's never been scared of me. Even at the beginning when I was such a gigantic, snarling prick, the kind of prick who makes armed police officers take an intimidated step back, she's never been afraid.

Even after the story I told her.

I say abruptly, "You don't have to cook for me."

Her eyebrows draw together. She shakes her head, like I'm making no sense. "I know. I want to."

My chest feels like there's a thousand-pound weight on it. Jesus Christ, hope is fucking terrifying.

"And . . . you don't have to stay with me now . . . I won't try to stop you from leaving."

I specifically don't say I won't beg. There will definitely be begging and pleading, but I won't try to stop her. She'll just have to listen to me crying like a goddamn infant while she walks out the door.

She touches my face. Her eyes are soft. "So you'd let me go, just like that? You think it's fair to introduce me to the best pancakes on earth and then expect me to live without them?"

Do I hear a chiding tone in her voice? Is she . . . *teasing* me?

The faintest smile touches her lips. "You used to have such a good poker face, sweetie. And now look at you. You might as well have that Jumbotron from Times Square on your forehead."

Everything inside me comes to a screeching, rubber-burning stop.

Sweetie. She just called me *sweetie*.

I can feel my face doing something strange. Watching it, Chloe's eyes get even softer.

"Don't get all mushy on me now, rock star, you've got a bad reputation to uphold. How are we going to keep convincing everyone you're such a grouchy dick if you go around with that face from now on?"

I can barely speak, such is my burning, agonizing hope. "Which face is that?"

She leans in and kisses me softly on the mouth. "Your madly-in-love, glowingly happy, finally-sprung-from-hell face." She purses her lips and looks at the top of my head. "We'll have to do something about that black cloud that's missing, too. Everyone's going to wonder what's happened to that."

I grab her, roll her onto her back, and stare down at her. Hope and love and anguish and pain and a million different emotions bang around the inside of my chest, bursting inside my skull. "What are you saying? What are you telling me? Just say it!"

I'm panting and shaking. My face is hot. My throat is tight. I might be having a heart attack.

But my angel is calm as a buddha. She reaches up and cups my face. "I'm saying that I'm going to make us some spaghetti, A.J. Everything else you need to know I told you just a little while ago after you carried me in from the rain."

It can't be. I can't be hearing this right. I whisper, "You said you belonged to me."

When she nods, it feels like a light blinks on inside me. Somewhere in the blackest, loneliest pit of my soul, someone has flipped a switch, and there is light.

I'm staring down at that someone.

She's staring back at me, and she's smiling.

I swallow around the rock in my throat. "And you said . . . you said . . ."

"Hmm?" She gently pushes my hair off my face, calmly waiting for me to get my shit together and speak.

"You said you loved me." It's a gasp, like I'm out of air. Because I *am* out of air. I'm breathing underwater. None of this is real.

Chloe winds my hair around her wrist and uses it like a leash to pull me down, until my body is fully against hers. Her breasts are so soft against my chest. I want to bury my face between them.

Against my lips, she murmurs, "Not loved, A.J. *Love*. Present tense."

She kisses me. That light inside me gets brighter and brighter. It gets so blindingly bright it blocks out everything else, even the clock in my head that's been steadily ticking down to zero all along, and still is.

We make love again. A.J. handles me like I'm made of the most fragile porcelain: breakable, irreplaceable, and rare. All his walls have crumbled, all his defenses are stripped bare. He's totally open to me, vulnerable and emotional, and the feelings I see in his eyes as he gently thrusts into me are blowing my mind.

He looks at me like I'm a miracle. Like I'm his savior. But it's really he who's saved me.

Every breath I've ever taken has been leading me to this.

We spend the rest of the afternoon talking. I make the spaghetti, we eat it in bed, sitting cross-legged on the mattress, and then talk far into the night.

He tells me about the train he took from Saint Petersburg to the Netherlands, two days of rocking cars and clattering tracks and nightmares so bad he'd wake screaming. From Rotterdam he took a cruise ship to New York—on the train, he'd stolen the passport of a man who looked like him—and arrived in the US with the cash he'd saved from his fights, rolled in fist-sized wads wrapped with a rubber band, stuffed inside a backpack. He lived for a while in a youth hostel, whose manager was a drummer in a local band. When the manager was killed crossing the street by a taxi driver, A.J. asked his widow if he could buy the drum set. She gave it to him with a "good riddance," convinced the drums had brought her husband nothing but bad luck.

"A toy drum was the last thing my mother ever gave me," A.J. says, staring out the windows at the midnight sky. It's clear now; the rain clouds have disappeared, and the sky twinkles with stars. "I loved the sound it made, the harshness of it. The colors it made when I banged on it were so raw. Is it the 'Star-Spangled Banner' that goes, 'And the rockets' red glare, the bombs bursting in air'?"

I nod.

"Its colors were like that. And the kit I got from the hostel manager's widow was the same, all angry and brassy and loud. I loved it. I'd thrash on those drums all night sometimes." He laughs. "And nobody ever had the balls to tell me to stop."

"Why New York?"

He looks at me. He's lying on his back with his arms under his head, his feet crossed at the ankles. I'm sitting up beside him with my arms wrapped around my knees, listening raptly to every word.

"Sayori once told me there are only two cities in the world where a person can really disappear. Where someone can go and become anyone else he wants to be, arrive invisible and stay that way, no matter how long he lives there. New York and Las Vegas." He looks out the windows again. "At least New York has a soul. It's a tough soul, pretty unforgiving, but it has one. Vegas is where souls go to die. It's a fucking graveyard of souls, that city."

I remember all those "facts" I read about him on Wikipedia. "So all that stuff about you on the internet, your bio and everything, that's all made up."

He glances at me, amusement in his eyes. "You Googled me?"

I blush. "Don't judge. I had to know who I was dealing with. The internet's the best place to start."

"The internet's full of shit," he says, holding my gaze.

He has a point. Perfect example: anyone with a computer can edit a Wikipedia entry. For many pages, you don't even need a user account to do it.

He reaches out and grasps my ankle, as if he just needs to be touching me somewhere, and continues to talk. "I was in New York for less than a year. The winter reminded me too much of Saint Petersburg, that fucking merciless cold that ices your bones. So I moved to sunny, soulless Vegas. Pretty soon after, I ran out of money. I couldn't get a real job because I didn't have a Social Security card, plus I was paranoid about anyone finding out about my past, so I washed dishes at a restaurant for cash under the table, then got a job as a bouncer at a strip club. That paid a lot better than dish washing. I was sixteen, but I was big, and rough-looking, and could get away with saying I was anywhere from twenty-one to twenty-five."

As he speaks, he rubs his thumb absentmindedly over my ankle-bone. I find it comforting.

"Then one night I got into a fight. In Saint Petersburg, we fought with our fists, sometimes with knives, but the hardware was usually only if you were in a gang. And there were rarely guns. They were just too expensive. But in Vegas, everybody had money. And guns were cheap. So everybody had a gun."

He lifts his arm and shows me a tattoo on the side of his ribs. *Faith is being sure of what we hope for, and certain of what we do not see.*

"Is that scripture?"

He nods. "Hebrews. You see the three scars, inside the F in faith?"

There's a trio of almost identical puckered scars, lighter in color than the surrounding skin, inside the wide flourish of the first letter where the tattoo starts.

"I was shot three times that night. Never even had a chance to throw a punch. Some dirtbag with a Glock semiauto who was high on coke didn't like it that I told him not to touch the girls. He left me flat on my back on the sidewalk, bleeding out. I was sure I was going to die.

"But I woke up in the hospital after surgery with some guy in a cardigan holding a Bible sitting in a chair next to my bed. I have no fucking idea where he came from, he was just there. When I looked at him, he said that line from scripture. I called him a name and threatened to rip off his head. He smiled at me and said he'd been told I was coming, and he was glad I was finally there. I thought he was a complete lunatic. Then his wife shows up, all Mrs. Ingalls in *Little House on The Prairie*—"

"You watched that show, too?" I find it impossible to imagine.

He says solemnly, "There's a lot of waiting around in brothels, angel. You watch a lot of TV."

"American TV?"

"You ever watch socialist TV?"

"No."

"Neither did we. Watching paint dry would be time better spent. And even in the slums we had this thing called satellite."

"Oh. Right."

"Anyway, his wife. She's as batshit as he is, at least that's what I think. At first. I'm in the hospital for two weeks, recovering, and every day these two crazy fuckers show up with homemade muffins and brownies and a shit ton of talk about the Lord and his plans for me, and I'm convinced they're trying to recruit me for a cult."

I'm hooked. "So what happened?"

"So when I was well enough to leave the hospital, they asked me to come and live with them."

"And did you?"

He snorts. "*No.* I went right back to my old life, working as a bouncer. But every fucking night at some point during my shift, this crazy pastor would show up, smiling like he's got some freaky secret, talking about the Lord. I can't tell you how many times I threatened to kick his ass just to get him to shut the fuck up."

"But eventually you moved in with them."

He nods, smiling faintly. "I think I did it just to get him off my back. Like, 'Here I am, you got your wish, sucks to be you, motherfucker,' but somehow . . . it worked out. They were actually just *nice.* I never woke up in the middle of the night with his dick up my ass like I was expecting."

I can't help it; I laugh. I drop my head to my knees and dissolve into laughter. A.J. laughs along with me.

"I know, right? Insane. Even more insane was how they encouraged me to play drums, take music lessons, join a band, read books . . . those people were ridiculously supportive. They only wanted the best for me. They were proud of me; they told everyone I was their son who'd been away on a mission."

"And no one questioned your sudden appearance? This unknown sixteen-year-old son shows up out of the blue and it's business as usual?"

He gives me a look. "You ever spend much time around really religious folks, Chloe?"

I shake my head. "My family's Protestant. That's about as non-religious as you can get without being atheist."

"Yeah, well, it's called faith for a reason. Total suspension of disbelief is pretty much the only requirement. Matthew's congregation was small, but they were super-religious. In other words, they were all allergic to anything that resembled logic. He said I was their son, and it might as well have been carved on a stone tablet for all the questions those people didn't ask. Plus my chromesthesia helped; they thought I was gifted, specially blessed by God. I got the feeling more than once that people were expecting me to walk on water, or turn a fish and a loaf of bread into Sunday brunch.

"Anyway, after I moved in with them, they set me up with all the right paperwork: birth certificate, Social Security card, everything. So Alexei Janic, fatherless bastard of a Russian whore, became Alex James, beloved son of an American pastor and his wife."

"What about that whole not bearing false witness thing? How could a pastor not have a problem with lying?"

A.J. smiles. "Funny thing about the Bible; people glean from it what they need to hear. Maybe that's its whole reason for existence. For Matthew and Marjorie, lying about who I was didn't technically count because it didn't hurt anyone, and because God Himself had told them to take care of me. The faith thing again. They basically got a holy hall pass."

"Wow." I stare again at the scripture tattoo. Then I look at all the other tattoos on his chest, abdomen, and arms, and feel overwhelmed by the weight of the stories that I sense behind them.

"I never shared any of their religious convictions, because I thought if God did exist, he was a serious fucking douche bag with a crap sense of humor who in no way deserved to be worshipped by anyone, but it got to the point where I respected their beliefs. So when they died, I got the tattoo in honor of them. Because of all they'd done for me; it was the least I could do in remembrance."

"What happened to them?"

He sighs. "The stupidest thing in the world: carbon monoxide poisoning. They had an ancient propane space heater in their bedroom that leaked, filled up the room with gas one night. That was it."

I reach out and take his hand. As I thread my fingers through his, he watches with a strange, dreamy expression on his face, almost as if he can't believe what he's seeing. His eyes flash up to meet mine. His dreamy gaze turns melancholy.

"Death follows me, Chloe," he murmurs. "It's always been all around me, ever since I was born. It's a part of me. It's one of the reasons I didn't want to get close to you. I didn't want anything bad to happen to you. I didn't want to stain you with my bad luck."

I unfold my legs and stretch out beside him, snuggling tight against his warm solidity. "Now who's not being logical?"

He wraps both arms around me and squeezes me tight. "It has nothing to do with logic. Bad luck is a real thing. Just ask any gambler."

"You're just looking at it all wrong."

He lifts his head and stares at me, brows raised.

"How many of your friends made it out of Saint Petersburg alive?"

His eyes darken.

"And what if you hadn't been big? When you were six years old, if you couldn't fight, what would've happened to you?"

His eyes get darker and darker.

"Exactly. And how many orphan slum boys are taught to read and to appreciate music and art by a kind, intelligent stranger? And if you weren't there to help Sayori at the end, what would've happened to her?"

He's perfectly still and silent, his normally bright amber eyes the color of dusk.

"So then you emigrate to a foreign country with a stolen passport—without getting caught for theft, or followed by any authorities who might be interested in the arson of a local house of ill repute—and find a place to live. You're not murdered in your sleep. You're not mugged by a gang of thugs. Even after all you've seen and experienced, you don't develop a life-threatening drug addiction. You *do* inherit a drum kit—"

"From a dead man."

"And no one around you tells you to stop playing, even though, as you said, you 'thrash' on it. From what I know of New Yorkers, they aren't exactly shy about speaking their minds."

He looks as if he's considering what I'm saying. His brows have lowered, and drawn together.

"From there you move to another city, and just as your money runs out, you meet a man who thinks God has sent you to him."

"Because he was insane. And I was shot, remember?"

"Yes, and when you wake up after being shot, there's a pastor sitting in a chair beside your bed who's convinced you're a gift from the heavens above. And he and his wife adopt you, and furnish you with a loving home and all the necessary documentation to cover your past. I mean, really A.J., that's a movie-of-the-week special right there."

"They died," he says flatly.

"As everyone does eventually," I respond, my voice very soft. "And through no fault of your own. Wouldn't they have had that space heater on in their room, even if you weren't living with them?"

He's silent.

"And Sayori would have died, too. Only not with the help of someone she loved. And not with the same peace of mind."

He says harshly, "And Pavel? Maksim? *Matushka*? In what fantasy world am I excused for them? How can you wash their blood from my hands?"

I press my hand to his cheek and look into his eyes. "You were born into hell, A.J. Everyone in hell has blood on their hands."

He sits up abruptly and turns his back to me. "I don't accept it."

I know I'm on fragile ground with him here. I also know I'd do anything—*anything*—to make him feel better, even if it's only for a little while. I decide to go out on a limb.

"Have you ever considered the possibility that maybe you're being tested?"

He turns his head. I see him in profile, straight nose and thinned lips and a hard, unyielding jaw, softened by candlelight.

"I'm not saying by God; I don't even know if I believe in Him. Her. Whatever. But I do believe in Fate, A.J. I believe things happen for a reason. And everything that's happened in your life, and mine, has led us to this moment. Right now. Us, in this room together. Would you ever have predicted something like this would happen to you? That you would feel this way for another person?"

His throat works. His lashes lower. After a long time, he says, "No."

I touch his strong, bare back. "Me neither. Maybe, in a way, that line from scripture is actually true. Faith doesn't necessarily have to mean faith in God. Maybe being sure of what you hope for, and certain of what you don't see . . . maybe that's about *us*."

He turns and stares at me.

"Maybe it's not about religion at all. Maybe it's about love. Because I've hoped for something like this my whole life, and now here it is. Here you are. And honestly—please don't think this is stupid, but it's the only word that fits—it kind of feels . . . holy."

There are no words to describe the expression on his face. His eyes, though, I've seen that look before. His eyes are haunted.

I crawl into his lap. He holds me, and as I always do in his arms, I feel utterly safe. I rest my head in the crook of his neck, and listen to the sound of his breathing.

We stay like that for a long time, not speaking. Finally A.J. exhales, and presses a kiss to my hair. I tilt my head back to examine his face. He looks calmer now, but there's still something behind his eyes, some worry or pain that hasn't been relieved by either his confession, or my reassurances.

With a little shiver of anxiety, I wonder if it's because he still has secrets left to tell.

I whisper, "What are you thinking?"

While he strokes his hand over my hair, I hold my breath, praying he's not going to shut down, shut me out, or run away from me for good.

"I'm thinking we need to spend some quality time in the bathtub," he says, voice husky. He traces his thumb over my lower lip, and I can't help but smile.

"Oh, yeah? You need a good soak?" I tease, relieved.

His eyes flash up to mine. The darkness recedes, and they kindle. "It's your hair, Sunshine. I wasn't going to say anything, but you're starting to look like Ziggy Marley's little sister."

"Hey! I've been sick!"

He stands, lifting me with ease in his arms as he rises. He's smiling now, and my heart soars. He carries me into the bathroom, sets me on the toilet lid, and bends over to turn on the water to get it hot for the bath. When he straightens, he says, "Be right back."

"Where are you going?"

Looking down at me, his hair falling into his eyes, he smiles at me so tenderly my breath catches in my throat. "Bath time calls for music, baby. I've got the perfect thing."

He goes into the other room. Moments later, above the sound of running water, I hear a song begin to play. It's "Take Me to Church," by Hozier.

A.J. returns with his arms full of unlit pillar candles. He sets them on the floor in the corners, around the sink, on the ledge above the tub. From the medicine cabinet he takes a matchbook, and lights all the candles, one by one. When he flicks off the overhead light, the room glows gold.

He steps into the bathtub, turns to me with eyes like fire, and holds out his hand.

"Don't move."

"I promise I'm trying not to."

"You're not trying very hard."

"You're not making it very easy for me."

A.J. presses his erection against my bottom. "For you, it will always be hard."

"Not funny," I gasp, gripping the sides of the tub.

A.J. sits behind me in the bathtub, his knees on either side of my hips. I'm reclining on his chest. One of his hands has a firm grip on my wet hair, keeping my head against his shoulder. The other hand is between my legs. His fingers stroke me slowly, around and around, up and down, gentle pressure and delicious, wet heat. Hot water swirls over his hand, my hips, my spread thighs, sloshing when I fail to hold still, as he's commanded.

His fingers slip inside me, and I moan.

He turns my head and kisses me deeply. As his tongue invades my mouth, I yield to him, concentrating on the sensation of his lips and tongue against mine, trying with all my might not to rock my hips as he begins to stroke my clit with his thumb as two of his other fingers delve deeper.

"Please. I have to move."

He murmurs against my mouth, "Move and I'll spank your pussy."

My eyes fly open. "You wouldn't!"

Slowly, his lips curve upward. He releases my hair and cups my breast, rolling my hard nipple under his thumb until it's all I can do not to arch my back and purr.

Jesus, this man is a genius with his thumbs.

"Try me and find out."

He pinches my nipple. I suck in a breath. *God that feels good.* Then he slides his hand across my chest to fondle my other breast. His cock is hard as an iron bar against my behind.

I have to grit my teeth to keep myself still. "Why are you torturing me?"

I feel his low, deep chuckle all the way through my body. "Call it payback." His laughter dies and he gently bites my shoulder, with just enough pressure to sting. "But mostly because I love to make you squirm, angel. I love seeing how you respond, how I make you feel. And watching you try to hold back is the sexiest fucking thing I've ever seen."

Oh. Well, since he put it that way.

He sucks on my throat. I let my eyes fall shut. Biting my lip, I hold perfectly still as he increases the speed of his fingers. When that gets him no reaction, he lifts me slightly and I feel, underwater, the head of his cock nudge my entrance. My mouth opens, but I manage not to make a noise, or otherwise move.

For this, I'm rewarded.

Gently, oh so slowly, he eases inside me, replacing his fingers with his throbbing, amazing cock, all the while continuing to stroke my clit.

I grip the sides of the tub so hard I can't believe it doesn't shatter in my hands.

He winds his arm around my waist. He holds me tightly against his body as he starts to slowly fuck me, his face turned to my neck, his hand working its magic between my legs. The water begins to slosh around our naked bodies in earnest, slipping over the edges of the tub, pooling on the floor.

"I can't—A.J.—I don't think I can stay still much longer."

His breath is hot against my neck. His beard is a rough scrape against my jaw. He bites my earlobe. "Do you *want* me to spank your greedy little pussy, angel?"

His voice is so sexy, playful yet so damn demanding, his words so dirty, I groan in frustration. I need him, the wild and unleashed side of him. And I need it now.

"Is that a yes?"

"A.J., please . . ."

Then I can't stand it anymore. Whimpering, I grind my bottom against his pelvis, taking him even deeper inside.

Suddenly he raises his hips, using the water's buoyancy to help lift me all the way out of the water, and gives me a light, stinging slap between the legs, right where I'm most sensitive.

I jerk, crying out as shockwaves of pleasure pulse through my body. I can't believe he did that!

I can't believe I liked it.

And dear lord, he knows. He *knows*. I'm trembling and panting and my nipples are diamond hard, and he realizes the effect he's just had on my body.

All humor gone, he whispers into my ear, "You want another, don't you?"

"I . . . I . . ."

"Yes or no, Chloe. We have to talk about this. You need to tell me what you like. I need to know your limits."

My heart pounds wildly, drunkenly, as if it can't decide whether to burst or faint. "I don't do kinky. I don't do *Fifty Shades* stuff. I'm . . . I'm . . . not into that."

He falls still. His lowered voice is full of concern. "Are you worried I'll hurt you? Are you afraid I'll try to push you into something you don't want?"

I have to admit the truth. "No. I trust you. I'm just . . . it's embarrassing. I'm not used to talking about what I like. No one's ever asked, to be honest. It feels a little weird."

After a moment, he relaxes. He begins to thrust in and out of me again, gently, controlling his speed, holding me steady with that strong arm wrapped around me.

"Don't be embarrassed. I only want to make you feel good, whatever that means to you. I won't ever do anything you're not comfortable with. But that means communicating with me. So if you want something, you have to ask for it, baby."

The room is almost unbearably warm. Everything smells like hot wax and sex. My breasts bounce with every move of his hips. His muscular thighs bunch and flex around mine. Candlelight dances over the walls, and I'm slowly going mad with passion.

Subtly, I arch against his chest, tilting my hips, giving him a better angle to slide inside. He's so big, stretching me open. It feels like paradise. I love the way he claims me. The way he owns me. The way he takes control.

Cheeks flaming, my eyes squeezed shut, I say, "Yes, I want you to do it again. But not too hard, okay?"

I feel the tremor that passes through him. His fingers dip lower between my legs, to where our bodies meet, and he exhales a rough burst of air. "How about like this?"

He raises his hips again, lifting me from the water, and slaps my exposed pussy. I twitch, moaning. It feels so good I almost come, but I'm still trying to be good for him, I'm still trying to hold still, hold back, hold on to my sanity.

"Harder or softer?" His voice has gone all low and rough. His breathing is deeper, more irregular.

"A little softer. And . . . *more*."

He stretches out his long legs, braces his feet against the wall above the tub, thrusts into me with more force, and gently slaps my pussy four times in quick succession.

My reaction is instant and violent.

I scream. My body bows toward the ceiling. I come, hips jerking, muscles contracting, blindly exploding with pleasure.

Beneath me, A.J. gasps. "Fuck! Angel! Fuck!"

He loses control. He grabs my hips and pumps into me fast and hard, riding out my orgasm as I writhe on top of him, completely helpless to stop any of the wanton sounds or movements I'm making. My cries echo off the walls.

When he bucks and groans and I feel a spreading warmth deep inside me, I'm still coming furiously. Water flies everywhere. The candles on the floor nearest the tub are extinguished with a hiss in a hail of drops. Smoke drifts lazily up into the air, and hangs in widening coils near the ceiling.

It doesn't occur to me until much later that he isn't wearing a condom.

For the next two days, A.J. and I exist in a strange and beautiful kind of suspended animation. It feels as if all the clocks in the world have stopped ticking, that for us time itself holds its breath.

The hotel becomes our lovers' playground.

We make popcorn the old-fashioned way in the large downstairs kitchen, frying hard kernels of corn and butter in a sizzling cast iron skillet on the six-burner stove, laughing and ducking when they explode. We put the hot buttered popcorn in paper bags and take them to the screening room, where we eat while watching old movies, the plush upholstered chairs we sit in draped with clean sheets so we don't get covered in years' worth of dust. We play hide-and-seek in the vast, dim attic, crouching behind antique armoires, peeking around floor-standing mirrors, darting in and out of the forgotten remains of decades of prior owners.

A.J. always finds me. Or maybe I always let him. Because I know when I'm caught there will be hugs and laughter and sweet, sweet kisses that quickly turn hot.

We spend hours exploring the library, the laundry, the overgrown gardens, all the upstairs guest rooms and downstairs storage rooms. In the subterranean parking garage, we discover one entire room A.J. didn't even know existed dedicated solely to broken televisions, cracked mirrors, and lamps missing their lampshades, relics from when the property had paying guests. In the cavernous ballroom with the vaulted ceilings and grand piano, I learn A.J. knows how to play more than drums.

"What, you thought I was a one-trick pony?" he asks with a wink while I sit transfixed beside him on the wood bench, watching his big, tattooed hands bring Mozart to life with an effortless dexterity that leaves me awed.

"Where did you learn to play the piano?"

"Church."

He says it like it's the most normal thing in the world, as if everyone learns to play Mozart in church. The most interesting thing I learned in church was how to sit still for long periods of time without falling asleep.

We talk and nap and shower and eat and make love.

Everywhere, we make love.

He shows me his music collection. I'm introduced to jazz greats John Coltrane, Nina Simone, and Thelonious Monk. From jazz he moves to opera, much of which I'm already familiar with. We listen in silence to Maria Callas sing "Madame Butterfly," and I'm moved to tears.

"She wasn't the most technically gifted soprano who ever lived, but she was the most honest, the most passionate," says A.J. reverently at the end of the song. "She lived for her art. I see it in the colors of her voice. Opera was the love of her life."

He turns to me with his gorgeous golden eyes ablaze with emotion, those words hanging between us. *The love of her life.*

I turn away before I make a fool of myself, and ask him to show me more.

We cover big band, swing, blues, hip-hop, R&B, soul, grunge, reggae, Goth. His knowledge of his industry is remarkable. He talks at length about the origin of punk rock, the best musicians who never made it big, why disco was the worst thing ever to happen to music. He knows the lyrics to a seemingly infinite number of songs by heart, singing along as the song plays, carrying a tune perfectly. We play a game where he bets me I can play any song in his collection and he'll be able to immediately recognize it, and correctly sing the first line.

"If I'm wrong, or I miss any of the lyrics, you win. But if I'm right, I win."

"Anyone can get lucky and guess one song," I scoff, folding my arms across my chest.

"Okay . . . how about twenty songs?"

He's already told me he has over five thousand CDs in the wall unit in his room. I'm crap at math, but figure if each CD has roughly ten songs, that's around fifty thousand songs we're talking about. I begin to feel smug.

"What do I get when I win?"

He grins. "A kiss."

"Hmm. And if you win?"

His grin grows wicked. I roll my eyes, pretending that smile doesn't do all sorts of bad things to my body. Bad and very wonderful things.

He wins, of course. I halfheartedly accuse him of cheating, just before he throws me over his shoulder and heads for the bed.

Those forty-eight hours are the most magical of my life. I don't want our time together to ever end.

But, of course, it does.

Just not how I've been expecting.

The smell of coffee wakes me. When I open my eyes, A.J. is kneeling on the mattress beside me, holding a freshly brewed cup. He's shirtless and smiling, two of my favorite things.

Smiling in return, I rub my fist into my eye and sit up. "What time is it?"

"Eight a.m., baby, Monday morning. Time for you to go back to work."

Oh my God, it's Monday. I freeze. My mind goes blank. My pulse begins to pound so loudly in my ears I have to concentrate on what I say next. "That's right. Our . . . our week is up."

Looking completely unfazed, A.J. hands me the coffee. "Technically, our week was up a few days ago."

I've overstayed my welcome. I look down at the mug in my hands. My face is so hot my ears are scalding.

"You hungry? There's cereal."

The thought of food turns my stomach. "No, thank you." I can barely form the words. *I'm leaving. This is it. It's over.* "I . . . I'll just get ready then . . . take a shower . . ."

"Okay." He says it with so much cheer I'm gripped by a violent urge to slap his face.

I'm leaving today. Our time is over. And A.J. doesn't give one single fuck.

He rises from the bed and goes into the bathroom, his step light, his posture untroubled. I hear the water go on; he's started the shower for me. He's so eager to get me out, he can't even wait long enough for my shower to get hot!

I shake with humiliation, pain, and a deep, aching sense of betrayal. Worst of all is the knowledge that I've done this to *myself*. He was completely up front with me; he told me we'd have a week, and now that week, plus a few extra days, is over. I knew this was coming all along.

What did I expect, a marriage proposal?

Blinking back tears, I take a swallow of the coffee. It's strong and black, just how I like it.

Son of a bitch.

I finish the coffee, take my shower, dress and blow-dry my hair, all while fighting tears and failing miserably to try to convince myself this isn't the end of the world.

Only it really feels like it is.

When I emerge from the bathroom, A.J. is in the kitchenette, washing my coffee cup in the sink. He rinses it, dries it, and puts it away in the cupboard. Watching that drives a stake through my bleeding, shredded heart. In his mind, I'm already gone.

Ignoring the tears that are now sliding down my cheeks, I cross to the sofa and reach for my suitcase, which is propped up beside it, but then I freeze with my hand on the handle when A.J. calls out, "So what do you think for dinner tonight? Are you sick of my pancakes? Because I was thinking of getting fancy and trying to make an omelet."

It takes what feels like four hours for me to straighten and turn to look at him. "Dinner?"

He's still at the sink, tidying up, with his back to me. His hair is loose around his shoulders. He's wearing ancient, holey jeans and nothing else. The sight of his strong, bare feet against the floor makes me want to weep, they're so beautiful.

"Yeah. You should be home around what, six? Seven?"

I can't think. My mouth refuses to form words.

He turns to look at me. When he sees my face, he blinks in shock. "Angel! What's wrong?"

And I totally lose it. I go completely, utterly nuts.

I shout, "Are you kidding me? Are you just screwing with me right now? First you're throwing me out and then you want to know what I want for dinner?"

A.J. looks left, then right, like he's wondering who this crazy person is and if there's anyone else nearby who can help him handle her. "Who said I was throwing you out?"

My hands are balled to fists. I can feel how red my face is. My chest heaves up and down, and all I can do is stare at him, shaking. Through gritted teeth, I say, "Our *week* is *up*."

Understanding dawns over his face. "Oh angel. Jesus."

He drops the dish towel he's holding and strides over to me. In several long, swift strides, he's in front of me. He gathers me into his arms and hugs me, hard. "You're not going anywhere without me, except work. And even *there* I'll be lurking in corners, watching, making sure nothing happens to you."

In a move I thought only happened in romance novels, my knees go weak. Now I shake even harder, clinging to his waist so I don't slide bonelessly to the floor. "W-what happened to one week? What happened to our deal?"

He takes my face in his hands. "What happened is that I told you all the worst shit I've ever done, and you told me you belonged to me. You told me you loved me. *Love*," he corrects himself, "present tense. I'm not letting you go, Chloe. You belong to me, and I won't spend another day without you. I can't live without you, don't you see? Without you I might as well be dead."

I burst into sobs and start to ugly cry so hard A.J. laughs.

"It's not funny, you jerk!"

He kisses me all over my wet, red face, holding me tight, murmuring how much he loves me, how much he needs me, how he'll never, ever let me go.

Mondays are officially my new favorite day of the week.

That day at work goes by in a dream. I'm surprised how well Trina and the staff handled everything in my absence; no fires had to be put out, no major mistakes were made. I make an appointment to have the stitches removed from my cheek, and another with the plastic surgeon my father recommended to see what can be done about any residual scarring.

I'm so happy I almost don't care about the scarring. I'm so happy I feel like the sun is shining out of the top of my head.

Grace, however, is *not* happy.

"So you spent about a week and a half playing house with the drummer, and now you're back at work avoiding all my questions like it's your mother you're talking to, and not your very best friend. Well, your *other* very best friend. Not acceptable, Chloe!"

Even her scathing tone can't put a damper on my glorious mood. I sigh and sit back in my office chair, propping my feet on my desk. "I missed you."

"Lie," she shoots back without hesitation. "Who do you think is on the other end of the line, babe? I know you like I know the back of my hand. Other than those thirty-second check-in phone calls, you didn't think about me once."

I smile because she's right. "Well, now I miss you. When can we get together? How's Kat?"

She snorts. "Other than being worried sick about you and driving me crazy about the wedding, she's her usual foul-mouthed, wonderful self. She and Nico are planning a party at their house next Monday for Memorial Day; I assume you and the Russian spy are coming?"

I see the dangling fishhook a mile away, and avoid it. All of A.J.'s secrets are safe with me, and always will be. "I don't know. I haven't even talked to Kat yet. Maybe?"

"No maybes. You're coming." Her firm, no-refusals tone softens. "How are you doing, really? Have you heard anything about dickface Eric?"

At the mention of his name, my stomach tightens. Feeling vulnerable, I lower my feet and sit up straight at the desk, hugging my free arm around my waist. "We got the restraining order, so that's good. And apparently Eric's out of the hospital, though he's not back to work; he's been suspended without pay."

Grace mutters a few choice epithets about Eric's manhood. "They should have fired that worthless prick on the spot."

"They have to do an internal investigation first, though it looks like it's just a formality. I think he'll be fired soon. I guess there were quite a few skeletons in his closet his bosses could no longer overlook."

"Well, good riddance. Honestly if I ever see his face again, I think I'll break it."

I love her for refraining from saying "I told you so."

"So do you want me to spend the night with you for the next few days, until you get settled back in? Or you're always welcome to crash at my place if you don't feel comfortable at your apartment since Mr. Law and Order left you with such nice memories there."

"No, I'm good. I'm staying with A.J. for the foreseeable future."

The silence on the other end of the line is deafening.

"I love him, Gracie," I say, much softer. "Wherever he is, that's where I need to be."

I wonder if Grace has bought a cat, because from the other end of the phone issues a sound like a cat trying to cough up a stubborn hairball.

"Okay, *best friend*, I'm ending the call now."

"Wait!"

Her panicked shout makes me pause. I can't remember the last time I heard Grace panicked. "What?"

"I just have one more question for you."

"Which is?"

It's her turn to pause. "Are you sure?"

There's not even a second of hesitation when I answer. "Yes. I've never been more sure of anything in my life."

I hear a deep, resigned sigh. "How the hell did I, badass bitch that I am, get stuck with two such *ridiculously* romantic girlfriends?"

I have to smile; that sigh means she's got my back, even if she thinks I'm insane. She'll never again say another negative or unsupportive word about my relationship with A.J.

"Are we in rhetorical question territory here? Or are you seriously expecting an answer to that?"

"Rhetorical, rhetorical," she mutters. "And now *I'm* ending the call so I can pour myself a large glass of water."

"Water? That's not like you."

"Of course I like water. Especially when it's frozen into little cubes and completely surrounded by vodka. Good-bye."

She hangs up on me, leaving me grinning at the phone.

I love my friends.

Over the next week, A.J. and I settle in to a routine. I go to work; he drives by on his motorcycle at least four times during the day to check on me. I come home after work; he cooks dinner. (He graduates from pancakes to omelets to French toast. The man has a serious addiction to eating breakfast foods for supper.) I clean up; he plays the piano or does some amazing drum solo on the practice kit he keeps in what used to be the lobby bar, whaling on it until his fingers bleed like that kid in *Whiplash*. Or he reads to me. Or we watch a movie. Or, or, or one of a thousand different things.

Showers and baths are taken together.

Everything, in fact, we do together, right down to folding laundry.

I had no idea living with another person could be so much *fun*.

"I never thought I'd meet a woman who has worse-looking hands than I do," he teases one afternoon after I yelp in pain when the juice of a lime I've cut to use in guacamole seeps into a deep cut on my finger. We're in the main kitchen downstairs, making lunch. The surface of the stainless steel table I'm standing at is covered in various dents and gouges, but is otherwise a perfectly competent prep area. I like having so much space to spread out; the kitchen in my apartment is miniscule compared to this. And A.J.'s kitchenette in his room is even smaller than that.

I flick a piece of avocado from my fingers at A.J. It lands on his cheek. "Gee, sweet talker, keep 'em coming. Those compliments of yours really get me hot and bothered."

He smiles at my sour look, swipes the avocado from his face, licks his fingers, and pushes away from the opposite counter he's been leaning on as he watches me work. He moves behind me and wraps his arms around my waist. "Yeah? How bothered?" He slides his hand up my ribcage under my shirt and fondles my breast, tweaking my nipple between his fingers. It instantly hardens.

I've given up wearing a bra at home, because A.J. takes it off as soon as I walk in the door anyway.

Pretending to ignore him, along with the flush of heat that spreads from my lower belly down between my legs as he continues to pinch and stroke my nipple with his rough fingers, I shrug.

His other hand slides down my hip, then between my legs. I'm wearing jeans; he rubs me through the fabric, his fingers warm and hard. Automatically, I spread my thighs a little for him, but keep right on making the guacamole, mashing the ripe avocado in a bowl with a fork as if I'm not being wonderfully molested by a big, brawny male with whom I just happen to be madly in love.

He takes my indifference as a challenge. "Not so bothered, hmm? How about hot?"

Unbuttoning my jeans, he pulls down the zipper, and slides his hand past it, into my panties. When his fingers brush over my clit, I almost moan, but catch myself in time.

I shrug again and go right on with the guacamole, which I now have zero interest in.

"Oh, yes, definitely hot," he whispers, his mouth at my ear as his fingers probe deeper. "Hot and *wet.*"

My hands fall still. I close my eyes, breathing shallower as A.J. puts his lips against the pulse in my throat and sucks me there, one hand pulling and rolling my nipple, the other buried between my legs, stroking and slipping in my wetness. When he pinches my clit between two fingers, I finally give in and moan, long and low.

His voice turns to a growl. "I'm going to fuck you on this table, angel."

He shoves the bowl of guacamole aside, yanks my jeans and panties down and off, turns me around and grabs my hips, then lifts me onto the cold metal table. Moving fast, he pushes me onto my back, takes both my legs and sets them on his shoulders, then bends and puts his hot, expert mouth where his fingers have just been.

I moan louder, arching against the table. My fingers dig into his hair.

"Fucking delicious, baby." I look between my spread thighs to find him staring up at me with glittering eyes. He swipes his tongue slowly through my wet folds, and I shudder. "Mmm. But we can't let this guacamole go to waste."

Before I realize what his intentions are, he scoops a big glob of fresh guacamole from the bowl beside me and smears it between my legs. I gasp. It's cold and wet and—

And oh dear God his clever, clever tongue. His full, luscious lips. He's eating it out of me. He's licking me clean.

I fall back against the stainless steel. Out of my mind with pleasure, I cup my breasts in my hands, pinching my nipples as he'd done moments before, every ounce of my focus on that amazing, carnal feast going on between my legs.

I feel something new, slippery and a little stinging. I open my eyes to find A.J. grinning wickedly at me while he squeezes the juice from half a lime into my exposed cleft. Without taking his gaze from mine, he lowers his mouth again and begins to suck.

The pressure builds. I feel it, coiling tighter and tighter deep inside me, sparking my nerves. Our eyes stay locked together as he eats me, his tongue flicking faster and faster, his teeth scraping over my clit.

"A.J." It's a warning; I'm right there. I'm just about to come.

He unzips his own jeans, frees himself, takes his jutting cock in his fist and starts to stroke it, still sucking my pussy, his gaze still on mine.

"Please. Please. A.J., God, please give it to me, I need you now now *now—*"

He rears up and plunges deep inside me, burying himself to the hilt. I groan, flexing my hips to meet his thrusts, holding on to his forearms to keep from sliding as he grips my hips in his hands and fucks me mercilessly, his face hard, his eyes ablaze with lust and love.

"You belong to me." He sounds like an animal, snarling and wild, his voice almost unrecognizably rough.

Knowing that I've affected him as much as he's affected me sends a thrill straight through my body.

"Forever," I whisper. My eyes slide shut. My head falls back. I come.

Within seconds, he follows with a roar, pulling out abruptly before he comes inside me. He collapses on top of me, takes my face in his hands, and kisses me so hard I forget everything else. There is only me and A.J., joined in perfect harmony.

Joined forever.

Chapter 32

"Forever," says my angel.

With that one word, she not only breaks my heart, she breaks what's left of my miserable, selfish soul.

The Memorial Day party at Nico and Kat's ultramodern compound in the Hollywood Hills is less of a party, and more of a wild, celebrity-studded, booze-soaked bacchanal.

Hundreds of people are here—many of whom I recognize from film or television—splashing in the pool, lounging on sleek deck chairs, dancing to the DJ who's set up on a raised platform by the pool house across the lawn. It's a catered affair, with black-tie waiters hoisting trays of hors d'oeuvres above the heads of laughing, half-drunk guests. The whole thing is a scene right out of *Entourage*. In fact, I think I see Adrian Grenier, the lead from the show, across the yard doing body shots from the cleavage of a bikini-clad girl.

We've only just arrived, but I can tell A.J. wishes he were anywhere but here. Maybe this wasn't such a good idea. Kat begged me to come because we haven't seen each other in weeks, but now I'm wondering if I'll be able to really spend time with her at all. This crowd is insane; she must be crazy busy playing the good hostess.

We make our way through the crowd. It seems everyone recognizes A.J. He's clapped on the back and nodded at, he shakes hands with several people but doesn't stop to talk. The women who ogle him he ignores completely, making me feel all sorts of smug. We take up a spot next to a white Lucite bar in one corner of the yard, and I order a chardonnay from the bartender.

Because it's mandated by law, the weather is a perfect seventy-two degrees. The view from the backyard is spectacular; I see all the way from Malibu to downtown. The ocean is a shimmering strip of navy in the distance.

"You okay?" I only ask because A.J.'s face is about as warm as a slab of granite.

"Parties," he says, gazing around the scene.

I take that to mean he doesn't like them, because he doesn't add more. I'm about to tell him we can go as soon as I see Kat, but then I spot Grace across the pool, waving madly at me.

"Grace!" Excited, I wave back, motioning for her to come over.

Her martini held high over her head, she shoulders her way through the crowd. When she gets tired of being jostled and spilling vodka down her arm, she throws her head back and downs the drink, and then sets the glass on the tray of a passing waiter. Then she's standing in front of us, flaming red hair and a tight white dress and a pair of leopard print Louboutins that add six inches to her already statuesque frame. She looks like an Amazonian goddess. Several people nearby are gawking at her, girls included.

Almost half of her life is missing from her memory, and yet she's stronger and more self-assured than anyone I know.

She pulls me into a hug, enveloping me in the scent of vodka and Clive Christian, her signature perfume.

"You look great," she murmurs into my ear. "I can't even see the scar."

I had the stitches in my cheek out last week. The plastic surgeon I went to did a little laser resurfacing afterward. The skin is still pink, but I've covered it with a special redness-reducing foundation and powder Kat recommended. I'm almost as good as new.

Almost. Every time I see a cop car now, I break out in a cold sweat.

"Thanks, Gracie. I missed you."

She pulls back, holds me at arms' length, and examines me. She smiles broadly. I can tell what she's thinking: *Someone's finally been properly fucked.* I grin back at her, nodding.

"A.J.," Grace says, turning her warm gray eyes to him. "Thank you."

He smiles at her, befuddled but interested. "For what?"

Grace gives me a little shake. "For *this.*"

Then she shocks the hell out of both of us by throwing her arms around his neck and giving him a big kiss on the cheek. At the end of it, we're all laughing.

It feels so good.

We stand and talk for a while, about nothing particularly deep or important. I know I'll get the third degree from Grace as soon as she can get me alone, but for now I just enjoy the sun, the conversation, and the wonderful feeling of A.J.'s arm slung over my shoulders.

Then Grace, looking across the yard toward the house, does a double take. "Holy shit. Is that Bono?"

A.J. says with a smirk, "Stupid wraparound purple glasses give it away?"

"Haters gonna hate," she replies, not looking away from the surprisingly short lead singer of U2. "I'm going to get an introduction. Judging by the way he's fondling that cocktail waitress, I bet he and his wife need a *lot* of marriage counseling. God, I can't wait to hear all about it. Back in a sec."

She sails away. I have no doubt she'll get her introduction; there are few things Grace wants that she doesn't get. Actually I can't think of a single one.

Then suddenly A.J. stiffens.

"Just a few more minutes and then we'll go, sweetie. I just want to make sure I say good-bye to Kat on the way out. I wonder if Kenji's here?"

When he doesn't respond, I look up at him. But he's not looking back at me.

He's looking at the raven-haired, large-breasted, incredibly beautiful siren in the skintight red minidress headed our way.

My stomach drops. My eyes flash to his face. It's clear from his expression that he's not looking forward to speaking to her, which makes me feel a little better, but it's also clear that there's some history here that he's very uncomfortable with.

Or maybe he's just uncomfortable because I'm standing beside him.

The siren stops in front of us. I've never seen a woman with such perfect skin, hair, or teeth. She's absolutely stunning. A model, no doubt.

And he's had sex with her, no doubt. Her knowing smile and bedroom eyes are proof enough of that.

"A.J. Good to see you."

He replies with a curt nod. "Heavenly."

Heavenly. Dear lord, I've come face-to-face with the infamous five-thousand-bucks-a-pop whore.

In spite of how much I instantly hate her, how I'd like to scratch out her eyeballs and tear her glossy hair right out of her scalp, I miserably understand why she can charge what she does. I'd bet men would pay her thousands just to look at her naked, and not even touch her.

She turns her eyes to me. No joke, they're the color of sapphires. I pray they're as fake as her boobs, or God is exactly as much of a bastard as A.J. thinks he is.

"And who is this?" she asks pleasantly.

"Heavenly, meet Chloe. Chloe, Heavenly." A.J.'s voice is wooden, his back stiff.

If any other part of his body is stiff, I will murder him where he stands.

"Of course," says Heavenly, looking me up and down. Her smile widens. It almost looks genuine. "It's a pleasure to finally meet you."

Whoa. *What?* He's told her about me? When? It takes me about three point five seconds to control myself, then I slip into sphinx mode, and calmly return her smile. "And you."

Her smile falters. She glances at A.J. I can tell she's wondering what he's told me about her, which, as we know, is nada. But I'll be damned if I'm going to let this Rodeo Drive ho get the upper hand over *me*.

Heavenly decides to up her game. Her smile returns. In a throaty purr, she says to A.J., *"Vy byli pravy. Ya lyublyu yeye."*

As if she's kicked me in the stomach, all the wind is knocked from my lungs.

This is no ordinary hooker. This hooker *speaks Russian.*

Instantly, I've conjured dozens of imaginary scenes of the two of them post-screw, sweaty and beautiful, murmuring sweet nothings to one another in their native language. I assume it must be her native language, too, because what prostitute has the time or energy for Russian lessons? And she has that Euro Bond Girl look about her, all slink and sophistication.

I've never felt jealousy like this before. Not ever. It's like I swallowed a bowl of razors.

I know my face is beet red, just as I know the smile I've got plastered on my face has turned sickly. For some bizarre reason, my mouth is watering. Probably because I'd like to spit a big loogie in her perfect, stupid face.

Then A.J. says something to Heavenly that confuses me even more.

"I told you you would."

"Would what?" I ask before I can stop myself.

A muscle flexes in A.J.'s jaw. "Like you."

My head is exploding. I can't believe what I'm hearing. A.J. told Miss Five K a Blow Job she'd *like* me? When, while she was bouncing up and down on his cock? Completely at a loss, I chug my drink, just barely managing to restrain myself from smashing it upside his head.

He had a life before me, this isn't his fault, you knew about his "experiences," he seems really uncomfortable so let's cut him some slack, shall we?

The voice in my head makes far too much sense, so I remind it that there is a very real possibility this girl knows even more about A.J. than I do.

Which means I'm really not all that special.

Which makes all the blood drain from my face.

"Won't you excuse me for a moment? I think I see someone I need to speak to," I say, prim and proper, in my best Julie Andrews *Princess Diaries* impersonation. My intention is to turn and run, but A.J.'s arm clamps down over my shoulders, preventing me from moving. He holds me tight against his side. I don't want to make a scene in front of *her*, so I stay put, face burning.

"You get an invite to this party, Heavenly?"

I can't tell from his voice whether A.J. is angry or merely curious. I swallow and look away, heart pounding.

"No, I'm here with Slash."

She came with the guitarist from Guns N' Roses? This girl really makes the rounds. I wonder what Slash's wife thinks about that.

Then A.J. says something to her in Russian. She answers back. I have no idea what they're saying, which obviously is the point. And now I'm so mad I could scream.

Just as I'm about to peel A.J.'s arm off me and throw the rest of my chardonnay in his face, Heavenly says, "You know my number." Then she turns and glides away. Heads turn in her wake.

I vibrate with fury. Also I think I might puke.

A.J. takes the glass of wine from my hand and sets it on the bar. Then he takes my arm and steers me past the pool and into the house. People scatter in front of us like scared mice; A.J. is wearing his serial killer expression. The thunderclouds have returned over his head.

He takes me to a first-floor bathroom, locks the door behind us, and backs me up against the wide marble sink. "All right. Say your piece."

Breathing hard, I cross my arms over my chest. "No, I think *you* should go first. And I'll give you five minutes to cover all the important points, specifically *why* and *when* you talked to her about me, when the last time was that you slept with her, and what the *hell* you two said to each other at the end there, when it looked like you were making plans to hook up later."

He says instantly, "I haven't been with her since we've been together."

"And when exactly did we get together? When you were visiting me at my apartment in the middle of the night, when you were grilling me about my entire life story but refusing to sleep with me, or after I moved into your place?"

He glowers. "You think I'm lying to you?"

That muscle in his jaw is really getting a workout.

"Don't you dare try to turn this back on me! I had to stand there like an idiot while you and your ho had a nice little chat *in Russian* about God only knows what!"

"She's not mine," he says, voice hard, "*you're* mine, and you know it."

He crushes his mouth to mine.

I struggle, but he holds my jaw in one hand and pins one of my arms around my back with the other. It's easier to give in than to fight him, so I let him kiss me, and pretend I don't like it. When he finally breaks the kiss we're both panting.

"I told her about you long before we ever got together, right after I heard you sing that day in your shop, back when you hated my guts. I haven't fucked her or anyone else since that day."

His voice is rough, but his eyes are soft, and I want so badly to believe him. But the way Heavenly *looked* at him . . . the intimacy of her eyes, her voice. It's eating me up inside.

"You're forgetting about that brunette you left with, the one you met in my candle aisle!"

"I just did that to piss you off, angel. I didn't fuck her. I didn't even kiss her. She gave me a ride to my manager's office, and then I took a cab home."

He kisses me again, another demanding pull on my lips, and I can't keep my head straight. I'm losing my train of thought. I draw back, but he doesn't let me go far; he keeps his hand on my jaw, his lips very close to mine.

"What about what you said to each other at the end? What was that?"

He's been looking at my lips, but his gaze drifts up, and he meets my eyes. He stares into them with sizzling intensity. "I told her she should go back to Slash."

"And what did she say?"

"That she was glad to see me happy. That I deserved it."

I look away because my eyes are filling with water. A.J. kisses my cheek, then murmurs into my ear, "I'm going to say something you won't want to hear, angel, but it's the truth so you need to hear it."

"What?"

He turns my face so I have to look him in the eye. "For a long time, she was the only friend I had."

That hurts and it also makes me incredibly sad for him. "Does she know about you? About your past?"

He shakes his head. "You're the only one I've ever told that story to. She's not stupid; she knows I'm not from Vegas. But she never cared. She never asked anything of me. Before you, with her was the only place I felt safe."

Oh God, my heart. I don't know how much more of this it can take. In a shaking voice, I say, "I can't compete with that, A.J."

"You don't have to, baby. There's no competition; all of me belongs to you. It has from the very beginning."

He kisses me again, hungrily, his hard body pressed against mine. I break away just long enough to say, "I never want to see her again! Promise me you'll never talk to her again!"

Against my mouth, he promises, "Never. Never. You're the only one I need."

I cling to his shoulders as he lifts me up onto the sink counter. His hands slip under my dress, pushing the fabric up my thighs. He pulls my panties down, and drops them to the floor.

"Yes," I groan when he slides his fingers inside me. I need this.

I need him. I'm going out of my mind. Beyond the locked door, the party rages; the bass from loud music pulses through the walls.

I fumble with his belt buckle, yanking at it until it comes undone. Tearing at the fly of his pants, I manage with my shaking hands to free his erection. He moans when I curl my fingers around it.

He pulls my head back with a hand fisted in my hair. "On your belly, baby." His voice is husky with need; he flips me over and pushes up my dress, exposing my bare behind.

I watch him in the mirror as he stares down at my body. I see the overwhelming desire in his gaze, and it calms me, as well as excites me. It only takes him a moment to don the condom he pulls from his wallet. Then he positions himself between my spread legs, and eases his hard cock inside my wetness.

In the mirror, our gazes lock. Holding on to my hair with one hand and my hip with the other, he starts to fuck me from behind.

Someone tries the door handle. We ignore it, consumed by watching each other, the heat building hotter and hotter with every stroke of his beautiful, rigid cock.

Through the door comes an aggravated shout. "Oy! Anybody in there!"

A.J. growls, "Go away or lose your fucking head!"

He thrusts harder. I moan brokenly, my palms flattened against the mirror so I can push back against him as he thrusts.

From outside the door comes laughter. "Get it, brother!" There are two short, approving raps on the door, then nothing but the music and the sound of the party.

A.J. moves his hand from my hip to down between my legs. His fingers expertly stroke me, sliding over and around my throbbing nub until my whole body quakes with pleasure and I'm so wet I feel it slipping down my thighs. He quickly brings me to two orgasms before he finally lets himself go.

As he shudders and moans, I rest my cheek against the cool tile, close my eyes, and pray that's the last we've seen of the woman who used to be A.J.'s only friend.

Unfortunately, it won't be. And if I thought I knew what pain was before, the two of them will soon give me an education in pain that will last me a lifetime.

"Honestly, Chloe, it's time I met this young man. You've been living with him for two months, for goodness' sake! When Bunny asked me the other day at the club how you were doing, I had absolutely nothing to say, did I? I don't even know his last name!"

My mother. Within minutes of calling the shop, she's in harassment mode. I smile to myself. Not even Mommy Dearest can knock me off my high.

It's been a few weeks since the Memorial Day party, and everything in my world is about as perfect as it can be. We haven't seen or heard from Eric—he didn't press charges against A.J.—and Heavenly feels like a distant memory. Best of all, everything between A.J. and me has been great. As in, *amazingly* great.

As in, I'm so in love with that man it seems like a dream come true.

"His last name is Edwards, mother, which I'm sure Dad has told you on more than one occasion. And you'll meet him at the wedding. I'm not ready to release the hounds on him just yet."

She makes a sound like she's deeply insulted, which I know is manufactured strictly for guilt-inducing purposes. We both know what A.J. would be subjected to if my mother gets him alone. *When* she gets him alone; I can already picture the scene at the wedding. I feel sorry for him in advance.

Lucky for us, my father is on our side. He and A.J. have spoken several times on my burner phone, and I get the feeling they like each other, though neither one admits it out loud.

Men.

"So if it wasn't for Kat having the good manners to invite us to the wedding, we'd *never* meet him?"

"Let's not get carried away on the exaggeration train, mother."

My parents have known Kat for years, since we went to high school together. Her mother was sick all through high school, and died our senior year, so Kat spent a lot of time at my house. My parents are like her godparents, so of course they were invited to the wedding. My brother, too. It's just over two months away; I can't believe how fast time is flying by. Grace and I haven't even planned what we're going to do for Kat's bachelorette party yet.

"Well, James had a few good things to say about him, anyway," she admits grudgingly.

I perk up at that. "Really? Like what?"

There's a fraught beat of silence. "He says he can tell this young man really cares for you. He thinks you're safe with him." She exhales heavily. "And after what you've been through, that's all that really matters to your father and me."

I'm touched. "Thanks, Mom. And I agree with Jamie on both counts. In fact . . . I can't remember ever being this happy."

Is that a sniffle I hear? No. Impossible. My mother isn't sentimental in the least.

"I'm glad you've kept your apartment anyway, Chloe. That's very sensible of you. Just in case."

I scowl. I've only kept my apartment because I signed a contract, which isn't even close to being up. If I walk away from it I'll get hit with a lawsuit, so it's been sitting empty, gathering dust. My mother must sense the storm clouds building, because she quickly changes the subject.

"How's work?"

I nearly fall off my chair in shock. "Um . . . great, actually. Thanks for asking. Kat's mentioned a few things about the wedding on social media that have been really great for Fleuret. I've picked up three big new clients this week alone."

There's a small pause, then my mother quietly says, "Your father and I are very proud of you, Chloe. I know we don't tell you enough, but we are. And we love you."

Now I'm completely blown away. I wonder if she's been drinking. "I love you, too, Mom."

The bell on my shop door jingles, indicating someone's come in. I've been expecting Kat and Nico; today I'm showing them the samples of their dining table centerpieces.

I look at the clock, wondering why A.J. isn't here yet. He confirmed just this morning he'd be here, and he's not one to be late. He said he had a meeting with his manager at ten o'clock, but that was hours ago. A twinge of worry pinches my stomach, but I push it aside.

"Gotta go, Mom. I'll talk to you soon, okay?"

I hear the sound of a kiss through the phone. "Take care of yourself, darling."

"I will. Bye."

When we hang up, I cross my fingers that Nico and Kat will like their samples. Trina and I spent all morning setting up two square banquet tables in the shop so they could see how the final table setup would look at the wedding. I've rented linens, silver, and glassware, and have set the tables for eight guests, mimicking the setup for the reception. In the center of one table is the low arrangement we'll be using, with the tall, dramatic arrangement on the other. They're alternating tall and low for the reception tables, which is one of my favorite designs for a large party. It gives the room more visual interest than just a sea of tall arrangements, which can easily look overdone.

I hurry to the front, where I find Nico, Kat, Grace, Kenji, a stout, fortyish blonde named Jennifer, who's the wedding coordinator, and Brody Scott, aka "Scotty," the lead guitarist for Bad Habit and one of Nico's groomsmen, standing in a semicircle around the display table with the tall arrangement.

Jennifer is snapping pictures of the arrangements on her iPhone. She looks impressed.

Grace is fingering the linens. She also looks impressed.

Kat is staring at the flowers with her hand over her mouth. She looks like she might cry. When she sees me, she says in a trembling voice, "Holy fucking shit, Chloe. I can't even . . ." She bursts into tears.

Nico puts his arm around her, pulls her against his chest, and smiles at me. "She loves it, darlin'. So do I. You've outdone yourself."

Flooded with relief, I beam. I've been stressing about this moment for a week. "Really?"

Brody is looking at the flowers like they've just arrived from outer space. I think he must hate them, but then he asks, "Where'd you get peonies in June?"

Everyone turns to stare at him, even Kat. Grace looks him up and down as if *he's* just arrived from outer space.

"Israel. But their production will be finished in August, so we'll get the peonies for the wedding from my grower in Amsterdam."

"Man," he says with awe, staring at the arrangement, "I don't know what you're paying for this Nico, but it's worth every damn cent."

Grace glances at me. We're thinking the same thing, because she asks, "Are you a big flower fan?"

He turns to look at her. He's what I think of as the "cute" member of Bad Habit. He's got a boyishly handsome face and a killer smile, with flashing dimples partially hidden by scruff. He's also got great hair, thick and brown, and an even greater sense of style. Today, for instance, he's wearing a pale blue button-down shirt rolled up his forearms, a smart navy vest, a pair of trendy jeans that fit so perfectly they look tailored, and black leather shoes I recognize as Ferragamo, because my father owns a pair. He's tall, but unlike Nico or A.J., who are both bulky, he's on the slender side. I think he looks more like an Abercrombie & Fitch model than a rock musician. A.J. calls him the fashionista.

With a hint of heat in his voice, Brody says to Grace, "I like all beautiful things."

Grace ignores his obvious come-on and turns away. I guess musicians aren't her style . . . though I actually thought all men with working genitals were her style.

Meanwhile, Kenji is bored, which is what happens when he's not the center of attention.

"Lovey, do you have anything to drink around here? I'm so dry I'm practically Mormon."

"Now that you mention it, I do."

I yell for Trina to bring out the bottles of champagne I've bought for this occasion, hoping it would be a success. Now that I know Kat and Nico like the flowers, I feel like celebrating.

So does Trina; grinning like a madwoman, she bursts from the back room with two bottles of Perrier-Jouët held aloft. "Woot! We nailed it! Par-*tay*!" My other designer Renee follows with a sleeve of plastic champagne glasses. They were obviously eavesdropping.

Kenji curls his lip. "Oh, lovey, you know Kenji doesn't drink from petroleum-based glassware."

"You will today, Divalicious," I answer, "because I don't have anything else."

Kenji points to the table. "What do you call *those*?"

I look at the rented crystal champagne flutes beside each place setting on the table, and start to laugh. "I call those a giant oversight on my part. Trina, trash the plastic. We're drinking in style."

She snorts. "I bet I know who's going to be washing these suckers, too," she mutters good-naturedly.

Kenji looks appalled. "Well I'm certainly not!"

Which is a given.

Once the champagne is poured and we've raised our glasses in a toast, the coordinator pulls me aside to go over some details, while Kat and Nico neck around the side of the flower cooler. Kenji, Trina, and Renee squeal and launch into an impromptu zombie dance-off when Michael Jackson's "Thriller" plays over the radio, and, most interestingly, Brody follows Grace as she drifts away from the sample floral arrangements and starts to peruse the display of glass and ceramic vases along the wall.

Musicians might not be her thing, but it certainly looks to me as if redheads are *his* thing. I try to remember if they've met before . . . maybe at the House of Blues party last year? Or on Memorial Day? I make a mental note to ask her about it later.

Jennifer and I finish our talk, and rejoin the rest of the group.

"So where's A.J., Lo?" asks Kat. "I thought he'd be here."

"Me, too. He said he would. I'm not sure what happened."

She and Nico share a look that scares me. It's an "uh-oh" look, one that has my heart beating a little faster as soon as I see it.

"I think I'll leave a little early to go check on him," I say, trying to keep my voice light.

"He still doesn't have a phone?" asks Nico, his arm around Kat's shoulders.

I try to make my shrug look nonchalant. "He's got a burner so I can call him in case of an emergency . . . you know, because of Eric. But I don't want to use it unless it's a real emergency."

"Chloe, he's not going to be mad at you if you call him and the shop isn't on fire," says Kat, exasperated.

"I know. It's just that phones aren't his thing. He doesn't like the idea of people being able to bother him whenever they want. So . . . I'm respecting that."

Nico smiles at me. "He's a lucky son of a bitch to have you, Chloe."

"Yes, he is," agrees Kat firmly. "If Nico refused to talk to me on the phone—"

"He hasn't *refused*, there just hasn't been an emergency. If there was, I'd call him." My voice comes out louder than I intended because I'm feeling defensive all of a sudden. When Kat blinks at me in surprise, I look away, embarrassed.

Then she's hugging me. "I'm sorry. I didn't mean to make you feel bad. It's none of my business."

I release a pent-up breath and hug her back. "Don't be sorry, I'm acting like a weirdo. I think I'm more worried than I realized about him not being here. Is that stupid of me?"

She pulls away and squeezes my arm. "Of course not. I know exactly how you feel. If I don't know where Nico is every minute of the day, I can hardly breathe."

That makes me feel a little better. We smile at each other. Grace interrupts us by saying, "So, Vegas for the bachelorette? Or is that too much of a cliché?"

Kat wrinkles her nose. "Do we have to do a bachelorette party? Aren't we a little old for that kind of thing? I'll just spend the entire time pining away for my hubby-to-be, anyway. I doubt if I'd be any fun."

Grace looks at her as if she's off her rocker. "The bachelorette party isn't for you, silly; it's for the bridesmaids, as a reward for all their hard work toward the wedding."

"I'm pretty sure that's not the case," I say.

Grace waves a hand in the air, dismissing the subject. "Anyway, Vegas is on the table. If either one of you girls," she nods at Kenji and me, "has a better idea, let me know."

I say, "Where's Nico going on his bachelor party? Maybe we should go to the same city and stay in adjacent hotels."

Grace and Kenji look like they might throw up. Kat, on the other hand, squeals in delight. "Yes! What a great idea!" She turns to Nico. "What do you think, honey?"

He smiles down at her, and brushes a lock of hair from her forehead. "I think I'm up for anything that makes you so happy, darlin'."

She claps. I can tell from the glare Grace shoots me she is less than thrilled with my suggestion, but I blow her a kiss and she rolls her eyes, and I know I'm forgiven. She'll have fun no matter where we end up going.

"Anything else you need from me, Chloe?" asks Jennifer, packing away her notes, schedules, and timelines into a shoulder bag.

"Nope. We're good."

She nods. "I'll be in touch next week, then. Call me if anything comes up in the meantime." She blows me an air kiss, hugs Kat and Nico, waves good-bye to everyone else, and leaves.

"I think I'm on my way, too, guys. I've gotta go find out what happened to my man."

Everyone hugs, we say our good-byes, and after they're gone, I get in my car and head home, trying to not worry.

The first thing I notice that's wrong is the chain-link fence on the dirt road leading to the hotel is open. Wide open, not just unlocked.

I pull to a stop several yards away, staring at it. I've never seen it unlocked before. In fact, I lock it behind me every morning when I go to work.

I swallow, assuring myself it's nothing. I drive past it, unsure whether to leave it open or lock it behind me, but there's this strange feeling in the pit of my stomach and I don't want to dally, so I drive on. At the top of the hill when the hotel comes into view, I see the second wrong thing.

A car, parked next to the fountain in the driveway. It's a beauty, too, a brand new Rolls-Royce Ghost, black on black, sleek and shiny. For a moment, I'm confused.

Did A.J.'s manager come here?

The strange feeling gets stronger. I park my car next to the Ghost. I try to look inside, but the windows are blacked-out limo tint; no luck. I hurry inside, take the staircase two steps at a time, and run down the hallway toward room twenty-seven, my handbag bouncing at my side.

Calm down! I tell myself. But it doesn't work. I'm panicking. I know, on a deep gut level, that something is very, very wrong.

When I open the door to the room I've been living in for the past two months, it only gets worse.

A.J. is in bed. He's lying on his back with his hands beneath his head, staring at the ceiling. He's bare chested, the lower half of his body under a sheet, but I can tell he's naked. Though it's midafternoon and still light outside, all the candles are lit. It's warm in the room, too warm, and it smells like . . . perfume?

I step inside. He turns his head and looks at me. What I see in his eyes—the deadness, the total lack of light—stops me short.

"A.J.? Are you all right, sweetie? You missed the meeting."

Before he can answer, I hear a sound that stops my heart cold in my chest.

The toilet flushes.

Someone is in the bathroom.

A.J. is naked in bed, *in our bed*, and someone is in the bathroom.

Then the bathroom door opens and my world comes to an end.

Heavenly steps out, brushing her long, wet hair with a brush I instantly recognize as mine. My grandmother gave it to me for my fifteenth birthday; it's a sterling silver boar's hair brush with my initials inscribed on the back. She looks up, sees me standing in the doorway, and freezes.

She's nude. She's beautiful. She's just taken a shower.

She's just fucked the man I love.

A noise comes out of me, an ugly, choked groan from deep within my chest. It sounds like an animal in agony.

Heavenly drops her arms to her sides. She makes no move to cover herself. She doesn't even look surprised to see me. "I'm sorry," she says quietly, looking away.

Sorry for what? Killing me? Because that's exactly what she's done. She's just stabbed me a thousand times in the heart with a dagger. She's just shot me in the gut with a shotgun. I can't breathe. I can't move. Everything is suddenly too bright, too loud, too close.

I feel like I'm suffocating, drowning, like I've jumped off a building and am falling at top speed toward the ground. My heart pounds and my hands shake and my throat is closing up.

For the final blow, Bella ambles from the bathroom, sits at Heavenly's feet, looks up at her, and barks.

I know that bark. It's her "feed me" bark. It's a bark she'd only make with someone she's comfortable with.

With someone she loves.

Oh God. They've been doing this all along. I've been going to work every day like a stupid, naïve little girl, and my man and his whore have been fucking in the bed that we share. If I hadn't come home early, I'd never have caught them. I would have let A.J. put his hands and mouth on me tonight, I would have believed every murmured word of worship and love that passed his lips.

I feel the exact moment when my face crumples. I back up a step, clutching my stomach, tasting bile in the back of my throat. I look over at A.J., but he's gone back to staring at the ceiling.

In a voice devoid of any shred of emotion, he says, "I'll pack up your things and have them sent to the shop."

I've been dismissed. Just like that, I'm no longer needed.

I'm no longer wanted.

It's all been a lie.

There's nothing left to say or do, so I simply turn and run.

Chapter 35

After Chloe's gone, Heavenly stares at me for a long time from her place near the bathroom door, while I lie flat on my back with tears leaking from the corners of my eyes.

"You should tell her, A.J."

I sit up and rest my elbows on my knees. I don't know if I can answer; the crushing weight on my chest is almost too much to bear. But finally I manage it. "I know what I'm doing. It's better this way."

"She loves you. She'll stay with you if you tell her the truth."

I bow my head and close my eyes. "That's exactly what I'm afraid of."

I hear Heavenly cross the room. Fabric rustles; she's pulling on her dress. Then she kneels beside me on the mattress and rests her hand on my arm.

When I look up at her, I can't stand the pity in her eyes, so I look away.

In Russian, she says, "You can still be happy, old friend. It's not too late."

"It *is* too late," I whisper, my voice breaking. "I knew this was coming, and I took it way too far with her. I should have ended it sooner. I should have never started it in the first place."

She sighs. She knows it's useless to argue with me, and we've been over this before. This is the way it has to be. This is the only thing I can offer after how selfish I've been. It's easier to leave in anger than in sadness, and now Chloe will hate my guts forever. That, at least, will give her some strength.

I know from personal experience how motivating hatred can be.

Heavenly stands and stares down at me. "You're a fool. If I had a chance at real happiness like you do, there's nothing on earth that could stop me from taking it. And you're just throwing it away."

The laugh that tears from my throat is more like a moan of despair. "Don't be stupid. There are no happily-ever-afters for people like you and me."

"Maybe you're right," she softly agrees, "but if I had what you have, it wouldn't stop me from trying."

She turns and walks to the door, picking up her clutch from the sofa on the way. She steps into her heels, then pauses for a moment before looking back at me one last time.

"And it's never too late, A.J. As long as you're still breathing, it's not too late."

She lets herself out, gently closing the door behind her.

Chapter 36

I don't remember the drive to my apartment. I don't remember parking the car, or taking the elevator, or unlocking the door. I move like a sleepwalker, blind and deaf, only coming to consciousness when hot water pours over my head.

I take a shower fully clothed, shivering violently, my teeth chattering though the water is almost scalding. I can't get warm. Everything inside me feels frozen. Beneath my skin lies nothing but a vast, deserted tundra of ice.

A lie. It was all a lie. He never loved me at all.

Finally, the full force of the pain hits me, and I bawl. My body is wracked with the strength of my sobs. I can't stand up anymore, so I slide to the floor and lean against the shower wall, crying hard, snot running down my face, my arms wrapped around my knees as the water pounds over me.

I don't know how long I stay under the spray. Long after the water turns cold, I sit in the corner of the stall with my arms around my knees, shaking. Somehow I eventually find the strength to stand, turn off the water, and strip out of my clothes. I leave them in a sodden pile on the bathroom floor. I don't bother to dry off. I make it to my bed before my strength gives out, and I curl into a ball with the covers pulled over my head.

For hours uncounted I lie there in silent misery, rising only once to lean over the toilet and puke.

That day passes. I don't eat. I don't drink. I don't answer the house phone or my cell phone when they ring. I know I'm in some kind of shock, and that this isn't healthy, but I can't find the strength to care. I have nothing left. I've been hollowed out, scraped clean.

I sleep.

I cry.

I die a thousand deaths, each time I remember it.

Another day passes. I wonder how my heart keeps beating.

I wish it wouldn't.

After another day or two or ten later, a loud pounding noise wakes me.

The clock on my nightstand reads four p.m. I have no sense of how long I've been in bed, of how much time has passed. When I lift my head and look around, I'm dizzy.

I can't remember when I last ate.

The pounding comes from my front door; someone is furiously knocking.

Go away. I'm not here. Send flowers to my funeral and go the hell away.

"Chloe! Are you in there? It's Kat! Honey, please, if you're in there, open the door!"

Her voice is muffled, but the frantic tone is clear enough. I can't muster the energy to feel sorry that I've worried my friend. I can barely muster the energy to sit up in bed, but I do because she won't stop her insistent hammering. I run a hand through my hair, shuffle to the bathroom and get my robe, and shrug it on while moving like a zombie through my apartment.

When I open the door and she gets a good look at me, Kat cries out in shock.

"Chloe," she says, her eyes huge, "my God, honey! What's happened? Where've you been?"

"I've been here. I'm fine. Don't worry. I need to go back to bed now."

My voice is strangely flat. I try to close the door, but Kat slams her hand against it and pushes it wide open. She takes me by the shoulders, steers me to the couch, makes me sit, then goes back and shuts the front door. She returns and kneels on the floor in front of me, taking my hands in hers.

"Chloe, you've been missing for four days. No one knows where you've been. You haven't been answering your phone. You haven't showed up for work. You haven't called anyone."

She speaks to me slowly and with very clear enunciation, as if to someone with a shaky grip on the English language.

"Your parents are freaking out. They thought Eric . . . well, you can imagine what they thought. They filed a missing person's report. When the police came by, all your neighbors said you hadn't been here in months, but the building manager was going to check on the apartment later today to make sure there wasn't a dead body in here."

There is a dead body in here, I think.

When I don't respond, she repeats more forcefully, "Where have you been?"

"I was here," I repeat woodenly, staring past her at the wall. "I've been here the whole time. I'm fine."

She sits beside me on the sofa. "You're *not* fine, obviously! What on earth *happened*?"

I think about it for a moment, and arrive at the only logical conclusion. "I died. And now I'm in hell."

When I turn my head and look into her eyes, all the color drains from her face. "You're scaring me."

My stomach growls. I try to swallow but my throat is so dry I can't. I'm dizzy again, so I close my eyes so the room will stop spinning. "I need to be alone now, Kat. Please tell everyone I'm fine. I just need to be alone." I try to stand, but my knees give out and I end up sagging back to the sofa, breathless, the room spinning.

"That's it," Kat says firmly. "I'm calling your father."

My eyes fly open. "No! Kat, no, please, don't call anyone. I can't see anyone. I can't . . . I just can't . . ."

Suddenly I'm struggling for breath. I feel as if all my organs are failing. I look at her, at her worried eyes and pale face, and realize with a painful intake of air that I don't want her to leave.

I'm afraid of what will happen if I'm alone for much longer.

I gasp, gulping air, beginning to shake all over. I blurt, "He doesn't love me, Kat. It's over. It was all a lie. I found him with Heavenly . . . I walked in and he was . . . they were . . ."

Her face goes through a number of expressions before it settles on fury. Her lips thin to a pale, hard line. "Don't think about it right now. We can talk about it later. Or not, whatever you want. Just lie back and rest." She gently pushes me back onto the sofa, and covers me with my fluffy chocolate cashmere throw. Suddenly I can hardly keep my eyes open.

"I need to make a few calls, but I'm staying here with you. I'm not leaving, okay?"

You'll never have to be alone again, not if you don't want to be.

I remember A.J.'s promise, and all the broken things inside me grind together, making me bleed.

I don't answer, but Kat doesn't seem to require it. She sets about turning on lights, opening windows, letting fresh air into my dank, stuffy apartment. I hear her on the phone, ordering food, then she calls several other people. My parents, I assume. Probably Grace, the shop. I drift in and out of a hazy sleep/wake state, lulled by the soft cadence of her voice in the other room.

I fall asleep once again.

One small mercy: I don't dream.

Over the next few days Grace and Kat take turns looking after me. They fill my refrigerator with food, do my laundry, make me meals, hold my hand in silent support when I begin, out of nowhere, to weep. I've refused to speak to either one of my parents, but the girls take care of that, too, reassuring them I'm okay, and that I just need a rest.

I might need more than a rest. I might need a prescription for strong painkillers and a long, pleasant stay at one of those places where a nice lady in a white uniform speaks very softly while pushing me around tranquil gardens in a wheelchair.

But slowly, over the next few weeks, my strength returns.

With it comes a terrible, burning rage. I find myself staring at random sharp objects—knives, scissors, the sharpened point of a pencil—and imagining myself plunging them into A.J.'s neck.

It's a little frightening, but it's better than the bottomless despair that swallowed me before. At least the rage gives me energy.

I go back to work. I relearn how to smile. Though it's not genuine, most people either don't notice or don't care. Kat and Grace do notice and care, but I think they're just glad I'm out of my pajamas and back into what passes as the real world.

Not that it is, of course. The real world is back in a crumbling ruin of a hotel in the hills, in a candlelit room with opera music and a three-legged dog and a man who taught me what happiness looked like.

Here, there, all an illusion. Everything is make-believe. Nothing really matters to me anymore either way.

Though part of me wants to burn them, I carefully pack my collection of beautiful origami birds into a box and bury them under a pile of old blankets in the back of my closet. Maybe someday I can look at them without wanting to scream, but for now they're entombed, like my heart.

June passes, then July. I don't look at newspapers, I don't watch television, I don't surf the web. I don't want to accidentally catch a glimpse of him. And I can't bear to listen to the radio. I don't want to be reminded of all I've lost.

Of all that never existed in the first place.

Several times I get the hair-raising feeling I'm being watched, but when I turn to look, there's never anyone there. I convince myself it's wishful thinking. No one's watching over me, not anymore.

Then August arrives, and the wheels of Fate turn once again.

Vegas. I've only been here once before, and now I remember why I've never been back. I can smell the desperation in the air.

"Now *this* is what I'm talking about, bitches!"

Kenji, wearing black suede platform boots, skintight purple velvet pants, a fuchsia silk scarf, and a long, black leather trench coat even though it's over one hundred degrees outside, sails into our suite at the Wynn with his arms held out, a giant grin on his face.

I admit the room is spectacular. It's actually not a suite, it's a three-thousand-square-foot villa, with balconies, a private massage room, floor-to-ceiling views of the golf course, and a dining room that seats ten. Fresh flower bouquets are everywhere, scenting the air with the delicate perfume of orchids and roses. The biggest gift basket I've ever seen sits in the middle of the mahogany dining table with a personal note from Steve Wynn, welcoming us to his resort.

It's weird having a famous friend.

Kat and Kenji are sharing one bedroom; Grace and I have the

other. It's Kat's bachelorette weekend. I'm determined to smile constantly so they'll all stop looking sideways at me, so obviously wondering how I'm holding up after being jettisoned like shit from an airplane toilet that it makes me want to scream.

"Okay, who needs a drink?"

Like Kenji, Grace is also rocking a definite Vegas style: sky-high stilettos, tons of black eye makeup, hair teased out to *there*, and a teal Valentino minidress so short I'm sure her coochie is about to make an unscheduled appearance. She stands at the large, curved bar over a three-deep row of bottles, wiggling her fingers in anticipation.

"You know what I need, girlfriend." Kat drops her handbag on the sofa and kicks off her shoes. She heads toward the bedrooms.

Grace nods. "Margarita: rocks, salted rim, Patrón silver. Coming up. Kenji?"

"Do we have any Hendrick's?"

Grace looks over the display of bottles, then holds one up. "Yes."

"I'll take a gimlet." He doffs his leather duster, flips the collar up on his shirt, then throws himself dramatically onto the long butterscotch leather sofa, where he sighs in bliss.

"Chloe?"

When I think about having a drink, my stomach turns. It's been doing that a lot lately. I've gone off half a dozen foods; everything from salad dressing to the tofu I usually love disgusts me. And I've been craving *meat*, for the first time in years.

A.J. not only broke my heart, he broke my appetite.

"I'll just have a sparkling water, thanks."

Grace stares at me as if I've just told her I'm plotting a government coup. "Sparkling water?" She looks at Kenji. "What language is this strange woman speaking? I don't understand a word coming out of her mouth." She turns her attention back to me. "Is this, or is this not, a bachelorette party?"

The argument isn't worth it. I can always dump my drink down the sink when no one's looking. "Fine, I'll take a vodka rocks."

"That's my girl!"

From somewhere deep in the bowels of the villa, Kat shouts, "You guys! Come check out the bedrooms! They're *huge*!"

Before I make a move, a bout of nausea hits me so hard I'm slapping my hand over my mouth as I run to the bathroom. I hear Grace calling my name, but I can't stop; the contents of my stomach are coming up, and they're on the express train. I barely make it to the toilet before I'm bent over, retching into the bowl.

"Jesus, honey, what did you eat?" Grace has followed me into the bathroom. Like the good friend she is, she holds my hair away from my face as I cough and spit.

"Nothing. I haven't had anything to eat all day." Those strange, unemotional tears that always accompany vomiting stream down my cheeks. I slump to the floor and lean against the wall, panting, my stomach in knots. Grace hands me some tissue and I blow my nose. I drag the back of my hand across my face, wiping at the wetness on my cheeks. "Whoa. That just hit me out of nowhere."

"You should see your face, it's totally green." Grace turns on the sink faucet, runs water over a hand towel, and passes it to me so I can wipe my face. She jokes, "It's not morning sickness, is it?"

The world comes to a standstill.

Clocks stop ticking, birds stop singing, the earth stops spinning under my feet. A noise like a thousand wolves howling swells inside my head.

I count, then recount, then count again. Slowly, I raise my gaze to hers. My eyes, which I've just wiped dry, fill again with water. I whisper, "Grace."

Her lips part. She stares at me in wordless horror. She shakes her head in disbelief. "No."

"I don't know. I think . . . I think I missed my period. I can't . . . I wasn't paying attention. I've been so . . . I've been so . . ."

My mind blinks offline. It can't stand the possibility of what it's putting together, so it just shuts down completely, leaving me staring stupidly at Grace with my mouth hanging open.

She kneels on the floor in front of me. Her face is white. She grips my wrist so firmly it hurts. "Think. When was your last period?"

I swallow. In a thin, wavering voice, I say, "May. The beginning of May."

Her eyes go very wide. "And this is the beginning of August."

I start to shake. "No. It can't be. I'm . . . it's just because I've been depressed, and not eating right, and working too hard, and . . . and . . ." When I run out of implausible excuses, I look at her pleadingly, begging her with my eyes for another explanation.

She blows out a slow breath and slumps to the floor beside me. "There's only one sure way to find out. You need to take a pregnancy test."

Please, God. Please. Don't let this be happening to me. Not now. Not after everything I've been through. Not this, too.

"We can't tell Kat. It's her big weekend. I can't ruin it for her."

Grace and I look at each other, and I can tell by the look on her face she understands exactly what I'm referring to. There's an awful story in Kat's past about a pregnancy that didn't end well. There's no way I can bring up my fears without being one hundred percent certain either way.

Grace reaches over and squeezes my knee. "You're right," she says softly, "we'll wait until Monday to deal with this." Her eyes are so sad I feel like bursting into tears. "But, honey, you can't wait any longer than that. If it's really been since May, there are decisions you have to make . . ."

She keeps talking, but I stop listening, because I'm filled with a sudden, inexplicable relief.

I've gotten a reprieve from reality. For another two days, I don't have to face the possibility that I'm pregnant with A.J.'s child.

Yippee.

The weekend passes in a blur. I couldn't say what we did or where we went or who we saw, it's all a jumbled mess of memories. Flashing lights, rainbow colors, raucous laughter, and the smell of cigarettes, everything underscored by the worry gnawing my stomach. My insomnia doesn't help matters. No matter what I try, I just can't get to sleep. My mind runs on a hamster wheel the minute I lie down, and eventually I get up and leave Grace softly snoring in the other king-size bed in our room, and wander through the dark villa alone.

As I watch the sun come up over the desert, I say a little prayer of thanks that my suggestion to have Nico spend his bachelor weekend next door to Kat's never panned out. I have a secret suspicion Kat put the kibosh on that after what happened between me and A.J., but the idea was never mentioned again.

No one ever speaks his name around me. We've all adopted an unspoken "don't ask, don't tell" policy, which suits me just fine.

One thing I do know for certain: A.J. is still Nico's best man, and Kat is none too happy about it. I overheard a one-sided phone conversation in which Kat hissed, "I don't care what he's going through, Nico, Chloe walked in on him with a *hooker*!"

I turned around and walked away before I could hear more, before my mind could spend too much time dwelling on what he might be going through. I can't let myself care what his problems are. It will be bad enough seeing him at the wedding.

When I think of that it makes me ill.

We fly back from Vegas the same way we arrived: on Nico's private jet. Until we disembark—or is it deplane? I can never remember the difference—I'm confident Grace and I have done a good job of covering up any possible whiff that anything might be amiss. But as we're waiting for the limo driver to finish putting our luggage in the trunk, Kat pulls me aside and demands, "Okay, this has gone on long enough. What's up?"

I don't bother with evasions. She'll find out soon enough either way; I'm headed straight to the drugstore after she drops me off at my apartment. "Okay. Two things. One: I didn't want to say anything until I was sure, and I definitely didn't want to upset you. Because I think this might upset you."

She frowns, and I hurry on. "And two: before I tell you, you have to promise me you'll keep it a secret. You can't tell anyone. Not even Nico."

Her brows shoot up. "Honey, there's nothing I don't tell him. You know that."

I nod. "But that's my condition. He can't know. Because if he knows, there's the possibility that he might tell A.J., and I'm just not ready . . ."

I trail off because Kat's mouth has dropped open. Her eyes go wide in the same way Grace's did. "Oh, God, Chloe, *no*."

She's figured it out already. I should have known. "Are you upset?"

She figures that out, too. Faster than I can blink, I'm pulled into a hug. "No, you idiot, I'm not upset for *me*, I'm only worried about *you*!" She pulls back and clutches my arms. "How could this have happened? Didn't you use protection? I thought you were on the pill!"

Suddenly it feels as if gravity is working overtime, and I'm about to be sucked down into the ground and swallowed up forever. Which might not be such a bad thing.

"I haven't been on the pill in months, not since Eric. And A.J. and I did use condoms, just this one time . . . we got a little carried away." The laugh I make sounds disturbing, even to me. "And it only takes once, doesn't it?"

Kat moans. "Oh, sweetie. What are you going to do?"

"I don't know, Kat. Honestly, I don't know anything anymore. Just, please—don't tell Nico. Not yet. I'm not even sure yet. Fingers crossed, this is all just from stress." I try on a grim smile. "Or maybe I'll get lucky and it'll be cancer."

Kat hugs me with all her might. "I'm here for you, whatever happens. You know that, right?"

I look over her shoulder at Kenji and Grace staring with worried eyes at the two of us, and I'm grateful that I've got people on my side, because I have a terrible feeling I'm going to need them.

If my trip to the drugstore ends with a little blue line on a stick that I've peed on, I'm going to need them all.

Chapter 38

Three hours later, I stare down at the white plastic stick in my hand, laughing. I laugh and laugh and laugh, until eventually I start to cry.

Sobbing, I look up at my bathroom ceiling. "God, I'd just like you to know that I officially hate your guts. And don't expect to hear from me ever again."

I throw the stick in the trashcan and go into the living room to call my mother.

She's always wanted to be a grandma.

My mother reacts to my news with her typical aplomb; after a long pause, she simply says, "Oh, sweetheart."

Then, because it's the universe's new favorite thing to screw with me, my father picks up the other phone extension in their bedroom and demands, "What's 'oh sweetheart'? What's wrong?"

"Hi Dad. How are you?" I stall, because he's not going to react nearly as well as my mother. In fact, I'm betting that some time in the next five minutes he'll be threatening a lawsuit and throwing things at walls.

"Chloe," replies my father firmly, "I heard your mother's tone. Tell me what's wrong with you."

Ha. Where to start?

"Technically there's nothing wrong with me, Dad, it's just . . . I um . . ." I take a moment to try to gather my courage. When my courage remains cowering under the sofa, I close my eyes and go it alone. "I'm pregnant, Dad. I haven't seen a doctor yet, but I just took a home pregnancy test and it's positive."

Furious silence crackles over the phone. My mother says gently, "Thomas."

"It's all right, Mom. I'm mad at me, too."

"It's his?"

My father refuses to even speak A.J.'s name. I didn't tell them about Heavenly, or really any of the details of what happened that day. I only told them we'd broken up, but they've witnessed firsthand the state I've been in over the past few months, and dislike him intensely just for that.

Well, my mother dislikes him intensely. My father might actually be plotting A.J.'s death.

I listen to my father's irregular breathing on the other end of the line, and bow my head in shame. "Yes, it's his. Listen, I know this is . . . it isn't ideal—"

"Does he know?" my father interrupts.

The thought of informing A.J. he's going to be a father makes my stomach drop to somewhere in the vicinity of my knees. Talk about awkward conversations. It occurs to me with a blast of disgust that my child might grow up spending alternating weekends with a hooker named Heavenly.

But no. A.J. won't want any part of this. Remembering the look on his face when he dismissed me so callously is a grim reminder of just how much he won't want to be involved with anything that has to do with me.

"No. I just found out, right now."

"And I assume since you're informing us that abortion is out of the question?"

I'm shocked at the hardness in his voice. "I'm not getting an abortion!"

My mother says soothingly, "Of course you're not, darling. No one is suggesting that." Her voice gains an edge. "Are we, Thomas."

That last bit is directed to my father. I picture them on opposite sides of their bedroom, glaring at one another.

My father starts barking instructions. "You'll go to London. You'll stay with your grandmother until it's born. Dr. Mendelsohn will handle the prenatal care and you'll have to deliver at home, but it's the only way to keep it out of the press so that son of a bitch doesn't find out—"

"What're you talking about?" I interrupt, hoping that somehow I've misinterpreted what he's said. He can't be saying what I think he's saying.

My father growls, "I'm talking about doing the only logical thing that can be done with this disaster, Chloe: private adoption. The records will be sealed, so no one will be able to find out the child's identity. And once it's over, we'll put it behind us. You'll come home and it won't be mentioned again."

He *is* saying what I thought he was saying. The wind is knocked out of me. Immediately following that, I erupt like Mount Vesuvius.

"You are *not* telling me right now that you think I should *hide* a child from his father, right Dad? I'm *not* hearing that, because if I *am*, I'm hanging up this phone and it's going to be a very, very long time before you and I speak again. *If ever!*"

Dead silence on the other end of the line.

Finally, with chilling softness, my father says, "He *abandoned* you, Chloe. He took you in when you were most vulnerable, promised to protect you, promised *me* he would protect you, and then he threw you out when he was tired of you. You've refused to tell us the details, but I suspect that's the case. Tell me I'm wrong."

I can't, of course. He's exactly right. But the fact remains, I have an obligation to tell A.J. about this baby, even if I'd much rather stab out his eyes with a fountain pen.

"Here's what's going to happen, Dad. Because I know you're upset, I'm going to pretend we didn't have this conversation. Then I'm going to make an appointment with a doctor—*not* Dr. Mendelsohn, but a doctor of my own—and then when I'm sure everything is all right with me physically, I'm going to inform A.J. What he chooses to do with the information is his business. And then I'm going to prepare for being a single, working mother, who's going to make the best of things—" my voice breaks because I'm crying again "—and be the best damn mother I can be. And if you're interested in having any kind of relationship with *your grandchild*, you're going to give me moral support even if it kills you. If you're not interested, that's your choice. Now if you'll excuse me, I have to go vomit!"

I hang up the phone and run back to the toilet, over which I suspect I'll be spending the better part of the next few months hanging my head.

The two-week period between finding out I'm pregnant and the wedding are probably the two most bizarre and emotional of my life.

Because Kat and Nico both have posted pictures of their wedding flower samples to their various social media accounts with credit to Fleuret, the phones at work ring off the hook. Literally. I have to turn off the ringers because the constant shrill noise starts to drive me insane. Magazines request interviews. The local news requests a feature. Every socialite, event planner, and bride-to-be within the continental United States crawls out of the woodwork, clamoring for us to give them quotes on their parties. I have to hire three freelance designers just to handle the daily delivery orders that won't stop pouring in.

It's thrilling and exhausting, but most of all I'm grateful for the distraction. I've decided not to tell A.J. until after the wedding. It's going to be bad enough posing for bridal party pictures together, I can't imagine the hell it would be doing it after he's told me the baby isn't his.

At least, that's the kind of dick move I assume he'll pull. My expectations of him doing the gentlemanly thing and offering to be involved, even just financially, are nil. He's already proven he's not a gentleman. And if nothing else, he's taught me to expect the worst.

Though I learn that morning sickness should be renamed morning-noon-and-night sickness, the days fly by. I bury my pain in work. I see a doctor, who confirms what I already know, along with confirming A.J. didn't pass me any nifty STDs. I spend too much time surfing the web for homeopathic remedies for nausea and books with titles like *Surviving Pregnancy: A Guide for Mothers without Partners*.

I'm aware that I'm depressed, but there's not much I can do about it, so like everything else in my life these days, I just accept it as my lot. By the time *People* magazine calls to schedule the interview for the feature on Fleuret they promised Kat and Nico in return for the exclusive on their wedding photos, my emotional roller coaster has taken its toll and I'm strangely numb. I give the interview, smiling woodenly when they take my picture, answering all their questions with a sense of detachment, as if it's someone else I'm talking about. As if this hasn't been my dream for years.

I don't think I have dreams anymore. I think they all died the same day I did, back on that sunny afternoon in spring.

The morning of the wedding I wake early, with a terrible sense of doom hanging over my head.

I can't shake it. Even after I've gone for a run, showered, and dressed, I still feel like there's a laser target on the back of my skull, or that the major earthquake LA has been waiting for is finally about to strike. I gather my bridesmaid's gown, shoes, jewelry, and undergarments—I'll be getting dressed at Kat's suite at the hotel after I've supervised the setup of the flowers—and head out to my car. The wedding's at five o'clock, and all the flowers need to be in place for pictures by three, so I'm on a tight schedule. But when I open my driver's door I stop dead in my tracks, looking at what's been left in a corner of my windshield.

It's not an origami bird this time. It's a shiny, metal LAPD badge.

It's Eric's badge.

Fear grabs me around the throat and squeezes. I quickly look up and around, but he's nowhere in sight. I swallow, heart racing, and pick up the badge. I turn it over in my hand; one of those round, yellow smiley face stickers is stuck on the back.

I've never seen anything so sinister.

As fast as I can, I stuff the badge into my purse and load my things into the car. In less than two minutes, I'm pulling out of the parking spot, headed to the shop. On the way I call my father. He doesn't pick up on his cell, or at the house, so I leave a message on his machine.

"Dad, it's Chloe. I just found Eric's police badge on the windshield of my car. I have it with me. I'm a little freaked out. Can you call me when you get this please?"

I hang up, taking a corner too fast, ignoring the shout of the pedestrian I nearly run over. By the time I get to the shop I'm a shaking mess.

Trina's already there, loading the cocktail table arrangements into delivery boxes. She stops short when she sees my face. "What's wrong, boss?"

I dump my handbag on the counter and run a trembling hand through my hair. "Eric left his badge on my windshield this morning."

She gapes at me. "Holy shit! He was at your apartment? Isn't that a violation of the restraining order?"

"I don't know. The order says he has to stay at least three hundred feet away from me. But I was parked down the street because there's never any stupid parking at my place. And I don't even know if it counts if I don't see *him*."

"But leaving his badge, that's like, intimidation or something! Seeing as how you're the one who got him fired!"

I shoot her a death glare. "Thanks a lot."

"I don't mean he didn't *deserve* it, Chloe, I'm just saying that a former police officer leaving his former badge on the windshield of his former girlfriend—who just happens to be the girlfriend he beat up, resulting in his exit from the police force—that's totally fucked up."

"I'm aware. What I don't know is if we can do anything about it." I pull at my hair. "And he has to pick today, of all the days!"

Trina stops loading the boxes to stare at me. Behind her glasses, her brown eyes don't blink. "You don't think he'd do anything at the *wedding* . . . do you?"

Exasperated, I throw my hands in the air. "I didn't before!"

"Sorry." She's chagrined for a moment, then brightens. "Why don't you take my gun?"

I stare at her in disbelief. "I didn't just hear you say that."

"Seriously, it's small enough to fit in your purse. I carry it in my purse all the time. I've got it here now."

I shout, "You bring a *gun* to work? Why?"

She looks at me as if I'm dense. "Because, *duh*, your ex is a cop who went cray-cray and beat you up and got his dumb ass fired from the force because of it. That's a disaster waiting to happen right there! I'm not gonna crouch under the desk like some sitting duck if he decides to come in here, guns blazing; I'm taking his ass *out*!" She smiles. "Then I'll probably get my own reality show."

Closing my eyes, I massage my temples at the same time I draw a deep breath into my lungs. When I've calmed down enough to speak, I tell her, "Trina, I'm not taking your gun. And I'd really appreciate it if you didn't bring it to work anymore, okay?"

She looks insulted. "Dude, I have a CCW."

"I have no idea what that means."

She rolls her eyes. "A concealed carry license. It's totally legit if I carry a weapon."

I'm dumbfounded by this information. "*Why* would you *need* a license to carry a concealed *weapon*?"

"You think you're the only girl who ever got smacked around by a crazy ex?"

She says this deadpan. It's not even a question, really, it's just one of those rhetorical things you already know the answer to.

"No, of course not. But a gun?"

Trina's expression hardens. For a moment I see the Venice gang girl of her youth, all razor blade eyes and rough edges. "You know the old saying, 'Don't show up to a gun fight with a knife'? Well, my ex loves guns. So now, so do I. Because if he decides to come after me again, I have to fight fire with fire."

I don't even know where to go with this conversation. "Okay, for the moment let's forget about firepower and focus on what we need to do today. We'll continue this some other time." I hustle into my office and start checking all my lists.

Within a few hours, the entire staff is in, everything is loaded into the vans, and we set off for the Hotel Bel-Air.

Eric's badge is still in my purse, burning a hole through the fabric.

At the hotel, it's smooth sailing. The load-in is a pain in the butt because the ballroom is on the opposite side of the property from the loading dock, which means we have to take all the flowers through the guts of the hotel, winding through narrow, overcrowded back hallways, carefully avoiding in-room dining carts, ceiling-high stacks of crated glassware and banquet chairs, and all the housekeeping, restaurant, banquet, and kitchen staff who are scurrying around like oversized, uniformed rats.

Other than taking longer than necessary to load in due to the hotel setup, there's not a hitch. The lighting crew has already set up the pin spots for the dining tables and the gobos for the walls that will give the room that gorgeous, warm glow. The stage is set for the swing band—Bad Habit is supposed to jump in and play a song or two if they're not too drunk—and the videographers and photographers have arrived. Jennifer, the wedding coordinator, is having a meltdown in the corner of the ballroom and is screaming at the banquet captain about security, which means everything is right on schedule.

It's not a wedding until someone has a meltdown. I'm just happy it isn't me.

Yet.

When I'm sure all of Fleuret's setup has been completed, I put Trina in charge and head up to Kat's suite to get dressed.

When I knock on the door, I hear the pulse of electronica music and shrieks of laughter. Over the music someone shouts, "Come in!"

I walk inside the honeymoon suite and find myself face-to-face with a male stripper. He's young, overly tan, and is wearing a black thong and nothing else.

He's holding Kenji over his head.

"Best wedding present *ever*!" Kenji screams, throwing his arms in the air like he's flying . . . which he sort of is because Tan Stripper Boy has started to speed walk around the room.

Grace, Kat, and three girls in black shirts and trousers, who I assume are the hair and makeup team, are across the suite. Four director's chairs are set up in front of the open balcony doors, and in them sit Kat and Grace in white robes, sipping champagne, while the other girls fuss around with hot rollers and makeup kits.

When she sees me, Grace shouts, "Because she didn't get a stripper for her birthday, right?" and throws back her head and laughs.

"It looks to me like he's more for Kenji than Kat," I reply, watching Grace's wedding present bench press Kenji in front of a mirror by the wet bar. Every time the stripper presses up, Kenji shrieks, "Again, bitch!"

Clearly the party has started without me.

"C'mere, Lo, and give me a hug." I cross the room and set my garment bag and purse on the sofa, then hug Kat, noting the excited sparkle in her eye, the flush in her cheeks.

"You're looking happy, kiddo," I say softly. "Nervous?"

"Pshaw! I'm marrying the love of my life, what's there to be nervous about?"

A pang of pain shoots through my chest, and my smile falters.

Opera music was the love of her life.

I wonder how long it will take before not everything anyone says reminds me of A.J.

"Hey. Forget about me, are *you* okay?"

Kat peers at me with suspicious eyes, but I'll be damned if I'm going to put a damper on the happiest day of her life. I shove all thoughts of A.J. and my worries about Eric aside. "I'm great! It looks amazing downstairs, I know you're going to love it."

My grin must be convincing, because Kat grins back, all suspicion gone. "Really? How does the gazebo look?"

"Like a fairy tale. I even captured a unicorn for you. He's a little high maintenance, though, so we're going to release him at the end of the ceremony along with the doves."

Kat sighs in happiness. "When do I see my bouquet?"

"Trina will bring it up as soon as I text her we're ready. When does the photographer get here?"

"Forty-five minutes. He'll shoot the girls first, then get the guys by the lake before the ceremony."

The guys. My heart starts to beat faster, knowing that in a short while, I'll be in the same room with A.J., seeing him for the first time since he ripped my heart out with a claw hammer.

My thoughts must show on my face, because Grace insists, "It'll be fine, Chloe. Kat and I are going to get you through this."

"I'm good you guys, honestly. Don't worry about me. Today's all about *you*, Kat."

Behind us, Kenji squeals. The stripper is doing splits in the middle of the floor, and Kenji is standing over him, clapping. I turn back to Kat. "Okay, maybe it's not *all* about you."

She shakes her head, downs the rest of her champagne, then eyes my bust. "Just out of curiosity, honey, are you sure you're still going to fit into your dress? You're looking a little fuller up top."

I look down at the cleavage swelling from the V neck of my shirt. Though I'm slightly fuller through my tummy, too, I haven't really started to show. My boobs have gotten a jump start on all other parts of my body.

And, of course, I haven't tried on my bridesmaid's gown since the day I bought it.

I mutter, "Shit." Instantly, Kat and Grace break out into hoots of laughter.

It's only a matter of seconds before I join them.

An hour later, the stripper sent packing, we're all set.

Our makeup is perfect. Our hair is flawless. We're dressed and ready to go. I had a moment's terror when I zipped up my gown, but fortunately for me I must have lost weight from all the puking before I started to gain it back; the dress still fits. I think it even looks better than before, because now my B-cups are probably closer to a C, and for the first time in my life I have cleavage.

I text Trina to bring up the bouquets. When they arrive and I hand Kat her flowers, she tries valiantly not to cry. Her eyes get all huge and watery, and she looks at me with her lips pulled between her teeth.

"Don't cry!" I admonish, dabbing at her eyes with a tissue. "Not yet, anyway, you're supposed to save that for the vows."

She sniffles, staring at her bridal bouquet. In a small voice, she says, "It's so beautiful, Lo. It's just so beautiful."

Two photographers hover in the background, snapping pictures. I hear another sniffle from behind me, and turn to see Kenji staring down at his own flower bouquet that Trina's just handed him. He's wearing a pair of slim-fit silk pants in the same pale celadon-green as our dresses, but over it he's got a Saint Laurent couture tunic embroidered with gold peonies. His neck is swathed in a scarf trimmed with peacock feathers dyed a translucent green. On his feet are a pair of beaded gold Moroccan slippers with the curled toes. He looks amazing, like a character from the Wizard of Oz.

"What's wrong, Kenji?"

He looks up at me. "Always a bridesmaid, never a bride," he says, then sweeps his arm overhead as if he's waving farewell to a crowd. "But fuck it. I know one day my prince will come!"

Grace says fondly, "Probably all over your face."

Jennifer bursts into the room. "Girls! Are we ready? We've got to get down to the gazebo *now* for the photos if we're going to keep on schedule!"

The four of us look at each other. "Showtime," I say to Kat.

She takes a deep breath. "Okay. Here we go."

And we're off.

Right up until the second I set eyes on A.J., I'm pretty calm.

The groomsmen have taken their pictures separately from the bridesmaids, in keeping with the tradition that the groom not see the bride before she walks down the aisle. The guests have been seated in the garden, the string quartet from the philharmonic has started playing. The distant whir of helicopters is only slightly distracting; Nico has arranged for a no-fly zone directly over the hotel, so paparazzi and news choppers hover off in the distance. Security is crazy tight; even the streets around the hotel are blocked off, so that no one who doesn't live in this uber-exclusive area of Bel Air can get in.

I'm breathing a little easier because of that. Trina's question about Eric coming to the wedding spooked me this morning, but judging by the amount of cops and private security personnel lurking discreetly in corners, I doubt even the President could get in if he wanted to.

We're waiting in a small banquet room adjacent to the garden for the cue from Jennifer to start down the aisle. As the best man and maid of honor, A.J. and I should be walking down together after the rest of the bridal party, but for obvious reasons that won't be happening. Brody and I will walk together. We'll be followed by Grace and A.J., then Ethan and Chris, Bad Habit's keyboardist and bassist, will escort Kenji between them. Nico comes after, then Kat.

When Jennifer calls my name, my heart starts thumping, but I'm still holding it together. It isn't until I walk out of the room and onto the shaded brick walkway where the groomsmen are waiting that I fall apart.

Because there he is, standing a little apart from the others beneath the spreading boughs of a weeping willow tree.

I'd almost forgotten how gorgeous he is. How fundamentally *male.*

Like the other groomsmen, he's wearing a white button-down dress shirt with the sleeves rolled up his forearms, a tight black vest (no coat), a skinny black tie, black slacks, and black leather shoes. He has a wide leather cuff on one wrist that for some reason manages to make him look even hotter, sexier, and more dangerous than usual. His hair is shorter, just above his shoulders, a tousled golden mess.

He looks at least twenty pounds thinner than the last time I saw him. That shocks me, but not as much as the other thing that shocks me.

As if he's been watching the door, waiting for me to walk through it, he's staring right at me, piercing me through with those beautiful amber eyes.

And I just die all over again. All the scabs are ripped off. All the progress I thought I'd made is reversed with one giant bitch slap to my face. I start to tremble. My eyes water. My throat closes up.

I still love him as much as I ever did. I still want him just as badly. I'm still just a lonely, lovesick fool.

Thank God for Brody, because I wouldn't be able to tear my eyes from A.J. without his help.

"Here we go," he murmurs, firmly taking my arm and turning me away toward the path leading to the gazebo. "I've got you."

I almost groan with the excruciating pain those three words evoke. They're exactly what A.J. said to me the night Eric put me in the hospital.

But Brody's just being kind. He links his arm through mine, steadying me, and guides me out of the shade of the trees and over the little grassy rise to the ceremony area. When Jennifer cues us, we start walking slowly down the aisle. I barely notice the guests, the music, the flowers. I can only see A.J.'s face. His eyes. The way he looked at me . . .

How much weight he's lost.

Halfway down the aisle, after I've recovered the ability to speak, I ask, "Why is he so thin?"

Brody is smiling, staring straight ahead at the gazebo where a pastor robed in white awaits. "I don't know. We've barely seen him over the last two months. He hasn't been coming to sessions."

My heart goes wild, ping-ponging around inside my chest. What could this mean? Has he been sick? Why wouldn't he show at the band's sessions? My frantic thoughts are cut short when Brody clears his throat.

"Chloe, there's something you should know. I thought it would be easier for you if it wasn't a surprise. And just for the record, I told him not to do it. We all did."

My stomach clenches. I know whatever he's going to say will be bad.

But I don't know just how bad, until he drops a bomb on my head so powerful I stumble and he has to grip my arm and pull me upright so I don't fall flat on my face on the processional aisle.

"A.J. brought Heavenly as his guest."

The violins suddenly sound off-key and screeching. The sun shining so cheerfully overhead burns my bare shoulders. The white swans floating in the lake beside the ceremony area look sickly and mean. Everything beautiful about this day turns ugly, and I want to drop my flowers and run.

I don't, of course. I plaster a smile on my face, grit my teeth, and remain silent, because I don't trust myself not to start screaming if I open my mouth.

Brody successfully gets us down the aisle. We take our places on either side of the pastor. Though everything inside me is a wasteland of ashes, I straighten and smile wider.

I don't look down the aisle to watch A.J. approach with Grace. When he takes his place in front of Brody, I turn my head and watch Kenji, Ethan, and Chris head down. I watch Nico walk down, swaggering, grinning from ear to ear. Then the music changes, and everyone stands for the bride.

A murmur runs through the crowd when they see her, and I understand why. Kat has never looked so stunning. Her dark hair is gathered back on the sides and pinned beneath a long, trailing veil, which is edged in crystals and seed pearls. Her ivory silk chiffon dress is fitted across the bodice, cinches tight around her tiny waist, and flares out into a ballerina skirt. She's wearing over one million dollars of Fred Leighton diamonds Nico bought her, including a twenty-carat pair of drop earrings and a choker with a ten-carat center stone. She looks like a fantasy princess.

She looks like a perfectly happy, blushing bride, which I know deep down in my soul I will never be. I'll be the single mom everyone feels sorry for and tries to set up with their divorced friends. I'll be the bitter career girl who wrinkles early and drinks late.

I'll be the spinster aunt.

I swallow, looking down. Without thinking, I turn my head and find A.J. staring right back at me.

Like it always was, our connection is instant and electric: a jolt of sizzling heat, a plug into a socket.

I feel like I might faint. I suck in a breath. His gaze flicks to my mouth, then flashes back up to mine. When I see the look in his eyes, that endless dark longing he used to look at me with, my heart stops.

He doesn't look away. Neither do I. My hands shake so hard the flowers in my bouquet tremble.

I'm finally able to break eye contact when Kat meets Nico at the end of the aisle. The wedding officially begins, but I don't hear a word. I don't see a thing.

All I'm aware of is the burning heat of A.J.'s gaze on me the entire time.

Misery: noun, plural *miseries.* 1. wretchedness of condition or circumstances. 2. distress or suffering caused by need, privation, or poverty. 3. great mental or emotional distress; extreme unhappiness. 4. a cause or source of distress.

"Yep," I say, staring at the dictionary app on my cell phone, "that's just about covers it."

"Put away your damn phone and go dance," Jamie says, snatching my cell from my hand.

I grimace. "With who? My baby daddy, or his paid-for piece on the side?"

"There's no reason to wallow, bug, it's unbecoming. It's like the line from that Metric song, 'There's no glitter in the gutter.' "

I glare at him. "Don't you talk to me about gutters! You're the genius who told me I might find a diamond there, covered in mud, and mistake it for a turd. Well as it turns out, counselor, it actually *was* a turd!"

I'm at Jamie and my parents' table because I couldn't stand one more instant at mine, which was inconveniently right next to A.J. and the whore's. The reception is in full swing. The main course has been served, the band is halfway through their first set, and I've never been so miserable. Hence the dictionary lookup; when Jamie asked me how I was doing, I wanted to be sure I was using the right word to describe my current condition.

Jamie sighs and looks to my mother for help.

She pats his hand. "Leave her be, James. She's earned the right to be miserable."

I raise my water glass in a toast to my mother.

Glowering at A.J. across the room, my father mutters, "I've got half a mind to make someone *else* miserable right about now."

"Thomas," my mother says without moving her lips, "you will *not* embarrass us at Kat's wedding. For goodness' sake, behave yourself!"

Other than the four of us, our table is empty, as are most of the others in the ballroom. Everyone else is on the dance floor, having a blast. Everyone but A.J. and Heavenly that is, who are sitting at his table, deep in a heated conversation. They both look pissed.

I hope they're arguing about the virulent strain of herpes she's given him.

"Dad," I say, trying to distract myself, "did you get my message this morning?"

He turns back to me, frowning. "No. What message?"

"About what Eric left on my car."

My father sits up ramrod straight in his chair. *"What?"*

I nod. "When I went out to my car this morning, Eric's badge was sitting in the corner of my windshield. I put it in my purse."

His eyes bulge. "Did you see him?"

"No."

Jamie and my father share a look.

"Is it a violation of his restraining order?"

"Absolutely. The protective order covers your vehicle as well as you. I wish I'd known sooner, I'd have called it in."

"I left you a message!"

He shakes his head. "No matter. I'll report it now. And then we're going to get a civil contempt order for that bastard, too." He rises abruptly from the table with his cell phone in hand and stalks off, headed for the exit.

I want to drop my face into my hands, or, even better, crawl under the table and hide, but I'll be damned if I'm going to do anything that even resembles looking like I'm as affected by A.J.'s presence as I actually am. Though I'm not dancing, my face hurts from all the fake smiling I've been doing, especially after Kat came by to apologize for A.J.'s surprise guest. Apparently she and Nico didn't know what the rest of the band knew, and they're livid about not only his cruel stunt, but the fact that nobody had the balls to tell them about it.

I told her if that's the worst thing that happens tonight, she should count her blessings. At the last wedding I attended, a drunk guest fell onto the dessert table and destroyed the bride and groom's five-thousand-dollar wedding cake.

"I'm going to the bathroom," I announce, knowing if I don't tell my mother where I'm off to she'll assume it's to go have a good cry outside in a shrubbery and want to follow me.

Proving my point, she says, "I'll go with you." She starts to rise, but my brother puts his hand on her arm and gently pulls her back to her seat.

"Give her a minute to herself," he says, shooting me an understanding glance.

I mouth *Thanks* to him, then grab my clutch and scoot away before she can charge after me. I hurry out of the ballroom, releasing my breath only once I'm outside in the fresh evening air. The closest ladies' room is a short walk through a lushly landscaped garden. I take my time, replaying everything that's happened so far today in my head, blinking back stinging tears.

I sort of wish I hadn't told God he'd never be hearing from me again, because I have a strong urge to raise my eyes skyward and wail "Why?"

How do people survive this kind of pain?

I push open the door to the ladies' room. Inside it's quiet; I'm the only one here. I stand in front of the mirror and look at my reflection, wondering how long I can reasonably hide here before my parents send a search party.

The door opens behind me. I quickly look down and open the little clutch I've brought for my cell phone and lipstick. I don't want to be caught crying, so I bite the inside of my cheek and breathe deeply, digging inside my bag, trying to look busy.

A voice says, "He's never fucked me."

Startled, I look up. When I see who's followed me inside the restroom, my clutch falls from my hands and drops to the floor with a clatter.

Heavenly crosses her arms, leans against the side of the toilet stall, and shakes her hair off her face.

"Excuse me?"

"A.J. and I have never had sex. I thought you should know."

Blood rushes to my face. I square off with her, my fists clenched. "Whatever kind of game this is, I don't want to play."

Her face remains impassive. "It's the truth. He's never had sex with me. He's never wanted to; he just wanted someone to talk to. He pays me for my time, not my body."

I'm certain I'm going to vomit. And this room feels like a furnace; I start to sweat. I hiss, "You have a really bad memory, lady, because *I walked in on you both naked*!"

Her lashes lower; I think she's ashamed. "That little act was for your benefit. He knew finding me there was the only thing that would make you leave him, so he paid me to be naked while he waited for you to come home." She raises her eyes and meets my gaze. "It was his plan for you to find us, understand?"

I'm staggered. My legs are suddenly so weak I have to lean against the sink for support. "No. No, I don't understand."

She sighs, straightens, uncrosses her arms. She moves to the sink beside me and fluffs her hair while looking in the mirror. She's wearing a sleeveless, long lavender gown with a side slit practically to her navel, and no bra. Her nipples show right through the fabric.

"He didn't look at me the entire time. I think he was too embarrassed. He thinks of me like a sister. Who wants to see their sister naked? No one." She turns to and fro in front of the mirror, checking herself out. "Even if their sister looks like me."

Her tone, expression, and manner all indicate she's telling me the truth, unbelievable though it is. There's a chair in one corner; I sink into it. I ask hoarsely, "Why? Why would he do that? Why would he want to make me leave him?"

There's a moment of silence as she stares at herself in the mirror. Then she turns her head and looks at me. In her eyes I see pity, and also a deep, frightening sadness.

"Because he's dying."

I can't breathe. I can't move. I can't even blink. I just stare at her, my heartbeat thundering in my ears.

She turns around, rests her weight against the sink, and stares down at the floor. "It's a brain tumor. He's known for years. It's very slow growing, but he's refused surgery. The doctors didn't think he'd even make it this far; they thought he'd be dead by twenty-five. That's where he was that day, when he told you he was going to see his manager. He sees his doctor every three months. And that day . . . they told him he'd run out of time."

This isn't real. I'm having a nightmare. This can't be happening.

I don't realize I've spoken aloud until Heavenly glances up at me. "They think the tumor is what caused his chromesthesia. It presses on the optic nerves. He's probably had it since childhood, but he only found out about it four years ago, when he had a CT scan after he was hit in the head by a bottle someone threw onstage. That little scar above his eyebrow? It's from that bottle."

With a shudder of horror, I remember something A.J. once told me.

So you started fighting for your keep.

Earlier than most, because I was big, and always angry anyway. I didn't understand why I was so different, why I saw colors in sounds and no one else did. I felt like a freak.

"So because he refused surgery to remove the tumor, they gave him a year. He was stronger than they thought, obviously." She laughs softly to herself, shaking her head. "He's too stubborn to die on schedule."

I'm sick and reeling, but I manage to ask, "Why would he refuse surgery?"

She pulls in a deep breath through her nose, then lets it out all at once. "Because even if they could successfully remove the tumor, he'd be blind. He said he'd rather die." She looks at me, her eyes glittering. "That's what he thinks he deserves, anyway."

Tears stream down my cheeks. I don't bother to wipe them away. They don't matter. Nothing else matters.

Heavenly looks at the ceiling. "He used to talk about you. All the time, all he could talk about was you. You know it was him who had the elevator and security gate fixed in your apartment building, right? The management company didn't move fast enough when he threatened them with a lawsuit, so he paid for it out of his own pocket. Twice what it should have cost, not that he cared. He would have paid any amount to make sure you'd be safe."

My mouth is open. No sound is coming out. But Heavenly isn't paying attention; she keeps on talking, telling her story as if she's grateful to finally be getting it off her chest.

"We watched this movie together once, *Moulin Rouge!*. There's this part where someone sings something like 'Suddenly my life doesn't seem such a waste,' and he turned to me and said, 'That's it. That's how I feel about her.' This was before the two of you were together. And then when you got together, I didn't see him again until the Memorial Day party." Her voice breaks. "And I was really happy for him. For you both. And also, really, really sad because I knew you didn't know. He didn't want you to know."

She looks at me again, and now her eyes are wet. "He hated himself for letting you fall in love with him, knowing he didn't have much time left. And at the end, he thought it would be better if he made you hate him, too. He thought it would be easier for you, when the time came, if you'd already put him far behind. He didn't have the strength to walk away from you, so he made it so you'd be the one to leave. And he knew the only way he'd be able to stay away from you today is if he brought me, so you'd hate him all over again. He thought he was doing the right thing. For you."

Heavenly pauses, swallowing. She whispers, "Right or wrong, Chloe, everything A.J.'s done since the day he first met you has been for you."

I'm moving. The decision wasn't made in any conscious part of my brain; my feet are just obeying some urgent, subconscious command. I run out the door, flying over the short path back to the ballroom with my heart in my throat.

Dying. Dying. Dying. It echoes inside my head. I can't let that happen. He can't die, not now, not ever. I have to tell him, I have to let him know about the baby, make him change his mind about the surgery—

The sound of people screaming makes me falter, then stop. Abruptly, the music inside the ballroom cuts off. The shrill, high-pitched squeal of feedback from a microphone fills the night air, and then there's an eerie silence.

From somewhere behind me, a cop comes running. He pushes past me, barking into a handheld radio. In his other hand he holds his gun.

I bolt toward the ballroom. People have started streaming out in panic, some of them screaming, some silent and white faced with fear. I run past them, shove my way through one of the doors, and look wildly around, trying to find the cause of the uproar. Twenty steps in, I come to a dead standstill.

In the center of the empty dance floor stands Eric. He's got my terrified, crying mother in a chokehold.

He's holding a gun to her head.

"Where is she?" he screams, looking around wildly. He drags my mother backward toward the abandoned stage.

Everything takes on the quality of a dream. I move in slow motion, my feet heavy, the sound of voices muffled and distorted like I'm underwater. Someone is calling my name; it's my brother, standing near our table, his arms stretched out toward me, his eyes terrified. I ignore him and keep moving, walking numbly toward Eric.

This isn't about my mother; she's only a placeholder. I know he'll let her go when he gets what he's really come here for.

He spots me. His lips pull back over his teeth. I notice he's favoring his right leg, the one that A.J. broke. He snarls, *"You!"*

My mother sobs.

Several police officers with drawn weapons advance slowly through the retreating crowd, shouting for him to drop his weapon.

Eric raises the gun and points it right at me. "You ruined my life," he yells, his eyes wild.

I'm frozen in terror. My vision narrows to a circle with my mother's face and Eric's behind it. I know this is the end. Instinctively, my hands cover my belly.

Just before Eric squeezes the trigger, I'm shoved to the side. I start to fall, arms flailing. A shot rings out. I hit the floor hard; my breath is knocked from my lungs. I hear several more gunshots in quick succession—*bam bam bam bam bam*—and I scream.

Someone else is screaming. It's my mother; she's standing stock still, her shaking hands covering her face.

Eric is lying on the floor behind her. A widening pool of dark liquid surrounds his head.

I turn to see who pushed me aside, and moan in horror.

A.J. is lying on his back on the floor a few feet away, eyes closed, unmoving. A single, perfect hole is punched through the fabric of his shirt, just above his heart.

Blood flowers from the hole, staining the pristine white fabric red.

"Let me see him! I need to see him!"

I'm screaming at the nurse who's holding me back from the doors that lead to the corridor of surgical suites at the hospital. She's trying to calm me, but I'm out of my mind.

I can't lose him again. I can't. I *won't.*

"Chloe, shhh, let them do their job! Stop! Come with me now, stop it, bug!" Jamie envelops me in a bear hug, tearing me away from the nurse. I cling to him, sobbing hysterically. My parents are in the waiting room, along with the band; their manager, Saul; Kat and Nico; and Grace and Kenji, with about fifty cops stationed outside.

"I have to see him," I wail, my face buried in Jamie's neck. "It can't end like this."

"Nothing's ending, Chloe. He's in surgery, they're taking care of him. He's going to be all right."

"You don't know that! You saw how much blood there was!"

Jamie holds me tight, letting me cry on his suit jacket. He strokes a hand over my hair. "He's going to make it, bug. And so are you. Now please try to calm down. Hysteria can't be good for the baby."

He's right. I'm probably dousing my baby in some really bad panic hormones. I try to breathe, and only manage to start hiccupping. Jamie gives me his handkerchief and makes me blow my nose.

"We're going to go sit in the waiting room until they have something to tell us, okay? There's nothing else we can do now but wait."

I nod, whimpering as I try to hold back sobs. I know Jamie's right, but waiting around doing nothing when I have so much to tell A.J., when we have so little time together left anyway, seems like cruel and unusual punishment.

Jamie guides me through the quiet, sterile hallways of the hospital to the waiting room. Everyone rushes me when I come in. Kenji, Grace, and Kat—who is still in her wedding gown—surround me and get me into a group hug. My parents are right there with them, putting their arms around us. My mother is crying; I think she's still in shock. My father is grim and tense, as is Nico, who stands behind Kat with his hand on her shoulder. Ethan and Chris stand a little apart with heads bowed, their arms folded across their chests. Brody is in the corner with his hands on his hips, shaking his head.

Saul is the only one who remains sitting. From the look on his face, he might not be able to stand.

"Nico," I whisper.

"Yeah, darlin'?"

"Did you know? About A.J.'s brain tumor?"

He blinks. His cobalt-blue eyes widen. "Brain tumor?"

So he didn't know. I look at Brody, Chris, and Ethan, who are all staring at me in horror. They obviously didn't know either. But when I look at Saul, he just looks defeated.

"Saul," I say, my voice choked.

He sighs. "He swore me to secrecy. He didn't want anyone to know he was dying."

The room erupts into chaos. Nico, always a hothead, stalks over to Saul and starts barking questions. While Chris tries to get him to calm down, my parents look at Kat and Grace, and all of them start talking at once. Kenji is jabbering to himself like a crazy person, Brody is grilling Ethan for information, and he's denying any knowledge of anything. My brother is the only one not saying anything, and that's because he's looking at the door.

My heart leaps; is it the doctor?

I whirl around to follow his gaze, but it's not a doctor. There in the doorway stands a very ordinary-looking man in a suit, carrying a briefcase, gazing in bewilderment at the scene.

"Miss Carmichael? Is there a Chloe Carmichael here?"

The room falls silent.

"Yes, that's me. Who are you?"

Saul rises. "This is Mr. Wells, Chloe. A.J.'s attorney."

Saul and Mr. Wells shake hands. "I got here as soon as I could," says Wells, his voice subdued.

Saul replies, "Thank you for coming." He looks at me. "There's some paperwork for you."

Hearing the word "paperwork" in relation to an attorney immediately raises my father's hackles. He steps forward and demands, "What kind of paperwork?"

Looking around at all the people staring back at him, Wells uncomfortably adjusts his tie. He glances at me. "Is there somewhere more private we could talk?"

"Whatever you have to say you can say it in front of everyone. I'll just tell them all anyway."

Wells lifts a shoulder. "As you wish." He crosses to the coffee table, sets down his briefcase, and opens it with a flick of his wrists.

From it he pulls a bound black notebook. He holds it out to me. "Mr. Edwards' estate planning documents."

When I just stare at him silently, he adds, "Will, living trust, durable power of attorney, advance healthcare directive." His voice softens. "He had a long time to prepare."

With shaking hands, I take the binder. "What does it have to do with me?"

"You're the beneficiary of his will, the trustee on the trust, which holds all his assets, including property, and his attorney-in-fact appointed to make financial and healthcare decisions on his behalf."

When I just continue to stare at him, openmouthed, he sighs.

"If he can't make decisions for himself, you're authorized to make them for him, do you understand?"

Saul says gently, "For instance, if he's . . . in a coma."

In a flash, I understand. If it comes down to it, I'm the one responsible for making the decision whether or not to pull the plug.

My brother catches me just before my legs give out. As I clutch the binder to my chest, he drags me to a nearby chair.

"Someone get her some water," Jamie barks.

"On it." Brody runs from the room.

"Let me see that, Chloe."

I numbly hand the binder to my father. He flips it open, scans the first few pages, then flips around to several tabbed sections, reading quickly, his finger skimming the page. After a moment, he mutters, "Jesus."

"Thomas?" My mother's voice pulls his attention back to the room, and everyone standing around waiting for him to speak.

He looks around, then back at me. "Well, you'll never have to worry about money again, that's for sure. He owns property all over the US. Looks like hotels, mostly."

I close my eyes.

Was it empty a long time before you bought it?

Years. It was originally built as a resort hotel but never made it. I bought it because it looks how I feel.

Alone?

Corroded. Decayed.

I'm certain all the hotels in A.J.'s will are just like the one he lived in, lonely, abandoned places with checkered pasts. Birds of a feather, he'd said. Birds of a feather.

"There's a mistake here."

I open my eyes. My father is frowning down at a page. He looks at Mr. Wells.

"This is dated July 1 of this year."

Wells nods. "That's correct. Mr. Edwards updated his living trust on that date to include Ms. Carmichael in the documents."

"But you and he were already finished by then," my father says, looking at me.

Tears stream down my cheeks. "He was never finished with me. He just wanted me to be finished with him, because he knew he'd be going away. He didn't want me to have to watch him die. But I'm going to anyway." Then I break down sobbing all over again.

Brody comes back with a cup of water, which Jamie sets aside. He then kneels in front of me and takes my arms.

"Bug, listen to me."

Devastated, I look at him.

He says softly, "No matter what happens, you'll always have a part of him. The baby, Chloe, that's not just yours. It's his, too. It's yours together. And always will be. You'll always have a part of A.J. with you."

I whisper, "Thank you."

In unison, Nico, Brody, Ethan, and Chris say, "Baby?"

Kat goes to Nico and hugs him around the waist. "I wanted to let her tell A.J. first, honey."

He stares down at her. "A.J.'s having a baby?"

"Actually it's Chloe who's having the baby, dear. Although your friend certainly did his part," says my mother, who seems to be a little steadier on her feet. Probably because she's just found out I'm a real estate heiress.

Nico looks at me, his eyes alight for the first time in hours. "Kat and I are gonna be an aunt and uncle?"

I shake my head slowly. "No. You're going to be godparents."

Kenji says proudly, "Me and Grace are going to be the aunt and uncle!"

Grace says, "Aunt Kenji does have a nice ring to it," and smiles at Kenji.

He replies, "So does Uncle Grace."

For a moment there's a lighter quality to the air, but it's shattered when a woman in a white coat and scrubs walks in the room.

"Mr. Edwards' group?" she asks, gazing at us. She's a tall, slender brunette in her midforties, businesslike and cold, her face absolutely expressionless.

My stomach drops. I stand, holding on to Jamie's arm for support. "Yes?"

Her cold gaze rests on me. Her eyes are the color of flint. "Are you the next of kin?"

I mutely nod my head.

She says, "I'm Dr. Rhoades. Come with me, please."

"What's happening?" my brother demands. Everyone draws closer.

Dr. Rhoades pauses for a moment. "We need to get some information. And I'm afraid we don't have much time. Now, if you'll please follow me?"

She walks out of the room.

"He's in critical condition, I'm afraid. The bullet damaged the right ventricle of his heart, and he's developed a hemopneumothorax—"

"English, please!" I cut in, desperate to understand what Dr. Rhoades is saying. My brother, parents, and I are standing near the nurses' station outside the operating room where A.J. is still on the table.

"There's an accumulation of blood and air in his chest cavity, causing one of his lungs to collapse. Also his heart isn't pumping efficiently due to the damage to the ventricle. The wound is severe; we don't know yet if it can be repaired."

"Oh God." I clutch my mother's hand.

"When I get an update from the surgeon I'll let you know, but in the meantime, does he have a DNR?"

"DNR?" my mother repeats.

"Do not resuscitate," explains my father. "She needs to know if he wants to be on life support or not."

"Not only that, but what measures should be taken to revive him should he go into cardiac arrest—"

"Do everything!" I blurt, so loudly Dr. Rhoades blinks. "Do anything and everything you can to save his life! Do you understand me? Do everything!"

My father puts his arm around my shoulders. I turn my face to his chest and cry.

"She has power of attorney," he explains calmly to the doctor. "Do whatever you can."

"All right. I'll let you know when I have more news. Do you have his healthcare directive with you by any chance? I'll need to get a copy of the paperwork."

"Here," says Jamie, handing her the folder.

She nods. "I'll just photocopy what we need and bring it back. You can have a seat in the waiting room and I'll send it out shortly. Thanks, folks."

She turns and walks briskly away. I know she must deal with this kind of thing every day, but I think she's heartless.

Maybe that's *how* you deal with this every day.

My family leads me back to the waiting room, and after we give the group the update, we all sit down in silent misery, to wait.

Four hours pass, then five. Nico and the guys bring in sandwiches and coffee from the cafeteria, but I can't eat. I'm going over and over it in my head, everything A.J. ever said to me, every time we were together.

It all makes complete sense now. Everything makes awful, perfect sense.

The police take everyone's statements about the events at the wedding. We're told Eric was dead on arrival to the hospital. When I hear that, I feel nothing at all. Numbness has seeped into every cell and nerve of my body, and for that I'm grateful, because it's the only thing keeping me going.

Then, at exactly twenty minutes after two in the morning, Dr. Rhoades comes back.

Everyone stands. No one says anything. She looks exhausted.

Finally she says, "He's in recovery. The surgery went well."

My heart squeezes to a fist. "How is he?"

She looks at me. For the first time tonight, she manages to smile. "We think he's out of the woods."

Everyone screams. I start to bawl, sinking to my knees on the ugly gray carpet. Kat and Grace fall onto me and we crouch there in a sobbing huddle on the floor, three women in designer wedding attire with their arms around each other, crying their eyes out, until the doctor calls for everyone's attention.

"If he remains stable, he should be moved into a regular room within the next hour." She looks at me. "I'll come and get you, okay?"

I stand, supported by Kat and Grace on both sides. Then I quickly close the few feet between us and throw my arms around her neck.

"Thank you," I whisper, "thank you so, so much."

She chuckles, patting my back awkwardly. "You're welcome. But you should thank the surgeon. I'll have him speak to you when he's finished."

I release her, nodding, too exhausted to do much more than smile. She pats me on the arm, then leaves.

Then, once more, we wait.

When I walk through the door of A.J.'s hospital room, I have to slap my hand over my mouth so I don't cry out in horror.

He looks like death.

His skin is a waxy, lifeless gray. His eyes are sunken deep in his head. His hair is matted with blood. There's a tube in his nose, more tubes stuck in his arms, chest, and the back of one hand, and he's hooked up to all kinds of blinking medical equipment that make disturbing chirping and sighing noises as he breathes.

Shaking, I go to his bedside and stand over it, looking down. He's asleep or drugged, I can't tell which; either way he's unconscious. The surgeon has told me he'll be in a lot of pain when he wakes up, and not to expect him to have the strength to speak.

I don't care if he speaks. I just need him to see me. I need him to know I'm here.

I take his hand and lean over and press a kiss to his forehead.

Both are ice cold. Despite the doctor's reassurances that A.J. is stable for the moment, he looks to me as if he's hanging on by a thread.

Everyone's given me time to come in alone and see him first.

I drag a chair next to the bed and sit in it, taking his hand again. I wrap both my hands around his big, motionless paw, lean over and press it to my cheek.

I sigh. "You idiot."

It's the first thing I think of. I decide it's probably not the right thing to say, so I blunder on, working myself up until a stream-of-consciousness tirade is pouring out of me.

"I can't believe you'd think it would be better for me to hate you than for us to be together. That's all I ever really wanted: for us to be together. And you were always holding back. I get it now that you were just trying to protect me, but what you don't get is that you just cheated us both out of months of time we should have spent together. I'm seriously pissed with you about that, sweetie.

"Your friend Heavenly is a real piece of work, by the way. Is that what you two were arguing about at the table at dinner? She wanted you to tell me and you were being your normal stubborn self and refused? Well, she followed me into the ladies' room and gave me an earful, so now I know everything. And it didn't work, anyway, your little plan to make me hate you. I didn't move on. I mean, I couldn't have anyway, because I love you too damn much, but also because of little A.J., junior. Or if it's a girl, I was thinking Abigail. Do you like the name Abigail? We could call her Abby. Abby Aleksandra, would you like that? My mother will probably kill me if I don't get her name in there somehow, so she might have to have two middle names. Abby Aleksandra Elizabeth Edwards. That's really beautiful, actually. Unless you don't like it. I suppose we could figure it out later." I sigh again, exhausted. "We have so much to talk about, sweetie. When you wake up I'm going to talk your ear off."

A weak, scratchy voice says, "You already are."

I look up, heart leaping. A.J. is looking back at me with a little half smile quirking his lips. I jump to my feet, already crying, and hug him.

He hisses in pain.

"Oh God I'm sorry!" I yank myself away, aware that in my eagerness I've hurt him, but he grabs my wrist with surprising strength, not letting me get far. He looks straight into my eyes.

"You're pregnant?"

I nod, wiping tears from my cheeks with the back of my hand.

He inhales, lashes fluttering, then whispers, "You're carrying my child? We're having a baby?"

I nod again, breaking out into a slightly hysterical laugh.

His grip on my wrist loosens. He opens his hand, reaching out for my face. I lean down, much more carefully this time, and press a soft kiss to his lips. His eyes close. His fingers stroke my cheek, tracing my jawline. "Well, then. I guess this won't be the only surgery I'll be having this month."

Hope surges through me. I stare at him, waiting, not daring to speak.

Faintly, he says, "I don't know if they can get it all; it's too big now. They said I only have a few months left. But it might buy me more time."

"But . . . Heavenly . . . she said . . . she said if they take out the tumor that you'd go blind."

His lashes lift, and he looks at me with so much love and adoration my heart swells until it feels like it will burst. He whispers, "Small price to pay to hear someone call me 'Daddy,' don't you think?"

My supply of tears is inexhaustible, because here they come again. "If you wanted to be called Daddy, I would've happily obliged!"

He smiles. His eyes drift shut. "I thought you said you weren't into the kinky stuff."

I sob, laughing and crying at the same time. "We never got much of a chance to try out any of your advanced moves, did we?"

His smile turns wicked. "Not yet."

Carefully, because I just can't contain myself, I kiss A.J. all over his face. "I love you," I murmur with every press of my lips against his skin. "I love you. I love you so much. You saved me, A.J. You saved my life."

"We saved each other, angel," he murmurs, and then falls back asleep.

Five weeks later, after A.J. has recovered enough to undergo brain surgery, he's admitted to the hospital again, this time to have the tumor removed.

We've moved into a small house we rented in Laurel Canyon while we decide what the next steps should be. So much depends upon the outcome of the surgery, it's difficult to plan in advance, but I didn't want to stay in my apartment and A.J. no longer wanted to live in the hotel, so we found a place that would serve as our new temporary home together, with Bella, where there are no bad memories to spoil a single second.

We're living on borrowed time.

There's no guarantee the surgery will be a success. In fact, the surgeons have informed us it's highly risky; blindness might not be the only side effect. The list of terrible things that could go wrong is daunting, including paralysis, but A.J. is insistent he wants it. If there's even a small chance it will allow him a few more years, he's taking the chance.

In the meantime, we've prepared for the worst.

"Do you have all the paperwork? I can't find the paperwork. And what have I done with my reading glasses? I'll definitely need those. I bought the new Grisham book, but I can't read without my glasses, especially in hospital lighting."

"Mom, calm down! I've got the paperwork. And your reading glasses are right there on the counter, next to your purse."

My mother is coming with us to the hospital. Since she found out that A.J. was, in his own messed up way, trying to do the heroic thing by letting me go, she's his new biggest fan.

Also taking a bullet for me didn't hurt.

My father still has his reservations, but he's stopped growling at A.J. and is begrudgingly giving him some respect.

Naturally, I never mentioned my little walk-in on A.J. and Heavenly. I think even the most supportive parents would have a hard time with that one, no matter how well-intentioned they are.

Speaking of Heavenly, we've reached a truce. I still don't like her—probably because she's too beautiful to have any sympathetic feelings toward, *and* she was naked in the same room as my man—but after several discussions, I'm convinced she really does just want the best for A.J. and me. She's meeting us at the hospital, along with the rest of the gang.

"Here they are!" My mother beams momentarily as she finds her glasses, right where I told her they were, but just as quickly her face falls. "Should we bring pillows? Those waiting room chairs are terribly uncomfortable."

"Mom, stop! We're going to be late as it is! Help me with my handbag, please, I've got my hands full with all this other crap."

"Language, dear," she scolds.

I'm the only woman in the western hemisphere whose mother considers the word "crap" foul language. She's even gotten A.J. to stop cursing. Around her, anyway.

"You upsetting grandma again?"

My mother and I turn to see A.J. amble into the room. He's smiling, looking relaxed, while I'm a bundle of nerves.

"No one's upsetting anyone, we're just running late." Scowling, I try to hoist my duffel bag containing clothes, toiletries, books, and other items to keep me distracted while I wait to find out how A.J. will fare in his operation. It will probably be another all-nighter, but regardless of the length of the operation, I'll be staying at the hospital until he's released, which could be anywhere from two to five days. I'm looking around frantically for my Kindle when a pair of strong hands encircle my upper arms.

"Angel."

I look up at him. "Yes, sweetie."

"It's going to be all right. I'm going to be fine." His gaze is warm and steady, the pressure of his hands reassuring; he knows I'm freaking out.

I swallow around the lump in my throat. "Okay."

He pulls me into a hug. I bury my face in my safe spot, the crook between his shoulder and neck, and breathe him in.

"How's my girl?" he whispers, stroking my hair.

I sniffle a little, determined not to cry. "I'm good."

"And the bean?"

I can't help but smile. We've decided not to find out the sex of the baby, so for now we're just calling him or her "the bean." I've started to show. I think my little pooch is cute, and can't stop running my hands over it.

"Snug in his momma's belly."

A.J.'s lips find my neck. "His? What if it's a girl? I kinda had my heart set on a little Abigail Aleksandra Elizabeth."

My face crumples. I squeeze my eyes shut, pulling in a breath through my nose.

A.J. pulls back and takes my face into his hands. "Hey. Listen to me now. I'm going. To be. Okay. We've got the house all set up right for when I get home, we've got the rehab specialist scheduled to help out, I'm learning braille. And if Stevie Wonder can play the keyboard without his sight, I can sure as hell play the drums without mine." He pauses. "Oh no."

Immediately, panic creeps up my throat. "What?"

He looks at me, completely serious. "I forgot to stock up on cool sunglasses."

I whack him on the shoulder. "Not funny!"

He grins. "C'mon, it's sorta funny."

I don't know how he's so calm. Part of me knows he's doing it for me, another part knows that's just him: strong. I hope our baby gets her strength from him, because it's taking every ounce of my concentration not to dissolve into a blubbering mess.

I'm pulled into another hug. A.J. and I stand there like that for a moment, silent, holding each other, until my mother gently clears her throat.

"I think it's time to go, loves."

"That it is," agrees A.J., giving me a final squeeze. He lets me go and smiles at both of us. "But I'm driving. And if this is the last time I'm getting behind the wheel of a car, you ladies might want to hold on to your hats. I might not be minding all the speed limits. Or any of them."

"Suits me," says my mother breezily. "Thomas drives like an old woman; it'll be a nice change to go fast."

The look on my face makes the two of them laugh.

We set off for the hospital, and A.J. is true to his word. My mother and I just hang on, while I keep telling myself one thing over and over again.

He's going to make it. He's going to make it. He will make it.

I break my self-imposed ban on talking to God, and start to pray.

The surgery lasts six hours. They are the longest hours of my life. Because I knew this was coming, it's somehow worse than when A.J. was in surgery after Eric shot him. The weeks and weeks of anticipation have wound every one of my nerves bowstring tight, and I can hardly breathe.

I pace. I drink coffee. I plead with God.

When the surgeon comes in to tell us A.J. made it through successfully and has been transferred to the ICU, no one erupts with cheers like they did the night of the wedding. There's still too much at stake; this is only half the battle. There is profound relief, however. Nico and Kat hug; Chris, Ethan, and Brody share a round of high fives; Kenji and Grace embrace, as do my parents. Jamie went back to New York weeks before, but I text him the news with shaking hands, silent tears streaming down my face.

Heavenly puts her hand on my shoulder. She looks almost as wrecked as I feel. Without speaking, we hug.

When it's time for me to go see him, my mother squeezes my hand. "Remember what the surgeon said, darling. It's too early to tell anything yet."

It's too early to tell if he'll be paralyzed, or be able to speak, or remember my name. It's too early to tell if my child will be growing up with a father who's merely blind, or one who can't function at all without a twenty-four-hour nursing assistant.

But he's alive. He's still my A.J. And no matter how disabled, I will love him just the same. Forever.

The surgeon leads me to his room. I stand outside the door, watching him. His head has been completely shaved; I've asked the nurse to save his hair.

"He looks peaceful," I murmur to the doctor.

He turns to me. "I have a few simple tests to do. I can come back later if you prefer."

"No," I say quickly. "I'm not leaving this room until he does."

A smile briefly flickers over his face. "All right. After you."

He holds out his hand, and we both enter the room. Feeling a massive sense of déjà vu, I stand on the side of A.J.'s hospital bed, and hold his hand.

It's cold again. The entire room feels cold. I get a chill, and shiver.

The doctor leans over A.J. and says loudly, "Mr. Edwards? Can you hear me?"

A.J.'s eyes dart back and forth beneath his lids, but he doesn't open his eyes.

I squeeze his hand harder. "Is that bad?" I whisper, trying to remain calm.

"No. He's still heavily sedated." The doctor takes a slender silver flashlight from his coat pocket, opens A.J.'s left lid, and shines the light into his eye. He repeats the procedure with the right eye, but, unlike with the other side, pauses and says, "Hmm."

Ice water is injected into my veins. Terrified, I ask, "What does that mean?"

He looks at me briefly before straightening. "There's some pupillary response in his right eye."

This damn doctor! Am I going to have to stab it out of him?

"And?" I holler.

He's completely undisturbed by my outburst. "And there shouldn't be."

I drop A.J.'s hand, lean over the bed, and grab the doctor by his lapels. "And what does that mean!"

He can obviously tell I'm losing it, so he quickly adds, "It means, at least in his right eye, the ocular nerve still has some function. It's a good sign, Ms. Carmichael. It's a very good, very unexpected sign." He carefully peels my fingers from his coat.

My heart soaring with hope, my lungs gulping air, I rock back on my heels. "When will we know more?"

He obviously has a lot of experience dealing with crazy relatives of sick people, because he blandly smiles at me instead of running away. "I'm going to give him another hour or so, and then we'll do a few more tests. There's a whole series we go through to assess his condition as he starts to regain consciousness, so I won't have anything definitive for you until later, but for now, he's stable. All right?"

I'm so relieved I want to slide to the floor. Instead I tear up. "Thank you."

He nods. "And if he wakes up, feed him ice chips. I'll have them sent in. He's going to be really thirsty, but he can't have water yet. And I'm sorry, but the time limit for visits in ICU is ten minutes, so I'll leave you to it."

He turns and strides out.

I look at A.J. There's some kind of weird jelly on his scalp, and the incision is hideous. I thought the stitches on my cheek were bad, but this is total Frankenstein territory. We're talking metal staples. I gently rest my hand on his forehead, and sigh.

"Mmrpph."

I jump. "What? A.J., oh my God, are you saying something?"

His lids flicker. His eyes are darting back and forth beneath them again. I grab his hand and lean close to his face, dying to rip out the tube that's stuck in his nose because maybe it's hurting him.

I squeeze his hand. "Baby, I'm here. You're doing great. Just rest, the doctor says—"

"Mmrpph!" he insists, frowning.

I don't know whether to cry or have a panic attack, so I just hold on to his hand as tightly as I can, my lower lip trembling. Will he not be able to speak? Is this it? Will that sound be all he can make from now on?

His eyes flicker open. They roll around in his head like he's spinning.

I stop breathing.

He blinks a few more times, squinting. His hand tightens in mine.

"Sweetie, I'm here. I'm right here. I'm not going anywhere, okay?"

He turns his head toward my voice. Watching him slowly open and close his eyes is heartbreaking. I can tell he can't see me standing there. His gaze is unfocused, like he's looking at something very far away.

I can't help it; I start to cry. I close my eyes, bow my head, and just let it go, because when he fully comes to I'll have to be strong enough for both of us. This will be the last time I can allow myself to break down.

From now on, I'm going to have to be the strongest one in the family.

It's several minutes before I calm myself. I swallow, sniffling, and reach for a tissue from the box on the little table beside A.J.'s bed.

And freeze when I hear a slightly garbled but still understandable, "Drama queen."

With a cry of shock, I straighten. A.J.'s eyes are closed, but he's smiling a drowsy, happy smile. He lifts the hand I'm not holding an inch off the bedcovers, and makes a motion with his forefinger. He's pointing at something across the room. The television? The little dresser?

"What?" I ask breathlessly. "What is it, honey?"

He swallows, running his tongue around his mouth like it's desert dry. He tries to say something else, but the nurse comes in with the ice chips and I lose whatever it was when she cheerfully greets us.

I snatch the cup of ice from her hand and bark, "He's talking! Be quiet, he's talking!"

She raises her brows at me, but doesn't say another word.

I turn back to A.J. and lean close, desperate to understand what he wants. "A.J. Tell me what you want. What are you pointing at?"

He swallows again. I feed him some ice chips, and he sighs in contentment. Two excruciating minutes pass as he slowly chews on them, sucking the moisture. Then he lifts that finger again and points. "Closet. Jacket." His voice is weak, the words slurred.

The nurse says, "I think he wants his coat."

I'm about to argue with her that it makes no sense that he would want his coat, but A.J. slowly nods.

"Please, would you get it?" I ask her. I don't want to let go of his hand.

The nurse, a slight Filipino lady in pink scrubs with her hair in a messy bun on top of her head, rummages through the closet and pulls out the big, zippered plastic bag that holds A.J.'s jacket. Everything was tagged and entered into a personal property log before surgery, which is good, because when they move him out of ICU, they'll make sure all his stuff gets moved with him. She hands the leather jacket to me. I stand there holding it, unsure of what to do next.

"Okay, honey, I have it. Are you cold? Do you want me to put this over you?"

A.J. smiles. It's an odd smile, one I don't think I've seen before, both cunning and satisfied. It causes me a moment's pause, but then he whispers, "Pocket."

Now I understand; there's something he wants, and it's in the pocket of his coat. Relieved, I hold it up and reach inside, feeling around for the inside pocket. There's nothing in it. I try the right pocket, but there's nothing in there either. I hope whatever it was he wanted didn't fall out.

But then I reach into the left pocket. When my fingers close around what's inside, I fall still.

A.J. moves restlessly in bed, his eyes closed, waiting for me to say something.

I slowly remove my hand from the pocket and look at what I've pulled out.

It's a black velvet ring box.

I drop the coat on the floor.

A.J. makes a "give me" motion. My hand trembling, I set the box in his palm. Slowly, with great effort, he lifts his other hand and cracks open the box.

Staring at the incredibly beautiful origami ring, I sob. Atop a braided circle sits a pair of small, fiery orange birds in flight, the tips of their wings touching. I've never seen anything so exquisite, so finely made.

"What are they?"

"Phoenixes."

I lift my gaze to his. In the faintest, breathy whisper, A.J. says, "Because even though it might burn the whole world to the ground, true love can never die. Marry me, angel."

And I blubber like a baby, even though not three minutes before I promised myself I'd be strong.

I take the ring from the box and slide it on my trembling finger. Then I lower the metal bar on the side of the bed and carefully crawl up next to him, ignoring the protests of the nurse. I kiss his neck and his face, crying and laughing, trying to be gentle as I hug him and rest my head on his chest.

Then I say the only thing that's left to be said:

"Yes."

Epilogue

For the hundredth time today, I check my phone to see if I've gotten any new texts from Trina.

It's a sunny, beautiful Sunday, five months after A.J.'s surgery. I'm supposed to be relaxing, but I can't because this particular sunny, beautiful Sunday is Valentine's Day . . . Fleuret's busiest day of the year.

And I'm at a barbeque at Nico and Kat's house.

I'm also as big as a whale. The bean—who has grown to the size of a watermelon on steroids—is due any time. Hence my being banned from the shop by A.J., who flatly told me a month ago I wasn't standing on my feet for twelve hours a day any longer. (If he could see the way my ankles were swelling he'd have banned me from the shop way sooner, but being blind does have its upside: no disturbing visuals of your pregnant fiancée's bloated body parts.)

A warm kiss on the back of my neck distracts me from my cell phone. I tilt my head back and see A.J. leaning over me, smiling. The sun glints gold and copper in his hair. As it always does when

I look at him, my heart skips and stutters before settling down into a normal beat.

"You're getting to be a ninja, sweetie," I grumble. "I can never hear you sneaking up on me!"

He chuckles. "Let me guess: you're out here checking your phone."

I guiltily tuck my phone under my arm. "I'm just enjoying the sunshine!"

His chuckle turns to a laugh. "Lying to a blind man? That's fucked up, angel."

My lips twist. "What's effed up is this heartburn. Seriously, it feels like I swallowed a habanero pepper. And my back is killing me. To top it off, I'm totally gassy today. You might want to go upwind. Ugh."

Moving carefully, A.J. lowers himself to the chair beside me, and then turns his head and smiles brilliantly, bathing me in a warmth even hotter than the sun. "Don't stop, baby, I love it when you talk dirty. Seriously, lay it on me—constipation? Spider veins? Stretch marks? Give it your best shot, all that shit gets me so worked up I might just throw you down on the grass and have my way with you right now."

You'd think he's kidding, but he's not. He loves hearing every detail about the pregnancy, no matter how raw.

"You're gross."

He reaches for my hand. I give it to him, and he raises it to his lips and kisses it. "I'm in love," he says softly. "Every little thing you do is magic."

Though I get misty-eyed at that, I still have to snort. "No fair quoting eighties song lyrics, superstar. You forget I'm the girl who knows every word to 'Bohemian Rhapsody.'"

"That's from the seventies," he shoots back with a smirk.

"Shut up."

He playfully bites one of my fingers. "Make me."

"Ha! Be careful what you wish for."

His smile fades. He opens my hand and presses my palm against his cheek. "You're all I wish for," he says in a husky voice, and my breath catches. Suddenly I can't wait to go home and get him alone.

Always, always this heat between us, this sweet, crackling urgency. I can hardly believe it's real.

I lean over and press a kiss to his lips. I whisper, "And you're everything I need."

He deadpans, "Except maybe some charcoal underwear. How many of Nico's extra spicy Tennessee ribs did you eat, babe? Because I'm totally getting that gas thing you were talking about—"

Cursing, I smack him on his muscular bicep. He falls apart laughing, then grabs me, hauls me onto his lap, and nuzzles his face into my neck.

"You're lucky you're so cute," I say with mock sternness.

"Or what? You'd kick my ass?"

I harrumph. "Into next week, buddy!"

He tickles me, I squeal and squirm in his lap, and then from behind us someone clears his throat. I look up and Nico is standing at the sliding glass patio door, looking a little embarrassed.

"Don't mean to interrupt playtime," he drawls, "but your man is supposed to be helpin' me clean up the mess in the kitchen. Considerin' he made most of it."

"I can't help it if I have a big appetite," says A.J., sounding unconcerned. "I'm eating for two."

Nico looks at me with his brows raised.

"Sympathy hunger," I explain with a shrug. "It's a weird pregnancy partner thing. He even thinks he has morning sickness. I swear he'll be screaming louder in the delivery room than I will be."

Nico mutters, "And here I thought penis envy was weird."

A.J. quips, "Aw, that's sweet, man! But don't worry, I'm sure your average-sized junk does the job just fine. Kat seems real happy." He beams, and Nico rolls his eyes.

"Fuck you, brother."

"Right back at you, brother."

They both grin.

I lumber from A.J.'s lap, groaning as I straighten; my lower back is in knots. "Okay, I've had enough of the male bonding. C'mon, Big Daddy, let's go inside."

Yeah, I know what you're thinking. But now that A.J. *is* a daddy—or a daddy to be—calling him "Big Daddy" seems to fit, even if I did have such a stick up my butt about it before.

Plus, the way it makes Nico cringe is totally worth it. There's not much that makes that man blush.

A.J. takes my outstretched hand, and I gently lead him across the sunny patio to the house. He can still see light and shadows, and some colors, but shapes and faces elude him. Driving is out of the question, as is going anywhere alone outside of our house, which he's learned to navigate expertly. He wears sunglasses much of the time because he thinks it makes people uncomfortable to look into his unfocused, faraway gaze, but around the band and close friends he doesn't bother.

And, thank God, his sightlessness hasn't affected his ability to play drums at all. Sit him down behind his kit and he still whales on it until his fingers bleed. I think his timing might even be better now that he's relying fully on his other senses.

I can definitely vouch for how acute his other senses have become, especially his nose. I swear he can *smell* when I'm horny. I don't even have to say a word. From all the way across the house he'll make a beeline toward me, and then we're in bed.

Silver linings, people. You either focus on the bad, or the good.

I've chosen to focus on the good. It's not hard; there's a lot of it.

Inside, Kat is trying to feed Barney another one of Nico's amazing ribs. Barney protests that he's already had enough, but the way he's looking at the plate Kat's holding makes it obvious he hasn't. Ethan and Chris are lounging on the sofa in the living room, playing a video game and insulting each other with good-natured name-calling, while Kenji sits to one side, examining his manicure and looking bored.

I don't see Grace or Brody anywhere.

"Okay, A.J., I'll wash, you rinse," says Nico. He's standing in front of the kitchen sink. One side is filled with fluffy white bubbles; beside the sink on the counter is a stack of plates and a mess of cups and silverware from all the food we devoured for lunch.

I lead A.J. to the counter. He follows with one hand resting lightly on my right shoulder, and then positions himself in front of the sink beside Nico, feeling for the edge of the counter, the water faucet, and the dish rack. Once he's set, he holds out a hand for the first plate.

I love it that no one treats him as if he's any different than he was before. He still has to pull his own weight. With the band, with everything. There's no pity, another gift for which I'm grateful.

"Who'd have thought our men were so domestic?" I say to Kat, watching two of the most famous rock stars on the planet soap and rinse cutlery.

Kat snorts. "Oh, please, it's all for show. As soon as everyone leaves, Nico will call the housekeeper. He doesn't even wash his own underwear."

A.J. jokes, "That poor fucking woman. I hope you're paying her six figures."

Nico hands A.J. another fork. "At least I own underwear."

"Bet it has little flowers on it, too."

Nico shakes his head, chuckling.

I set my cell phone on the big marble island in the middle of the kitchen and ease my bulk into one of the chairs around it, groaning. Kat comes over and starts to rub my back.

"Sore?"

I groan again when she digs her knuckle into a knot in my shoulder that's been growing bigger in direct proportion to my belly. I had no idea pregnancy would be so *uncomfortable*. It's a miracle anyone has more than one child.

"Yes, but that's helping. Thank you." I close my eyes for a moment, enjoying the massage, then ask, "What're Grace and Brody up to?"

Kat's hands falter. I turn to look at her and she's frowning.

"I don't know. She left to go to the bathroom like . . . ten minutes ago. And now that you mention it, Brody was pretty much right behind her."

Nico turns to share a look with Kat and me. "Well," he drawls, "ain't that interestin'."

Before anyone else can comment, Grace breezes around the corner of the kitchen, looking like a cat that's just swallowed a mouse.

Or a lead guitarist.

"That front powder room is fantastic, Kat—all those mirrors! It's like a fun house in there." She fluffs her hair, sits at a chair across from me, crosses her legs and sighs. There are two spots of color high on her cheeks.

"Emphasis on 'fun,'" I murmur, looking at her pointedly.

She cocks her head, furrows her brows, and says innocently, "What do you mean?"

At exactly that moment, Brody strolls into the kitchen and takes a seat beside Grace. She doesn't look at him, but the spots of color on her cheeks darken. She stands abruptly, announces, "I think I'll go get some sun," and whisks past us, headed to the patio doors.

As soon as she's in the backyard and out of earshot, Kat says, "Sun? She hates the sun, she can't tan."

Brody, looking all sorts of cocky, leans back in his chair and folds his arms across his chest. Without a word, he grins.

Nico says, "Oh it's like that, is it?"

Brody's grin grows wider. "I'm working on it."

I say, "Oh my God!"

A.J. turns from the sink. "What am I missing?"

"Brody's into Grace!"

Nico winks at Kat. "Told you."

Now I'm confused. "Wait, you guys knew this?"

Kat sits beside me. "According to Nico, Brody has a long-standing fetish for redheads. They're like his kryptonite; he goes weak in the knees every time he sees a ginger."

Brody says, "Guilty. And your friend makes me weak in every part of my body except one."

I wrinkle my nose. "TMI, Brody."

He grins wider.

Kat excitedly asks, "Is she into you?"

Brody shrugs. "So far she's told me I'm too young for her, she doesn't date musicians, it would be weird if it didn't work out because she'd have to see me all the time because of you guys, and she couldn't be with a man who dresses better than she does."

A.J. says, "Sounds like you're striking out, bro."

But Brody doesn't look convinced. His grin hasn't faltered. "Maybe. Or maybe she likes the chase as much as I do. Never met a woman who tells me to get lost while she's staring at my crotch like it's the Rosetta Stone."

A.J. and Nico laugh, but Kat and I are too busy having a wordless conversation to join in. By her face, I can tell she's thinking what I'm thinking: One, wouldn't it be awesome if they got together; Two, what's the real story about why she's not going for him; And three, why the hell hasn't she told us about any of this?

We are *so* going to find out.

In the meantime, I'm going to help Brody along.

"A word of advice? Ease off a bit. If she thinks you're too serious about her, it'll scare her away."

Brody cocks his head. "What do you mean?"

I look at Kat. She nods, knowing what I'm going to say, and approving. I think a moment, trying to find the right words. "Grace isn't the girl who wants the roses and the love poems and the happily-ever-after. Thinking too much about the future makes her uncomfortable. So just keep it casual and you'll have a much better chance."

For the first time, Brody's cocky grin fades. He puts his elbows on the table and leans toward me. "Did she have a bad breakup? Someone hurt her?"

I glance at Kat. She says, "Go ahead. If she finds out, I'll tell her it was my idea."

Looking confused, Brody says, "Okay, now I *really* have to know."

Thinking, I tap my fingers on the marble. I don't know how much detail to go into. This is Grace's story to tell after all, not mine. But the temptation to see Grace with a man who understands her, who gets why she never talks about the past or looks forward to the future is too great. If Brody really likes her, and he knows what makes her tick, maybe they'll have a chance.

"Okay, it's not a big secret or anything, and she's never sworn us to silence, so I'm going to tell you, but I'd appreciate it if you'd be careful about how you bring this up with her. If you ever do."

Eagerly, Brody nods.

"When she was eighteen, Grace was involved in a bad car accident. Her parents were killed."

"Shit." Brody looks distressed. "Was she badly hurt?"

I glance out the sliding glass doors to the patio. Grace is lying on the chaise lounge, eyes closed, her face turned to the sun. Though she's well out of earshot, I lower my voice. "She lost her memory. She can't recall anything before the crash. She had to relearn who she was when she woke up; she didn't recognize anyone, she didn't remember anything about her life. So now she has this whole 'live for the moment' philosophy. Especially with relationships. If she thinks someone she's dating is getting serious, that's it. It's over. Because she thinks it could all be taken away again, like *that*." I snap my fingers.

Brody sags back in his chair, stunned. "That's awful. I can't even imagine."

I sigh. "Yeah. It doesn't help that they never found the bastard who ran into them."

Brody's gaze flashes up to mine. "Sorry?"

"It was a hit-and-run," says Kat. "Some asshole ran a red light, then hit the back of Grace's parents' car just right to send it into a tailspin. They wound up wrapped around a telephone pole, and the other guy just took off."

Brody's face pales. He swallows. "Hit-and-run?"

"At least the bastard had the decency to stop and pull Grace from the car. If he hadn't, she would have . . . the fire . . ." I shake my head. "Anyway, she made it out and her parents didn't. So my point is—"

And then I'm doubled over with the worst pain I've ever felt. It hits me out of nowhere, radiating out from my stomach in violent waves. This is different from the mild discomfort I've been having over the past month, the twinges and pinches in my abdomen. This is *aggressively* painful.

"Honey!" says Kat frantically, grabbing my shoulders. "Are you all right?"

A.J. is beside me before I can even catch my breath, his worried face inches from mine. "Angel?"

"Contraction," I gasp. "Oh, God, it *hurts*—"

Warm fluid saturates my underwear and begins to slide down my legs. Holy Jesus, my water just broke.

I'm going into labor.

I shout, "The baby's coming!" and everyone leaps into action.

Kat jumps up and runs to the patio door, screaming for Grace. Barney yells, "I'll get the car!" and runs toward the garage. Kenji, clapping and squealing, leaps from the sofa in the living room, while Ethan and Chris abandon their video game and run into the kitchen, whooping. Nico grabs the small duffel bag with my toiletries and clothes that I've been carrying everywhere with me for the last two weeks, and A.J. lifts me into his arms.

"Honey put me down, you can't carry me!"

"Hell if I can't," A.J. growls. "I'm not letting my woman walk to the car when she's about to have my baby. Nico, lead the way."

So Nico, moving as quickly and carefully as possible while leading a blind man and a pregnant woman, guides us through the house and into the garage. A.J. only releases me to help me climb into the backseat of Nico's Range Rover, which Barney has ready and waiting, then takes me in his arms again. Kat and Grace pile in with us, while Kenji, Ethan, and Chris jump into Ethan's Hummer.

Then we're off, flying down the narrow, winding road toward the hospital.

"We're gonna have a Valentine's baby, angel," A.J. whispers into my ear.

I can't help it; I start to cry. I never knew I could be this happy.

It isn't until I'm in a wheelchair being pushed through the hospital doors that I realize we've left Brody back at the house, motionless and silent at the kitchen table, his face as white as bone.

Acknowledgments

This book wrecked me.

I wrote it in nine weeks, jumping up in the middle of the night, running out of dinner parties, and hanging up the phone mid-sentence to write obsessively about A.J. and Chloe whenever inspiration hit. I cried a lot. I'd wander into the living room, sobbing, a wad of soggy tissues in my hand, and my husband would look at me, laugh, and hold out his arms.

Thank you, Jay, for sharing your life with a woman who cries over her imaginary friends, for having the good humor to deal with it, and the good sense not to ask too many questions. Without you, I'm lost. (No, wait—I do what I want!)

Thank you to my editor, Maria Gomez, and my team at Montlake Romance for being so incredibly supportive, easy to work with, and fun.

Big thanks to Melody Guy, my developmental editor, who pointed out so many ways to make this book better I can't count them all. Your advice and input is invaluable, as it has been on all my books since the beginning. I so appreciate you.

Thanks to my Street Team, Geissinger's Gang, and my readers, whose enthusiasm and support make it all worthwhile.

I don't know where it comes from, but the urge to create has always been with me. Whoever or whatever is responsible for that, I thank you/it as well, because it's been an incredibly positive force in my life. Universe, you rock.

About the Author

J.T. Geissinger is an award-winning author of paranormal and contemporary romance featuring dark and twisted plots, kick-ass heroines, and alpha heroes whose hearts are even bigger than their muscles. Her debut fantasy romance, *Shadow's Edge*, was a #1 international Amazon bestseller and won the Prism Award for Best First Book. Her follow-up novel, *Edge of Oblivion*, was a RITA© Award finalist for Paranormal Romance from the Romance Writers of America, and she won a Golden Quill award for the final book in the Night Prowler series, *Into Darkness*. Her work has also finaled in the Booksellers' Best, National Readers' Choice, and Daphne du Maurier Awards.

She lives in California with her husband, on whom all her heroes are based.

Get notifications on new releases by signing up on her website at www.jtgeissinger.com.

Made in United States
Cleveland, OH
08 February 2025

14165146R00236